From **TANSTAAFL** Press:

CorpGov Chronicle novels by Tom Gondolfi
An Eighty Percent Solution – CorpGov Chronicles: Book One
In a world where corporations suborn governments as a part of good business practice
and unregistered humans can be killed without penalty, Tony Sammis, a midlevel
corporate functionary, finds himself unwittingly a pawn in a guerilla war between a
powerful cabal of business leaders and an elusive but deadly underground movement.
His final solution to the biological terror unleashed mirrors Tony's own twisted sense
of justice.

Thinking Outside the Box – CorpGov Chronicles: Book Two
Winning one war doesn't seem to be enough. Tony Sammis and the Green Action
Militia are once again thrust into the center of a conflict that will change the lives of
everyone in the solar system. This time they are allies with the fledgling CorpGov and
even the United States government against the ravages of the corrupt Metropolitan
Police Force. The GAM and their allies are fighting a losing war with few soldiers and
even fewer weapons. Behind the scenes, a humble and unsuspected power block lurks
with its own axe to grind.

Self-interest, romance, freedom, and a lust for power are stirred together in this chaotic
soup of tension, intrigue, assassination, and war.

Also by Tom Gondolfi
Toy Wars
Flung to a remote world, a semi-sentient group of robotic mining factories arrive with
their programming hashed. They can only create animated toys instead of normal
mining and fighting machines. One of these factories, pushed to the edge of extinction
by the fratricidal conflict, attempts a desperate gamble. Infusing one of its toys with the
power of sentience begins the quest of a 2-meter tall, purple teddy bear and his pink,
polka-dotted elephant companion. They must cross an alien world to find and enlist
the aid of mortal enemies to end the genocide before Toy Wars claims their family—all
while asking the immortal question, "Why am I?"

By Bruce Graw
Demon Holiday
Torval, Demon Third Class, Layer Four Hundred Twelve of the Eighth Circle of Hell,
has been in the business of chastising sinners longer than he can remember. Delivering
punishment is the only job he's ever known—the only job he's ever wanted. After
Torval witnesses something unexpected, his demonic Overseer demands that he take
time off to resolve this personal crisis. And so Torval, the demon, finds himself sent on
vacation...to Earth, the proving ground of souls!

Demon Ascendant
Torval, Demon Third Class, Layer Four Hundred Twelve of the Eighth Circle of Hell,
on *vacation* to Earth has managed to find another demon, has dated an angel and
inadvertently explored some of the sins of humankind: greed, gluttony and lust. Through
all this his biggest struggle involves deciding if he wants his holiday to end or to continue
forever.

The Bardess of Rhulon

Verna McKinnon

TANSTAAFL PRESS

TANSTAAFL Press
891 PH 10
Castle Rock, WA 98611

Visit us at www.TANSTAAFLPress.com

The Bardess of Rhulon

Second edition—TANSTAAFL Press
Copyright © 2021 by Verna McKinnon

First Edition by Sky Warrior Book Publishing, LLC
Copyright © 2018 by Verna McKinnon

Cover art: Kristin Bryant at www.kristindesigns.com

Printed in the USA
ISBN: 978-1-938124-67-9

Book layout by Hydra House Books

Chapter One

Rose Greenleaf wanted her recitation of the epic poem to be perfect for her Bard Master, Belenus Aylecross. She conjured images of blood-soaked battlefields and valiant warriors as she prepared to recite the epic story of King Gregor Ironheart. Her focus waivered as her mother's shrill voice returned to haunt her.

You're wasting your life on nursery rhymes instead of filling a nursery! Selfish girl, are you a changeling? No true daughter of mine would refuse marriage and children. It's unnatural!

I'm a person with hopes and dreams, Mother! I'm not breeding stock just because you want grandchildren.

Belenus struck a match, lighting the tobacco in his pipe, puffing away as smoky clouds masked his expression. He rapped his staff on the wooden floor, snapping Rose out of her tortured thoughts. "Come in Rose, don't dawdle. Recite the poem." The old Bard reclined in his over-stuffed crimson chair, the velvet threadbare and musty with age. Low lamplight cast amber-hued reflections on his wrinkled face as he leaned his staff against the wobbly side table.

"Sorry, Master," Rose mumbled. Her mother's grating voice continued to nag inwardly, disrupting Rose's focus.

Foolish girl! Why do you study this poetry nonsense when there are pies to bake! No wonder you're a spinster!

It wasn't just the fight with her mother. Since she woke this morning, Rose suffered ominous feelings all day, as though a black cloud loomed above her, threatening a terrible storm. *Karta help me,* Rose inwardly prayed to her patron goddess to banish her mother's stubborn presence from her mind, especially before reciting her favorite epic poem. She inhaled deeply the woodsy pipe smoke. It calmed her because it reminded her of her father, who enjoyed a good smoke, though her mother always fussed about the smell. The fusty odor of ancient books and scrolls was like perfume, and always beckoned adventure if one only dared to read! Rose exiled her mother from her mind. She invoked instead the memory of a king long dead, from a war long remembered.

The story transported her to the grim battle fields where Ironheart's forces stood against the demon armies of the goblin king, Raziel Drujaesh. Raw sensations coursed through Rose's veins as her mind's eye envisioned the grueling battle trek of Ironheart's soldiers during the goblin wars. Her tongue parched and belly rumbled as she recounted their sufferings when the field rations had long been consumed. Her bones rattled with stampeding horses screaming across the rocky terrain as they charged the demon hordes. It was a dark and terrible age that bristled with adventure and intrigue. Tales of sorcery, heroes, and love-struck maidens filled countless volumes from that mythic era.

Rose's poem reached its heartbreaking final battle when Gregor Ironheart stormed Raziel's stronghold in Fire Skull Mountain. In that fiery chamber of demons within the mountain, Gregor faced Raziel, a demon born of that rare Kobalos goblin breed, seven feet tall with crimson skin and black eyes. They clashed in the heated shadows. Gregor unsheathed his secret weapon, the legendary Sun Blade; the enchanted blade's light blinded the demon. Raziel managed to thrust his colossal black iron sword into King Gregor's heart. Broken and bleeding, Gregor shouted a final war cry and thrust the Sun Blade into Raziel's side before he collapsed. Raziel perished, howling as he was consumed by the mystical light until he burst into flaming ashes.

Tears welled in Roses eyes as she spoke the final words and she envisioned Gregor Ironheart carried away on a great shield by kings of old, his sacrifice for the world complete and the demons banished to the dark. The tragic fate of so many heroes is death. That loss resonated in her soul as she came to those final lines. She paused for a heartbeat, and then spoke deeply as the valor of the ancient king reverberated in her heart-

> *Light's glory dimmed as Ironheart's mortal life ebbed.*
> *Gregor, King of Rhulon, fell to his stony deathbed.*
> *Comrades lifted him upon a shield of victory so hard won.*
> *His triumph over darkness done.*

Finished, Rose wondered if her effort was worthy of Gregor Ironheart's legacy, and more importantly, would Belenus approve? Frustrated, she knew she would torture herself later over her performance, so she folded her hands together and bowed her head with practiced patience as Master

Belenus pondered his judgment.

After what seemed an eternity of torment, but was really just a few ticks of the wall clock, Belenus bellowed and rapped his staff on the scuffed floor. "Well done, Rose. Well done! Wonderful telling."

"Thank you, Master Belenus."

"What's the matter, Rose? You don't seem pleased, girl," he replied, studying her expression with sharp eyes.

She shrugged and sat down. "Well, I wasn't *perfect*."

He burst out laughing and Rose bit her lip in irritation, and then laughed at herself.

"You take things too seriously, Rose." Belenus tapped his pipe on the copper ashtray. "You had another argument with your mother, didn't you?"

"You know we fight every week now. It's getting worse. Still, it shouldn't matter. A true bard must perform no matter how they feel personally. I must be serious, Master Belenus. Teaching a girl to become a bard is not, well—"

"Not common? Not accepted?" Belenus huffed and slowly pushed himself up from his chair. "I've seen much of the world, Rose. It's not blasphemy to teach a woman. Many kingdoms accept women for more than housewifery and child bearing. Our people are noble, but have grown very isolated and traditionalist. They do not suffer change well. Compliance and stiff traditions are the greatest threats to any culture. That's why I was surprised to find a girl so eager to study the art, when most maidens your age have already snagged husbands and are bouncing squalling brats on their knees."

Rose shivered in mock horror. "That sounds more terrifying than facing Raziel the goblin king! Still, it's springtime again and the season of weddings. You know what that means."

"It means that mother of yours is on the bridal warpath again." He laughed, and put down his pipe. He coughed and waving a hand toward the cupboard. "Dear Rose, fetch me a bit of brandy. My throat's dry after my smoke. Take some water for yourself, for surely your pipes must need it after that long poem."

The faded green pine cupboard was crammed with old dishes and cups, mismatched utensils, a loaf of bread, a wrapped block of cheese, and several leather pouches of tobacco. She took the bottle of brandy from the top shelf and found the carafe of water, pouring herself a cupful.

It was warm but soothed her thirst. "My spinster status irks my mother like a nasty plague. Simon Split-Oak has been trying to court me since last winter, much to my mother's delight and my annoyance."

"Isn't Simon that big, thick lad? He's your father's apprentice at his smithy, isn't he?"

"Yes. Mother forced me to sit with him at church last Solday. We have nothing in common. He hates reading and cares nothing about music." She poured the brandy into his favorite cup, an old ceramic mug with chipped painted flowers and handed it to him. "Most of all, I just have no desire to marry anyone."

"What does your father say?"

"Very little in front of Mother," Rose replied dryly.

"With your mother Gerta, that's probably wise."

"Oh Master Belenus, I just need to survive a few more months and I will be free. Then I will be eighteen and of legal age. I can do what I want then. It's so unfair. A boy turns sixteen and he's considered a man. A girl has no say about her life until she's eighteen, and by then she is usually married off to some buffoon. Then it's all moot."

Belenus chuckled. A sturdy knock on the front door froze them both into muteness. Rose tiptoed to the window and peeked through the tattered curtains. It was Simon Split-Oak, the bane of her existence. A burly young man with a dull wit, pampered by an overprotective mother, he could not take no for an answer about courting her. What was he doing now—tracking her?

"Rose, you in there?" Simon bellowed through the door. "You mum sent me to walk you home. A girl needs a proper escort."

As if I need an escort! What's going to happen to me in this sleepy, tiny village? Will a swarm of ogres attack? A pack of wild beasts devour me?

Belenus pushed himself up, grabbed his staff and motioned for Rose to hide. She cursed the fact he had no backdoor. She grabbed her precious lute and went to the far corner opposite the door and crouched low next to a crowded shelf, crammed with old books and scrolls piled haphazardly.

Belenus opened door in mid-knock. "Stop your bloody knocking. What the hell do you want, boy?"

"I'm supposed to walk Miss Rose home. Her mother sent me."

"Rose left half an hour ago, Simon. Go away." Before Simon could utter another word, Belenus slammed the door. He peeped out the window and after a moment, motioned Rose from her corner of sanctuary.

"Is it safe?" Rose whispered.

"Simon's gone now. What the hell does his mother feed him anyway? He's big as a house and smells like cooked onions."

"I know," Rose giggled. "It's very odd."

"Why did your blasted mother send him here to fetch you?"

"Mother hates it when I come here. Thinks I have better things to do—like knitting or whipping lace for my wedding veil. This morning she had me running all over the village like a madwoman doing silly errands. I didn't even get breakfast. I was tempted to eat the apple pie I took to old Widow Brook. It smelled so good, I could have devoured the whole thing, but I do not steal food from old widows. I didn't even have time to grab a bite when I returned home. Mother fretted over a gooseberry pie while I obediently peeled the potatoes, watching the clock on the wall to chime my hour of freedom. Before the vegetables made it into the pot we were arguing. When it came time for me to leave for my lesson with you, she made me wash the dishes and sweep the floor, knowing it would make me late. When I asked to leave, she demanded to know where I had to go that was so important. Her face puckered like a wormy apple when I reminded her about my bardic lesson.

"Mother put my trousers in the wash, so I had to run in this damned heavy skirt, my lute bouncing on my back. I'm sure my back is riddled with bruises. I tripped twice, and since the ground was muddy from last night's rain, my dress and shoes are caked with it. I left the shoes outside to dry." She brushed at the dried mud on her skirt, which dropped off in flakes. "Ever since I started coming three times a week, it has become a war. Whenever I have a lesson, my house duties triple." Rose dropped down on the stool, exhausted. "But enough about my silly woes. I want to hear more about your adventures as a bard on the road or the kingdoms you visited. Last time, you told me about your time in the Tirangel court in White Thorn as a young man. Is it true that it never snows in Tirangel? Did the old Emperor truly have six mistresses at once? Tell me about your years as Chief Bard to our King Grimkel Ironheart at Rhundoran Keep. Is it true Rhundoran Keep is carved right out of the mountain? What happened to the Sun Blade they always talk about in the poems?"

"Stop, stop!" Belenus waved his hand in defense, laughing as he sank back into his chair. "Yes, yes, that charming seaside kingdom of Tirangel was one of my favorite haunts when I was younger...and spryer of foot.

The honor of being the Royal Bard to King Grimkel Ironheart was my greatest achievement. I lived in Rhundoran Keep for a long time, and the King was a good friend as well as a benefactor."

"That is an honor few can boast," Rose nodded, hugging her knees. "It must have been wonderful to be at the court of King Grimkel."

Belenus chuckled, his mood lightened by her enthusiasm. "There are many mysteries, my dear. That's what makes life a wonder. That mystical sword vanished centuries ago. Still, the luxury of court life did not calm my restless feet. They itched for adventure and new kingdoms to explore. I learned much about life as I journeyed. The best way to learn the culture and history of a land is to live there my dear, research their ancient fables and legends. Eat their food and drink their wine. This emersion fermented my own poetry and tales with fresh vision. A bard best serves the way—*the art*—on the road. A king or noble merely provides the purse for the bard to feed himself. If you are good, you eat well. If you are bad, you starve. There is a sacrifice in wearing the bardic mantle. It is a nomadic life—a lonely life. Do you really want that?"

"Yes," Rose replied with such swift conviction that Belenus raised his eyebrow.

"Are you sure you're not driven by the desire to be free of your mother's...coddling?"

"Mother doesn't coddle, though she curdles a bit," Rose grinned. "I dream of seeing the world and all its wonders. I want to sing and tell stories. Becoming a bard, a true bard, is all I have ever dreamed of. I love my family, I really do, but I feel trapped here, as though a spider has me caught in its web; but instead of being cocooned and eaten I am condemned to drudgery and a life without music or epic poetry. Whenever I talked about this to my best friend and cousin, Peony, she looks at me like I am a madwoman, but at least she does not ridicule. Do you think me mad too?"

"To be a bard is to be a little mad. We have the souls of wanderers. It's a curse, Rose, though you're too young to understand. But what you have is the talent; else you would not be under my tutelage. Your singing could enchant the Fey and your storytelling is masterful for one so young. I even endorsed you to the Bard Academy, but—"

"They don't accept girls," Rose finished sadly. "It was kind that you tried."

"Damned fools. The Academy in Rhungar is not the only school,

Rose. Every land worth its salt has a bard academy."

"It doesn't matter," Rose insisted smiling with pride. "I have you to teach me, and I can think of no better teacher."

"And I am glad I could teach someone with the talent. Those arrogant, pompous bureaucrats at the Bard Academy are just a pack of ignorant fools—the whole lot of them. You bring the words to life and have fire in your song. You have the memory too, which is rare and necessary. All you need do is read a page once or twice and you have it committed to memory. What is your tale and song choice for next week?"

"I'm looking over some tales now. For the music, the Song of Talasyn," Rose answered brightly.

Belenus nodded approval. "Fine and challenging choice. Talasyn had the glam rhapsodé, a magic so rare among our caste that perhaps one or two a century are blessed with this gift—or cursed." Belenus sipped his brandy. "There are many tales of glory and sorrow for those with this magic. A bard named Ailínn actually summoned the ocean waves with his song to crush an armada of invading warships. Javid, who hailed from the eastern lands of Uragon, used the magic to enchant a maiden to fall in love him, but when he grew tired of her, he could not break the spell. She killed herself out of grief and he never sang again. They had power, but their magic can be a bane as well as a blessing. Some even went mad."

Rose hugged her knees, her eyes wide with worship. "Talasyn was touched by the glam rhapsodé, but he never abused it, nor did he seem to suffer for it. I read the great biography of Talasyn Peony bought for me last Solstice. She had to order it from Rhungar. I have committed every poem and story he ever wrote to memory. There is a legend he was so beloved by the Fairy Folk that they made him immortal and took him to their misty Otherworld. In the Fairy Country, they restored the old bard to his youthful vigor. Talasyn still sings in their enchanted woods beneath the starlight."

"Damned Fairies were never that considerate of me," Belenus gruffly laughed. "For the best, I think. I'd get bored." His smile faded and his eyes became serious. "The magic of the rhapsodé touches few of us. What would you do if you were touched?"

Rose laughed and then stared at Belenus quizzically. "I don't know if you are testing me or joking? I don't know what I would feel. It's both frightening and marvelous to imagine. People treat you differently when you are different, and folks in this village already look at me like I am an oddity. Maybe I could enchant my mother to stop nagging me and leave me in peace."

"Speaking of peace, a drop more brandy please."

Rose refilled his glass and handed it back to him. "There are rumors you were also a spy for the King? I've read many tales of minstrels and bards acting as spies."

"There is some truth to those rumors in that some bards have also added *watchers* to our list of talents, but few ever speak of it," he grinned.

"Do you have regrets?" Rose asked.

"Only about a few comely maidens I had to leave behind."

"Rogue," she teased and pushed her stool forward, eager to hear more.

Belenus leaned forward, his eyes bright as a child. "Has any young man ever tugged at your heart, Rose?"

"Love starts out with flowers and honeyed words. It ends with smelly diapers and squalling babies. Doesn't seem like a fair trade."

"You're so young to be so cynical."

"The love stories are good," Rose shrugged. "Still, war sagas are much more interesting. I'm glad you came here, Master. At least I had the opportunity to study with one of the great bards of Rhulon. I know the Academy will never accept a girl, so you were my salvation. Tell me, why didn't you go back to Rhundoran Keep in Rhungar when you retired? The King would have welcomed you at court."

"I could have, but I decided to retire here in blessed obscurity and rest my weary bones in peace. This old cottage belonged to my grandfather and he left it to me many years ago. It's decrepit, the roof leaks, and I think there are mice living in the walls, but it's a quiet nest for me in my old age. Of course, when folks heard Belenus Aylecross, Bard of the First Order, had settled here, parents dragged their sons here to be instructed. Not one of them was worth salt. Then you banged on my door, with your lute on your back and a scroll of poetry in your hand. You announced that you wanted to be a Bard! I almost laughed, but something inside me whistled caution. Then, when I heard you sing and listened to your poetry and storytelling, I knew you had the gift." He looked pensive now, his green eyes shadowed. "But what will you do with my training, truly? There are no female bards among our clans. None have held that rank in more than a century."

Rose picked up her lute and fiddled with tuning the strings. "That's why I want to travel. I must find my own path. You've spoken of women in other lands that are considered equals among men. I don't belong here. I don't want a husband or wailing babies. My dream is to be a Bard. It has been since I was four years old when I saw an old Bard perform during Solstice that year in the village. He told marvelous tales of adventure and sang with the most wonderful voice. I knew from that moment that was what I wanted to be. I studied on my own until you came to our village. If I want to become a true bard, I must leave here. You know that, Master."

"Where will you go?"

"South to Tirangel, I think. The land of the tall folk seems daunting, but you did it. I'm not sure, but I must find my home on the road. Tell the stories. Sing the songs. Maybe I'm cursed, as you say. I'm saving the money I earn from singing. Last week I sang at the spring festival, plus there are always weddings and christenings. Until I reach adult age, I will do my best to please mother, barring marriage to some oaf, of course."

"What about your father? It will be hard on him to see his only girl leave."

"I will miss Papa. I know he tolerates my love of poetry and music as a childish dream, but he's never berated me for it. Papa overrode my mother's refusal for me to study with you-even though she raved liked a banshee for days. She burned supper three nights in a row to punish us both. Papa always spoiled me a little; sometimes I think to compensate for mother's strict demands. I'm their only child. Still, if I were a boy, they would praise me for my bard ambitions; as a girl, I am rebuked for it. They think I will put on a matronly apron and bake pies, but how many pies must suffer a scorched death before they realize I'm not like other girls?"

Belenus put down his cup and walked over to the window, his slight limp not slowing his step. He opened the curtains to let in the last of the day's sunshine and fresh air. "You're only seventeen. That's so young. I'm passed seventy winters now, beyond the time of supple youth and hot hearts. The decades have turned me gray and stiffened my joints, yet if I could walk a few good miles a day, I would still be on the road singing for my supper."

Rose tried to imagine Belenus Aylecross, still in his youthful prime and her imagination erased the crippling of age and gray hair. Yes, she could envision the young bard, defiant and strong, storming through the world with his lute. She could sense his captivity now, here in their insignificant village of Stone Haven. She felt a sorrow for him at that moment, but concealed it, knowing he would chafe at her pity.

He turned to Rose, his gaze serious. "What do you want Rose?"

"Freedom," she replied.

"Freedom has a price," Belenus warned. "It takes more than a sharp memory or a singing voice to be a bard, so much more and you have it, but it involves sacrifice. It can be a stark life touched with loneliness."

The wall clock chimed. Rose jumped to her feet. "Oh blast! Mother will have a fit if I'm late for supper tonight." She carefully slipped her lute into its leather cover and slung it across her shoulder.

"All that fuss just to eat at a specific time? Odd to be so persnickety about time tables when folks don't go anywhere."

"We're having company. Simon and his mother are coming to supper. At least Mother invited Peony and Tom too." She opened the front door and stepped outside for her shoes were caked with mud. She pulled them on and kicked against the outside wall, breaking off the dried earth in crusty chunks. "If I'm late again, I'll never hear the end of it." She hiked up her skirts and bolted. "Thank you, Master! See you next week!"

"Be careful not to fall in the mud this time," Belenus shouted as she jumped over a fallen tree branch without breaking her stride.

As Rose rushed home, the black storm cloud in her mind still hovered with mysterious threat, no matter how fast she raced from it.

Chapter Two

Knowing her mother would never tolerate a speck of dirt in her immaculate kitchen, Rose slipped her filthy shoes off outside. She tiptoed through the back door, listening for her mother, but the kitchen was empty and silent. Good. Exhausted, she lifted the lute case off her shoulder and laid it on the table. Her stomach growled painfully. The dinner platters were neatly arranged on the kitchen table, like a wicked temptation. Mashed potatoes, rolls, and fried chicken made her faint with hunger. Sweet corn bubbled on the stove. The heavenly smell of gooseberry pies cooling on the window sill tempted her with yummy sin. The basket of rolls sang to her. Golden and fluffy—and there were so many, her mother would never miss just one! She was so famished! Rose reached for a plump biscuit just as her mother burst into the kitchen. She jerked her hand back like it had been burned.

"Where have you been?" Gerta demanded. She twisted a dish towel in her hands, curly tendrils of dark hair dared to stray from her tight hair bun as she waited for an answer.

"With Master Belenus for my lessons," Rose answered simply. "You know that, Mother. We spent half an hour arguing about it before I left."

"Oh, that nonsense!" Gerta sniffed and glanced down at Rose's bare feet and the muddy hem of her skirt, frowning. "What happened to your nice dress? And where are your shoes, Rose?"

"They got dirty," Rose murmured, eyes downcast. "I'm sorry, Mother. The shoes are outside so I would not mess up your floor. I was going to clean them—"

"Never mind!" Gerta threw up her hands in disgust and turned her back on Rose. She stirred the corn in the pot, adding a pinch of salt. "Don't just stand there. Go wash up. Supper is almost ready and they'll be here any minute. Hurry down when you're presentable as a proper lady. I need your help to set the table."

"Yes, Mother."

"And wear your blue frock. I ironed it for you while you were out doing your foolishness. I laid it out on your bed."

"But Mother, that's my church dress for Soldays." Rose *hated* that dress. It was stiff as wood and itched like poison ivy.

"You will wear it tonight. Please do something with your hair too! You look like a wild ragamuffin. Now scurry, missy! Your father will be home soon." Gerta pointed to the lute. "Take that thing upstairs."

"Yes Mother," Rose replied evenly, knowing it was insane to even try and reason with her mother when she was flustered about dinner guests. She did not understand the fuss—it was only Simon and his prudish old mother. Why the hubbub about tonight?

Away from her mother's sharp demands in the sanctuary of her small bedroom, she breathed deeply and closed her eyes in the only safe and calm place. Rose carefully put her lute in its designated corner. Her shoulders and back ached. She had a raging headache from hunger.

"Best to get this over with," she mumbled.

Rose stripped off her muddy dress and underclothes and stuffed them in the hamper. Rose lathered her face, neck, hands, and feet with homemade honeysuckle soap. Sweaty from running, she lathered her armpits too. Her mother had a sharp nose, so it was best to be cautious. She splashed her face with cool water, hoping it would ease her throbbing head.

A raven outside her window cawed shrilly and her head throbbed violently. The raven was Karta's symbol, and because Karta was her patron goddess, Rose usually liked ravens. Today its cries rattled her nerves. "Oh Karta, goddess of fate, stop me from losing my temper with Mother and spilling gravy on my best dress," she prayed. The nagging feeling of dread she had suffered all day did not diminish, but deepened with every breath.

Rose tried to shake it off as she brushed out her long chestnut hair and tied it back with a blue satin ribbon. After donning a fresh chemise and bloomers, she slipped into the coarsely starched blue dress with the flounced skirt and buttoned the front bodice with the tiny rose-shaped white buttons. The lace collar of her dress tightened around her neck—like a noose. She sighed and pulled on her white stockings and stepped into the ivory shoes with silver buckles. They were pretty but pinched her toes.

Rose checked herself in the mirror, hoping to satisfy her mother's pristine standards, but looked more like a rigid, lacy doll. A gruff tomboy with no graces was her mother's usual taunt. Rose was a smidge over four feet tall. Her mother was relieved when she stopped growing last year.

Freckles dusted her tanned face from running about in the sunshine—not a proper creamy complexion most girls prized. Not even her mother's constant application of buttermilk lotion faded her offending freckles.

Rose felt incomplete, as though fate was still weaving her image; like a caterpillar ready to emerge from its warm, concealing cocoon—but what will I become?

Gerta's piercing shout snapped Rose from her inner musings. Goodness, how her voice carried. It was enough to scare the gods!

"Rose, hurry up! I need you downstairs now! The table will not set itself, you know."

"I'm coming, Mother!" Rose shouted back.

Rose took careful steps down the stairs, since her good shoes hurt. In the dining room, Gerta had already set the table, placing her best hand-painted plates on the crisp white linen tablecloth which was topped with a delicate lace cover that was usually reserved for Solstice dinner. Apparently, Gerta was too impatient for Rose to do this simple task.

Gerta folded the napkins, frowning. "Such a slow girl. Lazy as an old cat. No common sense for what's proper. Why can't she behave like a normal girl? That's going to change! What did I do to deserve such an ungrateful child?"

"I *can hear* you, Mother."

"Then get to work," she snapped without missing a beat for an apology. "We have much to do, young lady. Much to do!"

Rose finished setting the table, acutely aware of her mother's verbal barbs in an unrelenting bitter tirade. Rose tried to ignore her by gritting her teeth. She prayed for the arrival of the guests which would provide deliverance from her mother's oral assault.

"Why all this fuss over Simon and his mother?" Rose asked, trying to change the topic from Rose's failure and her mother's incessant scorn to something safe and neutral. "They've been here for dinner before. It's not like an Ironheart is coming to dinner. And Simon's table manners are not exactly princely."

"Don't be disrespectful. This is a big occasion. Simon's finished his apprenticeship with your father. He may go into business with him now, which is a blessing. Old widow Agnes has all that money her husband left her. Simon could buy into the business. Then your father could spend more time at home, if he had a partner to shoulder some of the burdens. The village is growing and a good blacksmith is never short of patrons."

"I hope Peony arrives first. I haven't seen much of her in a few weeks and I'd like to catch up."

"Well, being a *proper* wife and mother is very demanding work."

"I know, Mother," Rose sighed wearily, lining up the good silver on the table.

"If you realized that then you'd be married by now and I'd have grandchildren to cuddle."

Rose smoothed the lace tablecloth and bit her lip to prevent the retort that burned on her tongue. She took a deep breath and said, "I do hope Simon and his mother don't stay long tonight. His mother hates me and I don't care much for him."

"What's your problem with young Simon? He's a fine young man with prospects. He certainly speaks well of you."

Rose wrinkled her nose and shrugged. "His hair is greasy and he reeks of onions and soot."

"Rose Greenleaf, what an improper remark!"

You insult me at every turn. How is that proper?

Jack Greenleaf stepped through the front door, preventing her mother's tirade before it exploded. "Where are my ladies?" he shouted.

Gerta's brow creased in agitation, but she closed her mouth. Jack Greenleaf always tried to soften Gerta's ridicule and thankfully her mother was too busy for another argument on Rose's unwed status.

"Papa!" Rose cried, relieved at his arrival. She ran to him and hugged, her arms barely reaching around his broad chest. "Here, let me take your coat." Rose hung it on the front peg by the door.

"Thanks, Rose," he sighed wearily.

"What's wrong, Papa? You look so tired."

He patted her shoulder and smiled. "It's just been a long day, my dear. How was your lesson with Master Aylecross?"

"Wonderful, Papa. I learn so much from him." Her father always asked about her lessons and Rose loved having someone to share it with. "I learned three new songs and recited the war poem of King Gregor Ironheart."

"The whole thing!"

"The whole thing! I didn't miss a line. It took me almost half an hour to do it too. My rhythm was a little off though, I think. I also asked Master Belenus about his time in Tirangel and Rhundoran Keep. He told me that—"

"Don't bother your father with that rubbish now," Gerta interrupted, rushing into the room with a basket of biscuits. "Jack, go clean up and put on your nice wool jacket and a clean shirt. The Split-Oaks will be arriving any minute."

Gerta permitted Jack to kiss her on the cheek in passing, while she placed the linen napkins in perfect alignment with the plates. "Yes, dear," Jack nodded, climbing the stairs to do his wife's bidding. After many years of marriage, Jack learned to comply with Gerta's domestic demands.

Gerta kept Rose running to and fro with final touches. When Rose placed a crock of fresh homemade butter next to the steamy hot biscuits, they smelled so good she almost snatched one, but her mother's brittle stare stayed her hand. Her look would have frightened off a ravenous troll.

Thankfully, Peony and her husband Tom arrived first. Peony was more like a sister to Rose than a cousin. They all hugged in the foyer. Peony usually softened her mother's mood. Tom was a cheerful and stout fair-haired man who had his own bakery. He adored Peony and that made him golden in Rose's eyes.

"Peony, you look wonderful," Rose gushed. "That pink frock becomes you. Is it new?"

Peony, a delicate, petite blonde with kind hazel eyes, smiled and took her hand. "Yes, I made it last week." Peony whispered in her ear, "You look so...*starched*." The two giggled while Tom and Jack allowed the girls their moment until a knock on the door interrupted their happy chat.

"Answer the door, Rose," Gerta ordered, placing a large bowl of mashed potatoes on the table. Rose salivated at the sight of the buttery mash and rushed to obey, hoping they would eat soon before she fainted from hunger.

Simon Split-Oak and his mother, Agnes, entered with solemn importance. Simon Split-Oak was tall, but a bit shorter than Rose, so he always puffed up when she stood next to him. What he lacked I height he made up for in girth, built like an ox, thanks to his mother's hearty meals and an even heartier appetite. Simon was a beefy specimen. Only the hard work of the forge kept his bulk from turning into fat. He had been her father's apprentice since Rose left school at age thirteen. She rarely talked to him though, since he disdained books and music. He wore his good brown suit and looked cleaner than usual, but his wavy black hair was greasy as ever and he still smelled like onions.

Agnes was an obstinate old woman who despaired about anything young or new. She was middle-aged when she bore Simon; a miracle since Agnes believed she was barren for most of her life. A widow for eight years now, Agnes was the epitome of the proper Dwarf matron. She was petite, modest and somber of dress, for she always wore black, except for her white widow's cap trimmed in black lace. She hobbled on a polished black cane topped with a silver handle. Frail of bone and gray of hair, in contrast Agnes' character was hard as iron. Agnes clung to her son with tenacity and looked down on every girl in the village as not being good enough for her strapping young son.

Rose curtsied, keeping her eyes downcast and voice soft in front of Agnes. That old crone would snap at you like a spiteful old turtle if you crossed her the wrong way. Rose did not want any squabbles to lengthen their visit or bring further reprimand on her. She just wanted to eat and go to bed. Rose took their cloaks and hung them on the pegs. "Welcome to our home."

"Hello Rose," Simon nodded with a smile. "I went to Belenus Aylecross's house this afternoon to walk you home, but he said you had already gone."

"Oh, what a shame," Rose whispered with downcast eyes. "I'm sorry I missed you." She hated lying, even to Simon.

"Good evening, Miss Greenleaf," Agnes snickered, clinging to her son's arm. "A young girl should not be rambling about without a proper escort. People may get the wrong idea."

"Of course, Mrs. Split-Oak," Rose replied with forced gravity. "Please go into the dining room. Dinner is ready to be served."

Agnes skimmed Rose with rheumy eyes and snickered, "What…no trousers today, Miss Greenleaf? Afraid someone might take you for a boy instead of a girl for once?"

Rose replied in the most submissive and gentle tone. "Not tonight, Mrs. Split-Oak. My trousers are upstairs, if you prefer that I change?"

I'm going to pay for that.

Rose knew it was risky to spar with Agnes, but sometimes the old lady just irked her good nature. Agnes did not reply to her ill-timed humor, but wrinkled her nose as though she had a whiff of something fetid.

Agnes squeezed Simon's thick arm, her eyes bright with pride. "Well, Miss Greenleaf, don't you have anything to say to my boy about his accomplishment?" Agnes wheedled.

Agnes always referred to unmarried girls with a sneering '*Miss*,' as though being unmarried were a state of shame and degradation.

Rose curtsied with demure modesty. "Congratulations on finishing your apprenticeship and becoming a blacksmith, Simon."

"Thank you," Simon answered haughtily.

"My son's good at everything he does. He'll soon be best blacksmith in all the southern counties."

Rose's father rescued her from further cruel examination by stepping between them and shaking Simon's hand and then deftly took Agnes hand in welcome. "Welcome, Agnes and Simon! Come on into dinner before it gets cold. So glad you could sup with us tonight. We have much to celebrate now that Simon has achieved the status of blacksmith. You raised a fine young man, Agnes."

Simon patted his mother's hand and guided her to the table. "Come Mother, let's not fuss. Is that chicken I smell?"

Rose mouthed a silent thank you to her father and went to the table. Rose and Peony exchanged grins as Agnes continued to moan about the deviance of youth.

Despite the formality of tonight's dinner, the meal was splendid. It took her mother's home cooking to mute Agnes Split-Oak's opinions. For such an infirm old lady, she ate with gusto. Baked chicken, mashed potatoes whipped with heavy cream and butter, biscuits, sweet corn, and gravy. Rose was too ravenous to think about taking tiny ladylike portions, and scooped large heaps of everything onto her plate.

Embarrassed, Gerta put down her fork and hissed, "Rose, your manners! Goodness, people will think we never feed you!"

You didn't today, Rose mused in silent revelry. *You shoved me out the door with a very long list of ridiculous errands before I could even have a cup of tea.*

Gerta passed the crock of butter to Agnes. "I must apologize for my daughter. Rose is usually a very delicate eater."

Peony mixed her corn and mashed potatoes together, surprised by Geta's words. "No she isn't, Auntie. Her appetite is boundless."

Tom buttered a biscuit, agreeing with his wife. "Rose usually eats like starving bear after hibernation. If more folks ate like Rose, my bakery would make me a rich man."

"I'm always a bit jealous at how she keeps that trim figure," Peony said. "I'm envious of her tiny waist while my waistline just keeps expanding, especially after having two babies."

"A small price to pay for the sacred role of motherhood," Gerta added, chewing tiny bites of chicken and nibbling her biscuit with delicate care.

"More to love, sweet," Tom said, kissing Peony on the cheek.

Rose was glad Tom and Peony were so happy. It was a love match, not arranged like some weddings. Rose liked Tom too. He did not treat her like a silly girl or think her crazy for her love of music and poetry. He also gave her free sweet rolls whenever she stepped into the bakery to visit.

Peony put another biscuit on her husband's plate and said, "Remember the cake eating contest a few years ago? Rose won after eating a whopping—"

"I must check my pies," Gerta said quickly. "Please help me, Peony. I so miss you, my dear. Tell me about little Nettie and Cody. They are getting so big!"

"Yes, Auntie Gerta," Peony said, rising from the table and throwing Rose an apologetic glance.

Soon dinner was over and the plates cleared away for the best part— dessert! Gooseberry pies and a bowl of fresh whipped cream were brought to the table by Gerta and Peony. Rose still looked forward to pie despite the large meal she just ate. Rose was obligated to pour the coffee and Gerta served the sherry in her finest citrine-colored glasses with delicate stems. Peony cut the pies into generous slices and served them on the good dessert plates with clean forks. She passed them around to each person. Rose sat down and added lots of cream and sugar to her coffee and piled a few good spoonfuls of whipped cream on her pie too. She had been looking forward to this all day. Despite their disagreements, her mother was one of the best cooks in Stone Haven. Gerta's pies and cakes often won top ribbons at the local fairs and festivals, which she accepted with modest pride.

Jack Greenleaf stood and raised his glass of sherry. Everyone followed his example. Rose impatiently waited for him to toast Simon, eager to eat her dessert. Let it be full of praise but brief, Rose wished fervently. That pie looks so yummy!

Jack cleared his throat. With solemn pride he raised his glass. "Today is a special day. My apprentice and a fine young man, Simon, finished his training as a blacksmith. We have also decided to become partners and will expand our business together."

"Here, here," they all joined in. Rose took only a small sip, for she was more anxious for the sweet confection before her.

"There is more to celebrate," Jack declared, his expression serious. "Simon will not only be a partner of the forge, but of this family. He has asked for my daughter's hand in marriage." He paused, looking down at his shoes, until Gerta stood up and took his arm tightly. "Go on Jack. Tell everyone our happy news."

Jack nodded and raised his glass again. "I have accepted his offer for my only daughter, Rose. We have agreed on a dowry and the marriage will take place next Solday at noon."

Rose froze, the glass of sherry paused at her lips. She could not breathe or make a sound or even think with clarity. Married to Simon? Next Solday? That's in six days! She felt as though she had died in that instant and no one was polite enough to notice. The starchy lace collar strangled her and each breath was a struggle. Her fine meal was a heavy brick tormenting her stomach. She managed to register the shocked gasps from Peony and Tom.

That unknown black storm cloud of chaos was unveiled now. It had chased her all day, always at the back of her mind, haunting her. Her silly fear that nagged her all day exposed to a fate grimmer than even she could imagine.

Rose did not fail to notice Simon's proud stance, accepting the prize he had won—Rose. His arrogance was only surpassed by his mother's. Agnes glanced at Rose with narrowed eyes, as though she could not wait to torment Rose when she was under her strict thumb in Simon's house. Rose looked at her mother, who beamed with smug satisfaction at her domestic conquest as she sipped her cordial. Arranged marriages were common enough, she just never realized her parents would do this to *her*. Wordless, Rose looked to her father, but he turned away from her questioning and desperate gaze.

Her mother poured more sherry for everyone, giddy in her triumph. "Well, speak up Rose. What do you have to say about the fine match we have made for you? Don't you want to thank your Mother?"

All tender feelings for her mother vanished in that instant.

The dining room fell silent and Rose finally felt the air escape her lungs. Rose gently set down her glass of sherry and finally spoke—soft, barely above a whisper, but with firm conviction.

"No. I will not marry Simon."

Chapter Three

Agnes Split-Oak, insulted by Rose's refusal, gasped with shock. Her eyes popped as though struck by an anvil. Her wrinkly face twisted with such searing anger Rose thought the aged woman would burst into flames, like some terrible creature of myth. "Come Simon, we're done here!" Despite her infirmity, she hobbled away with amazing speed, her cane scuffing Gerta's gleaming oak floor. Simon said nothing. He simply turned away from Rose and followed his mother out.

"I'm so sorry, Simon," Rose called after him. He did not acknowledge her words. She hadn't wanted to hurt anyone.

"Oh dear, oh dear—Agnes, Simon, please WAIT!" Gerta cried after them, dropping her fragile cordial glass on the table. The contents spilled and stained the snowy cloth. Gerta cast a furious glance at Rose, pointing her finger at her like a sword of doom. "Don't you *dare* say another word or even move, Rose Elisa Greenleaf!"

Gerta chased after the Split-Oaks, wailing her apologies. Rose remained standing in the same spot, her anxiety rising with each ragged breath, nervously smoothing her skirt with her hands and wishing the earth would swallow her up.

Desperate, Rose turned at her father. "Papa, I'm so sorry but I can't marry Simon—"

With brusque finality, he held up his hand. "No, Rose. I don't want to hear it." He walked out of the dining room.

Rose's pleadings fell silent. Her tenuous hope for her father's support vanished. She thought she would crumble right there if it were not for Peony's support. Her plump hand brushed Rose's cheek affectionately. "Are you all right, Rosie? Did you know—?"

"She didn't tell me a thing, Pea. How long has she been planning this? I can't believe Mother tried to trick me into this marriage. How could Father go along with this! He never pressed me to get married. Mother thinks announcing it in front of witnesses will make it truth and I would have to marry Simon. It will never happen, not if the god's demand it! Did she tell you anything, Pea? Please don't lie."

"Of course she didn't tell me, I swear! I would have told you if she did. You know that."

Rose clung to Peony, fearing she would collapse otherwise. "What am I going to do?"

Peony hugged Rose and stroked her hair, like she did when they were children. "Goodness, I've no idea, Rosie. This is pretty bad. I've never seen your mother look this cross, even with you."

Rose took deep breaths, trying to calm herself. "Cross? CROSS! Try livid, furious, and murderous. Instead of a wedding next Solday, there may be a funeral—mine!"

"Your bard training has really expanded your vocabulary," Peony said lightly.

They both burst out laughing, though only for a single breath before the panic reasserted its brooding presence again.

"What should I do?" Tom asked, still sitting at the table, uncertain and sweating a little, clutching his napkin to his chubby chin.

"I've no idea," Peony shook her head. "Wait! Tom, you try talking to her father. But for goodness sake, do not challenge Auntie Gerta right now."

"Yes, Dear," Tom nodded and left the dining room.

Without Pea's support, Rose would have crumbled into a heap. Rose wished she could cry, but the tirade of Agnes in the hallway echoed through the house prevented further emotional outbreak. Dangerous curiosity pulled them to rush to the corner and peek at the confrontation between Gerta and Agnes.

"That girl needs a whipping," Agnes declared loudly, pulling her cloak around her stooped shoulders and swatting Simon with her cane when he tried to help her. She then pointed her cane at Gerta. "Your daughter is unnatural, Gerta Greenleaf. This is what happens when you let them read books and play outside," her raspy voice wheezed. "Mark my words; I'll announce to the whole village what a wretched mother you are and what a trollop your daughter is if you don't fix this. My Simon wants the little fool, though I can't fathom why. She's worthless. She cannot cook or bake or sew like a normal girl. She possesses no feminine virtues. She's tall as a man and plain as dirt. Your brat won't be courted by a better offer of marriage than from my boy. Talk sense into your daughter else I'll show her what's good for her."

"It's a maiden's panic, that's all," Gerta begged as she opened the door and showed them out. "All will be well, Agnes. Young girls are so flighty you know. Please stay silent about this embarrassing moment. Your Simon will be partnered with my husband soon. We must remain friends, after all. I will take care of this misunderstanding. Just give me a little time."

"See that you do," Agnes warned. She grabbed Simon by the elbow she marched out the door.

Rose and Peony rushed back to their original places at the table just as Tom bounded down the stairs and ran into the dining room. Rose looked at him for a hopeful sign, but with a glum expression he shook his head. Her father was not going to come between Rose and her mother this time.

Rose prayed Peony and Tom would be allowed to stay, but Rose was deprived of further emotional support when her mother sent them home. Peony and Tom's sympathetic faces was the last hopeful thing she saw before Mother pushed them out the door.

Rose's mind was barren of ideas. Her quick wit and sharp mind always capable of tough debates and reason deserted her now. All her courage drained away when she declared her refusal to marry Simon.

Now what?

But from Gerta's hostile expression when she returned, it was far from over.

# # #

The war of wills lasted three days.

Gerta locked Rose in her room for daring to refuse marriage to the noble Simon Split-Oak. It was unbearable. Rose tried reasoning with her mother through the door, but in the end her temper would snap. She would beat on the door with her fists, begging her father to help her—but he did not come to her aid by word or deed. That was the worst part of this vile situation. Her mother had always been vocal in her disapproval of everything Rose liked or enjoyed—hiking, horseback riding, fishing, music, books, poetry, and writing stories. Anything that involved living! Rose's resistance to marriage had been a constant battle for years.

It was her father's betrayal that stung Rose's spirit. He had always been a gentle shelter against her mother's harsh demands and old-fashioned opinions. Her father's abandonment in this terrible madness was a bitter revelation. During her incarceration her father did not visit once, though she cried out to him that first day of her confinement until she was hoarse.

Peony and Tom came every day, but were forbidden to see her. Mother took away her lute, scrolls, and books to further deprive her of any solace. She unlocked the door only to bring her food and drink. The food was barely edible. A deliberate tactic her mother used to demonstrate her power. Plain porridge without milk or honey, bread, and water were all her mother permitted Rose to have. No other food was permitted—not even butter or jam for the bread. It gnawed at Rose, who longed for even an apple, a sweet slice of sponge cake, or a salty slice of ham. She craved steaming cups of tea infused with heavy cream and sugar. But those were denied to Rose as part her punishment. She was treated like a convict in every way.

The final humiliation was the refusal for her to visit the water chamber in the back yard to do her personal business; instead she was forced to use a chamber pot like an invalid.

Her Mother also found her stash of money that first day they locked her in. Rose had been keeping it in her pretty wooden trinket box she had bought at a fair two summers ago. She earned every coin from her talents too. Gerta gloated over her discovery and confiscated that too.

Desperate, Rose she prayed to all the gods of her faith, not just her patron goddess, Karta. She doubted the mother goddess Ishar or any of the other gods would rage down from the heavens just for her benefit. They would have better things to do.

Rose would have to manage her own troubles.

Belenus Aylecross even came to the house. Rose's only solace was sitting at the window, since she could not expense the sunshine any other way as a prisoner locked in her room. She saw her bard master walk to her front door, staff in hand, and knock on the door. She pressed her face close to the glass, trying to see what was happening. Belenus hated coming into the village and did not like her mother. He wobbled the three miles from his cottage, using his staff to propel his aching hips, to speak for *her*. If Rose could have climbed out that window to thank him, she would have, however, Jack Greenleaf nailed the window shut that first day of her incarceration to prevent Rose from escaping. Fresh air was also not permitted for the prisoner.

The war of wills that erupted between her mother and Belenus was quite loud, though she could not understand all of it. Rose made out words about wedding, bard nonsense, minding your own business, and foolish old hag. Her mother, usually a stickler for proper manners, did not invite the venerable Bard, a man who performed for kings, inside or offer him refreshment for his pains to visit. Then the door slammed and the fighting ceased.

Devastated, Rose watched Belenus walk away from the house. She wished she could have spoken to him! He stopped by the front gate. His perceptions must have picked up on her desperate plight. He stopped and turned around, and gazed up at Rose peering through her bedroom window. He smiled up at her, a sad smile that broke her heart. He then bowed, touching the rim of his wide-brimmed hat, before walking away.

She wept only when he had gone from sight.

Each visit from her mother brewed only more embittered fights, recriminations, pleadings, and threats.

Mother, I don't want to marry. I want to be a Bard. Please don't force this false marriage on me.

Foolish spoiled girl. A female Bard! Bah—unheard of! A woman's place is with her family. No daughter of mine is going to gallivanting around the countryside singing for her supper like a beggar. Think of the shame!"

Shame? What of the shame I must endure being married to an oaf who sweats like a pig and smells of onions?

People are beginning to talk about you, Rose. An unwed maiden at your age speaks ill for your whole family. All these silly fantasies of yours have made you forget your proper place in life. Marriage is the only thing that will restore your place in the village. Simon is a man with prospects.

Can you only describe a man by whether or not he has prospects, Mother? I don't even like Simon. How can I grow to care for such a man? He hates books and poetry. He hates music.

You're an old maid, Rose. You cannot be choosy now.

I'm seventeen, Mother, not a crone.

My daughter is a changeling!

If only I had a changeling to switch places with, I could escape this damned fate.

Ingrate!

Jailer!

The fights always ended with Gerta storming out and locking Rose in with the key that she now wore at her waist on a chain.

After nights of racking sobs, Rose came to a difficult conclusion. To win this war, she had to forfeit this battle. To restore her freedom, she must lie and pretend to submit to their parental will. Rose was good at telling stories and even making them up, but to actually lie to her parents galled her. It distressed her to deceive the people she loved—even her wretched mother. Rose must now lie or become Mrs. Simon Split-Oak.

Freedom has a price.

Rose would not only have to lie, but she must leave her home, perhaps forever. To remain free and follow her heart, she had to suffer the loss of family, home, friends, and even country.

So, with a bowed head and sullen manner, as her parents would never believe joy, she agreed to marry Simon.

Her father, now willing to show himself, gently patted her on the shoulder. "That's a good girl. It's for the best, Rose. It's time to put aside girlish games, like your mother wisely advises. You'll thank us in time. You'll see."

He did not look her in the eye when he spoke those words.

Her mother's triumphant smile for her submission galled her. After they seemed certain of her docile obedience, they unlocked her room and restored her freedom as a reward for her submission. Rose's favorite dishes were served at meals too. Always a robust eater, Rose could not stomach food now. Lying to her parents made her feel dirty and withered her appetite. For once her mother had to coax her to eat the succulent dishes.

Gerta blamed Rose's lachrymose state on bridal jitters and eagerly planned the wedding with the efficient strategy of a warlord.

Freed from the prison of her room, she rarely left it now. Her family did not impose anything, though they still watched her guardedly. She needed to focus and gather courage to escape. She asked to see Belenus, on the pretense of inviting him to her wedding, but her parents refused to let her see him or even to send him a letter.

Tomorrow was Solday, her *wedding* day.

Not if I can help it, Rose fumed inwardly.

She endured the last fitting of her wedding dress in silence, despite her mother's constant chatter. A broad border of lace fabric had been added at the hemline to lengthen the skirt, since Rose was so much taller than her mother and the sleeves were altered to little puffed sleeves to update the fashion for a spring wedding.

"You'll love being a bride," Gerta beamed, stitching the hem with practiced whips of her needle. "It's the one day of a maiden's life when she is treated like a princess. She is the center of attention, except of course when there is a christening. That's another great day. I cannot wait for grandchildren. Being a mother will give you joy, Rose."

After the dress had been refitted to her mother's satisfaction, Rose took it off and changed as her mother hummed and laid it out on her bed like a grand prize.

"Supper will be in a little while. I need to run to the kitchen and check on your wedding cake. Can't you smell it baking? It's your favorite—yellow cake. I used extra eggs and vanilla too. Tom offered to make it, but it's a mother's right to prepare her daughter's wedding feast. I hope you're hungry tonight. We're having baked ham with sweet potatoes and peas for supper. You love sweet potatoes, dear. Do eat something tonight. You will need your strength for tomorrow. Why don't you rest for a bit and think about what kind of flowers you want to carry at the ceremony. I have a big box of ribbons to choose from to tie them with. Would you like that?"

"Yes, Mother."

Finally alone, Rose's hands, curled into tight fists, shook with frustration. All her mother cared about was Rose's submission and marrying her to that oaf Simon. She did not hate Simon, but his very existence made her cringe now. He was allowed to visit once since Rose accepted the marriage, but they only sat on the porch in awkward silence while her mother chattered about the wedding plans. The reality of the wedding night also loomed in her mind. Did her mother actually expect Rose to tolerate Simon touching her? She shivered at the thought and realized her happiness meant nothing to her mother. This truth stung, but it eased Rose's guilt a little about her deception.

That night, after a celebratory supper for her last night as a maiden, which Peony and Tom attended with false cheer, Rose retired to bed early. She could not find the courage to face Peony and Tom another moment. She could not look at her parents for that matter.

Her mother stopped her on the stairs and took her hand. "You'll see everything will be better now. You must accept your place, Rose. Life will settle in. You will find happiness with Simon and children. Trust your mother's wisdom."

"Yes, Mother."

Her father did not embrace her, as though he suspected her deliberate distance was the broken trust between them. He bowed his head and turned away, whispering, "Good night, Rose."

He looked so sad. She wanted to run to him and hug him one last time, but dare not do so.

"Goodnight, Papa," she whispered evenly.

In the quiet of her room, she stared at the wedding dress that lay across her bed. It had been her mother's bridal gown years ago. Next to it was her bridal headdress, a wreath of silk flowers with long blue ribbons. Rose fought the urge to rip it to shreds. The dress was a white threat, the moonlight shining on its cruel lace. It looked like a shroud. The sounds of life downstairs gradually faded. Later, the soft pads of footsteps in the hall and her parents going to their bedroom finally cast a mollifying silence in the house.

Rose lay for hours; it was well past midnight before she finally stirred from the warmth of her narrow bed. Efficient and quiet as a mouse, she went to work. Even in the dark, she knew where her clothes chest was, topped with the quilt her mother had made for her twelfth birthday, the row of ragdolls on the window sill she had collected as a little girl, naming each one after some famous heroine or goddess, which annoyed her mother. Dolls were intended for a girl's practice for motherhood, but Rose was not interested in that. Her dolls fought battles. All memories of innocence before deceptions and lies threatened to damage the soul.

Rose decided to travel as a boy, having read about such a ruse in stories and hoped she could do it with success. She was tall as a boy and not that pretty anyway, so why not? She balked at cutting her hair, her one flaw of vanity. She settled on braiding her hair back tightly and pinning it up. She found an old hat with a wide brim and also wrapped a scarf around her face. She pulled on her trousers and wore a plain shirt and jacket over that. She took out her sturdy walking boots, but carried them. She would wait until she was outside before putting them on. She feared creaking floors would expose her.

She grabbed her old satchel from under the bed and stuffed it with an extra set of clothes, socks, writing styluses, and a roll of paper. It burned her that she had to leave her treasured books behind. With regret and longing she glanced at her old birthday quilt and snatched it; she rolled it up tight and tied it to the satchel. Her cautious search for her lute and money was fruitless. Her stolen property was well hidden, since her parents did not fully trust her submission. The lack of her money was annoying, but her lute was precious. She needed it to help her earn her keep. She could still sing without it and tell stories, it just would have been better with her lute. She did not know when she would earn enough coin to buy another.

There was one last thing to do before she left her bedroom. She reached under her mattress and withdrew the farewell letter she had written this morning.

Dear Mother and Papa,

I cannot marry Simon. I must find my path in life, so I am leaving home. Do not worry for me and please do not hate me. I cannot be the daughter you desire, so I must become the woman I was meant to be. Forgive me. In time, I will send word that I am safe.

Farewell.

Rose

She folded it and laid the letter on her dresser. She picked up her satchel and opened her bedroom door a crack and listened to be certain all was clear. Silent, she crept down the stairs to the kitchen. Her wedding cake loomed in the center. A large sheet cake smothered with thick white icing; pink and blue candy flowers rimmed the cake. Such temptation of confection would have been hard for her to resist before, now she could not stand to look at the array of cakes and goodies. Instead, she grabbed a loaf of bread and block of cheese from the pantry. *Now I am truly a thief,* she thought with irony. She added a few apples to her loot, since they kept well. She took the water bag her father used when they went fishing. Sad memories of happier days threatened tears.

She stepped outside into the bright moonlight. It was a chilly night, still a long way to summer, and she pulled her jacket close. She slipped on her boots and began to walk. Her eyes filled with bitter tears, for she never thought she would have to leave home this way. She felt like an outcaste skulking away in the dark with stolen goods.

Freedom has a price.

A strange shadow by the gate caught her eye, just a few steps away. Curiosity pulled her toward it. Upon close inspection, she gasped and fell to her knees.

It was a lute!

She dropped her satchel and picked up the lute with care. As Rose held it in her hands, feeling its smooth wood and touching the strings, she knew it was not her lute even in this darkness. It was Belenus' lute, with the familiar worn leather strap attached. Her master possessed four fine lutes, but this was the one he used when he played. How long had it been there, lying against their white-washed fence, waiting for her? Why had no one taken it in passing or inquired? She looked around, but could neither see nor sense anyone nearby.

How did Belenus know I would run away?

Tucked in the strings was a letter. She plucked it carefully and unrolled its mystery. She risked standing in the bright moonlight to read the contents. It was sketchy in this light, but she could see it was a letter of recommendation and introduction, commending her skill and talent as a Bard. She could use this letter to gain entry to a noble house or even an admission to audition for the Bard Academy in White Thorn. She recognized Belenus' flourishing signature at the bottom. She folded the letter and tucked it in her jacket.

She thanked Belenus aloud, as though the wind would magically carry her words to him. "Thank you, Belenus. I will make myself worthy of your gift, Master," she promised aloud, fearless of discovery. "I swear by my gods and by my soul, I will make you proud of me."

With head held high, Rose walked the moonlit path out of the village. The lute slung over her shoulder, her heart was light again. Her bravery restored and spirit strengthened by the faith of one man.

Chapter Four

After days of hiking through overgrown trails choked with wild grass and thick leafy vines, Rose finally found a tilted guidepost with a cracked wooden sign hanging from a rusty chain, forlorn and forgotten in the wilderness. The words were painted in both Rhulonese and Tirangeli, faded and cracked by time's weathering hand. "Here marks the border of Tirangel," Rose recited in Tirangeli.

Rose had expected to be more inspired by this hard won feat. In secret, she had studied the old maps in the library before running away, but they were much older than she realized. Three days ago she reached a fork in the road; she chose this path based on her hand drawn maps from those books. But it only led deeper into dense wilderness instead of civilization. Now she felt like the village idiot.

Too late now.

"At least I'm not completely lost," she shrugged, speaking Tirangeli, which Rose often practiced on her journey. She had only herself for company and decided to put this lonely time to good use. Belenus had tutored her in several languages of the western kingdoms, and she was grateful for this. Her sharp memory always helped her to learn fast, however, it was still going to be difficult.

She recalled her mother's reaction to Rose learning Tirangeli. *Goodness, whatever do you need that nonsense for? You speak one language just fine already.*

At this forgotten border, she observed no difference in the landscape between the two countries. The dirt, grass and rocks looked the same; the trees were just as tall and the sky as blue, though overcast with rain clouds again today. What destiny awaited her in this strange land? What mysterious trials did the elusive Karta, Goddess of Fate, have hidden for Rose in her shadowy wings?

Taking a deep breath, she crossed into the new realm with a broad step. The ground was spongy from rain and her boots made squishy sounds. It doused her moment of liberty. "I'm in Tirangel," she announced. *And I'm so hungry.*

She treaded on, shoulders stooped with her lute and satchel. The strange forest that surrounded Rose dusted her imagination where ancient fey myths and monsters loomed. It would be so easy to become lost in these shadowed woods, so she stayed on the path. She put her childish fears down to being alone for so long. Still, Rose was watchful for the ancient Fairy Folk, for if they existed, such primordial woods would be home for their elusive race. Perhaps a sprite waited for a hapless wanderer like Rose, eager to lure her into the Otherworld groves to be lost forever. She imagined an ogre lurking in the dark corners of a cave nearby, hideous nose sniffing out the scent of a frail solitary girl, licking his chops hungrily. A troll crouched beneath a bridge loomed in her thoughts, ready to snatch her away and drag her into the darkness. These creatures lived in dark, dank places and preyed on innocent travelers. She had often told these fey tales at fairs and festivals.

Rose hoped they were only *tales*. She cursed her imagination. A family of red squirrels caught her eye. They chased each other around a tall cottonwood tree and she laughed at their antics, relishing the silly distraction. Her stomach gurgled, and she took a long drink of water from her flask in a vain attempt to appease its demand for food. The tepid water tasted stale. There had not been a fresh stream or river in sight for two days, and she was afraid to stray too far from the road.

She hoped to find a village soon. The way stations built for travelers were sparse along this route and were quite run down. In the wilderness, she just as often slept in cramped, moldy tree holes or beneath bushes. How she longed for a real bed with soft, clean sheets smelling of lavender sachets her mother always slipped into the linen closet! Her poor birthday quilt was filthy now, but it was comforting to wrap herself in at night.

Rose had endured the grueling task walking miles alone. In the beginning, she hitched the occasional ride with farmers and merchants traveling southward. That eased her way, though she was careful not to be too friendly. She played the lute to pay for her ride and supper and even told a few stories, keeping her voice low and raspy. She claimed a sore throat whenever they asked for a song. She did not know how to sing like a boy. Still, her disguise as a young boy searching for adventure was successful. It's strange how boys seeking adventure are applauded and girls are considered unnatural for it.

There were a few blessed days spent with a kind family. She told them her name was Robert. They gave her a lift in their farm cart and she rode atop large flour sacks, comforted by its homely scent. She was grateful to them for their generosity and kindness. They were an older couple, with a daughter about Rose's age. The girl was shy and quiet around Rose, thinking her a boy of course. It would be improper for an unmarried maiden to be otherwise, unless she was officially being courted and chaperoned. Rose let the mask conceal her true sex, though it would have been nice to have someone her own age to talk to. She missed Peony's companionship. The family shared their meals and campfire with her, which helped stretch Rose's meager provisions. They felt sorry for the boy they came to know as Robert, not Rose, going to a strange country. They told 'Robert' to take care among the strange tall folk in the southern kingdom. Before they parted company, the wife pressed a small basket into her hands, packed with pears, apples, cheese, and a loaf of nut bread. The generous gift brought tears to Rose's eyes, but to her relief, her boyish facade remained intact. The family seemed happy too. She had not been happy living with her mother for years and that thought made Rose very sad.

After they dropped her off, she was truly alone for the first time in her life.

That was her last ride and since then the days were grim and lonely. She had eaten her gift of food sparingly, though in better times she would have polished it off in a day. Now she was hungry and alone in a strange land.

Stop moping, Rose chided herself.

The city of White Thorn was her future now, but homesick memories haunted her. She cried herself to sleep almost every night. The physical pangs of hunger assaulted her again. She ignored it and tried to pass the time by reciting her favorite tales and poems. When she began the epic of King Ironheart, she stopped in her tracks, realizing it was the last poem she performed for Belenus. She wept for a moment, wiped her eyes with her sleeve, and walked on.

Recollections of home haunted her like a vengeful ghost, refusing to vanish. In the kitchen, Rose only excelled at burning toast, but her mother ruled the kitchen liked a warrior ruled a battlefield. Memories of pancakes dripping with cinnamon butter and maple syrup, mashed potatoes whipped with baby onions and cabbage, chocolate cake, fried chicken, pot roast simmered with new potatoes, carrots and gravy, and fluffy egg pie stuffed with spinach, cheese, and mushrooms baked in a flaky crust, made her salivate. These were the dishes her mother cooked for her during her last days at home before she ran away. At that time, Rose's appetite had vanished due to emotional stress and was unable to eat more than a bite of her favorite foods. Now her deprivation demanded vengeance and it cursed her frugal eating during those final days when delicious hot meals had been abundant.

"But all the food in Stonehaven would not make up for being forced into an arranged marriage," she reminded herself. "I can't go back home, so why torture myself?" Rose said firmly in Tirangeli, and trudged further into the new territory with heavy steps.

Rose tried to concentrate on her new life in White Thorn. She realized her high expectations might not be realistic, since women in most realms faced some prejudice. Still, Tirangel was a logical choice for many reasons, not just because it bordered Rhulon. Women were allowed education beyond the rudimentary needs, they owned businesses and property, and some even served as warriors! Rose had read many stories and poems about women warriors from Belenus' library. She hoped to meet a real one.

A chance to study at the Bard Academy in White Thorn enticed her dreams, but she had no funds now. Her hoarded savings had been snatched by her mother during the turmoil of refusing Simon's proposal, if you could call it that. He never asked her, she was merely informed of it. That made it worse somehow. Still, she vowed that one day she would study at the Academy.

She wondered what people would think of her. Could they accept her as her own people had not? Would she be an outcast? No matter, she would make do in a new world and not whine about it. But even these intense thoughts did not distract her from shivering in the chilly morning air and being so damned hungry. She knew even if her mother did not speak of her running away, she knew Agnes Split-Oak would be wagging her tongue.

Foolish Rose. Imagine a girl traveling alone in the strange land. She must surely be mad. Why else would she turn down my handsome Simon? What a fool!

Better a mad fool than a married one, Rose thought.

She wondered about the tall folk. She had read about them, but had never met one. Blast! What she wouldn't do to talk to Belenus again.

Rose stumbled down the hill and a lump in her boot forced her to stop. She rested on a fallen log and pulled off her boot and shook it until the source of her irritation, a small stone, tumbled out onto the muddy ground. "Oh yes, this is high adventure worthy of a great poem! A huge pebble has invaded my boot. I shall cast it out anon by my mighty hand." She laughed and rubbed her foot, and slipped her dirty boot back on.

Loud male voices alerted Rose to take cover. Though her tortured feet begged for a ride, wisdom prevailed over comfort. Even though she wore a boy's disguise, she took pains to be careful with the people she begged rides from. Not everyone would be kind and Rose had enough sense to take that to heart. The sounds were coming from inside the forest—not the road! That was oddly suspect. Frantic, Rose took refuge off the road behind a hawthorn tree as the first tall folk men she had ever seen appeared.

What giants! She spied two men in leather jerkins rode in a rickety wagon pulled by two horses. Dirty and rough looking, they openly carried swords. The horses mesmerized her, their gargantuan size giving rise to the mythic stories of the flame-winged mounts of Celestial Warriors created by Ursas. The shaggy Dwarven horses of Rhulon were miniature toys compared to such majestic, albeit frightening, horses of the tall folk.

The driver stopped the horses when they reached the road and the wheels of the wagon creaked to a stop. He did not seem so godlike. He was mortal to a fault. A thick fellow with a head of shaggy, dark blonde hair; he looked disheveled and grimy. His companion, a lanky man with greasy black hair, jumped down from the wagon.

Fearful, she crouched lower, her mind racing with prayer. *Please Ursas and Ishar, creators of all things, protect me from my enemies. Save me from a terrible fate if these men be evil.*

The man wandered over to her side of the road. She should have fled deeper into the woods when she had the chance. Better to face trolls than such strange callous men. He was so close she smelled his rank odor of stale sweat and beer. Rose held her breath, afraid of making a sound. He stood on the other side of the hawthorn tree she hid behind and pissed. She squeezed her eyes shut when the flow of his urine showered the tree and he moaned with relief.

"Hurry it up, Albin!" the driver shouted.

She closed her eyes, silently begging, *Go away! Go away! Go Away! Don't walk around the tree! Dear gods—will he ever stop!* Her heart hammered in her chest, thumping with violent thunder. She was certain the giant men would hear her and drag her out. She would suffer a gruesome death as his pitiless lands, never to be discovered in this feral grove. She would haunt the forest as a pale phantom, the bleak fate of the dead cast away without proper burial or prayer.

Curse my imagination!

Finally, Albin stopped urinating and returned to the wagon. What did he do to relive so much water—drink an ocean of beer? They drove away, urging the horses to a fast gallop; the mud caked wheels moving southward down the path.

She exhaled, dizzy from holding her breath for so long. She remained hunched over in her hiding spot until they were long out of sight. When she finally stood up, her legs tingled with pins and needles. She rubbed her legs and tried to get the blood flowing again. She picked up her lute and satchel, relieved for the first time to be alone. They were going in her direction and that frightened her.

Afraid to walk out in the open, she kept off the road but stayed close enough to follow it. She hiked a few miles, until she saw a stream. The morning sun shone brightly on the clear water, making it shimmer like magic. Fresh water! She ran to the stream's edge and knelt to refill her canteen. She splashed handfuls into her eager mouth. The clear, chilled water tasted so good! She washed the grime off her hands and face. She knew she must keep moving and find a proper shelter and sleep without fear of strangers.

A flock of black crows burst out of the trees. They shadowed the sky with dark wings. Rose shivered, thinking of the goddess Karta. Crows and ravens were her sacred symbols. She stood up to leave, grabbing her canteen. The snapping of a branch to her left stiffened her spine. From the corner of her eye, a dark-haired man stepped out from behind a pale birch tree, a dagger dangling in his filthy hand. It was Albin, the one who pissed on the poor tree.

"What have we here?" he grunted. "A little boy? You lost? Come here boy." His accent was guttural and she found him hard to understand, but his malicious grin made his intent quite clear to her.

Forsaking her satchel, she grabbed her lute and ran. Horses charged into the grove and blocked her way, the corpulent blonde man holding the reins. The horses reared up, and she spun away, terrified they would trample her with giant hooves. The stranger's long strides matched her speed with ease and he seized her by the waist. His companion laughed as he grappled her. She had dropped her lute in the clash for survival. He lifted her high in the air and spun her around. She dangled from his arms, thrashing at him with her fists and kicking her feet.

"Be still, little boy!" he ordered, holding her out like a ragdoll and shaking her.

Her hat flew off and her hair tumbled down her back in a thick braid. He roughly threw her face down to the ground. Her nose and mouth filled with the tang of moist forest loam followed by the sour taste of sweaty skin as his enormous hands cupped her mouth. Mad with terror, she bit his hand hard. Warm salty blood stained her tongue. He yelped and snatched it back. She scrambled away, but strong hands dragged her back and rolled her over on her back. He pinned her down with large hands.

He growled in his throat. "I told ya' to settle down!" He cuffed her hard with his fist. Pain and dizziness overwhelmed her. She screamed as he straddled her little body with ease, a terrible victorious giant. He leaned in and pressed the tip of his dagger to her throat.

The blade's threat silenced her.

"Can't escape old Albin," he laughed. He looked her over and grinned. "Hey, you're not a boy. Hey Fendrel, we got us a little girl."

Terrified, jaw throbbing and bleeding, she lay still. Afraid he might indeed kill her, she obeyed him. She read stories about highwaymen and cutthroat thieves. Their cruelty was not an exaggeration. He was too big to fight off. He must be nearly six feet high! It might as well be a troll or ogre holding her prisoner.

Fendrel hollered, "Little girls fetch a good price in the whore houses. Tie her up and put her in the wagon."

Whore house! Never! Not even if the gods demanded it, Rose silently fumed.

Albin's greasy smirk revealed stained, broken teeth. "Hey, you ain't no child! I think you be a woman by that body! Look Fen, a tiny woman. That's funny. Tiny woman."

"Brilliant observation," Rose spat in Rhulonese.

"Huh?" he said. "What's that gibberish? You some kind of foreigner?"

She realized she lapsed into her own tongue. Forcing her voice to remain calm, she formed the words slowly, hoping not to mangle the speech, especially since her life depended on it. "You are quite right that I'm a woman. I'm a bard from Rhulon, good sir. You're doing me a great injustice and more to yourself." A small window of reason rationed how she might deal with these thugs. She had no hope to fight them off; perhaps she could talk her way out of this madness.

"You talk funny," Albin grunted.

She smiled up at him, as though she were having tea and crumpets with a friend. "Albin, I have just arrived to your kingdom. I know you're gentlemen of adventure, but I must warn you that I do have friends. They are meeting me here. They will be here very soon, so for your own sake, let me go! I will not say anything if you free me. Be wise! My companions will be angry if you hurt me."

"More little folk like you?" Albin smirked. "We can handle 'em."

"No, they are not little folk. They are quite tall-taller than you even." She added in her own tongue, "Except that they bathe."

"Hey, what did you say? Sounds like rubbish to me."

"Sorry, I am trying to say your words correctly. Do you think I would be traveling alone in such bleak territory without protection?" Rose maintained her lies so smoothly she stunned herself. "If you hurt me, you will bring trouble on yourself and your friend, for I am the newly appointed Bard to the House of Astriad in White Thorn." She plucked the name from an old Tirangel poem.

"They sound like noble caste?" Albin grumbled, trying to gage her words.

"Yes, an old noble family, good sir. A *powerful* family. They will react violently if one of their own is harmed. I know you have your reasons for being outlaw, but take pity on a lone woman making her way in the world. Think of the harm you would do to your business adventures should you act *hasty*. My friends will be back soon. We have journeyed long from Rhundoran Keep in Rhulon. I just wanted to walk alone for a spell, to work on a song for my new Master. My muse demands solitude. A smart man like you must understand such things. If you let me go, I'll compose a poem about you, Albin, a highwayman who spared a poor maid out of kindness. People will admire you."

He nodded at her words, agreeing with her bold assessment of his intellect.

"Listen to me Albin; I'm just a simple bard. I am poor, like you. I rely on the kindness of benefactors. Often I have gone without food and shelter, as I know you have in your life."

He scratched his scruffy beard and his bushy brow furrowed trying to work out if she was lying or speaking the truth. "I been hungry and poor," Albin agreed. "I've never had a song written about me."

"Let me sing for you to prove I'm a bard." She began to sing a simple ballad. She feared her voice would crack from stress, but her vocals were smooth as honey. As she sang, a strange shiver rushed through her body; her face and hands suddenly felt hot. It made her dizzy. Rose was terrified, but she continued to sing. Albin's expression wavered and he slowly drew back his dagger, smiling like a child. Even Fendrel paused, his scowl softening to a smile. Rose finished, a little stunned at the effect of her song.

Fendrel blinked and shook his head. Albin still stood there like a moon-eyed puppy. "ALBIN! Snap out of it," Fendrel hollered, shattering the fragile charm Rose had nearly woven over them both. "She's lying, except about being a bard. Only a foolhardy bard would talk that much with a dagger pointed their way. Just put her in the wagon. We can sell her for a good purse to an eastern slaver. We can't let folks talk their way out of being slaves. Bad for trade."

Albin lingered in confusion, his jaw working as he digested her pleas. She had placed a seed of doubt at least.

Fendrel barked, "Put her in the wagon now or I'll take care of *both* of you myself. NOW ALBIN! And gag her too. She's too yappy."

"All right, all right!" Albin leaned in close to her, his breath fetid. "I'm still gonna sell ya' tiny woman. Don't get many dwarf girls in the south. Your price just went up!"

He dragged her toward the wagon by her feet and roughly tied her hands and feet with coarse rope. Albin gagged her with a filthy cloth. It tasted foul and she winced. He scooped her up and dumped her into the back of the wagon like a sack of potatoes.

"Take care with this one," Albin warned Fendrel, climbing into the front seat. "Her talk is as dangerous as her bite," he groaned, wrapping the bloody hand she bit with a dirty kerchief.

"You don't say?" Fendrel grumbled and leaned to spit again.

The wagon jostled along the rough road. The ride was brutal as she felt her body bruising with every bump and hole the wagon drove over. In her prison in the back of the wagon, she tried to wriggle free of her bonds, but Albin had knotted them too well. The long wooden boxes roped together unnerved her. She feared a heavy box would topple and crush her.

She blinked back tears for her lute, lost to her now forever. The satchel she could do without, but the loss of the lute was heartbreaking. Belenus had left her that lute and she failed him.

It was as though Karta, Goddess of Fate, decided to mock her foolish bravery with a cruel storm. Hard rain poured down on Rose with vehemence and she shivered with cold. Fate had more trials for her, it seemed.

Soaked and miserable, Rose scolded herself for believing that sprites, ogres or trolls were a danger.

Human men were much more terrifying.

Chapter Five

The wagon rolled over every bump and fissure in the road, jarring her body until she feared her bones would snap. The abrasive ropes cut tightly into her wrists. The crude remarks of her captors burned her ears. If her mother heard such vulgar language, she would perish from shock! Rose morosely dwelled on her bleak fate, plagued by her own overactive imagination, tormented by visions of her mother's frowning image gloating over her prone and trussed up form, tapping a rolling pin in her plump hands with stern satisfaction.

You should have listened to your poor old mother! If you had married Simon you would be baking an onion pie right now.

Rose was not sure which fate was worse.

The sun dipped low in the sky and flocks of crows, hundreds of them, roosted in the surrounding trees as dusk settled upon the forest. Their deafening caws rattled her nerves. The sparse trees soon drooped with black-feathered leaves. Rose flashed to the mythic tales of crows she had studied to keep her mind focused but distracted from her pain. Crows appeared in many legends and could be omens of good or evil, and often acted as messengers for the gods, especially Karta. Crows are smart and clever. If Rose were as clever as those mysterious black birds, she would not be a prisoner of evil men.

She winced at the constant gutter language of her captors, despite her attempts to ignore them. If only they would be silent for just five minutes! She fervently wished a pack of vicious trolls lurked nearby. She imagined a garish tale where snarling trolls attacked these smelly ruffians and devoured them, crunching their bones with daggered teeth. As trolls chewed grimly on her enemies, she also wove an image of her rescue with hundreds of crows flying down and carrying her far away to safety.

Her imagination could be a solace, after all.

Despair returned to torture her thoughts, which Rose crushed with forced optimism. But all her fantasies could not erase the fact her stomach growled angrily. *How can I risk flight and freedom when I'm so weak from hunger?*

The wagon finally stopped. She relished the relief to her battered body, but shifted to panic again as a gruff, new voice spoke to her captors with clipped authority.

"You're late! Any trouble along the way?" he asked gruffly.

"None at all, Rebec," Fendrel answered. "We mostly kept to the back roads and wooded pathways. Not a ranger in sight neither, even on the main highways. Since the crown built those new roads, these routes have fallen into disuse—and to our advantage."

"Good," Rebec replied. The stranger walked over to the back of the cart and peered down at her. What the hell is this?" he bellowed, pointing at Rose. "A child? They're too much trouble."

"Nope—it's a *tiny* woman," Albin snickered, jumping down from the wagon.

Rebec jumped into the back and coldly gazed down at Rose. A swarthy man in black leather and a dark turban, she cringed as his large hand cupped her face and examined her worth. She marked his cruel eyes, a jagged red scar that ran down on his cheek, and sour breath.

"A Rhulonese dwarf? They don't come south often and they certainly don't let their women wander neither," Rebec said suspiciously. "I don't like this." He sat back on his haunches, looming over her like a fearsome titan. "Rhulonese women are a unique prize and she may fetch a nice clutch of gold on the auction block. Still, it bothers me."

"She was alone," Fendrel insisted. "Carried a lute and blabbered about being a bard. She was dressed up as a boy too, but we weren't fooled."

"Big lies for tiny woman," Albin replied, still amused by his term for her. "She speaks fancy. She nattered too much, so we gagged her to shut her up," he added, unhitching the horses. "She'll fetch a good price from a whore house, being a rare piece of tail."

"Just feed the damn horses, Albin," Rebec ordered. "Tomorrow we ride east with the cargo."

"When do we get paid?" Albin asked.

Rebec's voice tightened with impatience. "After we cross the border and collect our payment for the women—got it?"

"I got it. Man needs to watch out for his interests, you know. I ain't stupid, you know," Albin muttered.

"No Albin. Stupid isn't the word I'd use," Rebec replied sharply.

"How much they gonna pay us this time?" Albin needled.

"Just shut your mouth!" Rebec commanded. "Now do as I say or you'll get a lashing! My whip hasn't been used today and it feels neglected."

Albin ceased talking. Rebec must be the leader of this lewd group of ruffians, judging by how Fendrel and Albin deferred to him.

Rose's mind worked furiously. Snatches of their conversation offered fragments about what her fate held. Crossing the border? Head east? But to where?

Rebec jumped down from the wagon. "Lock the dwarf up with the others. She'll sell fast. Not many Rhulon women in the whore trade. If she's virgin, that can triple her price."

Albin opened the back of the wagon and pulled her out, feet first. He dropped her on the muddy ground. He looked down on her and said, "Never had a dwarf girl before." He scratched his scalp and cocked his head. "She's a pretty one. Ripe as a plump peach, she is. She could be a virgin. Never had one of them before neither."

"Keep your lust tucked in or I'll slice it off," Rebec warned. "She'll bring a higher price if she ain't split between her little legs."

"How can they tell if they've been split?" Albin pondered, scratching his head again.

She shuddered at that question. She did not want to know and blocked further thought about it by wondering if Albin's scalp itch was a nasty habit or lice infestation.

"Just do as I say," Rebec ordered and stomped away.

Albin lifted her easily with one hand and carried her into the cave. Inside the cave's mouth, there was a cooking area where a fat man squatted, stirring a large iron pot over a low fire. Rose smelled the thick slabs of bacon that sizzled in an iron skillet and spied thick loaves of round bread and yellow cheese laid out on a cloth.

"Hey, Borlon, I'm hungry. When's supper ready?" Albin asked in passing.

"It's coming," Borlon shouted back. His frayed clothes were patched and he carried more than a spoon, eyeing the dagger in his belt. Tatters of crumbs and twigs clung to his frizzy black beard like an old nest. She wondered if those ended up in the cooking pan. What Borlon stirred in that pot had an odd pungent spell, but hunger trumped taste. She might just eat anything, including that mystery stew! Albin shifted her in his arm like a sack of potatoes. The cave was even bigger as they moved deeper inside, the darkness lifted by rows of torches on the walls. They moved into a vast chamber where several rough looking men milled about. The homey scent of bacon was vanquished by the foul odors of human waste and unwashed bodies.

Albin dumped her on the ground and snatched a ring of keys off the wall. Women were confined in tall metal cages. She did not see any male captives, so their trade must be women only.

Albin unlocked the nearest cage and bellowed, "Stay back wenches."

The women remained huddled together at the back of the cold jail, defeated and mute. He cut her ropes and removed her gag. Her relief diminished when he pressed the tip of the knife against her cheek. "You behave, tiny woman," he threatened, "or I'll cut your pretty face." He roughly shoved Rose inside and slammed the door, locking it with a quick turn of the key.

She landed face down in the dirt. This final act of humiliation, along with the long hours of being bound up and terrified fractured her temper.

"*Wicked Scum! Goblins have better manners! A scourge on your lice-ridden head! May the gods shrivel your balls into dried-up walnuts!*" she muttered violently in Rhulonese, pushing herself off the dank ground.

"What'd the hell you say?" Albin asked, squinting down at her.

Rose looked up at him squarely. "I merely extolled your refined charms, Albin," she replied coolly.

He grunted, confused by her smooth reply. "Well, keep yapping in gibberish, tiny woman, and I'll gag you again!" Albin threatened. He walked away, scratching his scalp vigorously.

"The smell is doing that already!" Rose choked, covering her mouth with her hand. The source of the wretched smell was a small wooden bucket in the back corner of the cage–and that was overflowing with filth. Obviously, it was the only place for the poor women to relieve themselves. These brutes did not intend on letting anyone out of their prisons for any reason.

Several women were clustered together in the cage. They stared dully at Rose. Rose studied the large cavern. Torchlight enabled Rose to see coarse, mean looking men in shabby armor carrying swords or spears. The cave itself was enormous and she noticed paths leading upward to caves and tunnels. From where she sat, she counted several sturdy cages all crammed with women just like this one. The stink was so horrible she thought not think. Rose held her arm up to her face, but it did little good.

"Your nose will go numb soon enough," a deep, feminine voice commented.

"I doubt that," Rose choked.

A tall redhead stood up from the pitiful group. Though her clothes were stained and torn like the rest of the women, she possessed a regal air this dreadful jail could not sully. The woman lifted her skirt, ripped a thick strip from the hem of her petticoat and handed it to her. "Here child, it's not much, but it does help until you get used to it. Tie it around your face to block the smell."

"Thank you," Rose replied, accepting the cloth.

The stranger was kind to her, even in this grimy place where cruelty reigned. In fact, this was the first kindness she received since entering Tirangel.

The woman moved closer and squatted down to eye level with Rose. "My name's Meg," she offered.

"I'm Rose."

"You have an interesting accent. You've got quite a temper too. I can relate to that. At first I thought you were a child, but upon closer view, I see you're a young woman. Are you from Rhulon?"

"Yes, I just crossed the border today. Sadly, the first men I met were these highwaymen."

"The roads are dangerous. You should never talk to strangers."

"I didn't!" Rose replied sharply. "I even hid from them off the road and thought they had long passed me by, but they found me anyway." She instantly regretted her anger. "Sorry. I shouldn't have snapped at you. I should not unleash my temper on a fellow prisoner. Especially one who has been so thoughtful."

"It's all right. You've had a tough day. You look rather young to be traveling alone on such a long trip."

"I'm eighteen—well I'll be eighteen in a few months. I'm quite able to take care of myself, though current circumstances may not accurately represent that fact," she added dryly. "How'd they capture you?"

"Me? I live on a dairy farm near a small village outside of the city. I was walking home from the market and they ambushed me on the path. They hit me over the head and I woke up here two days ago."

"That's terrible. I overheard them talking when I got here. They're leaving tomorrow. If we don't escape before that, our fate is to be sold to slavers when they cross the border." Rose dropped her head to her knees and whispered in a shaky voice, "I'm just so damned scared."

Meg knelt down next to her. "You hid it well from that idiot, Albin."

"My bravado is a hollow defense, I'm afraid."

Meg grinned and stoked her head gently. "What did you really say to him?"

Rose whispered it to her and Meg burst out laughing. "It's best that you lied to him. Albin is stupid, but he has a violent streak."

"Thanks," Rose remarked. "He didn't actually believe me when I said I extolled his charms, did he?"

Meg shrugged and settled next to Rose, crossing her legs. "With that moron, it's possible. Why were you traveling alone?"

"I wanted to come to Tirangel to be a bard. White Thorn has an academy. I planned to work and save money."

"What about the academies in Rhulon?"

"They don't accept girls. My choices of a vocation back home were limited. In the end, it was either run away or succumb to marriage."

"Arranged?"

Rose hugged her knees closer to her. "Yes, in the worst way possible— by my mother. His name was Simon Split-Oak."

"Was Simon at least handsome?"

Rose laughed. "He always smelled of soot and onions."

"Best to run then," Meg replied, smiling lightly.

"Simon wasn't horrible. He just wasn't for me. We had nothing in common. I don't think I'm made for marriage, so I decided to follow my dreams and become a bard."

"You couldn't do that in Rhulon?"

Rose shook her head. "In Rhulon, things are very traditional when it comes to girls. I was going to leave the proper way when I came of age. I wasn't of legal age yet in Rhulon, so even if someone wanted to give me work, they couldn't without my parent's permission." Rose turned her face away, unwelcome tears of frustration brimming. "I'm not like other girls. I was terrible at all the girly things, like cooking and sewing. I was the opposite of what my mother wanted in a daughter. I was her bane and she mine. My mother arranged the marriage bond with Simon and I had only a week to plan. I had no one on my side but Belenus, but he had no legal rights to speak for me."

But my father did, Rose thought sadly. *He abandoned me to mother's machinations. How could he allow something so wrong and think it was for my own good? I always thought papa would stand up for me, but he did not speak for me. That hurt more than anything.*

"I understand. Being different is something of a curse," Meg answered softly, eyes somber.

"It's a curse," Rose agreed, "that's gotten me into loads of trouble. They locked me in my room until I agreed to marry Simon. That was the only time I ever lied to my parents. As my matrimonial fate loomed I plotted my escape. I thought it was destiny too, because the night I ran away, Belenus, my Bard Master, left me his favorite lute. It was a symbol of his faith in me and it's gone now. Albin tossed it away when they kidnapped me on the road. Now I have nothing. Well, that's my story. I must sound silly."

"No, you're not silly. Sometimes flight is the only path to take," Meg whispered.

Rose did not know why she confided her heart's secrets to this stranger. For some reason, she trusted her. Meg shared her cloak with her to ward off the chill and for the first time since she saw those dreadful men on the road, she was not afraid.

"Hungry?" Meg asked.

"I was, but this smell killed my appetite."

"Just as well. I doubt they'll feed us," Meg whispered. "Even if they do, it might be drugged. So take care."

A thickly-muscled man with a flat nose and a bald head covered with intricate blue tattoos strolled toward her cage. Shirtless, his tattered black leather vest and his muscular arms encased in brass armbands strained against his girth. Rose noticed his left eye was swollen and bruised. He carried a water bucket and a tin cup with a long warped handle.

"Come and get it, ladies! Jardo has a treat for you. Nice clean water," he called, stirring the dipper in the bucket.

The frightened women were desperate for any sustenance and rushed to the front of the cage. Rose would have been knocked aside if it were not for Meg, who remained steadfast by her side in the chaos, her strong, gloved hand a firm comfort on her shoulder.

The women desperately crowded together and gulped water until he kicked the cage and growled, "Get back now! One at a time, else sweet ole Jardo will get mad!" He allowed each woman a quick drink and then barked at them to move back. When Meg took her turn he jerked the dipper away. "No water for you! You're too much trouble, Red."

Meg kicked at the bars and sneered, "What's the matter? Still smarting over that black eye, Jardo?"

He thrust his hand through the bars and grabbed Meg by her bodice and pulled her roughly against the cage. "You'll suffer more than that before we leave, whore!"

Meg jerked away and spit at him. "You don't scare me, baldy!"

"Bah!" he roared and stomped away. "You're not worth a piss!"

Meg glanced down at Rose. She then kicked at her cage. "Hey Jardo! Come back! The little dwarf girl needs some water. Have a heart! It's her first night in hell."

Rose held her breath and waited tensely, parched for water despite the foul smell around her.

He glanced at Rose and grunted. He marched back and quickly shoved the dipper through the cage bars and ordered. "Hurry up and drink!"

She barely swallowed before Jardo jerked back the reviving cool water and stomped away to another cage.

Rebec strolled by, swilling from a brown jug. She doubted it was anything wholesome.

"Jardo, how are the sluts?" Rebec asked.

"Scared and witless, just the way you like'em."

"Good. We'll fetch a nice fat purse off these sluts this go round."

He strutted away like a ridiculous rooster. She had known this wretched man for less than an hour and she loathed him with every pulse of her body. This time, she began to imagine a combination of drooling ogres and goblins falling upon Rebec. His end was not pretty.

Borlon carried in a bucket that sloshed with something that vaguely looked like soup. He filled small tin cups with the gruel and handed them out to the women.

"There now, sluts," Rebec announced loudly, strutting around the cavern. "Remember I offered you all this fine meal before your journey to a new life better suited to your talents. Rebec takes good care of his property."

Frantic women rushed to snatch the tiny cups of thin soup. Rose and Meg each grabbed a small cup. Rose held the cup to her mouth, but hesitated. It smelled like the strange concoction Borlon was stirring. Meg's gloved hand covered the cup and shook her head.

"Ladies, stop!" Meg hissed. "Don't eat this swill. I think it's drugged."

But the famished women had gulped down the soup, oblivious to reason. Only Meg and Rose did not drink the soup. Meg dumped hers in the bucket when the men were not looking and Rose followed her example.

"Why do they need to drug us?" Rose whispered.

"To keep us docile and quiet on the road," Meg answered bitterly. "It's a long way to the border. This many women would take a caravan of wagons. Slavery is illegal in Tirangel, but there are other kingdoms not so enlightened and do not ask where the slaves come from. They do not want the Emperor's Rangers to suspect."

"Rangers? Rose asked. "I have read about them since I was a child. They have a stellar reputation as warriors. They patrol the roads and forests of the Empire, to keep it safe for the people. Do you think the rangers might rescue us before we reach the border?" Rose asked hopefully.

"We must always hope," Meg replied.

Soon the drug-spiced gruel did its work and the women fell asleep. Rebec remained out of sight, so the men relaxed and indulged in the distractions of ale and dice, gathering in loose circles near the fire.

"We better feign sleep too," Meg suggested, propping herself against the bars with the unconscious women. "We don't want to arouse suspicion."

Rose's nerves were rattled. She was not sure she could even close her eyes, frightened by the grim fate of slavery and worse. She kept her head covered with her share of Meg's cloak and prayed to all the gods for deliverance, along with the addition of a few potent curses for these foul slavers. Meg's eyes were only partly closed, as she watched the guards carefully.

Borlon and Albin played dice for a while, but Borlon soon grew bored and crawled into a blanket near the wall, hugging his crock of ale. In moments he was snoring. The games broke up and the men drifted off to their corners to sleep or stand guard listlessly against the defenseless women. Fendrel stumbled in and wrapped himself in a leather cloak. Albin began singing. He sounded like a sick hound. Rose winced. He staggered toward her cage, swilling a jug of spirits and shaking a ring of keys.

"Want to play with tiny woman," Albin slurred, unlocking the door and swinging it open.

Rose feigned sleep, hoping he would not bother if she was unconscious. She had a horrified thought he would not care about that either.

"Wake up, tiny woman," he coaxed, grabbing at Rose.

"Leave her alone, scum," Meg demanded, throwing off her cloak and jumping to her feet.

"Out of my way, slut!" Albin replied gruffly and shoved Meg against the bars. He dropped the jug and seized Rose, pulling her out of the cage by her hair.

Rose screamed as he dragged her across the rocky floor. He let go of her braid and stood over her. Trembling, she raised herself on her elbows. "Albin, stop! Remember what Rebec said! He wants his cargo untouched."

Borlon grumbled from his curled position, "Keep it down!"

"Piss off," Albin shouted, swaying in his drunken stupor.

Rose scrambled to her feet and bolted, but even in his inebriated state, Albin was quick and strong. He grabbed her and flung her on the hard ground. He descended upon her small body, ripping her shirt open. She kicked and fought, but her exertions were useless as Albin pawed at her body. None of the men in the cave helped her despite her screams, but merely watched with dully amused eyes or turned over in their sleep.

Suddenly, Jardo was shouting. "Albin, you damned idiot! You heard Rebec's orders! No one touches the women! Get away from her!"

"Back off, baldy!" Albin mumbled, unlacing his trousers.

"Hey, Albin!" cooed Meg from behind. "Wouldn't you rather have me? You want me more; I've seen it in your eyes. I'm naked—just for you."

Albin's grin was revolting. "Knew that damn redhead lusted for me," he slurred and twisted around to look. His face blanched with panic when he saw Meg. He released his grip and Rose pushed herself away from him. When she glimpsed the weapon in Meg's hands, Rose scrambled to get out of her path of fire.

The bucket!

Meg hurled the foul contents at Albin. Howling with disgust, Albin crumpled to the ground, dripping a disgusting mixture of urine and fecal waste.

The other men in the background, roused by the ruckus, were equally repulsed by Albin's foul state. Some laughed at his humiliation and some threw things at Albin, swearing at him to go away. The drugged women in the cage were oblivious to the chaos and mess.

"Whore!" Albin spat, drawing his dagger and swaying from the stench. "I'll slit your throat for this."

Jardo's face twisted with disgust, but he jumped forward and immediately put himself between Albin and Meg. He kicked Albin to the ground.

"What the hell?" Albin sputtered. "Stay out of this, you bald shit-"

"Go to the river and wash off that muck, stinky" Jardo commanded. "You reek! Go now!"

Rebec stormed in and even he recoiled when he saw Albin. "What the hell happened?"

Borlon shrugged, scratching his armpits. "Bitches did it to him. Poor Albin just wanted some fun with the little dwarf. Wasn't his fault."

"Albin, you idiot! I warned you! No soiling the merchandise!" Rebec said.

Soiling was an ironic word choice, Rose winced.

"Get to the river now!" Rebec commanded.

Albin slunk away, leaving a vile trail of muck.

Fendrel walked up, holding a torch. "That dwarf girl and the redhead are the troublemakers. Stupid sluts! That dwarf tempted him like a whore and led him on. He couldn't help it."

It was a blatant lie, but it was useless to refute it among these barbarians. Rebec's vicious eye turned on Rose. She backed away, fear knotting her gut.

"You're to blame for this, Dwarf!" he accused.

She knew she would not talk her way out of this. Rebec was a monster. All she could do was shake her head and pray his punishment would not kill her.

"Who tossed the bucket?" Rebec asked coldly.

"I did," Meg confessed proudly. "Albin was going to rape her. He got exactly what he deserved. Leave the child alone, Rebec. Punish me instead."

Rebec's chilling grin as he unrolled his whip made Rose feel sick. "Shut up, bitch! I'll punish who I want and this red whore needs the discipline of the lash."

"No!" Rose cried, fearing Meg would suffer because of her. Fendrel grabbed Rose and pulled her away, holding her tightly. The men cheered Rebec on, roused at the Rebec's promise of savagery. Jardo pushed Meg closer to the fire. Rebec fingered his whip, its thin leather strips worn and blood-stained.

"Yeah! Thrash the redhead first!' Borlon begged. "That slut deserves a good thrashing for stinking up poor ole' Albin. She's got more fight in her anyway. That dwarf won't last three strokes of the whip!"

Jardo forced Meg to her knees before Rebec, her long red hair clutched in his thick hands. The men began to whoop it up and clustered together in a large circle around them.

"Leave her alone!" Rose screamed, struggling against Fendrel's grip.

Rebec pointed his whip at her. "Silence, Dwarf. You're next."

Rebec cracked his whip, the snap of it striking the ground made Rose jump. Meg did not even flinch. Rose sensed Rebec had moved past *punishment* to something more sinister now.

"Got any last words, whore?" Rebec demanded, striking his whip again.

Fearless, Meg stared up at her captor, smiling. "Yes, I do—in the name of the Emperor, you're all under arrest."

Chapter Six

Meg's bold announcement stunned Rose—but the daring lunacy of her declaration only elicited a bewildering burst of laughter from the circle of criminals.

Even Rebec snickered, albeit briefly. "You're funny, whore," he grunted. His expression blackened again and he raised his whip to strike Meg. A crossbow bolt speared Rebec's neck from high above. Rose gasped and her head jerked up, seeking the hidden saviors in the darkness. Rebec's eyes bulged and blood curdled from his mouth; he dropped the whip and grasped at his neck with quivering hands until his knees buckled and he slumped to the ground.

The laughing stopped.

Rose stared at Rebec's lifeless body. She had never seen anyone killed before. The brutal reality shook her hard. Death is often a theme in poems and tales, but its truth was harsher. She felt no pity for Rebec, but watching him die so violently unsettled her.

Silence filled the cave.

In the stunning turn of events, Jardo released his hold on Meg and now stood by her side, handing her a sword!

Undaunted, Meg and Jardo faced down the gang of thugs with chilling calm. Jardo extended his long dagger and shouted, "Surrender! Or everyone one of you pigs will suffer the wrath of the rangers! If you want to follow Rebec into the Underworld, I'll gladly to send you on your way."

Thunderstruck by the turn of fate, the outlaws hesitated in their attack, but soon curdled back into violence and unsheathed their blades. Meg flicked her hand and a shower of crossbow bolts struck the ground at their feet and forced them back.

Rose held her breath, both terrified and impressed by the lethal accuracy of the mysterious bowmen hidden in the cave.

Meg's fierce expression brooked no mercy. "That's your only warning. If Rebec's death has already faded from your dull memory, look up, gentleman," Meg commanded. "You're surrounded by the full power of the rangers—and their crossbows. Surrender or die. Your choice."

Shadowy figures appeared on the cave's ridges high above, the torchlight forming an eerie nimbus around several cloaked men holding crossbows. They drove their victory home when they kicked to the ground six dead slavers from those ledges. The heavy thud of corpses striking the hard-packed earth crushed the outlaw's fighting rage. They lost their battle spirit along with their vicious leader. One by one they relented, faces dark with repressed anger as they dropped their swords and knives and raised their hands in surrender.

"All right, you mangy dogs," Jardo barked, marching toward the sullen captives, "On your knees and keep those hands up where I can see them! Do it now!"

The criminals obeyed Jardo's commands. Suddenly, more than two dozen rangers in green cloaks swarmed the cavern with swords and crossbows in hand. They swiftly began to lock the prisoners in manacles and drag them away.

In the disarray they had forgotten Fendrel, who had restrained Rose. He had dropped her in the chaotic turn of events for his comrade, Rebec. Motivated by panic, he grabbed Rose, holding her before him like a shield. Rose cried out briefly, but fell mute when he pressed a dagger to her neck. His hands were shaking and she prayed he would not cut her throat by accident. The rangers around them reacted swiftly. They aimed their crossbows at Fendrel, their expressions hard and alert. Rose sensed these rangers would not comply with this criminal's demands.

"Stay back! Stay back all of you, damn it!" Fendrel shouted. "I'm leaving here, see! I leave safe or the dwarf girl dies."

Meg's flinty gaze was the only warning Fendrel received before she subtly flicked her hand. One of the rangers fired a crossbow bolt. It hissed over her head and Rose's scalp tingled from its swift passing. Her heart seemed to burst in its wake. It pierced Fendrel between the eyes and his startled gasp was the last thing Rose perceived before it knocked him backward, taking Rose down with him. Rose lay shaking on top of the dead man, fighting down a surge of hysteria that threatened to explode.

Jardo and Meg rushed over to Rose and detangled her from Fendrel's limp arms. Jardo picked her up gently, as though she was a porcelain doll. Indeed, even in her shock, she felt like one in the massive arms of this giant man.

"As I said—only one warning," Meg shouted, pointing to Fendrel's body.

"There now little one, Skullcap has you safe now." He cradled her like a baby, which was very strange. She forced herself to calm down now that the danger was passed. She also hoped all tall folk did not think her a toy. He checked her neck for any marks with his large, callused hand, but was quite gentle. "See, not even a nick. You're just fine. A ranger never misses."

"Good to know," Rose whispered.

Rose's mind clicked with questions and she caught his change of name. She glanced up at him and asked, "Skullcap? But, you said your name was Jardo?"

"Ah, that's just a name I used to infiltrate these scum. My real name's Skullcap Axton. I'm a ranger too, just like Red Meg there."

Meg looked her over too, like a mother hen inspecting her chick. "You sure you're all right, Rose? Did that bastard cut you?"

"No he didn't. I'm fine. I think you can put me down now."

He gently set her down and she prayed her shaking knees would hold her up. He gave her a canteen and she swallowed several gulps of water.

She nervously brushed off her trousers, trying to regain her calm. "You were very convincing as an outlaw. May I ask if Skullcap is your baptismal name or a sobriquet?"

Skullcap titled his head, confused.

Rose bit her lip and added, "Sorry-I mean, is it a nickname? Skullcap is a very strong and impressive name."

Skullcap grinned broadly and rubbed his bald head, shiny with elaborate blue tattoos, "Oddly fitting name, isn't it? Now my real name is not so impressive. Only my mum calls me by my blessing name of Robert."

Rose laughed, but quickly apologized when she saw the confusion on his face. "Sorry, I don't mean to insult your given name at all. It's just that I used the name 'Robert' when I was traveling here. I thought it would be safer to pretend to be a boy since I was alone. Who knew it would not make a difference?"

"That's all right, Rose. Anyway, but I've been Skullcap ever since my first captain nicknamed me when I took the ranger vows over twenty years ago. But once I had a full head of dark wavy hair. Years ago, a comely witch I courted put a curse on me and I went bald overnight."

"Goodness, how dreadful! I'm so sorry about that," Rose gasped.

"Thank you, Miss Rose. That's why I've had these runic symbols mystically tattooed on my head. A sorcerer wove spells into the tattoos to protect me in case she tried to curse me again."

"Clever and wise," Rose nodded. She was tempted to inquire about what he did to anger a witch so, but hesitated despite his jovial attitude about it.

Meg circled Rebec's corpse and scowled. She even kicked the body as though to make sure he was truly dead.

"Meg's still vexed with Rebec, even though he's dead," Rose whispered.

Skullcap shrugged. "That Rebec was very nasty piece of work. The foulest man you could ever meet. He specialized in murder and the slavery of women. He's been eluding us for years. Now the bastard's dead and can't run no more," Skullcap laughed darkly. "Now Rebec's condemned to the dark underworld of *Hel*. No escaping that place when you're a depraved soul like him."

The prisoners, who only moments ago were boastful of their cruelty, now bowed their heads in submission as Meg walked among them, fearful of her now. "I wish Rebec had lived long enough to pay the hangman. Merely robbing and murdering travelers must have gotten dull for Rebec. Still, death can have him," Meg sighed with resignation.

Skullcap bent down and whispered apologetically to Rose, "Sorry to scare you so much, Miss Rose. We wanted to warn the other women, but could not risk anyone knowing what we were up to. We had planned on raiding this operation tonight and everything was arranged."

"You were most believable," Rose gulped, surveying the thugs being taken away and the drugged women tended to.

"Thanks," Skullcap grinned broadly. "I'd like you to meet someone special." He whistled and a large black crow flew down from its hiding place high up in the cave and landed on his arm. "Miss Rose, meet Owena, my pet crow. She's also a ranger."

"Really?" Rose exclaimed, curiosity soothing her frayed nerves. "She's so pretty!" She longed to touch the sleek crow, but Owena gave her a wary glance, so she refrained from such familiar action until they were better acquainted. "Crows are very smart."

"Yes indeed, she's an official ranger for the Crown! My little crow for the Crown" he cooed lovingly. "My Owena carried important messages to our rangers during this operation. That's how we knew where to find this secret encampment."

"Very clever," Rose agreed, her mind buzzing with a story idea of her own. "Owena must be very clever indeed. And you must tell me all about this plan. It would make an incredible tale. I'm a Bard."

"Well, Owena's the best crow in the kingdom. Extra treats today for my little Owena, yes indeed." He gently stroked the crow's glossy black forehead and the bird obviously enjoyed his doting.

"When you are done conversing with Owena, I think you should fetch Albin from his bath," Meg suggested with a wicked smile. "We don't want him to feel left out of the festivities."

"Damn, almost forgot about him. Right away, Commander," Skullcap saluted and marched off with Owena settled contentedly on his muscular shoulder.

In the strange chaos, Rose stared at the fire for a moment, trying to get her bearings. Meg put a blanket around her shoulders.

Rose's eyes lit up and she turned to Meg. "I never met a warrior woman before."

"Never?" Meg laughed.

"Rhulon's warrior women are banished to song and legend now, I'm afraid. May I write a poem or story about you?"

"Ever the bard, I see," Meg laughed.

"I'm sorry. That must sound dreadful considering what's just happened."

"No, it's not. Artists and scholars are folk that see things differently. Same as a warrior does. Most women would still be weeping and wringing their hands, even after rescue. You're strong, Rose. Don't discount that."

"Thanks," Rose replied, heartened by her words.

Meg knelt before Rose until they were eye to eye. "Let's make a fresh introduction. I'm Commander Meg Sparrow of the Imperial Rangers—but you can just call me Meg."

Rose was sure she had found a friend in this tall woman as they shook hands. "I'm Rose Greenleaf of Stone Haven from Rhulon. "I've read about the rangers of course, but never knew they accepted women in their ranks. We have rangers in Rhulon too, but in my homeland, they would never permit a woman take that path and carry a sword or bow like a man. I've read about brave women in stories, legends and histories all my life. You're the first one I've met."

"Take a look in the mirror, Rose, and I think you will see a very brave warrior. You should tell a story about your adventures. Many would not have been as courageous as you have been this day."

Rose blushed at the unexpected compliment, but swayed on her feet and Meg reached out to steady her. "Dear me, that was embarrassing."

"Nonsense," Meg replied. "Lack of food, noxious smells, death, and the shock of, well everything, just caught up with you. Let's get you out of this damned cave."

Rose agreed and prayed she would not faint! She was never one of those frail girls who needed smelling salts.

Meg led her away from the carnage. "You just need some fresh air." They walked through the chaos of men busily rounding up the criminals and helping the drugged women from the cages. Outside, the cool night breeze revived her and now had a wonderful smell—freedom!

"You've had quite an adventure," Meg said. "You should tell your own story of your adventures coming to Tirangel. I know I would listen."

"Funny you should put it that way. It's peculiar because I never thought to be the subject of one of my stories. What you did was amazing though! How did you know the rangers were even up there?"

Meg answered, "Well, first off, I knew the rangers were in place because Skullcap and I had a secret code. When Skullcap grabbed me in the cell and refused me water, I knew the men were already in place. If he offered me water, I would know things were not yet ready. Spitting at him was just for show. We were just waiting until most of them were asleep before we attacked. We wanted to catch them when they were most vulnerable and minimize any threat to the captives. Sadly, Albin got other ideas."

"He and Fendrel captured me in the woods," Rose recalled darkly. "The only reason they didn't violate me was because Rebec wanted the women pure."

"Virgins sell for a higher price on the slave market," Meg replied somberly. "Fortunately, everything worked out. The slavers are arrested and the women weren't hurt."

Skullcap rode into the clearing on a light gray horse. Albin was dragged along behind, his arms bound to his sides by strong rope. He was half naked, soaking wet, and cursing. Another rope was used as a leash, which the rider kept a tight rein on.

He laughed and shouted, "Commander Sparrow! I got Albin all nice and tied up for the ride home. He still stinks to high heaven though."

"Lock him up with the other scum," Meg ordered.

"Happy to oblige," Skullcap replied. "Hangman's gonna love this batch. Shame Rebec died so quick though."

"You took quite a risk, going undercover like a spy and letting yourself be abducted by these wicked men. That was very dangerous," Rose commented.

"It was just as dangerous as you traveling alone, all the way from Rhulon," Meg added with her potent stare.

"Point taken, but in my defense, I was fleeing my own brand of slavery—matrimony."

They both laughed. Meg accepted a green cloak from one of the rangers and put it on. Her bright red hair was a striking compliment to the rich color.

"Will they all hang?" Rose had never been exposed to real criminals before and was still horrified that people could be so heartless.

"Not all. There will be a trial. Some, depending on their criminal records, will trade the rope for prison or the mines, especially if they give up valuable information about the slave trade," Meg replied. "I doubt if they will receive much mercy right now. The Emperor is in seclusion. His eldest son and heir, Prince Justin, died two weeks ago. They say it was a riding accident, which is strange. The Prince was a master horseman. All of Tirangel is in mourning."

"I'm so sorry to hear that. I will pray for his soul."

"Thank you. In the city, people are wearing black armbands in show their sorrow. I know you're new to our land, but I will give you one to wear if you like."

"Thank you. I'll wear it to honor your Emperor's loss."

Hoping to change to a less grim subject, Rose said, "I heard Skullcap call you Red Meg. Does he call you 'Red Meg,' because of your hair or your reputation as a fighter?"

"Both," Meg replied, grinning.

Skullcap strolled over to them, tossing a cloth wrapped piece of bread and cheese to Meg. He had changed into the official uniform of the rangers. His white tunic and brown vest were pristine and green cloak floated behind him like wings, Owena the crow perched on his shoulder. He was still intimidating to look at, but she knew his heart was good.

"Any callous criminals in your home village?" Meg asked.

Rose shook her head. "The biggest criminal act in my village of

Stone Haven was a rather elusive bread thief who turned out to be a ten-year-old boy."

"Sounds like a wonderfully quiet place," Meg said, breaking off some cheese and bread and handing it to Rose.

Rose accepted it gratefully and munched hungrily, fortified by the safety of the ranger's presence and real food. "It was, when my mother wasn't harping at me. But what you do must be very hard, yet is so noble. How long have you been a ranger?"

"About ten years," Meg replied.

Rose studied Meg and added, "You never really struck me as a dairy maid."

"Thank the Gods!" Meg replied.

"But you saved me from a dreadful fate and for that I thank you with my whole heart," Rose said solemnly. "I don't want to think about what grim fate awaited me if you had not been so brave. Thanks for protecting me."

Skullcap bit into his wedge of cheese and added, "You're a very lucky maid, little Rose. I'm glad we got you rescued before anything worse happened to you or these other poor women. They're free again and it's the slavers that are in chains. That's a good day for a ranger."

Meg surveyed the area. "Skullcap, let's use their extra wagons to carry the women back to the city. Then we can start contacting their families and get their testimony. Make sure everyone is safe. We leave at dawn. I want a ranger in each wagon with the women to make sure they're not suffering any ill effects from the drugged food."

"I'll arrange that. What about Rebec and Fendrel's bodies?" Skullcap asked.

Meg's expression was chilling. "Tie them to the back of one of the wagons and drag them back to the ranger station with a hangman's noose around their necks. Then the city watch will swing them from the walls as a warning to those who violate the Emperor's Law until crows do their work. I don't like slavers or men who abuse women. Rebec did both—and much worse. May his black soul burn in hell for eternity."

"I think that's a certainty, Meg," Skullcap agreed.

Albin whimpered, and Skullcap tugged impatiently at his rope. "Silence, you dog. Save your blubbering for the judge."

Rose sat down, but despite her exhaustion, amid the bustling rangers securing the prisoners and arranging the wagons, she could not rest. She missed her lute. She had no idea where she had lost it back there or how to find the spot where they took her. The loss of her lute did bring tears, which she brushed away.

"Let's get moving," Meg ordered and crooked her finger to summon her. "Rose, you ride with me. You can't travel alone. Not anymore," she added for emphasis.

Rose was grateful for any aid after what she had been through. She followed Meg to the giant horse that snorted at her presence and glared down at her with disdain.

"I don't think she likes me," Rose gulped.

Meg lifted Rose up onto the saddle of her horse and then mounted behind her.

"You're just not acquainted with her. Don't be afraid. Fayre's a good horse, aren't you, girl," she said, patting her neck affectionately.

Rose blanched at being astride the massive creature. Strange this horse made her so fearful after all she had been through, but she was only familiar with the smaller dwarf ponies of her home. She was a good rider, though her mother did not approve of her riding.

She decided after all she had survived; the horse was not really a big threat-as long as she didn't look down.

"Where are we going?" Rose asked, nervously holding on to the pommel of the saddle and praying she would not fall to her doom.

"White Thorn," Meg replied.

Elated that she would have protection to the city she had chosen for so long was more than she could ever wish for. Even so, being atop this giant horse was both daunting and she continued to look up at the sky.

"She seems like a sweet horse, but it's just so high up from the earth," Rose gulped.

"You're in Tirangel now," Meg grinned, "the land of the tall folk. A lot of things will be out of your reach."

"I'm beginning to realize that," Rose replied dryly.

# # #

Darius observed the sea gulls fly across the ocean with graceful abandon. He envied their careless freedom. The clear day brimmed with sunshine and the sea and sky were a vivid crystal blue. It was a sad day though, his last day here. He inhaled deeply, relishing the brisk sea air and the eternal serenity of the monastery. His life would never be calm again.

Your brother is dead, Your Highness.

Those terrible words changed his life forever. The royal messenger had been brief with this tragic news. His brother fell from a horse during an afternoon ride, as he had been informed by the contrite messenger who knelt before him yesterday. His neck was broken and he died instantly. All of White Thorn was in mourning. His parents commanded his immediate return home.

Darius could not imagine his older brother gone. Prince Justin, heir to the great Tirangel Empire.

He was the Crown Prince now. That did not fill him with joy.

He imagined his stoic father not revealing a flicker of emotion when informed of Justin's death. His poor mother would have not shed a tear in public, but would have retreated to her private chambers to weep alone. Darius had been stunned by the tragic news. He had loved his brother, even though they had little in common. His older brother was destined for many great things. Such a premature death at the peak of his youth was never considered or even imagined. Justin had been an expert horseman who learned how to ride before he could walk. How could Karta be so cruel in choosing such a fate for his dashing brother?

Darius had spent his life being the necessary but often useless second Prince. He never resented it—he relished it because it gave him a small bay of liberty to live his life. His brother Justin was bound for the austere crown of Tirangel. Darius was happy to remain in the background of his brother's glory. Darius was bound for the church or the military, a life which would have afforded him small but welcome freedom from responsibility.

Brother Osbert knocked on the door and entered, poking his tonsured head inside. "Your Highness, the ship has arrived."

"Thank you, Brother."

"They also delivered a letter for you, Your Highness."

"Just leave it."

Osbert put the letter on the table.

"We will miss you, Darius," Osbert said softly.

"And I you," Darius replied. "When do I leave?"

"Tomorrow at sunrise."

"Thank you, Brother."

Osbert quietly departed, leaving Darius to ponder his future. Darius did not want to leave this small seaside monastery. He would miss all the monks, especially pudgy, gentle Osbert. Darius loved it here. Home was a different story."

Darius pulled himself away from the sea to open the letter. To his surprise and joy, it was not from his stern father, Emperor Aristide. The wax seal bore the royal insignia of the House of Ironheart.

Darius opened the letter and read it. His old friend, Prince Culain Ironheart, was coming to White Thorn as the new Ambassador. Culain wrote that he looked forward to seeing his oldest friend and sent heartfelt condolences for the loss of his brother, Prince Justin. From Culain, Darius could believe those words. The Dwarven Prince had been a friend and regular visitor to White Thorn for years, in various diplomatic positions for his father, King Grimkel. He envied Culain, who had so many brothers and sisters; he never had to worry about being an heir.

Darius had always been the mouse prince. Now he must shine. How? He was not hard enough to be an Emperor. Darius recently learned from his father's dispatches, that he also inherited the responsibility of a future bride, Princess Lilias Rhodan. Along with his brother's rank as heir, Darius also inherited his royal fiancé.

"How can I worry about being a future Emperor and a husband?" Darius asked sharply to the flying seagulls. "I'm not even tall," Darius uttered. He had one secret jealousy—his brother's six foot height and muscular build. Darius was barely five foot six inches tall, and physically not very impressive.

Freedom was something he had never known except here in the monastery. As prince, he was bound with a golden rope. Dressed in velvets and silks, he dined from silver plates and drank from jeweled cups. Here at the monastery by the sea, he could run barefoot on the beach and fish with the monks for his supper. He was just Darius.

Now you are the only Prince.

Darius watched the sea birds on their graceful flight, wishing he could be as free. Suddenly the sky darkened with rain clouds and the omen unsettled Darius. It only fortified the gloom in his heart.

Chapter Seven

After her liberation, they journeyed to the ranger house that was just a few miles outside White Thorn's city gates. There was a great cheer for Meg and her team when they arrived with the prisoners and the freed women. It was exciting to see the green-cloaked rangers welcoming them back.

Less exciting was the cramped, stuffy office illuminated by low-burning candles, Rose gave a detailed testimony to a stern and dour-faced Captain Jesper Nerlis. Skullcap and Meg were with her, partly to verify her story as official witnesses and partly to give moral support. At times she felt like it was a great adventure story, and found herself resorting to colorful words and expressions until Captain Nerlis' sharp look forced her to state only the plain, bare facts.

Skullcap brought her a tin of hot coffee and she welcomed the sustenance, though the coffee was bitter. It helped keep her awake as she went over every detail. Captain Nerlis made copious notes as she spoke and his clipped manner was more infused with his pile of papers on his desk than Rose's predicament.

He was, however, concerned about a dwarf maiden traveling alone. Captain Nerlis raised a brow, arranging his notes with meticulous care. "Mistress Greenleaf, have you committed any crimes in your home country that would warrant such flight from Rhulon without proper escort? It's rare for a woman of your race to be without the protection of your family."

Rose sighed and wearily replied, "If fleeing an unwanted, arranged marriage to a boorish young man is a crime, then I confess. I am guilty, Captain. What is my punishment?"

Skullcap guffawed and Meg covered her grin, but Captain Nerlis did not crack a smile.

So much for humor.

He handed Rose her statement. "Do you know how to read and write, Miss Greenleaf?" Captain Nerlis inquired.

"Oh yes, Captain Nerlis, I can read and speak five languages."

"Excellent. Please read that report carefully and sign your name," he instructed, offering her a stylus. "It's a written statement of what you told me, minus the dramatic embellishments, and will be used during the trial as evidence. You also pledge to be in court as a witness."

Rose read it quickly, astonished by his impeccably perfect handwriting. She signed the document and Meg and Skullcap also signed as witnesses. Captain Nerlis then signed his name and affixed the official ranger seal, which she noticed used green wax and the image of a large oak tree.

"That's a lovely seal," Rose commented.

"I'm pleased you approve, Miss Greenleaf," Nerlis remarked without glancing at her. "The trial will in a few weeks. The courts are backlogged, as usual. You'll receive an official summons and an escort to the trial. Until then, you are required to remain in the city of White Thorn. After the trial is concluded, you're free to go anywhere."

"Yes, thank you, Captain." Rose pondered a moment, and asked, "May I seek work while I wait so I may support myself?"

"Yes, if that is your desire. What is your trade? Do you sew or cook?"

Rose laughed but Captain Nerlis' expression did not reflect her lighthearted response, but remained grim as gravestone. "Sorry, Captain. I'm a Bard. I sing for my supper, literally!"

"That explains your rather lively and flamboyant testimonial. Good luck, Mistress Greenleaf," Captain Nerlis replied and waved them all away. "I've other duties to attend to and more witness to interview now that the other women are finally rousing from their drugged state. I apologize for your ordeal but take heart—justice will be done. For your cooperation and since you are newly arrived to our city, we will pay for your lodgings at an inn until the trial, but after that you are on your own. Are you prepared for that, Miss Greenleaf?"

"Yes, Captain," Rose answered soberly.

"Good. Commander Sparrow will escort you to one of our approved inns for your stay since you are new to our city. Good day." He stacked his papers and neatly placed them to his right, looked at Meg and Skullcap and allowed a slight grin to crack his starched expression. "Your report states Rebec the Black was killed during the operation?"

"Yes, Captain," Meg answered.

"I'll send your condolences to the hangman," Captain Nerlis commented dryly. "I commend your fine investigative work, Commander. The Emperor will be pleased."

"Thank you, Captain," Meg saluted.

After a quick goodbye to Skullcap and Owena, who allowed Rose to stroke her head, Rose and Meg left for the city on Fayre.

"Where are we going?" Rose asked.

"I have friends who own a tavern called the Red Boar near the docks. It's one of our approved inns where you can stay."

Inside the city gates, Rose glimpsed White Thorn for the first time. It was like a mythological beast come to life, and its mysteries both exhilarated and frightened her. She blamed her fear on her exhaustion. She knew she had to shake it off if she planned to be an adventuress.

# # #

Rose waited on bench in the hall just outside the taproom of the Red Boar. Her feet dangled because it was so high, being been designed for tall folk. She imagined her mother's reaction to Rose being inside an actual tavern.

A young girl in rough tavern house like a common doxy! My reputation as a mother will be ruined forever.

Fortunately, this was just one of many things Rose's mother would remain oblivious about. Memories of home pricked her conscience. She missed her cousin, Pea and her teacher, Belenus. She banished her father's image from her mind. Their breach was never mended. Her mother would always be a trial, but her father had been her rock until he abandoned her to a forced marriage. Troubled by her past, Rose leaned over and resumed eavesdropping as Meg argued on her behalf with the stout innkeepers, Digby and Becky Crofton, for a job and place to stay.

"But I don't need no new barmaid!" Digby protested.

"You always need help," Meg retorted. "Becky agrees with me."

Despite the robust verbal exchange, Rose fought from falling into a stupor because of her exhaustion.

Now, Rose waited in the Red Boar Tavern for judgment again. This time from the couple who owned the inn.

"Rangers are always welcome in my house," Digby replied boisterously, greeting Meg with a big hug. "What have we here, Meg?" he asked, looking down in Rose's direction. "Is that a child?"

"No Digby, she's not a child. She's from Rhulon. Her name is Rose Greenleaf. If you have room, the ranger house will pay for her stay until the trial."

"Fine, we have the room. So you captured those slavers at last?" Becky asked.

"Indeed we did. Rebec is dead and his followers are in prison awaiting trial. Rose was one of the young women we rescued."

"That poor thing," Becky cooed.

"So she's one of them little folk from up north, eh?" Digby sniffed, squinting at Rose.

Becky, his wife, slapped her dish towel across his head. "Manners, Digby. Miss Rose is our guest."

"And I have a favor to ask as well," Meg whispered. Let's go inside and talk." She knelt down and whispered to Rose, "Just wait here for a minute."

So, Rose waited alone in the hall while Meg spoke on her behalf to the older couple. She folded her hands demurely, outwardly examining the earthy ambiance of the Red Boar tavern. She had nothing else to do. Huge nets with shells decorated the walls, giving it all the touches a sailor would appreciate. Tables and chairs were scattered in the taproom. Patrons sat, drinking spirits at the tables, and a few glanced at Rose with curious eyes. She forced herself to ignore them. Her ears burned with curiosity, cocked listening to Meg discuss with Digby and Becky Crofton, the inn's proprietors, her fate. Frustrated, she slid off the bench and moved closer. She watched them from the doorway to see what her fate would be.

Digby was short for a tall folk man, with a portly belly. Meg towered over Digby as he sweated in the darkened taproom. Digby wiped his moist face with the large blue kerchief he tucked into his brown vest pocket. His nose was porous and bulbous; his head mostly bald and what little hair he possessed around his ears curled and gray. His gray linen shirt and trousers looked worn, yet he possessed a fine silver pocket watch with a velvet fob in his vest pocket.

Becky Crofton, chubby and florid as her husband, carried a tray of mugs to a table for them. Her tightly-laced red bodice strained against her magnificent girth and her brown hair was twisted into a haphazard bun, strands escaping the hairpins. When Becky smiled, a few teeth were missing—but it was genuine and full of warmth. Becky's kind hazel eyes glistened as Meg explained Rose's predicament.

Digby wiped his furrowed brow and poured cider into the mugs for them all. "I'm sorry, Meg, but I can't afford to be giving charity to every stray cat that flicks it tail my way. Bad for business, you know."

"Surely, you can let her work for her keep. The ranger house will pay for her stay until the trial, but she needs a safe shelter after that," Meg begged.

"I don't like strays," Digby said mulishly.

"She's not a stray," Meg protested. "I know you need help around here. Your charming personality has chased away three barmaids in the last six months."

"I miss my daughter, Ellie," Digby said roughly. "She knew how to help out around here."

"Of course you do," Meg agreed. "But your daughter moved away last year with her new husband to their farm, so I know you could use someone to help out."

"I could use another helping hand," Becky commented.

"We do just fine," Digby blustered.

"Then you do all the cooking and cleaning and see how fine it is! All you do is keep watch in the bar and count coin, Digby."

"I do my fair share woman!"

Becky harrumphed and insisted, "When it suits you. You scared off our last barmaid a week ago."

"She was not very mannerly to our customers. Bad for business."

"Rose is well brought up and educated," Meg added. "She'll work hard for you."

Digby grunted and glanced over to Rose on the bench and sniffed. "She looks a bit too delicate. My daughter Ellie was strong and could even lift the beer kegs without aid. This tiny girl couldn't lift a pewter mug of my fine ale without toppling over. I can't use her here! Besides, those Dwarf folk make me nervous. You can never see them proper unless you look down."

"Oh Digby," Becky chastised. "You don't like anyone. I know you miss our Ellie, but her place is with her husband now. Rose is a poor maiden all alone in a strange new country. She doesn't have any folk here. We have to help her! You saw how pretty and sweet she is. She looks gently reared. It would be good for us to help her."

"No we don't have to help anyone!" Digby crossed his arms stubbornly. "And she's foreign. Too small to be of any proper use and I wager she can't even speak our tongue!"

Rose had had enough and purposely marched over to table; she picked up the great pewter mug of cider from Digby's hand and held it aloft firmly to display her strength. "As you can see I am quite strong. I can lift heavier things too. Trays. Chairs. Pillows. The list is endless. I also speak and read five languages. To be frank, I'm a terrible cook, but I can help wait tables and clean up. More importantly, I'm a trained Bard, taught by Belenus Aylecross of Rhulon. He has sung for kings and I was his favorite pupil. I can sing, tell stories and encourage patronage for your fine establishment. Consider this, Master Digby. I am from Rhulon and a woman bard—a rare commodity. Long ago, they use to call our caste *Bardess*, but we faded from prominence due to a demand for pie making apparently. Surely that will bring the curious to your door. As my master Belenus once told me, the curious are often quite thirsty."

"Ah, see now Digby, she can sing too! That would class up our ale house and attract some fine folk," Becky urged.

"Fine folk make fussy demands," Digby grumbled and took back his cider from her tiny hand. "And where's your lute or harp? Don't bards have fancy instruments to pluck upon?"

Throughout everything Rose suffered since she began her journey—kidnappers, hunger, the stark loneliness of the road, she had remained stoic and brave. But the loss of her precious lute pierced her deeply. This reminder shattered her reserves.

Rose burst into tears.

Digby's expression crumbled. Immediately contrite, he shoved his grimy kerchief at her, which Meg gently deflected. "No! NO! No weeping now! Please don't cry! It's bad for business! Meg, please make her stop!"

"What can I do?" Meg shrugged, sipping her cider.

"I'm so sorry," Rose sniffled, "I had a lute! Truly, I did! It was a beautiful lute too. A gift from my Bard Master, Belenus! I hate crying! Weepy girls always annoyed me." She wept uncontrollably now. Running away, missing her family (even her *mother*), Belenus, the lack of food, sleeping in trees, and the fright of being kidnapped by loathsome slavers gushed out like a raging flood.

Flustered, Digby wiped his sweaty face. "Meg, please stop her from weeping. Folks be staring now. It's bad for business!"

Becky snapped him on the shoulder with a towel, scowling. "Men always say the wrong thing and then expect us women folk to fix it!"

"Those wretched men stole my lute and tossed it into the woods when they kidnapped me. I have no idea how to even find it again. I'm so sorry. I've always prided myself on not being a useless fainting maiden. I'm tough. Really. I'm hearty. I'm hard as nails!"

"There, there, my sweet," Becky consoled her, hugging Rose tight to her massive bosom. "Of course you can stay with us. You can have Ellie's old room. No need to cry anymore, dear. We'll look after you."

Digby waved his hands, surrendering to the circle of determined women. "Alright, alright—you may stay. You'll work here for board and room, plus tips, on a trial basis. No barding, missy. We don't need no bard."

"But I can sing and tell stories," Rose protested between sniffles.

"Let's see how you do at washing dishes and serving my ale first," Digby insisted.

"Meg's one of our oldest friends and she wouldn't bring us this girl unless she thought she was worth the trouble." Becky finally released Rose and stood back, looking down at her, shaking her head. "Poor thing, you're so thin. Are you hungry? I bet you and Meg ain't had more than a measly crust of bread so far today, have you? Let me bring you girls something to nosh on."

"Oh, thank you," Rose whispered, the thought of food calming her. "I'm starved."

"I could eat," Meg smiled.

When Becky and Digby went to fetch them some food, Rose wiped her eyes with her sleeve. "I'm so sorry, Meg. I don't know what happened to me."

"Delayed shock," Meg remarked calmly, pushing a mug of cider her way. "I think you needed to cry, Rose. Being brave can only take you so far."

"I still feel silly," Rose sniffed, climbing onto the chair. It felt strange to do this, and made her feel like a four year old again. She would have to adjust to this too.

"You're not silly. Besides, I think your breakdown might have helped cement your place here. Digby is a good soul but he's stubborn as an old badger and a coin pincher. He has a soft heart but pretends otherwise."

"Thanks, Meg. You've helped me so much. I just wish he would let me perform."

"You will. Just give it time. Drink some of this cider until the food comes. Becky is a good cook."

Indeed, Becky served them all a fine breakfast of fried potatoes, eggs, bacon, fluffy biscuits with blackberry jam and butter, and real fresh coffee that did not taste like swill!

Rose hungrily ate the magnificent spread, hoping her manners were not too barbaric. She imagined what her mother would say.

"Don't gobble like a pig, Rose. Why did the gods curse me with such a strange child?"

Why indeed, Mother, Rose thought, and then resisted another urge to break into tears. Her mother was far away. As was her father and Pea— no more regrets, she told herself firmly.

The coffee was such a blessing and not at all bitter. Hot and dosed generously with cream, it flooded her with much needed warmth and soothed her. She loved coffee! Digby and Becky became busy with patrons and the two young women were left to themselves.

"You need to write to them," Meg mumbled between bites.

"Who?" Rose replied, a little tense.

"Your parents! Your Bard Master! Let them know you are alive and safe. It will make you feel better."

"I know," Rose sighed and nodded. "I was hoping to have more victorious news when I wrote them other than my new career as barmaid. Also, well I—"

"Go on," Meg prodded.

"I am not sure what to say. They must be furious with me. What do I tell them?"

"Let's start with basic truth. You're alive and well, living in White Thorn. You need not tell them about your more tragic or interesting adventures, at least not yet. But no matter what, you need to do this. They must be worried sick about you. A forced marriage is never a good bargain for any maiden, but you escaped that. Now it's time to be kind and forget the past. Forgive them, Rose."

"I know, I will," Rose agreed. "I promise."

"Good," Meg nodded, digging into her potatoes with gusto.

As they ate and her mind calmed, Rose noticed little things, like the dense smell of ale in the tavern, the peeling white paint on the walls, and that Meg never took off her gloves—even to eat. When they met in the cage, Meg was wearing gloves and Rose never saw her remove them. She wanted to ask about it and though she felt a kinship with her, hesitated to intrude.

She touched the black armband Meg gave her. She noticed several of the patrons wore mourning bands for their lost prince. He must have been loved.

"Maybe if I offer to sing for free, he will let me perform?" Rose said, smearing jam on her biscuit.

"Now you're beginning to understand old Digby," Meg laughed.

#

Wrapped in a hooded purple cloak, Crimson, the changeling, scurried through the woods, enjoying the freedom of night. Moonlight was strong and guided her path to the ancient deserted graveyard outside the city. The old chapel on top of the hill was an ancient building long abandoned of worshippers. The roof caved in and the walls crumbled, entwined by ropes of vines, weeds, and heavy moss. Once it had been a temple to one of their light gods. *These humans so love the light, even when they are wicked*, she thought. Now, this forgotten place was her refuge of evil.

Crimson enjoyed the irony of making this once sacred place where humans had prayed to Ursas and Ishar, a den of darkness. Humans were so odd. They go the trouble of building a fancy temple of stone and carve the gods of their imagination. Priests sanctify their temples and say mass within hallowed walls. Humans offer coin and flowers at the altar in sweet sacrifice. Then, when their sacred houses becomes inconvenient, they are forgotten. The stone statues of their gods abandoned to become victims of bird crap and squirrel nests.

Crimson salivated at the thought of fat squirrels, for she hungered for raw meat. Perhaps later she would hunt. The old chantry was on a high hill and from here she looked down upon the city of White Thorn, she saw many lights, spoiling the darkness and so many humans! The temptation to wreak havoc on them was strong. She loved to torment human folk, but she had a mission of high import.

Crimson had her own God to serve, and he was not made of stone. Her God was true. Her God lived—the new Goblin King! And he gave her an important task.

Crimson stepped gingerly through piles of leaves and chunks of stone until she reached the undercroft door in the floor. She pried it up and climbed down into the murky pit with its welcome smells of mold and decay. The old crypt, once crowded with the rich tombs of the nobility, was now a shambles of dusty coffins and scattered bones, except for one thing that Crimson tended to.

She lit the lamp and examined the large snowy cocoon on a stone crypt bed in the center of the hollow. The former occupant was a jumble of ancient broken bones on the floor. Crimson scrutinized the pale, feathery shell, smelling the enchantment burning around it. She removed her glove and touched the cocoon firmly with her gray, clawed hand. The heartbeat was still strong. Her red amulet shimmered with the magic again. The bonding surged throughout her body. Good. Her human mask was secure again. She looked down at her hands, which resumed the pale smooth skin so prized by people.

Crimson then walked to the altar, a circle of obsidian glass on the floor framed by red ochre. A mirror of dark magic that shimmered when she gazed into its shadowy fathoms and touched the glass. She recited the incantation in hissing whispers, though no one would hear in this forsaken place deep in the ground. The mirror flamed and this always startled Crimson, who gasped with reverence as her God's face became clear in the mirror's fire. The proud brow and flaming scarlet skin, the obsidian eyes! She bowed her head to the ground in reverence, shivering with joy.

"Speak Crimson of Mordok," the deep voice demanded. "What have you to report of our enemy?"

Shaking with joy and fear, Crimson rose and looked into the black eyes of Morziel. "They suffer, as you commanded. Prince Justin is dead. It was so easy. I sabotaged his saddle. May I come home now, Master?"

"Not yet. Wreck more havoc. I want the human realms disrupted and in chaos before I rise to war on them."

Crimson gazed upon the image lovingly. "Your will be done."

The fire dimmed and the magic subsided. Soon the old crypt was as damp and cold as before. Crimson remained until dawn, caressing the obsidian glass in longing and worship, before she slunk back into the world again. Soon it would be sunrise, and Crimson must walk among the humans again.

# # #

Fallon Gansis, bored by Crimson's worship, distracted himself with his other mirrors in the vast windowless chamber. Images of people and places flashed before Fallon as Crimson caressed each dark glass.

One of his shadow mages entered the mirror chamber, a whisper of dark robes. The mage stared at the groveling changeling, shaking his head. "I am still confused as to how this changeling is useful? They are not very reliable."

"It is not use, but loyalty, that I am testing. She thinks I'm her goblin king. The goblins are stirring again and I smell their wickedness, even in this lonely desert tower. I love chaos, and Crimson is providing it in subtle ways. It's a pity. She would be invaluable if she were not so stupid. If she knew what I truly was, Crimson would be terrified. What did you want?"

The shadow mage bowed deeply. "Forgive me, Lord Gansis, but rich supplicants have come to pay homage and offer tribute to the Sorcerer of Hazda, in return for a few favors."

Fallon pulled his scarlet hood up, concealing his opalescent skin and white hair. He waved a hand and the obsidian mirrors fell silent and void as he strode out of the chamber.

Chapter Eight

Rose loathed waking at sunrise, unlike her mother who woke at first light with the energy of a demented hummingbird. Rose scoured the kitchen's stone floor with pungent soap flakes and hot water. Kitchen duty was hard, but preferable to the vile task of washing the public privy closet. Surely, the forbidding Underworld of Hel was a befouled water closet, not fire and brimstone. The fetid odor was bad enough, but why can't men aim? Was it the alcohol they consumed before staggering to the water closets to relieve their ale soaked bladders? Why couldn't they flush? The metal chain was right there.

Digby gave her his cleaning gloves when he handed her the bucket and a brush, she blanched. She was hesitant to touch them. "Don't fret. I always boil them in soap flakes." He told her. "I use them solely for cleaning the public water closets and nothing else. Wrap a scarf across your face to buffer the smell. I wouldn't touch nothin' either with your bare hands, if you know what's good for you."

How comforting.

Rose accepted these smelly trials, because the goddess Karta had not finished testing her. She had jumped into the real world to find her fortune and the Goddess of Fate was making her scour her way to worthiness. She just had no idea her journey would reek this much.

Rose's affinity for Karta began when she was only five, after she accidentally shattered her mother's favorite teacup. She attempted to glue it back together, but it was hopeless. Rose prayed to Karta that day for her mother not to be angry with her. Rose tearfully confessed her crime and presented the sadly patched cup to her mother. Her mother told Rose it was all right and gave her a cupcake. Since that day Rose considered Karta her patron goddess.

"Karta, I know you're challenging me, but I would be grateful if you eased up just a little bit," she mumbled softly. "My hands are red and cracked like the desert."

She wiped her sweaty brow and resumed her vigorous rhythm of circular scrubbing with the brush. Her scullery duties in the morning were lonely and to break the monotony, she had fallen into a pattern of singing to ease the dull repetition. After she scrubbed the last corner, she sat back on her feels and flexed her aching back. "Thank the gods that's done, at least for today."

One thing had haunted Rose that she was almost afraid to pray to Karta about. She often thought about when she sang for Albin and Fendrel in the wilderness, and how they stopped and almost fell into a trance as she was singing. The moment was brief, but it stayed with her, like a curse she refused to acknowledge.

She looked out the kitchen window and the sun brightened the sky. She hauled out the filthy bucket of water and dumped it in the gutter. She returned to her room upstairs and changed out of her filthy cleaning garb and washed off the grime. Goodness, but those flakes smell! She donned one of the dresses Becky had altered for her and went downstairs.

She had finished brewing the coffee just as Becky walked into the large kitchen, yawning and her hair haphazardly pinned up.

"Morning, Becky," Rose said over her shoulder. "I made the coffee. I think I'm getting better at it." She used the step box Digby made for her so she could reach things like the pot of bubbling coffee. She used the kitchen pads to lift the hot coffee pot and carefully poured the fresh brew into two cups. "How's your hip this morning?" she asked with concern, noticing Becky's stiff walk.

"Better today, thanks love. It's just my poor age creeping up on me." She slowly sat down on the chair and then sighed with relief. She looked around the kitchen and smiled broadly. "Everything is so spotless. It looks wonderful, love. You've been such a help. Sit down for a spell and I'll whip us up some breakfast."

"Thanks Becky. Let's have our coffee first. Where's Digby gone to?" Rose asked, smoothing her green skirt after she climbed onto the chair.

"Oh, he's already at the market. You know he's so eager to get there early and haggle. Be prepared for loud complaints about the price of flour and sugar when he returns!"

"Digby does that daily." Rose sipped her coffee and added more cream. "It's like a ritual, but I think he actually enjoys it. If prices dropped, I swear that man would be miserable."

Becky chuckled as she sipped her coffee. "I'm tickled to see some of Ellie's old clothes get some use again. That green frock looks so pretty on you."

"Thanks, Becky. I'm so grateful to you for giving me your daughter's old clothes. You're really a marvel with the needle. I can't sew on a button without injuring myself."

Rose was unaccustomed to being the tiny one, a peculiar fact she had to adjust to since she was always the tall, ungainly tomboy in Stone Haven. Rose was glad of these hand me downs and despite her strange circumstances and Digby's gruff exterior, the Crofton's were good to her. Rose knew Becky and Digby missed their daughter, but life on a farm with her new husband was going well by the letters they received.

"I'm so grateful for your gifts, Becky. My shabby shirt and trousers do not make for much of a wardrobe, except for my more grisly cleaning duties."

"You're welcome, dear. I think I'll make porridge and bacon for us today. After breakfast, why don't you go out? Maybe check for letters from home?"

Rose nodded and stirred more sugar cubes into her coffee. She penned four letters home—to her parents, Pea, Belenus, and even Simon. She asked for forgiveness, but was resolute her decision to leave was for the best. The letter she sent to Belenus was full of optimism, that she made it safely to White Thorn and was pursuing her freedom, at least in a fashion, and thanked him for the lute. She did not tell him the lute was lost. She knew the mail could be slow, but was bothered her parents had not yet replied. Pea did, thankfully, and her letter was infused with joy and relief that she was safe. Pea added tidbits about Tom and the bakery, and how the children, Nettie and Cody, missed her. Belenus wrote to her with encouragement. It was a balm to receive those letters. She refrained from writing Belenus about her strange experience when Albin and Fendrel kidnapped her and how her song swayed them for a brief moment. In fact, she kept that harrowing part of her journey out of all her letters home.

Rose's life was at a standstill of cleaning and serving ale, so it was hard to feel artistic. She felt like a failure sometimes. Even the Bard Academy was a sore point. Rose finally summoned the courage to ask for an audition last week. The Academy's large stone building was four stories high and elegantly designed, and intimidating. She watched with envy the young people who studied there and the elder Bard Masters, denoted by their deep blue robes. She had gone there to inquire about her chances, armed with only the letter Belenus gave her. The Dean was impressed with her letter of reference from Belenus Aylecross and commended her talent when they tested her knowledge of stories, history, poetry and song, even without a lute. However, Rose discovered to her detriment it was not her fair sex that barred her from attending White Thorn's Bard Academy. It was money. The tuition was very high and they had no scholarships available until next year. Rose could not afford to attend on the tips she received at the Red Boar. She did not even have a lute anymore, though she was saving to buy another. The Academy Dean was kind but blunt. He had no place for her at this time, but suggested Rose acquire a noble benefactor. She was welcome to audition next year, should she choose to do so.

If only finding a rich patron were that easy. As a young woman, there was also the potential for a benefactor to expect more than gratitude and bardic duties from her. She flinched. Never, not even if the gods demanded it! It was a hard lesson that even true talent needed coin and noble connections to succeed in this world. She certainly would not find one at the Red Boar. Karta was indeed going to make her scour her way to greatness!

Rose often walked to the official department of posts and messengers to check for letters from home. She would stand before the doors with people milling around her, sometimes eyeing her curiously. She was getting use to that. She was not the only Rhulonese person in this city, but they were clearly a minority.

Despite the city's vast size, it was a congested conurbation. The contrasts were sharp here, often cruelly so. The poverty was brutal and the wealth extravagant. It unsettled Rose at first, but she began to warm to the excitement of White Thorn. People of many colors, from fairest ivory of races that lived north to the deepest brown tones of the faraway kingdoms came to post their messages home. Her ear was treated to some languages she had never heard before and her vision an array of exotic fashions. It was fascinating.

It contrasted greatly with her childhood home of Stone Haven, a quaint, pristine village that was picturesque with its modest stone or wooden houses and local trade. There were less than five hundred people living in Stone Haven. There were no folk of interesting foreign heritage that ever visited her modest hamlet. She found herself missing the humble village with quiet streets, where broad roads were lined with trees and small shops or homes; nearby the forest and river beckoned. She used to go fishing with her father and hike in those woods. She would probably never experience these familiar comforts again and that twinge of loss would darken her mood.

Rose walked home to the tavern, but when she reached the Red Boar, her mood bloomed bright again. Heartened to see two familiar horses tied to the hitching post in front of the Red Boar Tavern, and one of them was Meg's horse, Fayre, she ran inside. As she passed Fayre, the mare flicked her tail at Rose familiarly.

"Where you been, Rose?" Digby asked as blocked her with his girth and a scowl when she entered the barroom. "I need you to serve the tables. Bad for business if my help keeps vanishing like a ghost."

"Becky told me I could go to the post to check for letter."

"Again?" he replied, frowning. "Any news from your folks yet?"

Rose shook her head.

"Silly wench," he grumbled and handed her a tray with two jugs of dark ale. "Go serve your ranger friends and then get to work."

"Thanks, Digby."

She carried the tray to the table where Meg and Skullcap waited. She passed them their flagons. Then Meg and Skullcap each gave her a hug. Owena, Skullcap's crow, was perched on the back of an empty chair, enjoying her own regal space.

"It's so good to see you!" Rose gushed. "I haven't seen either of you for a few days, not since the trial ended."

"We're glad that's over. Most of those men are going to see the hangman shortly," Skullcap said. "I heard a few will be sent to the mines."

Rose shook her head. "I feel strange knowing my testimony helped send men to their death, even if they deserved it."

"That's because you have a heart," Meg consoled her. "But do not let it break on their account."

"Where have you two been?" Rose asked.

"We had a mission," Meg winked, "a very important mission."

"Is it a secret? Can you tell me?" Rose gasped, holding her tray to her lips, eager to hear about something more exciting than the cost of ale and wine.

Skullcap grinned and picked up a large canvas bag from under the table and handed it to her.

Rose's heart beat wildly and she dropped the tray. Even in the large sack, the familiar outline awakened long dormant hope. She opened the tie and lifted out her lute! It was scratched and scuffed, but it looked whole!

Even the old leather strap was undamaged. "Oh great Karta! My lost lute! Thank you! How did you two ever find it?" She examined it with loving care. Karta be blessed. It was a miracle. "There are just some broken strings and a few scratches. I can fix those. There's no water damage either!"

"Thank the end of the spring rains for that," Meg said.

Skullcap took a long drink of ale and shared some with Owena. "We just tracked the forest routes from their old plans and hunted around those areas. They left some pretty obvious tracks. Those men were not exactly brainy. We finally found your poor lute in some bushes some miles from the slaver's cave."

Rose hugged them both. "Thank you, thank you, thank you!" she cried. She even stroked Owena's beak in gratitude, which she tolerated. Clutching the precious lute close to her, Rose ran over to Digby.

"Now what?" he sniffed, filling a pitcher with beer.

"Look, Digby!" She held up her lute like it was the most precious object in the world. "They rescued my lute back! Meg and Skullcap found it for me! Isn't it wonderful?"

"It's a lute," Digby sniffed. "Lutes don't serve tables or clean the bar."

"Oh, Digby, you must let me perform now. Not just a shanty when I serve drinks."

"No, I don't," he grunted stubbornly.

"I'm really good. You've heard me sing. The customers will be cheered and ask for more ale."

"I told you no barding," Digby barked, carrying the pitcher to a table of dock workers, the foam sloshing on the rough wooden table. "And you sing anyway no matter what I say."

"Ah, let her perform, Digby," one of the dock workers shouted. "Rosie's songs will only raise the class of this dump."

"Then where would ya' go for drinks," Digby shouted grumpily. "And singing don't make you a fancy bard, girl. You ever performed for real folk proper like?"

"Of course I have!" Rose exclaimed. "In Stone Haven I performed all the time. Please, Digby! Besides, it will increase my tips."

"Don't I pay you enough, girl?"

"You don't pay me at all—that's why I need the tips."

"All right, all right, stop your nagging. What is it about women folk? You'll harp on and on until a man's bones shatter." He marched to the bar and wiped the wood down with a rag, scowling. "You can sing tonight if you stop torturing me. Don't get too fancy though and don't be pouting when you go back to filling flagons with my beer."

"Thanks, Digby," Rose grinned, hugging her lute like a lost love.

"No sad songs," Digby insisted gruffly. "Bad for business."

# # #

It was moonrise when Darius reached the royal port of White Thorn. His personal guards accompanied him, which was still new for him, having lived free of court rules for so long. The night air was chilly and he wrapped his cloak tighter around him as he waited on the docks.

"Hello, Darius!" shouted a familiar voice.

Despite the darkness, in the light of the torches and moonlight, he recognized his friend before even seeing his face. He strode down the plank with grace and confidence. His rich garments would have made a woman envious. Finely fitted brown leather doublet and black trousers, snowy linen shirt topped with a deep blue velvet cloak and wide brimmed hat crowned his head; superb leather boots expertly crafted to him alone adorned his feet. Darius knew only one man who had this dash.

Prince Culain Ironheart, youngest son of the King of Rhulon, Grimkel Ironheart.

"Darius!" Culain called out with open arms. "My dear friend! You came to greet me"

Darius smile was genuine as he bent down to embrace his old friend. "Culain, welcome! It's good to see you, old friend!"

"I was stunned to hear you accepted a post as Ambassador. But I'm glad of it. That means you will stay here for a while at least. It's good to see a friend."

"As am I," Culain replied, "My royal father has so many children he doesn't know what to do with us all. As his youngest and wildest prince, he finally found me a post so I would not be the wandering diplomat or lay about prince. Personally, I think they ran out of appointments in Rhulon. My older brothers and sisters and all of their children edged me out of any noble occupation. Rather rude of them, I think. Still, I am glad of it. I love your fair city. The south is warmer and generous with sun and lovely women. I can be freer here than at home."

Darius understood the restraints on freedom when your title is *royal*. He had experienced it his whole life, except at the Crescent Monastery.

"I'm glad you are here, Culain. It's good to see a friend, especially now that my brother has died so suddenly."

"I know. It is a tragedy. I've missed you, Darius. And tonight, we must drink together before returning to palace and duty. On our last quest together, we had a great hunt across the city for the best tavern in White Thorn before they shipped you off to that monastery. Remember?"

Darius nodded with a pained expression. "I vaguely recall that tempestuous night, but have vivid memory of the terrible headache I suffered the next morning."

Culain grinned, "It was well worth the pain, my friend. You're a better man than me. I could not live in a monastery for three years without going mad." Culain paused and his tone became serious. "I'm so sorry about your brother, Justin. He was a fine man and a great prince. How are your parents handling this tragedy?"

Darius hesitated a moment and asked, "My father and mother are heartbroken, even though they do not reveal this openly. We must put on a stoic face for the world. I have been able to spend some time with my mother, but my father is harder to talk to. He has been keeping himself shut away. We don't speak much. The death of Justin was unexpected. I know he was his favorite. That does not bother me. Truly, I just wish I could be the man he wanted."

"Give it time," Culain advised gently. "A lot has happened. I regret I didn't arrive in time for the funeral. I was on a diplomatic mission for my father and didn't hear the tragic news until much later. Forgive me."

"There's nothing to forgive. The imperial funeral was a sorrowful and strange day. All of Tirangel mourned that day. Now I am the heir and very unprepared for what lies ahead."

"You have fine qualities that will serve the crown, Darius. Do not discredit yourself. I'm truly sorry for your grief. My parents send their sincere condolences for your loss. I will need to speak with your father privately soon. I have some news for him from my father. But, no more sadness tonight. Let us share a toast in your brother's memory and catch up."

"Why do I suspect you have a plan?" Darius replied.

"One must always have a plan."

"I feel another headache looming in my future," Darius laughed,

"It will be worth it, my friend. Before you return to the rigors of imperial life, let us enjoy the evening as common men. Let's revisit a few of our favorite haunts of ale and cheer."

One of the royal guards brought his horse and a smaller, stout Dwarven steed for Culain.

"Where do we go first?"

Culain mounted the horse with effortless grace, winked and shouted, "The Red Boar!"

# # #

Rose dressed in a midnight blue skirt and red blouse with little puffed sleeves. It was her best outfit, fitted to her thanks to Becky's needle. She bathed with jasmine soap so she would not stink like the soap flakes she used for cleaning and nervously polished and tuned her lute. She drank a full glass of hot water with honey to ease her dry throat.

She tiptoed down the stairs and peeked into the main taproom. It was crowded with people in the golden lamplight and she strained to see where Meg was sitting. At the far end of the room she finally saw three long tables crowded with rangers. She could just glimpse Meg's bright red hair among them. Meg waved to her. Goodness! Did she bring the whole fort?

Digby impatiently summoned her. Rose tossed back her long hair and strode in with all the bravado she could muster. Digby banged on his tray with a tin cup until the voices abruptly ceased. "All right you bloody sots! Now be silent because the Red Boar has a special treat for you good folk tonight. We have our very own bard tonight, Rose Greenleaf, who will entertain you with a few songs this evening."

A hearty round of cheers and clapping greeted her. She assumed some of the sailors were all drunk and would clap for anything. The lamps generated a hazy yellowish shimmer in the taproom. She needed to be seen and heard, especially since it was so closely packed, so she stood on the sturdy pine box Digby placed for her, so everyone could see and hear her sing clearly.

Please do not let my voice crack, she silently prayed as she positioned her lute. Her nerves were forgotten and the strange faces faded before her as she began to sing a cheery tune about sailors and their love of the sea. She followed with a few more cheery songs about maidens and heroes, much to the delight of all. As she performed, Rose sensed she was being studied, not just watched as a performer. In the back of the tavern, she marked a pair of men at a small table in the corner. They were unlike the other, more common folk who frequented the tavern. A tall folk man, young with dark hair and gentle features never took his eyes from her. He wore a cloak with elegant embroidery, and flashes of velvet peeked through. His companion was a richly dressed Rhulonese man with a steely gaze that made her feel peculiar and oddly nervous.

After a brief applause, she sang about Iara, an ancient legend about a mermaid who loved a sailor, a tragic song which she was sure Digby would not like, but it was one of her favorites, a beautiful slow song of love and loss. Sailors love songs about the sea. When the song ended, she actually saw a few rough looking sailors wiped away a tear or two. She then sang about Talasyn, legendary bard of Rhulon who was so loved by the Fey, they carried him to their secret realm before he died, so he could live forever among them. He was gifted with the glam rhapsodé, and his powers were legendary. His bard magic sealed a terrible breach when the world was torn asunder by the Fairy Wars. She finished her last song and a brief silence fell, then a robust applause awarded her efforts. They did not throw rotted vegetables or mock her. Belenus would tell her that was a good sign.

Awash with relief, Rose gingerly stepped down from her box just as the richly dressed Rhulonese man and his friend approached her. The Rhulonese man pressed a velvet bag into her palm before disappearing. He wore an extravagant wide-brimmed hat and his sharp blue eyes unsettled her, but he was gone before she could thank him.

His tall folk friend did not flee as quickly, but bowed his head to her. His gray eyes were so sad it broke her heart. "You sang beautifully," the stranger whispered. His voice was deep as velvet and he kissed her hand.

"Thank you," she murmured, but he was already following his mysterious companion out the door.

She clutched the purse as Meg and Skullcap congratulated Rose on her performance. The regular patrons were full of praise and requests. Digby finally elbowed through the cluster of people, like a hound dog sniffing the gold in her purse. "Rose, what did those rich men give you?"

She opened the soft velvet bag and there were ten gold lions! Such generous alms were unexpected.

"All that gold for a few songs?" Digby guffawed. "That would buy my foodstuffs for a month!"

Bolstered and intrigued by the mystery and her success, Rose smiled up at Digby. "Good for business, though."

Chapter Nine

Rose and Meg savored Becky's sweet pecan loaf and strong hot coffee during a rare afternoon respite in the tavern's kitchen. Rose stacked two pillows on the high backed wooden chair so she could sit at the table without feeling like a three year old.

"Has Digby adjusted to your nightly performances?" Meg asked, pouring a second cup of coffee.

Rose grinned between bites. "He sullenly accepts the deviation of my duties, but as my performing has improved both patronage and coin, his grumpiness is all for show."

Meg stirred cream into her coffee, nodding. "Digby was born grumpy."

"I'm grateful to them, and to you, Meg. Starting a new life in a foreign country is more difficult than I ever imagined. And it's not just my lack of stature."

"Change is difficult, especially if you hadn't planned to alter your life so abruptly. Starting over from scratch is hard. I did it myself. I journeyed here alone from Juraca about ten years ago."

"That is very far away. Were you escaping wedlock too?" She said it lightly as a joke, but noticed Meg briefly frowned and looked down at her coffee cup.

"No. I ran from a broken marriage–a broken life. It's a long story and it was years ago."

"I'm so sorry. My tongue is cursed sometimes."

"It's all right, Rose," Meg grinned and cut another slice of pecan loaf with swift accuracy. "It's only the past."

"ROSE!" Becky cried, abruptly cutting off Meg's confession as she waddled into the kitchen, clenching a scroll with a dark blue seal.

"Goodness, what's wrong, Becky?" Rose jumped down from the cushions and guided her to sit down.

Becky plopped into the chair, flushed, breathless. "Imperial soldiers are here. They have come for you with a special invitation to the palace!"

"For me?"

Meg handed her a cup of water and Becky gulped it down. "One of the soldiers handed me this. He said it was for Mistress Rose Greenleaf only!" She extended her plump hand clutching the scroll. "

"That's the royal seal," Meg confirmed, examining the image of a lion in blue wax, carefully extracting it from Becky's quivering fingers and handing it to Rose. "I think you better open it."

Rose cracked the wax seal with the butter knife and unrolled it. Her eyes scanned the contents and she almost fell into Becky's ample lap. "It's an invitation commanding that I sing at the Imperial Court tonight, to celebrate the betrothal of Prince Darius!" She thought of Karta again, whose dusty wings of fate touch people in strange ways.

Meg plucked the scroll from Rose's shaking fingers and read it. "It's an official summons from the palace alright. They want you to sing at a royal banquet tonight."

Meg smiled and exclaimed, "You've been performing for large crowds for the last couple weeks, but the customers here are usually locals, rough seaman and dock workers, not aristocrats. No offense, Becky."

"None taken," Becky laughed. "Our patrons are common but good folk."

Meg squinted in thought. "Remember that first night you sang here? Those two richly dressed gentlemen and one was Rhulonese and gave you that bag of gold!"

"Yes," Rose brightened. "Digby still pouts over that generous tip."

"One of them must have praised you to someone powerful," Meg said.

"Oh, that's such good news!" Becky cried. "Our little Rose will sing for the Emperor!" The old woman wept with pride, dabbing her eyes with a dish towel.

"The invitation clearly states Bardess Rose Greenleaf is invited to entertain at the official betrothal ceremony of the Crown Prince, Darius. Why does the letter refer to you as *Bardess?*" Meg remarked with an arched brow.

Rose looked at the invitation again. "It's just an ancient title for female bards in Rhulon's history and legends, but the word fell out of fashion long ago." Rose explained. "Odd, I thought I was the only one who knew that rare fact."

Meg hugged her friend. "Well, I'm proud of you, Bardess!"

Becky's eyes widened with terror. "Oh dear, you can't go before royalty like that! You must have a proper gown. The Emperor and his kin will be seeing ya' sing, girl! You need some satin or brocade! There's no time for that anyway. They're waiting outside to take you to the palace now!"

"Now!" Rose gasped.

Rose looked down at her simple gray skirt and tunic of white cotton. "I'm not dressed for royalty, but it must do." Her lack of velvet and jewels were overshadowed as her hands flew up to her head as she spun around to Meg. "But my hair is dirty!"

"Just take a deep breath and relax," Meg told her calmly. "This mysterious patron must know of your humble surroundings. Nobles have the world at their fingertips and I think can provide you with proper attire, even for a tiny dwarf bardess. You will be amazing. You're singing makes songbirds jealous! You could wear a potato sack and it still would not matter. You're a *Bardess,* remember? Just do what you do best!"

Rose hugged Meg and poor, sobbing Becky. "I'll just get my lute. Wish me luck!"

A sudden revelation startled Becky. "Oh dear, what do I tell Digby?"

"Tell him he can do the singing tonight," Rose replied dryly.

"Oh dear, that would be bad for business," Becky moaned.

# # #

The minute Rose stepped from the lavish coach a bevy of beautifully gowned women swept her away to a large, elegant suite where she was bathed head to toe with exotic smelling soap and oiled up like a lamp. She was quite capable of bathing herself and tried to resist, but they only giggled and ignored her. It did not help that they were twice her size. She feared she would drown in the deep copper but the water was joyfully hot and bubbly. Still, it was unnerving having strangers wash her hair.

The chamber was opulent with golden brocade drapes and elegant furniture. The large bed with the blue silk coverlet was unnerving. She hoped this mysterious patron did not expect anything improper! Perhaps she was expected to spend the night because it would be so late when she finished her performance and she would be driven back in the morning? But who summoned her here?

Rose's distress regarding her humble wardrobe dissolved when a fine outfit was laid before her. She could not believe it. There were even under garments, which made her blush, made of pure ivory silk! The outfit was a proper bard ensemble for court performances, like those she read about in books. A suit of dark blue velvet finely made in the traditional bardic fashion for court wear. The trousers were comfortable and laced in the back easily. The fitted jacket had tiny copper buttons and was snug around the upper arms and widened into hanging sleeves, revealing the inner snowy linen shirt. Short black boots were extravagant, being constructed of soft brushed velvet and fit her as though made just for her.

The court ladies dressed and fussed over her, as though she were a doll to be played with before tea and cakes—and she so needed some tea and cakes! She was hungry from nerves and rattled by the unexpected. The constant chatter about how cute Dwarf maidens were tested her reserve, however, she remained mute. The women did not engage her in actual conversation; they just groomed her like a horse for auction.

They gently led her to a wall mirror when they finished. She gasped at her reflection in the polished glass set in elaborate gold. She looked pretty. The bardic outfit was finely made and her hair dressed in simple fashion, swept back into a loose braid that draped over her left shoulder and tendrils of chestnut hair curled around her face.

Rose refused the expensive lute with a jeweled strap they tried to offer her. She insisted she would play the lute of Belenus! It may be scratched and old and the strap worn, but she treasured that instrument more than any fancy lute in the world. In the mirror, she noticed the coat of arms embroidered on the jacket. The embroidery was so delicate and intricate her mother would have been envious, but it was more than that. She recognized the two grizzly bears with double–bladed battle axes that crossed, and the red rose woven at the center where the blades met, with a golden crown above.

"This coat of arms belongs to the royal house of Ironheart!" Rose exclaimed.

"Wonderful! I knew I was right to choose you," an unfamiliar male voice commented.

Rose spun around. It was the man with sharp blue eyes and the generous bag of gold.

"How long have you been there!" she asked, blushing.

"Not long enough, I fear," he quipped.

Seeing his rich attire and knowing he was indeed her mysterious benefactor, she curtsied, recalling her mother's lessons, sensing that this man from her home country was more than just a courtier. The women had flocked together like shiny hens, beaming at their fine handiwork. They all fell silent and curtsied deeply as he approached.

"You may leave us, ladies. You have done excellent work," he commanded. "Thank you!"

"No, please stay!" Rose begged as they fluttered out of the chamber and closed the double doors, feeling a knot of fear in her belly. After they were gone, she bravely faced him. "Forgive me, but I am confused." She dared to look up at him. He was quite tall, easily over four and half feet. "May I ask who are you, sir?"

"Well, you recognized my family crest."

"*Your* family crest?" Rose gasped. "That means you are an—"

"An Ironheart," he finished. "It is permissible to speak it aloud. The gods shall not smite you."

"I didn't think they would, being as they have better things to do," Rose retorted.

She bit her tongue, but he only burst out laughing. He approached, ever bolder, but did not touch her. He bowed deeply. "Allow me to introduce myself, fair lady. I am Prince Culain Ironheart, youngest of my father's vast brood of royal children. I am the official Ambassador to Tirangel. Welcome to White Thorn Palace, Bardess Rose."

She curtsied again, for lack of knowing what else she should do and she silently cursed both him and her ignorance. "I am honored to meet you, your Highness. I did not expect to meet someone from my homeland in Tirangel, much less a prince."

"We are a bit aloof, but even the Rhulonese have trade concerns in the world," Culain replied. "I do love Tirangel. White Thorn is the jewel of the Kingdom. My homeland is equally glorious, but alas it is too stifling for me there. I much prefer to be here where my expectations are low."

He poured two glasses of wine and handed her one. She accepted it, not wanting to refuse a prince, but did not drink. "Do they demand much of you in Rhulon that you seek the sanctuary of a foreign kingdom?" she asked carefully.

"There are few demands actually," he replied. "That is the trouble with being the youngest of fourteen children. They do not know what to do with us all."

"Fourteen!" Rose exclaimed.

"Yes, my dear mother, Queen Fiona, is so fertile they are thinking of deifying her as a fertility goddess. But in all fairness, twins do run in the family."

"My awe of your mother has just doubled as well," Rose gasped.

He laughed at that and drained his wine glass and poured another. "Yes, my brothers and sisters could start their own country. They are from oldest to youngest—Wulfgar, the oldest and crown prince and from childhood always first to push my face into the mud at every opportunity. Amber and Milka are twins and they are married to some noble dwarves in the eastern counties and have born twins of their own. Armon is general of father's royal army and very serious. Elgar and Dirk are twins as well, but they are quite different in temperament and look. Elgar is blonde and light of mood, whilst Dirk is dark and broody. Bathilda is very pious and serious; looks more like a forlorn horse than a sister, hence her piety. Eldora is the beauty in contrast and looks just like mother, only not as bright. Osrik is very scholarly and Valdis can think of nothing but glory and battle. Frida and Olga are so identical that only mother can tell them apart. Father just flips a coin and guesses. And then there is me, the wild card. I was a surprise gift from the gods. Mother thought she was done with childbearing, so I was quite a shock to her. The royal posts at home have been taken by my older brothers and sisters, and their children. So I am here enjoying the sun and warmth only the south can provide."

"I can only imagine what the holidays can be like with a family so large."

"It involves heavy drinking and violence ensues before the Solstice gifts are even opened," Culain replied dryly.

"Your name, Culain, rings from the northern provinces," Rose said.

"Yes, most of my clan was given the more common southern names of our land. My mother, Queen Fiona, is a northerner though and through. She insisted her last child be baptized with a proper northern name."

"Culain was an ancient hero in legends," Rose commented.

"You know your literary references. Good. My heroics are just a flair for diplomacy and an eye for troublesome situations that can threaten Rhulon, so my father sends me to other kingdoms to act as ambassador or to broker trade treaties."

It occurred suddenly to Rose she was speaking with a Prince of the

House of Ironheart as though she were speaking to a common man! "Why did you send for me? I'm just a poor girl working in a tavern. A simple maid finding herself in a palace is not always a good thing." Maybe she was too blunt, but she needed to know where she stood.

"You're many things, Bardess, but simple is not one of them."

"You know nothing about me."

"Ah, but I do. I have many eyes and ears that work for me, Rose. The benefit of a royal purse and an inquisitive mind. I also recognize potential and talent. You're from Stone Haven, a quaint but unimportant village in the southern part of our country. You are almost eighteen and ran away to escape an arranged marriage. Your father is a blacksmith and well respected in your tiny hamlet. Your letters have made it home by the way."

"How did you know that I—"

"I know you made it all the way here only to be abducted by slavers, and then you were miraculously rescued by the Rangers. One of them, Commander Meg Sparrow, helped secure you employment at a popular tavern called the Red Boar. A marvelous establishment, as I have taken to enjoying their ale, at least when Digby doesn't water it down."

"It's just cheap ale, he doesn't water."

Culain laughed and asked, "But your skill on lute and your voice are well trained, lady. Where did you learn? You knowledge of tale and song are very impressive."

"Belenus Aylecross taught me," she replied proudly. "He chose me as his pupil when he moved to our village. Many a mother dragged their son to him to be taught, but he picked me."

"I remember Belenus," Culain said fondly. "A crusty and irreverent Bard! It does not surprise me that he decided to teach a girl. He was revered and honored for decades in my father's house. He was wild of foot too, living in the lands of the tall folk like me. I always liked him. I like him even more now."

"So I am here to sing for the Emperor?"

"Yes. There is a special banquet honoring the betrothal of Prince Darius and Princess Lilias Rhodan of Uragon. We use the word honor rather than celebrate due to the recent death of Prince Justin, as celebration would be too cheery, Darius is also my friend. So you will be performing before the imperial court. As a student of Belenus Aylecross, I am counting that you will do him proud."

Her heart began racing, a combination of desire and fright in one great assault. "I'm relieved, Your Highness, I was afraid that, well, I mean, that your expectations of—"

Mercifully, he put up his hand and she stopped trying to phrase her question that she feared asking. "Your virtue is not in danger, so you may relax. My plans for you are more cerebral."

"Then I shall strive to make Belenus proud of me this night."

"Excellent. Should you prove pleasing to the royal audience, you will be in my employ as Bardess Rose Greenleaf and a part of my official household."

The opportunity seemed too wonderful to be true. A bard with an official patron of royal blood was a dream. Her wishes were being granted with such swift promise she felt a prick of suspicion. She reminded herself to curtsy again in gratitude. "Thank you, Prince Culain. It's unusual you know the female rank for Bard. I didn't think anyone knew that but me?"

"It's been an ancient and unused title for far too long. There is more you must learn of course. What I also need from you is a good ear and strong wit. From what I heard about you, you may fit quite nicely."

"I do not understand," she whispered with care.

"Oh, you will soon," he smiled, and poured more wine. "Now let us discuss the protocol for the banquet and your choice of music and stories to amuse this noble lot."

She listened, but all the while in her mind, deep in her thoughts, the black wings of Karta whispered to her to beware.

Chapter Ten

The spectacle of royal festivity was astonishing in its unvarnished reality. Chandeliers blazed above long tables covered with white linen. Guests in garish finery drank from jeweled goblets.

There must be hundreds of candles burning in this room tonight. And I've never seen so much food!

Guests gobbled freely of the exotic food provided by servants dressed in somber black. Towers of sweetmeats and nuts graced every table. Luscious berries swimming in rich sauces were spooned onto plates of shining silver. Most of the guests just looked pompous and did not impress Rose, though she pitied one elderly nobleman in a curly brown wig too young for his years. He longingly gazed at the confections spread before him, but only soaked his bread in wine to soften it before nibbling at it.

Poor old gentleman can't even enjoy a sweetmeat.

Succulent roasts and fowl on salvers garlanded with flowers were delivered to the tables of greedy courtiers. Rose found it humorous until the tragic sight of a white swan; its former glory forever frozen in death with feathers intact, stuffed and propped up on a huge platter carried by two helpers. It saddened her. Rose loved swans. She could never imagine eating one. She lost her appetite.

A discreet group of musicians played in the shadowed background during supper. Rose would not perform until after the main meal was finished. That was only proper. No singer who valued her voice would ever perform in such pandemonium.

The Imperial family and chosen guests dined separately at a private table overlooking the hall. Emperor Aristide De'Ruarc was an austere figure amid the forced gaiety of his court. His silver hair cropped very short beneath his gold crown and his black damask coat was plain. Empress Isabeau was regal in black satin, her dark blonde hair pinned into an elegant chignon that complimented her aristocratic beauty. They dined with genteel manners and took frugal bites of the rich food.

At least they look and act royal, Rose judged.

Her eager judgments of the guests paused. The dark-haired man sitting next to the emperor was the young man with the sad gray eyes who kissed her hand that night at the Red Boar. So this was Prince Darius De'Ruarc! She remembered that gentle kiss, which was her only kiss, even if it was on the hand. Simon never even kissed her hand—not that she ever wanted him to. Next to Darius must be Princess Lilias of Uragon, his betrothed. Flaxen haired, blue-eyed, and delicately beautiful—just like every princess she read about in fairy tales as a child.

Why must they always be blonde?

Unlike the others at the imperial table who wore dark colors, her satin gown was pink, embellished with pearls and trimmed with snowy lace. Darius and Lilias sat awkwardly together, picking at their food and avoiding eye contact. Rose was strangely satisfied at their discomfort together, though she could not fathom why.

Sitting next to Princess Lilias was the most exotic woman Rose had ever seen. She reminded Rose of a mortal embodiment of Tarani, the elemental goddess of love and hate. Her flawless beauty was unearthly and her green eyes watched the guests with a thinly veiled contempt. She wore no jewels and her sleeveless red silk gown must be of the Uragon fashion, for it was void of flounces, hoops, or laces. Her only accessory were long black gloves.

Prince Culain joined Rose in the hall and observed her study of the royal table.

"Who is the woman seated next to the princess?" Rose inquired softly. "She's certainly not old enough to be her mother."

"The ravishing brunette next to the Princess Lilias is Lady Thera Sule, and she's far more dangerous than any mother. She is the guardian of the Princess's virtue until Lilias is properly married. Lady Sule is also rumored to be King Krell's official mistress." He looked at Rose curiously. "How did you know it was me coming up behind you?"

"I recognized your perfume," Rose commented. "Don't your friends at the party miss you?"

"My only true friend is Darius. Alas, he is occupied with his future bride."

"Have you met the princess he is supposed to marry?"

"Twice, but she is a flighty creature."

"There is something odd about her, but I can't explain it." She rubbed her temples. Rose was also getting a headache. She put it down to nerves.

"Her beauty is disconcerting to most women," Culain commented dryly.

"That's not what I meant, Your Highness," Rose replied coolly.

She gritted her teeth and returned to her surveillance of the feast. "Look at all of them. Eating like pigs at a trough. No. Pigs are neater. Are these nobles always so crude? I've seen better manners at the Red Boar."

"Disillusioning, isn't it?" remarked Culain, leaning against the wall.

"There must be hundreds of people in that banquet hall."

"Free food and drink attract the court parasites like flies to a honey jar."

She was speaking boldly, but Rose reminded herself to take care. *He's an Ironheart, from an unbroken dynasty dating back centuries, even if his clothes are frillier than a woman's.* Yet Prince Culain seemed to encourage her honest speech without rancor.

"They are not what I expected, that's all," Rose shrugged.

"True. But not everyone at court is what they seem. That is your first lesson."

Rose whispered, a little shaky, "What if my voice cracks or a string breaks on my lute?"

"Fate did not bring you this far to fail. You will perform as a true bard, the way Belenus taught you. I have faith in you Rose; else you would not be here. I'm returning to the feast now. Be ready to enter at my signal," Culain warned.

"I will," Rose answered. "And I will do Belenus proud—and you."

Yes, Fate did bring her to this place. This was a dream she often wove over and over while sitting beneath her favorite oak tree at home. This was now her reality. She was grateful for this chance Culain offered her. She just wished he was not so exasperating!

Indeed, as the hour passed, by the time dinner ended and the servants cleared away the plates, she was anxious to run into the banquet to sing and get it over with. She breathed deeply, remembering Belenus' tutoring. She smiled to herself when she recalled his advice on performing for royals, his gruff voice vivid in her mind.

All men are born the same. Naked. Fancy velvets or rough homespun do not measure a man's worth.

Prince Culain rose from his chair, which was in an honored place at the end of the Emperor's private table. He signaled the musicians. They ceased their soft music and the chief drummer banged the drum in rhythmic beats until the guests fell silent. Culain walked to the center of the hall and bowed deeply before the Imperial family and the guests. "Tonight, I have arranged a great treat for you in honor of my good friend's betrothal to the pearl of the east, Princess Lilias of Uragon," he announced, bowing to the young couple. "I too possess a rare jewel, unseen by all until this evening. Her remarkable voice will enchant you. Her stories will enthrall you. In my kingdom, she is known as the beautiful Rose of Rhulon."

Beautiful? He's exaggerating that pitch. And he does not possess me!

"I now present for your pleasure the legendary, Bardess Rose Greenleaf!"

At least I am legendary.

A wave of cautious applause followed as she entered the hall. She was keenly aware of the amazed expressions and heard a few passing whispers. A female Rhulonese bard was not common. She must make that work to her advantage. She first curtsied deeply before the Emperor and his wife. A court musician placed a small stool for her to sit upon. She was grateful for the strong repertoire she learned for Belenus, for Prince Culain's requests were very specific and not easy songs either. A lesser trained bard would have been awash in panic, but Belenus had been a hard task master. She knew all of these songs by heart.

Rose immediately dived in, fearing any pause would freeze her voice and fingers forever. She played upon the lute a delicate but brief introduction to transition before she began with a song about the first Emperor of Tirangel. It was a rousing song of epic battle and conquest. The song recounted how the first Emperor rescued his stolen princess from an eastern warlord and defeated his enemies to found an empire. This established a dynasty that still existed to this day. With satisfaction, she noticed the song drew a slight grin from the stony emperor.

Rose smiled with a twinge of triumph as her tune reached its climax. Stronger in confidence, she strolled among the court, keeping within range of the royal family, and sang a traditional welcome song familiar to those of the southern lands, a cheerful ditty to lift the mood. Rose followed with several famous ballads. She then drew gasps when she sang a frightening fable about the goddess, Karta, and her judgment of forbidden lovers fleeing dark enemies in her sacred forest. She followed this with a traditional hymn about the mystical Garden of Valhalum, the sacred place ruled by the goddess, Ishar. She sang about the Vila, the elusive fey women who weave fairy rings in the forest.

She finished her last number and the applause resounded in her ears. Then the Emperor spoke directly to her!

"Excellent, Bardess Rose. Your talent is impressive. I commend Prince Culain for finding such a notable talent. I do have a request. Are you versed in the traditional heroic poem about your famous King Gregor Ironheart? I relish a strong war poem and the Rhulonese do their king's legend better than our tall folk. Can you perform it, Bardess?"

Rose was both petrified and ecstatic. The Ironheart war poem was her favorite. It was also not in the repertoire chosen by Culain. She bowed deeply and glancing at Culain, who for once looked surprised. "Your Majesty, I shall be honored to recite it for you."

Rose placed her lute upon the small stool and began the tale of Ironheart. The hall was silent as she spoke, bringing to life the heroic battles and the terrifying demons. Her memory was solid as she recalled each line. She let the adventure, victory, and tragedy carry her through each stanza. She forgot about everything but this moment as she recited the tale of her favorite legend and king, Gregor Ironheart.

During her precise oration, an eerie feeling pricked at Rose's nerves. It sent shivers down her spine. She continued her performance, but found her eyes scanning the great hall for any clue to the darkness she sensed. The poem's performance took nearly half an hour, but when she finished the poem, she closed her eyes and bowed her head. The vast hall was silent as a grave for a heartbeat until an enthusiastic applause boomed.

Rose opened her eyes and breathed, beaming at her audience with newfound confidence. The dark presence had not diminished, but she pushed it away. She focused only on the happy faces cheering her performance. Even the Emperor and Empress hailed her. When she dared to glance up at Prince Darius, a gentle smile lit up his face as he enthusiastically clapped. Princess Lilias applauded; however, she yawned openly. Her guardian, Lady Thera Sule, studied Rose with green eyes as she sipped red wine from a crystal goblet.

Culain stood up, loudly applauding, and at his designated signal, Rose bowed and departed the banquet.

After she passed through the curtains, only then did her nerves strike her down. Rose had never been anxious about performing before. Her knees felt like water! Singing and poetry was as natural as breathing to her. But something other than stage fright unsettled her in that great hall. She was unsure of the source. Was it the boredom of Princess Lilias? The calm scrutiny of Lady Thera Sule? A foreshadowing of something unknown? It felt strange and ethereal, like a whisper of darkness.

Rose did not see Culain after the performance, but a young maid was waiting for her in the hall. She led her back to her room, where a nightdress was laid out for her on the bed. A supper tray waited for her on the table. Rose was famished and could not wait to dig in. She was feeling better but still had a slight headache; she hoped some food would help.

"His Highness says he will see you in the morning," she told her. "Enjoy your dinner."

"Thank you," Rose answered softly and carefully put away her lute.

"Shall I undress you for bed, Mistress Rose?" the maid offered.

"No thank you," Rose replied. "I can do it myself. And just call me Rose. What's your name?"

The maid looked to be around Rose's age; she had dark curls peaking from her cap. She smiled and curtsied. "I'm Sally."

"Good night, Sally."

"Good night, Mistress—I mean Rose."

Rose was relieved Sally did not insist on undressing her. How do royals endure such intimate attention, especially when they are so distant in everything else? Rose was frantic with pent up energy. She was too excited to even finish her meal, though she sampled generous portions of tonight's delicacies arranged on the lovely platter on the dining table.

Was Culain pleased with her performance? What would be her fate now? Why did she feel so anxious? It was as though a Vanth, a herald of death and bad luck, touched her with her black scythe.

Despite her exhaustion, the combination of excitement and ominous feelings tormented Rose. She barely slept, tossing and turning on the downy bed and punching the fluffy pillows scented with lavender. Near dawn, she gave up on sleep. Rose had been too mesmerized by her new situation to notice until now, but she realized that not only the bed, but all the furnishings in the room, were scaled to her smaller size. This must have been a suite for a Rhulon noble perhaps?

A raven's sharp caw at her casement window drew her attention. A black raven perched on the windowsill as though waiting. It did not fly away when it saw her, but remained on the ledge, gazing at her patiently.

The raven was Karta's messenger, so she should honor her. Rose grabbed a chunk of bread from the food tray. "I best offer you a bite of food to thank Karta for last night," she said.

She opened the window and carefully placed her gifts on the window ledge. The raven was not threatened by Rose and inspected the bread. Deciding her food worthy of consumption, the raven cawed loudly, scooped up the morsel in its beak and flew away. She watched the bird fly away, hoping it was a good sign of her destiny rather than a warning. With Karta, you never knew!

In the twilight, Rose saw a lone figure in a purple cloak running across the grass. It was not a gardener or servant, for even at a distance, the cloak looked expensive. A large hood concealed the identity of the wearer and a flash of petticoat was the only clue it was female. The figure stopped suddenly right beneath her window–and looked up at Rose. She shivered, for the purple figure's gaze was almost a deliberate challenge. She could not see the face, only hooded shadow. She sensed something ill from the mysterious woman.

It was the almost same foreboding Rose experienced at the banquet when she performed for the Emperor. It sent an icy shiver down her back, it was not the same feeling, though it had a malevolent touch. That weird tingle of darkness she experienced was different. It still haunted her, and Rose retreated behind the curtains. After a few seconds, Rose dared to look again, but the cloaked stranger had disappeared.

# # #

Fallon Gansis observed the banquet that night. His enchanted mirrors revealed more than the opulence of the Emperor's court. A young girl who sang intrigued him. He sensed something within her. A seed of something unborn, but waiting eagerly to sprout. He was rarely curious, and knew there was something special about Rose Greenleaf. He needed to know more.

He knew the changeling would need to renew its human shape again tonight. He doubted Crimson could maintain the same guise for much longer. The last weeks of constant metamorphosis were becoming an agony and that would make Crimson a liability. The changeling was also becoming unstable. Fallon knew the cost of keeping a particular human shape for too long; it required complicated magic that was draining on the changeling. If the victim died, Crimson would lose the ability to hold that human form and its memories. She risked exposure if that happened. He could kill the changeling, but then he would lose his amusement.

Fallon waited for her before the mirror. Crimson soon appeared as he expected, her face only partly human now, a hideous duality. He touched the mirror, and the changeling saw what he intended–the image of her goblin king.

Crimson groveled. "My Lord!"

"You're taking too many risks, Changeling," Fallon warned.

"I do all for you," Crimson whimpered, cowering. "I live with smelly humans. I eat their bland food. Wear strange clothes. I go to their chapels with their foreign gods and pretend to pray. I kill, which I enjoy. Thank you for that. I run to this ancient boneyard and weave my magic to keep this human form, all for you."

"You should find another victim. Let this one perish."

Crimson stripped away the black gloves, revealing her true hands of gray mottled skin and long wiry fingers. "I know the human is slowly dying in the cocoon. Soon, soon, I will cast off this silly false form and be Crimson again. I have news, dread lord. Please forgive poor unworthy Crimson, majestic ruler of darkness. The ancient enemy of your blood is here. There is an Ironheart at court."

"Tell me more," his thunderous voice commanded.

Fallon Gansis grew bored as he listened to Crimson's ecstatic report. He was not interested in an Ironheart, but knew they would eventually have to be dealt with. The goblin clans did despise the Ironhearts. The goblins had sent their changeling slaves to several key kingdoms, but they were becoming too disruptive, too fast. He would have to put a stop to that until the time was right.

It was not Culain Ironheart, but the dwarf maiden, Rose Greenleaf, that intrigued him. He had watched the imperial banquet to keep an eye on Crimson. Something sparked within Fallon's core when he observed Rose Greenleaf through his mirrors. Her singing unveiled a fragment of untapped magic so uncommon she was not even aware of it. He did not sense she was a witch. Could it be? The glam rhapsodé was rare. Not even Fallon could be sure she had it unless he examined her personally. Such a young woman could be valuable–if turned to the shadows and tutored by him.

Rose had detected his scrutiny of her as she performed. That intrigued him further.

Fallon's used his sorcery to maintain his image of the goblin king in the mirror, but soon that would change, at the right time of course. Being a giant red-skinned goblin was becoming tiresome.

Crimson bowed. "What do you command?"

"There is a new bard at court named Rose Greenleaf. "Capture and cocoon her for safekeeping."

"You want me to take her place?" Crimson nodded eagerly. "So we can kill Ironheart?"

"No. I want you to bring her to me in this catacomb of bones. I will handle the rest. In time, Prince Ironheart will die, as will the rest of his family. I demand the girl first."

Crimson sniffed. "But why do you want the dwarf girl?"

"That is not your concern, slave. Bring her to me or suffer my anger."

Chapter Eleven

Queen Gurza was old, even for a hobgoblin of the Kobalos breed. They ruled the goblin clans since time began. Now her long reign was done. In her prime, Gurza stood over six feet tall; her skin red as blood; her fangs lethal and long. Now infirmity and age twisted her body and withered her skin; her fangs broken and stained; even her bones rattled for death. Let the Grim Gods summon her down to the underworld and be done with it. She had one last duty before she surrendered to it. Seven nights ago, she finally passed the bronze crown and sacred rod of Mordok to her son, Morziel. He was chosen to deliver them from the shame that had been their plight for centuries. At least that is what the oracles promised; but they would not dare say otherwise without risking being sacrificed and eaten.

One of her rock troll slaves shuffled into her chambers, its gray speckled face bowed in respect. "Forgive me, Queen Mother, but Beleth has come as you requested."

"Bring her to me." Gurza reclined on her throne.

Beleth entered the throne room like she already ruled as Queen. She was the prize of Mordok and knew it. Like Gurza, she was born with the markings of a queen–black swirls that marked her scarlet cheeks. Her black hair sprouted with tiny snakes that seemed to dance. A trace of envy burned in Gurza. She touched her sparse mane, stroking her own weary little serpents; even they were tired in their old age and rarely danced now. Beleth knelt and bowed her head in obeisance. Her eyes burned with lust and hunger. Yes, Beleth could endure what was to come.

"Rise," Gurza commanded.

"What may I slay for you, Queen Gurza?" Beleth asked, using the formal greeting.

"At the next full moon, I have decreed that you shall wed my son, King Morziel."

It was expected. Beleth was the only acceptable mate. Morziel was descended from Raziel himself–through Gurza. Beleth was descended from priest and oracles. These ancient lines, sacred among their demon kind, would give weight to her son's destiny.

Beleth's lips curved in a satisfied smile, her fangs pointed and sharp. "I pray to be worthy of King Morziel."

"You must be."

"Yes, Queen Mother. I will bear Morziel many warriors. I will prepare the way for the coming of the Grim Gods."

"Long have we waited. For generations we have remained hidden in caves and underground kingdoms beneath the realms of the humans. Mordok is our country, but we exist everywhere. Centuries ago, the last war left us near extinction. Raziel was killed by an Ironheart. The cursed dwarf used the sun blade, poisoned with fey magic. It destroyed Raziel. To die by fey magic is a fate worse than simple death. Ironheart died, but his legions decimated the rest of us. What little survived scattered and hid, like rodents. The ascendancy of our race has been the goal of my clan since that fateful day."

"I have dreams," Beleth whispered, "of long ago. The ancient fairy races ruled this world once. They have long since vanished, but still they exist. In my dreams they watch us, peering through the mystical veils that divide our worlds."

"The priests said you might be an oracle, touched by the Dark."

"My dreams only leave me confused, Queen Gurza."

Gurza rose sluggishly from her throne. "Help me up." With the aid of Beleth, she hobbled to the low altar of black stone. "Let us pray to the dark ones," Gurza invited.

"What else do the priests say?"

Gurza tittered, her frail skeletal body shaking with the exertion. "The priests cast bones and swing their stinking incense, not that they know any more than we do. We sent some changelings to infiltrate the human world and its weaknesses. They are making chaos. Killing. Spying. They can walk where we cannot. The changelings have begun reporting back, but there is one still missing. Crimson. I gave her to Morziel as one of his coronation gifts. She worshipped him. He sent her to scout the borders of our realm, nothing more. She should have been gone for no more than a few days, but it has been weeks."

"Such an insignificant slave is a trivial loss, even a favorite. If she is ever found, I will make sure she is punished," Beleth promised.

"The changeling would deserve it, but the pathetic creature worshipped my son. Morziel found her amusing. She just vanished. I must find him another gift, besides you of course. What would you do,

Beleth, if Crimson suddenly returned?"

"I would crush her skull and have her remains stewed for Morziel."

"Excellent," Gurza chuckled. "You are worthy of the bronze crown."

# # #

When Rose tried to get dressed, she discovered her own clothes were gone. She hoped they did not throw them away! That would upset poor Becky. She wanted to save the smart bardic uniform for performing, should she have a position. Maybe the maid put her clothes in the wardrobe? She opened the doors and found masses of exquisite clothes stuffed within, all fitted for her dwarf size—not tall folk. There was even an array of accessories. Shoes, nightgowns, cloaks, gloves, stockings, and even underwear, crammed together in the bottom drawers. Rose was disturbed. A single outfit was one thing to plan. This was something else.

I wonder if Culain keeps a Rhulonese mistress for his amusement and these are her clothes. Maybe he discarded her? Maybe he has many mistresses and he keeps an assortment of gowns for his harem!

These fantastic ideas infuriated her. This perplexed Rose, because she did not even care for Culain. He was too bold, arrogant, contradictory, and dressed like a frilly fop. Still, Rose needed to put something on. She chose the plainest outfit she could find, a forest green muslin skirt and white cotton blouse with a lace collar. She felt a little dirty wearing the castoff clothes of some fallen mistress.

Restless, she gravitated toward an ornate desk. Rummaging through the drawers, she found a ream of pale golden paper and an expensive writing stylus. The find broke her frantic hunt. She sat down and began writing about last night, as though only that could make some sense of it all. Writing always calmed her down. If she focused on a new story about Meg, she could not fume about Culain's secretive mistresses.

Knocking on the door broke her concentration. Rose reluctantly called, "Come in."

Prince Culain strode into her chamber. Sally followed him with a tray of hot coffee and pastries. The aroma was wonderful. She was ravenous again. Sally curtsied and left.

"Good, you're awake," Culain smiled and indicated the table for Sally to leave the breakfast. "I see you found the pen and paper. Excellent. A true bard is always creating."

Being alone with Culain made her uneasy now. She got up from the desk and reminded herself to curtsy, for he was still a prince. "Your Highness, do not be angry with me for asking, but I don't know if it is proper for us to be alone in my bedchamber."

Oh dear, I sound just like my mother!

"Don't fret so, Rose. Your virginity is safe. This is just business."

She felt her face flush and bit her tongue.

"You're in my employ now. There's nothing unwholesome about a breakfast meeting."

"So it's official. I'm your bard now?" she asked.

"I think we will revive the term bardess, as it gives you an edge. You are unique in the world, thus you should have a unique title. I rather like the sound of it. Bardess. And yes, you are my official bard. If you had not done well, I would have sent you packing back to the Red Boar last night."

"Good to know," Rose replied dryly.

"When you recited the Ironheart poem, you could not have made me prouder. Flawless! I was not expecting that request. You must perform it for my father someday. I commend Belenus for his tutelage."

She smiled, glowing with pride for a brief moment, until she recalled the wardrobe of mystery clothes.

"Now, let me explain more about your other duties," Culain said, pouring them coffee.

Was it normal for a prince to wait upon common folk? He was confusing her again.

"I'm not sure what you mean, Your Highness?" she replied quizzically, sitting down and adding cream to her coffee.

"In private, you may just call me Culain. Titles tend to grind my sensibilities. They are a facade people often hide behind. In public, just use the normal royal drivel." He chose a raspberry roll and leaned back in his chair. "In serving me, you serve Rhulon. Even something trivial could be important to the security of the state. I want you to listen and watch, Rose. My trusted valet, Robert Silverberry, will help you learn the ropes. You're talented, but naïve and young. Therefore you must be tutored in the ways of court politics. Do you understand?"

"Yes, Culain."

"Excellent," Culain replied. "Today, you'll perform in the royal gardens on the west side of the palace at tea time. No singing unless requested, just instrumental. Play your lute and listen. My valet, Robert, will take you there. Wear your bard uniform. That blue suits you by the way."

"I will be there."

"Until three this afternoon, you're at liberty to do whatever you wish. My private carriage is at your disposal. I have a long meeting with the Emperor, so I won't need it."

After Culain left, her mind churned. The purple cloaked woman. Her sense of dread, but it was probably just foolishness. The closet of fancy dresses vexed her. Her frets faded with the reality that she was appointed as a real bard! A bardess!

Taking Culain at his word, Rose summoned Sally and requested Culain's carriage. She had so much to tell Meg and the Croftons. She quickly wrote a message to Meg, asking to meet her at the Red Boar around noon.

# # #

Emperor Aristide laid a hand on the pile of reports gathered from all over the continent, shaking his head. "Are you sure about this, Culain?"

Culain reclined in the blue brocade chair and nodded. "Positive. My people are skilled in tracking facts and evidence. There have been numerous anomalous occurrences in several kingdoms in just the past year. Juraca has broken into a civil war, but we saw that coming for years. Not with the other kingdoms. Rulers are dying from mysterious illnesses or accidents in such quick account that they are worrisome."

Aristide looked exhausted. Culain had spent all morning with him, reviewing the stack of testaments. It grieved Culain to add to his burden, especially since he had recently suffered the loss of his eldest son, Justin.

Aristide rubbed his eyes after removing his reading spectacles wearily. "Generals and other important people of state and military are dying or just vanishing without reason or trace."

"It's happening everywhere and far too frequently to be the usual political games or sad event. Several states have been thrown into chaos."

"Could my son's death be part of this? Could this conspiracy of chaos you speak of have assassinated my son?"

Culain was hesitant to answer, because in truth he did not know. "I've no wish to cause you pain, Aristide, but it's impossible to know that."

Culain did not relish bringing this up to Aristide, but he had permission from his father to bring Aristide into the fold. "Tragically, this past year we suffered our own chaos. A changeling infiltrated our court and tried to assassinate my father."

"Why haven't I heard of this?"

"We kept it very quiet. I trust you shall keep this a secret for now. Several brave guards died saving my father. We tried to capture the damn thing. It died in the process, which was a shame."

"Why?" Aristide gruffly asked.

"Because I wanted answers," Culain replied sharply. "Unlike goblins and other similar disgusting species, a changeling can wear a human face and breach human populations. Such extremes points to a darker power, especially since changelings have squat for intelligence. There are even rumors that Mordok is swarming with goblins again. They have been sighted in other realms too."

Aristide looked skeptical. "This is speculation of course."

"Speculation can become fact."

"We exterminated those monsters centuries ago," Aristide affirmed. "A few strays roam here and there, easily put down by the sword."

"We know so little about them," Culain confirmed darkly. "I'm not saying goblins are planning world carnage, but past experience reflects their love of killing and mayhem. It's possible the goblin threat is a front to mask the real conspirators. There may be other more human factors at the reins, but I need to investigate this further. I trust you, Aristide. Our family shares a long bond. I would rather learn the truth now. I don't want to be caught with my britches down to discover it's all true and it's too late to do anything about it."

"My beloved son and heir is dead. And if that was not bad enough, he may have been the victim of faceless enemies we don't even know." Aristide looked so fragile for a moment that Culain pitied him, but he would never confess it.

"The loss of a child is a sorrow that can never heal," Culain agreed gently. "But avenging that loss is a worthy start, as long as we target the right culprits." He sipped his sherry and paused a moment, thinking. "If I may ask, don't you think Darius should be hearing this? This does involve him as your only heir now."

Aristide shook his head, standing up from his elegant desk and pacing around the room. "Not yet. This is too new for the boy."

"Perhaps, but the events indicate a threat to your kingdom."

"A ruler must be strong. Darius is not," the Emperor commented bluntly. "I may sound cruel, but I have known you since you were a boy, Culain. You've been my personal conduit to your father for years. I trust you more than any other except for my family. You know that Darius was never meant for the throne. Maybe that's my fault. I focused all of my energy and attention on Justin. I didn't even think about the possibility the crown would fall to Darius. He was the 'spare' as they often call the second son, marked for church or army—or an advantageous foreign marriage to a princess of wealth. Now I am paying the price. I grieve for my empire as much as for my son. He was a natural to succeed me to the throne, so bold and fearless, a great rider, noble, generous, and wise in statecraft. The perfect prince. Now he's dead and lost to me forever. I know you're his friend, but I fear Darius is too soft for the imperial crown."

"As Darius' friend and a fellow prince, I understand his position as well as yours. When you're not the heir to the throne and never expected to rule, such as myself, it's shocking when fate changes things. When you're a secondary prince, or like me, fifteenth, you have a choice. You hone valuable skills and talents to make yourself useful to king and country. Or you become an indolent prince who drinks all day. My liver would not tolerate the latter, so I decided to become useful. Darius is gentle of heart, but he is still a De'Ruarc, son of the great Emperor Aristide. He studied vigorously at that quiet monastery. All he has done for three years is study. He is patient and devoted. Now he's your sole heir and that's hard for him too. He wants to please you more than anything." In a softer, personal voice, Culain added, "He worships you, Aristide. He just needs time and your gentle guidance to help him."

"I don't know how to be gentle," Aristide confessed in a broken voice. "I have been an Emperor since I was seventeen. I don't remember what gentleness feels like. Darius looks like he would break if I pushed him too hard."

"He is more adaptable than you think. Princes tend to be quite resilient. It's in our blood. Invite him to counsel meetings. Let him watch and learn. You may both even enjoy it. Darius is stronger than you realize."

"You have a lot of opinions, Culain, but you also understand the sacrifice required in kingship. It's a shame you're not the heir to Rhulon.

What a king you would make! Together, we could conquer the whole continent."

"Ah, but if I were, I would not be enjoying your exquisite sherry. I wouldn't know what to do with that kind of power. I would suffer constant headaches." Culain gave a mock shudder and poured two more glass of sherry. "Horrifying notion." He passed one to the Emperor after he sipped it. "So as not to disturb your taster."

"Always considerate," Aristide grinned.

"As an ancient ally of Tirangel, Rhulon's interests have always aligned with yours. We have a wonderful balance of trade and military support. If we are threatened by outside forces, we must take care to watch our backsides as well as our borders. Monarchs are toppling in the east at an alarming rate. Heirs and kings are dying suddenly. Generals. Religious leaders. It is too strange for it all to be just a coincidence. I know this is painful, but we need to investigate this together. If we can find the source of these maladies, then we could strike them down before they do more damage."

"I will consider your proposition. Say nothing of this to my wife for now. Isabeau has suffered greatly since our son died in that cursed accident—if it was an accident. Right now Darius is home and it gives her comfort, and for that I bless him. Perhaps you're right, but let's keep this between us for now."

"I would never dream of upsetting your gracious Empress. I would sooner cut out my tongue. She's a sweet lady who does not deserve such grief. For that alone, I will discover what is behind all of this," Culain promised earnestly. "I know it would be easy for each kingdom to ignore each other's troubles. That is also the way to chaos and ruin. I think our enemies are counting on that."

"And what does the Raven say?" Aristide asked pointedly.

Culain arched his brow, leaned back in his chair and grinned. "You would know about Raven of course."

"Of course I know about the Raven, Rhulon's spymaster who directs your operatives throughout the world. I just don't know who it is. Hel, not even my Imperial Spymaster knows the identity of the Raven."

"Of course my patriotism prohibits my telling you, should I even know. All states have secrets. Please don't torture it out of me."

"I wouldn't dream of it, Culain. That could start a war, and neither of us wants that, at least not with each other."

Chapter Twelve

The Red Boar buzzed with noontime guests. Becky beamed with pride when she told them about her official appointment as a bard. Meg cheered and hugged her. Digby grumbled, wiping down the bar, complaining about losing his barmaid and almost in the same breath, boasting to his patrons that their Rose was now a real bard at the palace.

"I'm so proud of you, Rosie," Becky sniffled. "You girls have a nice sit down. I'll sit with you later." She shambled back to the kitchen, dabbing her eyes.

"I feel so bad about leaving them so abruptly," Rose murmured. "They've just been so good to me!"

"They're truly proud of you," Meg exclaimed. "And they will be just fine."

"We got some beef stew today if you're proper hungry, unless you're too fancy for my food now," Digby offered.

"I would love your stew," Rose beamed.

"Make that for both of us. I'm starving," Meg added.

They sat down at an empty table in the corner. Digby brought them two large bowls of stew, cider, and a small loaf of bread.

"I think there's actually some meat in this stew," Meg said and dug in, ravenous. "I'm happy for you, Rose. Who is your benefactor?"

Rose stirred her bowl of stew with the rumination of a witch over a cauldron. "Prince Culain Ironheart. He was the one who gave me that bag of gold."

"What's wrong?" Then Meg's eyes flamed with anger. "Did he try to bed you?"

"He didn't try anything improper. Prince Culain swears my virtue is not in danger."

"Good," Meg said gingerly, "then neither is his life. Until the spell breaks, just enjoy it. What's your benefactor like?"

"Prince Culain. He's very eccentric," Rose whispered. "I can't put it into words. He has very blue eyes. He's smart, yet acts like a court fop in public. I can't explain it. I'm at a loss for words."

"Prince Culain must be complex for you to be at loss for words. Language is your bread and butter." Meg tore off a hunk of bread and dipped it in the stew.

Rose spooned the thick stew into her mouth between sentences. "Culain wants to train me in court politics. And this outfit?" Rose exclaimed, pointing to the elegant lace trimmed blouse and whispering, "Was among many rich clothes in my new closet. There is a whole wardrobe full of feminine garments. Dwarf size—not tall folk." She put down her spoon and tore pieces of bread into her stew and stirred. "Perhaps he kept mistresses and these are leftover clothes from a court tart." She whisked her stew furiously.

Meg calmly put her gloved hand over Rose's to stop the stew from being whipped to death. "Is that what's bothering you?" Meg asked pointedly.

Rose dropped the spoon and sighed heavily. "I don't know. I suppose he doesn't seem like a man who keeps tarts." She went back to eating until she scraped the last of her meal from the bowl onto her spoon. "He's not ashamed to have a woman as his bard. I never expected that from a Rhulonese man. Most would laugh at my ambitions, but he doesn't." Rose pushed away the empty bowl and leaned back, exasperated. "And last night in my room I saw-"

A strange man approached their table. His face was shadowed by a wide brimmed black hat; his dress was somber and plain; black cloak eased only by a white collar, like a vicar.

Meg's expression was chilling when she looked at him.

"Meghan?" he said softly.

"Mathias," Meg replied coldly.

Meg jumped up and struck his jaw with such force it sent him crashing backward into the next table, scattering the occupants of the next table. The stunned customers mutely kept their distance from her and the stranger. Mathias staggered to his feet, cupping his chin.

"What's this all about?" Digby shouted, marching toward the stranger. "I don't want trouble in my place. What'd you say to our Meg? Who are you, villain?" standing protectively in front of Meg and Rose, raising the wooden club he kept handy for rowdy customers.

Meg stormed out of the Red Boar, the patrons giving her wide birth as she fled.

"Forgive me," the stranger apologized as he straightened his hat. He laid a silver coin on a table. "For your troubles and my short comings, sir."

He left the Red Boar without further explanation, his cloak billowing like raven wings with his stride.

# # #

Robert Silverberry, Culain's elderly valet, rested on his walking stick of twisted hawthorn wood outside her door when she finally returned. He was an imposing presence with his piercing stare and voluminous gray robes. He was also cranky.

"I take it you're Mistress Rose Greenleaf?" he asked bluntly.

Rose nodded, breathless. She ran all the way to her room from the moment she jumped out of the carriage. "You must be Robert Silverberry."

"I've been waiting to escort you to the gardens for almost a quarter of an hour."

"I'm so sorry, Mr. Silverberry."

Rose was still distressed about Meg. She went to the ranger house, but Skullcap had not seen her. He did confirm a gentleman had come to the ranger house asking about Meg that morning after she left for the tavern. Even with the speed of the carriage, Rose was very late and worried sick about her friend.

"The tea party is nearly ready to begin and Prince Culain is expecting you to be on time, young lady."

Rose rushed past him into her room and shut the door. "I'll just be a minute." She pulled off her blouse, unhooked and kicked away the heavy skirt; all the while his booming gravelly voice penetrated the thick door.

"Ha! I've heard many a maiden promise that and then take over an hour for dress and the crucial arrangement of hair. Never understood why girls take so much precious time to put on a dress. My master has invested his trust and time in you, Miss Greenleaf. Personally, I think Prince Culain is being foolish-"

Rose opened the door, dressed in her bard uniform and holding her lute. "I'm ready now."

His windy speech froze in mid-sentence when she abruptly appeared, fully dressed in her bard uniform. She even managed to plait her hair into a quick side braid and had her lute.

"You were saying?" she asked sweetly with a smile.

His eyes narrowed and crinkled, "You are a cheeky girl," Robert grumbled, but Rose caught a humorous twinkle in his eye.

"But, still not like *other* girls," Rose countered. She did not mind his crusty personality because he reminded her of Belenus.

"Well, let's move on, Miss Greenleaf."

Despite Robert's urge for speed, Rose had to restrain her walk to match his turtle pace. He gave her a list of songs to play and the order. Robert had amazingly thick snowy hair for a man of his advanced age. It puffed out from his head like clouds and also sprouted from his ears. She secretly named him Fuzzy Ears. Their march was slow and it gave her time to think about poor Meg.

"Why were you tardy?' Robert asked bluntly.

"My friend is in distress."

"Is this friend some frilly young maiden you share gossip with?"

"No, she's a ranger named Meg Sparrow. No frills, I'm afraid. Something upset her today. It was far from frivolous too. She's a good friend. She even saved my life. Honestly, she was more than just upset. I would describe it more like a volcano erupting with molten hot lava and-"

"Are you the one who upset her?" Robert asked pointedly.

"Of course not," Rose replied, confused.

"Are you sure?" he needled.

She answered him a sharp look.

"Just checking, miss," Robert smirked, chuckling.

She had been torn about Meg, but she had ridden away so fast.

They almost bumped into Prince Darius when he abruptly turned a corner. Remembering he was a prince, Rose curtsied deeply and bowed her head. "Your Highness," she stammered. "Forgive me."

Robert bowed stiffly and then could not straighten up.

"Please Robert, no fuss now," Darius insisted, looking uncomfortable. He helped Robert stand up straight and his spine made popping sounds as he recovered his posture. "You know you don't have to do that."

"It is only proper that I do, Your Highness," Robert insisted, rubbing the small of his back.

"I was hoping I would see you," Darius said quietly.

"You were? Really?" Rose gasped.

Robert remained a watchful and stubborn chaperone with furry ears.

Darius continued, "You were wonderful last night. Your voice is amazing."

Extraordinary joy filled Rose. "Thank you, Your Highness," she said formally.

"Even my father was impressed. No easy feat. Mother thought you were most charming. Please Rose, just call me Darius, at least as long as my noble parents are not in sight. I've never heard the Ironheart poem recited with such fervor. That was my favorite poem as a boy."

"Mine too," Rose replied. "King Gregor was the greatest hero in my country's history. It's ironic that my benefactor, Prince Culain, is his descendent. I always imagined all the Ironheart men as rough-hewn with massive beards braided with iron pins and carrying mighty battle axes dripping with blood."

Robert fussily leaned on his staff watching them. "The sad result of reading too many silly adventure tales," Robert Fuzzy Ears sniffed.

Darius laughed, "But a vivid description. I must admit I can never imagine Culain to ever resemble such an image."

They both laughed.

Robert leaned on his staff, scowling. "Yes, the legendary warriors of Rhulon are most impressive," Robert interjected. "Now we must be going now, Bardess Rose." He nudged her by rapping her leg with his gnarly staff. "I'm sure Prince Darius understands the obligation of such a famous bardess."

Robert said *bardess* with a sharp tinge of sarcasm.

"I'll see you there," Darius said. "Mother is looking forward to it."

"I'll be there with my trusty lute," Rose replied. She winced, feeling ridiculous.

"You bards are so clever with words," Robert snickered as he walked down the hall.

"And old gentleman too free with their walking sticks," she retorted, cursing her foolishness.

"A benefit of my gray years," he remarked.

"Have you worked for Prince Culain long?" she asked.

"I've served the Ironheart family all my life," Robert said proudly. "Prince Culain is just the youngest Ironheart in my charge."

The garden's lavish green and the subtle fragrances in the air instantly soothed her. There was such a great variety of flowers and trees! The flawless roses alone would make her mother curse with envy. A blue and cloudless sky allowed ample sunshine to bathe the gardens in light. She caught a brief glimpse of a hummingbird, tiniest and swiftest of birds, with soft green with shimmery red wings buzzing briefly above pink chrysanthemums.

Robert advised, "Stay in your spot unless summoned. Do not eat or drink unless invited."

"I'll behave, Robert."

She sat in the chair Robert indicated, a small cushioned seat beneath a tall oak a slight distant from the guests so as not to be intrusive. Robert tottered away slowly. "If you have trouble finding your way back, just ask one of the guards. They can show you."

"Thank you, Robert."

From her hidden place by the tree, they wanted to imagine their music is delivered by mystical fairies as they nibble their delicacies. The tea and little iced cakes brought by the maids looked scrumptious. She tuned her lute and waited, wanting this to be over so she could find Meg. Rose wished she could revel in the green beauty around her, kick off her shoes and run barefoot on the soft grass.

A raven flew down to the manicured grass, hopping about boldly in hope of tasty tidbits discarded by the wasteful humans. The bird boldly waddled near Rose. It was funny how majestic birds are in flight, but when walking on the ground become clownish.

"Did Karta send you?" Rose whispered. "I've no food, but after the royal party is over, maybe I can offer you some leftover cake?"

"Do you converse with ravens often?" a rich feminine voice inquired from behind.

Startled, Rose turned to see Lady Thera Sule standing amongst the trees in a jade colored gown. The silk clung to her curves as she moved.

"My lady, I did not hear you," Rose said.

Thera moved closer, delicate sandaled feet silent on the grass. "That is good. I whisper through the world. My caste is trained to be quiet in manner and deed. Forgive me if I surprised you, little bard."

"There is nothing to forgive," Rose replied. "I'm just fond of Ravens. They are Karta's symbol."

Lady Sule smiled and held out her sleek, gloved arm and whistled. The raven instantly alighted on her slim wrist. "I too respect the raven. Karta is one of the few gods our races share." Her voice had a liquescent accent.

Rose was shaken for a moment, seeing the wild raven fly so eagerly to a strange human. "What did you mean by *caste?*"

"I am priestess caste. I was born to poor barley farmers. Lowest caste next to slave, but my parents sold me to great temple when I was seven."

"That's terrible," Rose blurted out.

"Not at all," Thera replied. "They made a virtuous sacrifice for my future. In turn, they received a small bag of gold and a box of salt for me. I trained to be a priestess in the Temple of the Elementals. I have talents, of course, as the priests require more than beauty to serve. In return, I received an education and an honored place in the world. I am High Priestess now. Noble blood is an illusion, the invention of mortal man."

"And mortals are dust to elementals," Rose added, recalling the old tale. "Please call me Rose. "I've read about Uragon. It sounds so very wild and beautiful. Your people worship a race of elementals."

"Elementals are the creators in our faith. They are ancient beings beyond mortal comprehension." Thera gently stoked the raven's beak. It did not bite her, but welcomed her touch.

Was she a witch or sorceress?

"The sacred elements of fire, earth, air and water are the forces of all life and death. Elementals create power. They are power," Thera proclaimed. "The ancient ones do not grant it to mortals. The weak perish. The strong conquer. Destiny is an illusion."

"I never thought of it that way," Rose replied. "Which temple do you serve?"

"Hecubal, Elemental Queen of Wind and Sky. She rules the moon and reigns over the night. She wears a crown of stars upon her celestial head and her eyes are storm clouds."

"She sounds terrifying," Rose blurted out without thinking.

But instead of being angry, Thera seemed pleased with her response.

"Good. She should be terrifying. Elementals are not play things for human weakness." She stroked the inky feathers on the raven and added in a whispered tone, "Hecubal has three daughters. One of them is Karta, Elemental of Fate."

"Karta is my chosen goddesses," Rose confessed.

"Then we share a bond, for Karta is my mine as well." She lifted her arm and the raven flew into sky.

Time paused as Thera watched the raven vanish from sight. Thera Sule was a mystery, despite all she had said to her.

The vociferous giggle of a young woman broke the timeless moment. Princess Lilias arrived with the royal party. Her pink satin dress lavish with lace trim was in the western fashion and her blonde hair a mass of ringlets that framed her perfect, bland face.

Are all her gowns pink?

Suddenly, Rose had a painful headache.

"We will speak again, Rose," Thera promised. She joined the royal party and took her place by Princess Lilias.

They gathered around the table laid with rich foodstuffs and fine porcelain cups and a shining silver tea service. There was much about ado about the passing of cups and sweets as they settled. Lilias reclined in an elegant chair for her comfort. Her feet were encased in stiff satin shoes with ribbon laces peeking out from her petticoats. Rose played her lute, yet kept her focus on the conversation.

Prince Culain arrived much later for the tea party, flamboyantly dressed in black and white satin brocade coat with a jaunty matching hat trailing a long white feather. "Sorry I'm so tardy, my treasured Empress Isabeau. Forgive this unworthy wretch!" He paused to bow and kiss her hand. "Your husband kept me locked in his study for hours working. I'm exhausted!"

The Empress smiled genuinely as she accepted a cup of tea from her maid. "You always make my heart light, Culain. Aristide works too hard," she agreed. "Will my husband join us for tea?"

"Alas, he sends his regrets, Your Majesty, but promises to join us for dinner this evening."

"It's so boring," Lilias pouted, daintily dipping her biscuit in her tea. "Where's the music? Doesn't your servant know to entertain us, Culain?"

I am a bard not a servant, Rose fumed inwardly. Rose's head throbbed with pain. In her distraction, she realized she has stopped playing her lute. Angry with herself for being such a village idiot, she called out, "Forgive me, Princess Lilias, I was tuning my instrument so it would be perfect to your ears."

I hope they bought that! Rose grimaced, beginning a soft, cheerful tune on the lute.

Lilias and Thera were from the same land, the same court, yet they were as different as night and day. Lilias looked like any frivolous aristocrat. Thera was regal as a panther. Rose pondered if Lilias would have lucked into a better caste if she had been born to poor farmers like Thera?

Darius and Lilias fell mute after a few minutes of forced gaiety and conversation. Lilias slumped in her chair and stirred her cup listlessly.

"It's a lovely day," Empress Isabeau interjected, trying to revive the conversation.

"Sunny," Culain agreed.

"The only thing missing is the sound of crickets," Rose mused softly as she played.

"Dear Darius," Lilias began, boldly taking his hands. "I know we have not been acquainted long. There has been such tragedy. But your royal parents and my uncle, King Krell, have signed the new marriage agreement. Please Darius, I don't want to wait. Let's marry now. Well, not this minute of course. There is no need for a long courtship. We should marry before month's end. Don't you agree?"

Culain's eyebrows shot up, but he kept silent as he watched.

Darius changed from stiffly attentive to pale shock. "I am speechless," he sputtered.

At least that was honest, Rose thought. She frowned, her head throbbing.

"I promise you, dear Darius, I will make you the happiest of princes."

Prince Darius looked ashen. Rose thought her head would explode and suspected Darius felt the same way.

"I will speak with the Emperor," Isabeau affirmed with a gentle nod.

Lilias clapped her hands like a little girl. "Wonderful!"

Rose broke a string on her lute, but her playing was no longer necessary. A new interest had absorbed them all. A royal wedding.

After the royal guests departed, Culain accompanied her back to her room.

"Are you all right?" he asked. "You look pale."

"Just a headache. It's finally abating now."

"What did Lady Thera say to you?" Culain inquired. "I saw her talking to you from a distance."

"She's fascinating," Rose commented. "Did you know that she's a high priestess in one of their elemental temples? Her parents sold her to the temple when she was seven. She talked a lot about caste, elementals and power. We both have an affinity for Karta too."

Tea and cakes were already waiting for her when they reached her room. He poured tea and arranged some little cakes on a plate for her.

"Excellent work, Rose. Not even I knew her true caste origin or her temple affiliations. She must like you to confide her humble origins. The lady barely speaks to anyone here."

Though her headache was better, the heaviness of her sleep deprived state made her listless. She bit into one of the cakes, hoping it would help. "I'm not sure if she's that fond of me."

"Have you slept at all?" he asked, studying her. "That might be why you have a headache."

"No. I didn't sleep last night. It's something else too. Culain, I hate to ask a favor when I am so new to your service, but something happened to someone dear to me. It's hard to explain, but my friend needs me. It's complicated, but I need to find her. I would be grateful."

"Your friend is already here. Commander Meg Sparrow, I believe. Robert informed me. I took the liberty of inviting her. Robert's bringing her to you. Now, talk to your friend. Make it all better. Have some tea and cake. Go to bed. That is a command. You need to be rested and alert if you desire to remain in my employ."

"Thank you," Rose whispered.

"The wardrobe has ample clothes, including some nightgowns. Lucky for you the former ambassador's daughter adored the shops in White Thorn."

"Ambassador's daughter?"

"Yes. She's very close to your size, and her father indulged her amply. Her love of clothes and jewels was excessive, mostly because the poor thing was rather homely. She did have excellent taste, but her vast wardrobe was filled with gowns she never wore. When the former ambassador was summoned back to Rhulon, she left most of her clothes here, except for the jewels of course. She's a spoiled and extravagant lady, who discards gowns after a single wearing. Even your bard costume was a riding habit I had altered to a traditional uniform."

Rose was internally ecstatic the beautiful clothes were acquired innocently and not from a court tart. It mattered somehow. "Very lucky," Rose agreed happily, eating a small cake.

When Meg arrived, Robert Fuzzy Ears insisted on formally announcing her.

"Commander Meg Sparrow is here for an audience," Robert announced and Meg walked in, dusty from hard riding and her red hair wild.

"Wipe your feet," Robert admonished as he closed the door behind him.

"Who was that?" Meg whispered.

"Mr. Fuzzy Ears, but you should call him Robert. Help me finish these cakes?" Rose offered.

Meg nodded and joined her at the table. "I guess I owe you an explanation," Meg said, looking embarrassed.

"You owe me nothing, though I admit my storytelling curiosity had me weaving a lot of tales. This man upset you, so I curse him. Did he hurt you in the past?"

"His name is Mathias Prophett. He was my husband. He abandoned me when I needed him most." Meg removed her black leather gloves and rolled up her sleeves. Rose saw her bare hands for the first time. Now she understood why Meg wore gloves all the time—her hands and arms were covered with old burn scars.

"Dear gods, what happened?" Rose gasped.

"Fire. I was accused of witchcraft and condemned to burn at the stake."

Chapter Thirteen

Meg's right hand and arm had severe burn scars; the left hand was more whole, with faint discoloration patches. Meg studied her scarred hands with an abstract eye. "People find it difficult to look at them. Plus, I don't like questions. So I keep my hands gloved."

Rose gently took her friend's hands in her own. "I've no trouble, Meg. My problem is the pain they inflicted on you! I can't imagine the torture you endured! I can't believe they tried to execute you for being a witch! Witchcraft isn't illegal. "

"It's forbidden in Juraca. That's my old home. And I wasn't a witch, at least not then."

"I heard the country is embroiled in civil war now. Why is magic prohibited?"

"It's a long and gruesome story," Meg replied wearily. "One worthy of a good bard tale." She plucked out a flask from her hip satchel and uncorked it. "This might make it easier."

"What's that?" Rose asked.

"Rum. Go on. Try some. It'll add spark to our tea. You might just like it." Meg poured some into their teacups. "It's made from molasses."

Rose sipped the enhanced tea. She flushed as the warmth flooded her mouth and throat. "Oh my, but that's quite a spark!" She giggled. "But it's not at all like molasses."

Meg sipped her spiked tea. "I said it was an ingredient, not that it tasted sweet." She sat down and put her booted feet up on the table. "I got a few burn marks on my legs too, though not as bad. They've faded and healed over the years. I was wearing a heavy skirt and boots at the time, so my lower body was protected. My hands use to look much worse, but I know a witch who made me healing ointments. They helped a great deal. I still use her ointments. That and time softened the damage. Her name is Zula and her magic is amazing. You must meet her one day. Once I had beautiful hands the color of milk. Now they look like a demon's."

"Don't say that." Rose sipped the strong tea and added more sugar. "I read in school that Juraca was a forbidden country to outsiders. I know they're isolationists and practice an austere version of Ursas' teachings; my teachers didn't talk much about why magic was outlawed. We knew mages were persecuted."

"How long were you in school?"

"Until I was thirteen. Then my parents took me out of school like most girls to learn about being a proper Dwarf maiden. I had to learn everything else on my own. What changed in Juraca that made things so terrible?" Rose asked.

The King declared magic was evil."

Rose was incredulous. "Magic is natural part of the world, though few people truly have the gift for it. People respect the mystical castes in Rhulon."

Meg's voice tightened as she continued. "In other countries that's true. Juraca was once like that. They revered magic. That changed over ten years ago when King Josiah Ethanus converted to a new faith. He converted to a creed that hates magic of any kind. He expected everyone to become like him, for our own salvation. He declared that any form of magic was illegal and a sin; the penalty for being a witch, or any mage caste, was death by fire."

"I heard Juraca adopted a new faith some years ago. Even in our little corner of Stone Haven, we get some news. Not much was known beyond that, except that they closed their borders years ago. What was this strange new religion?"

"The Brethren of Ursas. They're also called the Red Brotherhood by some. The Brethren created their own bible scribed by its founder, a man named Bel Urgasa. His followers are fanatics who worship him as the prophet of Ursas. Tragically, Urgasa found a safe haven in Juraca. He converted our king. After that, not only were all other faiths banned, it became a strict theocracy."

"That's frightening."

"King Josiah decreed all the holy books of Ursas and Ishar be burned. It didn't stop there. Over the course of that first year, the Brethren scourged all traces of the old religion. The mage castes weren't the only ones threatened—everyone was. Churches and chapels were shuttered, torn down, or converted to the new religion. The clergy were the first victims under these harsh new laws. Bishops and vicars who refused to adopt the Brethren's faith were arrested. Some were burned as heretics as an example. Some languished in prison. Some capitulated. The holy sisters of Ishar suffered too. Their convents were razed. The nuns were stripped naked. They burned their robes and prayer beads. Those who did not convert to the Brethren's faith on the spot were burned as heretics. That was the fate of all other religions and magic in Juraca—absolute destruction and death." Meg drained her cup and refilled it, pouring a liberal dose of rum. "The bonfires burned with confiscated holy books from the old religion. Some folk hid or buried their books, but it was risky. The Brethren rejected all the old gods, except Ursas. They even called them demons. They even decreed Ishar was not a true goddess or Ursas' celestial wife."

Rose shuddered as she listened to Meg's story. "Ishar is the goddess of magic! How could anyone do this?   "Why would your king allow this madness? Especially when it hurt his people."

"When people become fanatics, reason and logic vanish. There's a lot of speculation. He ruled with justice once. He suffered tragedy, as most people do in life. His wife, Queen Parthena, and son, Prince Caleb, perished during a plague epidemic, similar to the one that killed my parents. Rumors say he became a broken man after that. That's when Bel Urgasas insinuated himself; after he converted someone who worked at court. That new convert brought Urgasa to the king. That's how it started. Some say Josiah's sanity broke when he suffered a battle injury that left him crippled. There are lots of stories, but no remedies."

"Did anyone try to fight him?"

Meg's grim smile was unsettling. She put down her teacup and leaned close. "Maybe in books and songs, justice prevails over wicked kings and dark curses—reality is different. Sometimes no one gets saved. Bands of folk, both noble and commoner, protested against the injustice and tried to overthrow Josiah. Most of those poor fools ended up with their heads stuck on spikes decorating the king's wall. For a madman, Josiah had a very powerful army ready to do his will—men willing to follow without conscience. Bel Urgasa became his general and brought his own fanatical soldiers of salvation from exile to fight this new holy war. After the uprisings were crushed and the immolation of the clergy, people fell silent and obeyed."

"Why didn't you leave?" Rose asked cautiously.

Meg moaned and threw her head back. "Oh gods, we should have! So many fled Juraca rather than endure the blood and madness. After a while, Josiah closed the borders and it became harder to leave. When things go crazy in your world, it's like a bad dream. Mathias and I had such a simple life. Our little village was an obscure footnote on a map, far away from the towns and cities. We thought we could hide; but no one was immune, not even a poor apple farmer and his wife."

"Did you stay for your husband, Mathias?"

Meg nodded and poured more rum unto her cup, ignoring the tea.

"So, are you a witch?" Rose asked. "Or were you a victim of the hysteria?"

Meg shrugged and looked at Rose. "Both." Rose's brow furrowed quizzically and Meg laughed. "It's complicated."

"And my head is spinning," Rose confessed, holding her head in her hands. "Give me more of that deadly molasses and continue."

"Well, drink up then." Meg poured the rum, draining the flask. "You will need it to hear the rest. I was only eighteen when we married. Mathias was gentle and sweet. Handsome too. His family gave us part of their apple orchard in Oak Hollow as a wedding gift."

"Is that were you were born?"

"No, I was raised in the north, in a town called Red Vale. Oak Hollow is in the southern part of the country. After my mother and father passed away, I couldn't stay in my hometown. It made me sad. So I left. I was working as a seamstress in Oak Hollow when I met Mathias."

"Somehow, I can't imagine you demurely sewing for your supper," Rose remarked with a raised brow.

"Ah, but I was very good at it. Before my hands were nimble with a sword, they were nimble with the needle."

"What was your mother's name?"

"Deirdre. I inherited her red hair, but only a fragment of her witchcraft. I miss her terribly, but I'm also glad she didn't live to see what Juraca became. It would have broken her heart to see people treated so evilly. I use to love to watch her do magic."

Rose smiled, swirling the last of the rum in her cup before downing it. "I use to play at being a witch when I was little. I would take my mother's iron cooking pot and pretend to be a powerful enchantress casting great spells in her cauldron to summon mounds of cream puffs and dozens of puppies."

"Very ambitious," Meg laughed, her sorrow broken for a moment.

Rose shrugged and laid her head on the table. "Of course, I was only five at the time."

"Even though I was shoddy at witchcraft, my mother loved me and was always proud of me. Father adored her. His name was Robert Sparrow, the best blacksmith in Red Vale."

"Our fathers are both blacksmiths!"

"Yes. I use to watch my father at the forge, wondering how he could stand the heat all day. Ironic. My mother's death was so sudden, you see. There was a plague outbreak. She worked day and night to help folk. She saved a lot of people. Eventually she fell ill with the sickness too. I knew about herbs and healing medicine from mother's training. I tried to cure her. She still died. I cried for days. More than half our town perished. Father lost his will to live and soon followed her soul to the Sacred Gardens. They said it was the plague, but the plain truth is his heart was broken."

"I'm sorry, Meg." Rose's homesickness swelled for her father's solid presence by the hearth, smoking his pipe. She even missed her mother's nagging.

Meg threw off her green cloak and stretched in the chair, lengthening her torso and arms. She reminded Rose of a cat.

Rose was sure she was drunk. The combination of lack of sleep and hard liquor made Rose dizzy.

Meg put her long gloves back on. "Mathias became my new family. When the trouble came, he didn't want to give up our orchard. He said to keep quiet and obey. He thought our king would come to his senses. That never happened. Then we heard about the burnings in other towns. The Brethren priests claimed fire purified the soul of evil and was necessary for the good of all."

"That's barbaric! What happened that caused them to accuse you?"

"A woman happened. A slutty woman named Levina."

"A tart name if there ever was one!' Rose agreed wholeheartedly.

"She lusted after my husband. Mathias refused her, but she was obsessed with him. Levina even told her father Mathias was in love with her. It didn't help that her father was also the headsman of our village. He openly accepted the king's new religion and watched everyone. Our old priest did not approve of what was happening. He just disappeared one day. He was replaced by man in red and gray robes with crimson runes tattooed on his brow and a shaved head. Levina accused me of being a witch during church services one morning. She wailed that I put a hex on her. She even put on a show, rolling on the floor and talking gibberish." Meg's eyes were bitter at the memory.

"How could they believe that?"

"It's not about belief, it's about fear. The priest wailed that Ursas sees all sin and called me a wicked witch. The magistrate arrested me right there in the church. I was dragged away and locked in a cramped cell with strange symbols painted on the walls to prevent my using magic or escaping, which was superstitious nonsense. My trial didn't even last ten minutes. I was condemned to burn the next day."

"What did Mathias do?"

"Nothing."

"Nothing!" Rose gasped. "But he was your husband!"

"I didn't understand. Damn it, he didn't even visit me in my pitiful jail. He did not speak one word in my defense at the trial."

Rose took her friend's hand and squeezed it gently. "Did this Levina know about your mother?"

"I doubt it. The sad truth is people were often accused out of spite or greed, because there was no defense against witchcraft. Very few actual mages were burned at this time as most had the sense to flee the country. The following morning, I was taken to the town square and chained to a wooden stake on a stone mount. It was built just for witches and heretics. Every town was issued one with the upheaval, but this was the first time ours was being used. The priest walked ahead of me, swinging incense, face blackened with ashes. He was stridently vocal praying about Ursas and sin as I was led to my doom. His droning got on my nerves. I snapped at him."

"Oh, Meg, what did you do?"

"I told him to shut up or I would turn him into a toad."

"Oh my, that was brave—considering your circumstances."

Meg shrugged. "I had nothing to lose. I think I scared him a little, because he kept his distance and prayed in a quieter tone after that. Mathias was there. Damn, the whole town came to watch me die, including Levina; clinging to her father's arm, carrying a prayer book with a sanctimonious look on her mousy face. The bitch! Mathias didn't protest or tell them to stop. He did nothing but watch. All of them did—like it was normal. I didn't expect rescue. All I needed was one word of love. That would have sufficed. Mathias just stood there as they piled the dried wood around me and poured the oil."

Rose was dizzy. Horrified and enthralled by Meg's tragic tale, she could not imagine enduring such terrors. "How did you escape? Were you pardoned? Or did someone rescue you?"

"I rescued myself. That was the strangest part of this whole travesty. I never had my mother's easy talent for witchcraft. I was awful at it. I gave up on magic as a child. Something happened to me at the stake. I remember how the priest smirked when his torch ignited the pyre. How the fire burned slowly around me at first, the flames fueling as they lapped the up the oil. I did not pray. I did not cry. I was just *angry*! It hurt me that people I once called friends came to watch me die. It hurt that Mathias did nothing! His desertion devastated me! He once promised to love and protect me. Then the hem of my dress caught fire and flames smothered my naked hands. It was excruciating. Desperate, I looked up at the blue sky, so clear and calm on my death day as the fire spiraled to engulf me."

Rose wiped away tears. She held her friend's hand in support as she recounted her tragedy.

"That's when my magic flickered within me." Meg's eyes bright with the memory, her haunted look vanished. "It was warm and comforting. Light as air and full of an energy I can never put into words. It bloomed with such force! I knew in a heartbeat I could save myself. I shouted at the flames to go and they fell away like leaves. I summoned rain. In an instant, black storm clouds filled the sky. It poured down in such harsh sheets my death fire was doused within seconds. My chains shattered with a thought. My hands and arms caught the worst of the fire, but I walked away from the inferno alive. The priest was the first to run away from me, screaming like a lunatic. My temper was raw and vindictive. I glanced at the sprinting priest and sent thin bolts of lightning sparking at his heels."

"Good. He deserved that," Rose affirmed. "Does that make me evil?"

"No. It makes you a realist," Meg replied. "I stumbled from the stake, my clothes scorched and smoking. Everyone fled, even the brave soldiers who dragged me from my prison cell bolted. Except for Mathias. He did not run. He fell to his knees and bowed his head. Though it was pure agony, I wrenched my silver wedding ring from my raw, burned finger and flung it at him. I told him our marriage was broken."

"Oh, gods, what did you do next? What did he do?"

"He bent over and cried, but I was deaf to his weeping. I had to escape, so I closed my eyes and summoned a horse. Believe it or not, a horse came galloping toward me in the rain."

"You conjured a horse! Yes, I believe you did."

"No, I didn't conjure. That takes incredible skill and training," Meg laughed. "There was a horse farm nearby. I think she came from there."

"Was it Fayre?" Please let it be Fayre, Rose wished.

"Yes, it was. She galloped toward me like she knew me. She looked at me with such trusting bright eyes in the smoking chaos. I named her Fayre right then. I rode away from Juraca that day and never looked back. That was ten years ago. I hadn't seen Mathias since the day they tried to burn me as a witch and a heretic."

"Until today," Rose added. "What could he want after all these years?"

"I don't know or care."

Rose did not believe that, but she did not press the matter. Such pain should never be poked at. "Maybe he wants forgiveness?" she suggested.

"Could you forgive?" Meg asked coolly.

Rose thought about the teachings in the holy book. The prophets of Ishar and Ursas give many examples of how people should forgive their enemies. The reality was she could never forgive something so terrible. "No. I guess I'm not as good a girl as my mother wanted," Rose confessed.

"We never are," Meg replied blithely, her mood lightening.

Rose fingered her empty cup, sorry the rum was gone. "Can you still do magic?"

Meg's eyes glittered. She leaned over and whispered in Rose's ear, "Yes, but I am cautious. Old wounds, you know. Skullcap knows about my witch talents, as do most of my rangers. My magic is not reliable though, so I rarely use it."

"You trust him," Rose smiled. "I like Skullcap too. His tattoos are so pretty."

"You're pretty drunk," Meg laughed. "Yes. We've saved each other's lives more times than I can count. I use magic when needed. I'm grateful for it, because it saved my life. It means I inherited something precious from my mother. After Juraca, I vowed I would never be a victim again."

More than a little intoxicated, Rose stumbled away from the table. "I think I need my bed. That rum is potent. Who knew molasses could be so deadly? Maybe it should be weaponized."

"Let's get you to bed. You need some sleep. I should start heading back anyway," Meg yawned. "It's quite a ride back to the ranger station."

"Wait, wait—you haven't told me how you became a ranger?"

"That is another story with another bottle of rum. Oh, wait! There's one more thing I want to give you before I leave." Meg handed her a dagger in a blue leather sheath from her cloak's inner pocket. "I was going to give you this at the Red Boar, but we got interrupted by my past."

Rose slid the dagger out of the sheath. The blade was sleek, sharp, and gleamed like silver. Fine craftsmanship that her father would praise. The blue enameled handle was lovely. "It's both beautiful and lethal. I think it even compliments my bard uniform," she quipped.

"Many bards carry a traditional dagger or staff. I have a collection of weapons, so take it. I don't like it when you walk alone in the rough parts of town without protection. Consider it a gift to commemorate your new position as Bardess."

"You collect weapons?"

"A lady needs a hobby. Consider it an accessory with purpose. Even in a palace, a woman is at risk. I suggest tucking it under your pillow at night." Meg threw on her cloak and walked to the door. "But don't play with it until I give you some lessons. I don't want you slicing your fingers off. That would damage your musical skill."

After Meg left, Rose put the dagger on her night table. Too tired to rummage for a nightgown, she undressed and managed to neatly fold her uniform. She fell into bed in her undergarments. After a few seconds, she pushed herself up, grabbed the dagger and slipped it under her thick pillow. She slept fitfully until her dreams became wild, fracturing her peaceful sleep.

Rose walked alone in the barren wilderness. The sky above her was swirled with storm clouds. From a distance, she saw Belenus Aylecross, alone on a distant mountain, calling to her. She ran toward him, but the sky darkened to a black maelstrom and the swirling clouds pursued her to the earth. Rose shielded her eyes as the shadows swarmed over her head, breaking into hundreds of ravens that cawed mercilessly, shattering her ears.

In her anxious sleep, the dream ravens continued to cry louder until Rose finally woke; covered with sweat.

Rose screamed when she saw a monster more terrifying than her nightmare staring down at her with bulbous black eyes. The beast hovered over Rose; it snarled as its clawed hands tightened their grasp around her neck.

Chapter Fourteen

Rose kicked and screamed until the beast struck her across the face. The heavy blow stunned her. She watched in dazed horror as it sniffed her. It touched her arms and legs and panic flooded away rational thought. She resumed thrashing and crying out. The monster bayed viciously. Its shrill hiss pierced her ears like a knife and shattered her nerve to fight. Rose's cries muted when it shoved its gruesome face against hers. Gods, how her head ached! Rose twisted her face away from its hot, curdled breath that smelled like rotted oranges. She squeezed her eyes shut, blocking its stare. It seized her hands and pinned them at her side. The beast loomed over her, threatening and resolute.

She was in a palace filled with guards and servants—*where the Hel are they?*

It inspected her body, as though choosing a roast for supper. In forced silence, she opened her eyes and forced herself to watch. Her brain absorbed every facet she could glean about the creature restraining her. A lamp near her bed highlighted speckled gray skin and tufts of black fur sprouted from its head. The body was lean and almost reptilian, with clawed hands, slightly webbed. Its opaque black eyes were enormous. It appeared to be naked, though she could not determine if it even had a gender.

What is this monster?

There was something familiar about it, but panic blotted out lucid reasoning. How could she verify minor facts and features about some beast when it might be preparing to eat her? Rose could not fathom what it was doing to her. It grabbed her face with leathery hands and cocked its grotesque head, as though it studied her. Then the hands secreted something white and sticky. It was deliberately violating her and acted with more than instinct. Its actions seemed very specific. Was it demon? A strange fey creature? It was not an animal. She liked animals. This was a hideous monster. It must be a demon. Her stomach was queasy. She forced down nausea and vowed to never drink again. Despite the creature's strength and viciousness, she concluded that it could have easily killed her by now.

"Stop fighting," the creature warned her in a raspy voice. It stroked her head. "Sleep. Sleep."

Terrified, she refused to obey its command. It was a demon. Sleep would be death, she was sure of it. She was sure this debility in her limbs was from more than a few cups of rum-laced tea. Her body went numb as the chrysalis began forming on her limbs and arms. It enthralled her with its strange powers. A black abyss dragging her down. She struggled to stay awake. Silent despite her inner panic, Rose endured the beast gingerly fingering her face and body. It shrouded her body with the white secretion that stiffened when it touched her skin. For an instant it loosened its grip. She seized her chance and bolted.

Rose dropped to the floor and sprinted for the door, fighting the heavy sensation in her legs. It howled and the scuttle of footpads pursued her. She grabbed the door handle, so close to her salvation. It grasped her by the braid and yanked her back hard. It dragged her back toward the bed.

"Bad dwarf," the demon hissed.

A palace guard kicked her door open and charged into her chamber. For a split second, Rose thought she would be saved. The guard visibly paled when he first eyed the demon, who shrieked at the man, its black hair bristling down its back. The guard recovered from his shock quickly and charged with weapon drawn. The demon dropped her, distracted by the assault. It evaded the sword's strikes. Rose's legs went completely limp. She beat at them for a heartbeat in frustration. She resumed her crawl toward the door, trembling and sweating from the struggle. The clash with the guard ended quickly when the beast seized the guard's sword arm snapped it. Rose flinched when she heard the poor man's arm break. The sword fell to the carpet, and the monster hurled the hapless guard across the room.

Then the demon brutally scooped her up in one arm and flung her on the bed. It punched her hard across the cheek and displayed its talons, warning her to be still. She cowered, but escape was all Rose could think of as the monster lingered over her prone body. A single clawed hand squeezed her neck, but not enough to choke her. She blanched at the rough, sweaty texture of its skin as it pressed its bony fingers around her neck. Impulsively, she screamed again. The monster snarled and its repulsive hand clamped firmly over her mouth. Savage and deliberate, it continued its mysterious ritual on her. Her muscles were turning to pudding. She could not run or even walk. Rose's consciousness waned. A glimmer of cogent thought trickled into her frightened mind. Despite her bewildered terror, she suddenly remembered Meg's gift!

The dagger.

How could she have forgotten the dagger! Idiot!

The monster hissed. Drool dribbled from its maw as it wove its white shroud. She wanted to strike that repellent look off its face. For a fleeting second, the black eyes were off her, absorbed by secreting the webs to bind her. She could still move her arms. Rose quickly slipped her free hand under her pillow, grateful for Meg's warrior mind. Rose struggled to find the blade, her strength weakening with each breath.

The demon's head snapped back and glared at her suspiciously, hissing. Her heart racing, she fumbled until she grasped the slim handle of the blade, sliding it out of its sheath beneath the pillow. She whipped it out, blindly stabbing at the monster. It yelped and shrank back from Rose, surprised it was the victim now. She pierced its flesh and black blood splattered her hand. It wailed. Rose blindly thrust her knife again, crying and screaming at the same time until it released her. The beast's gore seared her flesh, tainted with the faint odor of decay. It jumped back, howling in pain. Blood oozed from the wounds she inflicted. She ripped at the sticky webs, gripping her dagger like a precious talisman. She rolled until she fell over the side of the bed as it stumbled toward the door, trailing blood.

Several guards finally rushed in and blocked the demon's exit, surrounding the monster with swords and spears. Trapped, the demon howled and retreated slowly from the advancing soldiers. Then the demon charged for her window and crashed through it.

Unable to walk, Rose dragged her body to the nearest corner, clutching her weapon. She tried to scrape the beast's blood off her hands, but the thick substance clung to her like glue. Shouts rang in her ears. She recoiled in the corner shivering. The crunch of broken glass beneath booted feet made her cringe. The monster's blood was rank, like a fusion of burning iron and decayed flesh. It churned her already fragile stomach. The aftermath of drinking rum did not help matters.

More guards swarmed into her room, shouting. They sounded distant and strange, like an echo. Rose shut out the world and remained in her safe corner; holding her wonderful dagger with eyes shut tightly to blot out the harsh reality of demons and hot blood.

The clasp of warm, strong hands firmly on her shoulders startled Rose from her protected cocoon. A familiar and frantic voice shouted 'Rose' over and over until she finally opened her eyes.

Reluctantly, Rose looked up. No terrors stared back at her. Only the worried expression of Culain greeted her—not the dreadful fiend with hellish black eyes.

"Breathe," Culain tutored gently, slowly drawing her from her corner. "It's safe now. Take deep breaths. Breathe."

Rose trusted him and obeyed, breathing deeply for a moment until her mind cleared and she could speak again. "Culain?" she whispered in a small voice.

"Yes, Rose, it's me. It's all right. You're safe now. The creature is gone. Did it hurt you?"

She shook her head. "No. I don't think so. It held me down. I fought, but it was so strong!" She shakily showed Culain the dagger, smeared with the gray demon blood. "So I stabbed it."

"Good girl," Culain affirmed and flashed a smile of pride. "I think I'll take that blade for now," he said gently, carefully removing the dagger from her hands with a white handkerchief trimmed with lace. He carefully handed the bloody weapon to Robert.

"Is she hurt?" Robert asked with concern, his brow furrowed. "Should we summon the physician?"

"Just frightened I think, poor thing," Culain replied. "Bring some ice too. Her face is swelling. Get my gloves. Send for strong soap, hot water, and plenty of towels to clean the blood and webs off her skin. The towels should be burned after. Order a hot bath too. We want to make sure no traces remain that can harm her. Wake the maids, if they're not already up from this chaos."

"Sir, do you think it was-"

"Yes, I do. That blood is gray and its reek all too familiar." He spoke into Robert's ear. "Quietly inform everybody to refrain from touching the blood or anything stained with it as well. Anything it bled on must be removed and burned. They should wear gloves for safety."

She ignored their conversation. There was something familiar about the grotesque thing that attacked her. Why? It irritated her because her memory was usually so excellent. She was terribly embarrassed too. She acted like a five year old afraid of the boogey man. She picked at the white and webby residue the creature had coated her with, disgusted.

"I'm sorry I fell apart," she apologized in a small voice.

"Nonsense," Culain assured her. "You were very brave. You did the only normal thing anyone would do. You screamed to high heaven and fought back too, based on that blood-soaked dagger. That took courage. What happened? Can you tell me what you remember?"

"It's so strange. I was having a dream about ravens. The ravens kept crying at me, unrelenting. Then I opened my eyes. That *thing* was just there–looking down at me. I don't know how long it was standing over me as I slept. Oh that poor guard! He tried to help me! He's hurt badly. It broke his arm-"

"He's being looked after," Culain assured her in a gentle tone. "Don't worry. I will keep you safe now."

As her senses calmed, Rose's practical modesty reasserted itself too. She needed to wear something more substantial than a scanty silk chemise and drawers. Her mother would have fainted from the impropriety by now. She imagined her mother's incensed outburst and her father's stern expression over her undressed state in front of so many strange men. It restored a fragment of her sanity. She bowed her head and leaned over to Culain. She murmured, "I think I should get dressed now."

"Forgive me," he exclaimed. "You must be cold too." To her surprise, Culain took off his own robe and draped it around her shoulders. Much to her relief, he was fully clothed beneath the voluminous robe in a white linen shirt and black trousers.

"Thank you," she whispered. She tried to stand, but her legs were still limp. Panic returned. "I can't walk. What did that demon do to me?"

"The paralysis is only temporary. Your legs will return to normal very soon," he assured her. Culain lifted her in his arms and carried her to a chair. "Fetch a glass of brandy," Culain asked Sally.

"Yes, Ambassador," Sally nodded, hands nervously twisting her apron.

Rose's stomach curdled at the mention of alcohol. She leaned close to Culain's ear, whispering, "No brandy, please. My stomach is shaky. I don't want to throw up in front of everyone." She looked away, mortified as another wave of embarrassment took her. He probably even smelled the rum on her breath.

"Perhaps a glass of water might be better," Culain suggested.

"Thank you," she replied in a small voice, mortified and nauseous. She blamed the rum more than the beast for her ill stomach. At least her headache had faded. He was being so nice to her. Why was he always so nice? She could not figure him out. That vexed her. She could always figure people out.

Sally brought her a tall glass of water. Culain took it and held it to her lips as she sipped, because her hands would not stop shaking. The combination of shock and the dehydrating effects of alcohol made her quite thirsty. She drank down the water, trembling.

"Better?"

"Yes, thank you."

"Is Miss Rose going to be all right?" Sally asked.

"I'm fine, Sally," Rose said. "I just need for my legs to work again and scour myself in a bath until I don't feel so foul."

"Your movement should return to normal within the hour." Culain examined the dagger, careful to keep the kerchief around it. "I must say, this is marvelous crafting. Where did you acquire this splendid dagger?" Culain asked with a raised eyebrow.

"Meg Sparrow gave it to me for protection. She said a woman alone is in danger or- something? I don't remember. We had rum with our tea as we talked. I put the dagger under my pillow, mostly because she suggested it. I'm glad I did. When I finally remembered it was there, I grabbed it at the first opportunity. Then I stabbed the beast and kept stabbing it too." Rose saw the creature's bloodstains on her hands and blanched. "What was it doing to me?"

"Sir, they found six guards unconscious in the halls," Robert reported, returning with a bowl of ice.

"That explains why no one came when I screamed," Rose commented.

Culain's expression was grave. "It's wounded and dangerous. Judging by the trail of blood, it cannot have gone far in its condition. We'll send soldiers to hunt it down. I want this one alive, Robert. I want to interrogate it."

"Do you think they'll find it?" Rose asked.

"They will. Don't worry, Rose. I'm just relived you're not seriously hurt." Robert handed him a pair of gloves that Culain slipped on. Then he personally took a fresh steaming basin of water from Sally. He gently but thoroughly washed away the blood. He spoke to her in soft tones as he soaped her hands and arms. "I must thank your Ranger friend for her foresight," he remarked. "I would hate for my Bardess to leave my employ so quickly by such wicked means." He turned to Robert. "Take the blade to the palace alchemist, Robert. Don't let it out of your sight. Tell him what happened here. Then gather testimony from the guards. The alchemist should be able to confirm what attacked her. The Emperor must be informed of this at once."

She hoped that bath would be ready soon. A very, very, hot bath. The image of the beast was branded in her memory, taunting her. Then she had a revelation and her head jerked up with clarity. "It was a changeling!" She could not remember until now. She blamed the rum for that too.

"I know. But how did you know?" Culain asked curiously.

The comfort of knowledge and reason restored her equilibrium. "I read a lot growing up, and much to my mother's dismay they were not recipes. I read everything I could find in the Stone Haven library. I loved all subjects and studied history, languages, mathematics, philosophy, poetry, and science. There was a book on demons and monsters that belonged to my Bard Master, Belenus Aylecross. He had a very impressive library. I remember seeing a drawing of a changeling in one of his books back home. I asked for a copy of it for Solstice. My parents thought I was mad. It was the Encyclopedia of Mythical Beasts by a professor named Marcus Sage."

"That is an excellent book," Culain approved. "I believe my father has the first edition of the book in his personal library."

"Well, the changeling looked like that, only much, much worse in real life."

"They usually do," Culain agreed.

#

Crimson cowered in the shadows, bleeding from the dagger wounds the mean dwarf girl inflicted. Her blood left a trail in the grass, but night would conceal those for the moment, though not the odor. She stumbled across the grounds, evading soldiers when they appeared. There were so many. She was too weak to fight and needed to hide from her enemies. She could not even shapeshift into her other form. She could not shapeshift at all. Too weak. Master would be displeased that she failed to bring the dwarf to him. She shivered, fearing his wrath.

Feeble and crying, she sniffed the earth, slithering like a snake across the green until she found a metal circle on the grounds. The iron cover led to the underground sewers beneath the palace. She could hide there. Rats would be plentiful in the sewers. Bugs too. Could feast on rats and bugs to give her strength and help heal her wounds. Then find a human to feed on, to complete her healing. Rats would not be enough, but they keep her going until she found an unsuspecting human. But how to overtake a human in her wounded state? She must wait. Hide in the dark. Find plump rats and juicy bugs. She lifted the heavy iron cover and descended.

Crimson trudged through the damp underground until she found a dark crevice. She curled up, whimpering. There was no one to help Crimson in this dark hole. In her agony, she blamed one thing for her failure—Rose Greenleaf.

"The ugly dwarf girl caused my pain. Master will despise me now," she whined, talking to herself. "Master wanted Rose. I failed him! I could have killed the Ironheart too. I could have been rewarded. Master's wrath will fall on my poor head."

Anger consumed Crimson for the dwarf girl! Rose Greenleaf was so little. How could she fight her off? Where did that dagger come from? Deceitful little bitch. The changeling's ability to take a person in their sleep was old as time as itself. Rose should not have woken up! Rose should have remained asleep as she cocooned her body. Master would have rewarded her for bringing dwarf. Now she would be punished.

Crimson vowed to make Rose suffer for this agony and humiliation. She opened the grip of her gray hand, revealing her secret treasure, a few long strands of chestnut hair from the dwarf girl. This would be enough for Crimson's revenge.

Chapter Fifteen

Rose could easily count each inflamed vein on the Emperor's forehead. Aristide's booming voice and ferocious gaze reminded her of a wrathful god, like Taranis, the ancient force of storm and thunder. His long stride punished the elegant carpets as he paced back and forth in the grand study, a towering giant in purple velvet robes. A poem about him was actually forming in her head as she watched the Emperor with trepidation and intense curiosity. Aristide was a formidable man, and not just because he was over two feet taller than her.

"This is unacceptable. How does such a miserable demon like that infiltrate my palace?" Aristide demanded.

"We thought the same thing when it happened at Rhundoran Keep," Culain confessed.

"A changeling infiltrated Rhundoran?" Rose gasped.

"A fact we have kept secret, so now you must, Rose. Do you understand?" Culain asked.

"Yes, of course," Rose agreed quickly.

"Changelings are vile creatures, but not very bright." Culain pointed out. "That's how we caught ours. They're unpredictable and vicious. The creature left a trail of bodies before we finally stopped it. We must act quickly. I would rather that not happen here."

"Nor I," Aristide agreed. "I want this demon trapped and in custody before it kills anyone. Gods, what if it has already copied someone here." Aristide paused and a flash of pain shadowed his features. "Or perhaps it has killed already?"

Culain quickly raised a cautious hand. "Perhaps, but we will never really know if Prince Justin's death was truly an accident or the machinations of a changeling. We cannot assume anything yet, Your Majesty."

The door unexpectedly opened and Darius rushed into the room. Robert was stubborn as he tried to block Prince Darius from entering. Robert's expression was so cross Rose almost burst out laughing. The poor old valet attempting to keep a strapping tall folk man from entering was staunch loyalty indeed. She hoped the old valet didn't sprain anything.

"It's all right, Robert. Don't strain your back," Culain sighed, rubbing his brow.

Aristide's tone did not reflect welcome at his son's intrusion. "Damn it, Darius! I ordered that no on interrupt us! That included you. Now go. This is about state security."

Darius bowed deeply, but did not leave. "Forgive me, Father, but I just learned what happened. I want to help you."

"Not now," Aristide replied. "Leave us alone. We'll talk later."

"But Father, I can help you-"

"Damn it all, I'm busy. We've been breached by a demon at the palace and it's still out there. Now is not the time for a lesson about kingship," Aristide said bluntly. "We'll make time for a chat later."

"This is the perfect time," Darius insisted stoically. "I'm your son and heir. I must be useful."

"This is a security crisis, Darius. If you want to make yourself useful, go make sure your mother is safe and assign more guards for her protection. And stay out of my way."

"But Father, you can't just-"

The verbal sparring between royals ended abruptly when Empress Isabeau entered the chamber, graceful in a gold satin robe. Not even Robert dared to stop her passing. Everyone bowed respectfully as she rushed to her husband's side. "Aristide! I heard what happened. Is everyone safe? Will the poor guard recover?"

"It's being handled, my dear," Aristide told her gently and kissed her hand.

Rose was amazed at the transformation of the Emperor when he spoke to his wife.

The Empress turned to Rose and went to her. Isabeau gently cupped her cheeks and a look of genuine concern was on her face. "My child, how frightened you must have been. I am so glad you are safe."

Rose curtsied. "I'm quite well and unharmed. Thank you, Your Majesty."

"You're so brave, my dear. I would be in pieces after such an experience. See she is well looked after, Culain," Isabeau commanded briskly. "Rose is a treasure you should not risk."

"Her protection is my first concern, Your Majesty," Culain bowed.

Darius' face could have been carved of marble as he stood there. Isabeau's expression was full of understanding when she looked at her son. She extended her hands and asked, "Darius, would you mind escorting me back to my room. It is not safe with that demon on the loose. Then I am sure your father will charge you to assist him with this terrible situation."

"Of course, Mother." Darius stiffly bowed to his father and tenderly took his mother's hand. Rose's heart ached for him as she watched them depart the chamber.

Robert bowed his head to the exiled Prince and the Empress before closing the door and resuming his post, scowling, his arms crossed in front of his chest.

Culain watched the tense exchange between the Prince and the Emperor, but his expression was neutral. He did not comment or interfere. She knew the princes were good friends, but boundaries and allegiances are tricky when dealing with an irate emperor.

After Darius and the Empress departed, Culain did not remark on what just happened. He picked up the conversation right where he left off. She observed Aristide's temper softened after a moment and returned to the business at hand. Culain's calm tact and resolve was impressive as he handled this imposing ruler. Being the son of King Grimkel Ironheart must not be easy either. She wondered what her own king was like.

"Your Majesty, my concern is that changelings do not infiltrate to this high level alone," Culain suggested. "We know they're useful because of their ability to shapeshift. They possess a slight cleverness, though they're not very bright. Anyone or anything could be using it for other purposes that are a threat to all of us. It is not uncommon for humans to employ changelings. It is rare but it does happen. The rumors about the goblins stirring in Mordok bothers me. It may be nothing, but we must look at every aspect. In the meantime, we need to hush this incident and hunt it down."

"I agree," the Emperor replied sternly, accepting the glass from Culain. "We must keep this quiet. I want that changeling found immediately, preferably alive so we can torture the details out of the despicable thing before we kill it."

"We must ascertain why it's here," Culain said. "Find out what its agenda truly is."

"Well, it just tried to kill your Bardess," Aristide pointed out. "What would it have gained by that?"

"No, it didn't want to kill me," Rose mumbled to herself, but tragically loud enough for the Emperor to turn his stare on her.

"Forgive me for speaking out of turn, Your Majesty. The changeling could have snapped my neck quite easily. I think its plans for me did not involve killing me, but something worse.

"Go on," Aristide encouraged with a steely gaze.

"The changeling held me prisoner. I'm only four feet tall and a girl of normal strength. It could have killed me. I gave it reason to, as I was not a cooperative victim. Death was not its motive. I believe it wanted to copy me. It was covering me with sticky webs secreted from its hands." Rose shuddered at the memory. "It also was enthralling me somehow. I lost the use of my legs for an hour. I still feel wobbly. There are lots of legends about changelings. One is that it cocoons its victims. Sadly, a lot is unknown about the changelings. I am sure it wanted to take me. It seemed determined to do so. It may also have taken others."

"Rose is right," Culain agreed. "Who knows what it does to achieve its deception."

"Your bardess would have been a prize for the changeling," Aristide agreed. "Acting as a spy in the inner circle of your household undetected. You're lucky, Culain."

"Indeed I am, Your Majesty. My research suggests they kidnap victims they plan to impersonate for long periods. They can also emulate a person for a short span with nothing more than some blood or piece of that person, like hair or a tooth. I've done some research, but not enough. It's tricky to determine their weaknesses. The poor victims are rarely found. Even if they are, extracting them alive from the cocoon is chancy. Even a changeling's blood is deadly."

"The blood is dangerous?" Rose gasped.

"That's why I was so careful to wash it away and make sure they removed all evidence of it to be burned, except for the dagger. But all we know is that it can cause a nasty rash."

"There have been stories and assumptions, but we need facts," Aristide said coldly.

"And quickly, since the changeling has infiltrated this deep into the palace," Culain added. "It's hard to know how long it has been here or whom it has impersonated. We need to learn more about it. That is our first step."

"Find the answers," Aristide demanded. "Lead the investigation. Thank you for coming to me about this, Culain. Right now, I want every guard scouring the grounds and every room in the palace for it. It's been exposed and such demons are dangerous. I want to keep this investigation between us. I will inform the Captain of my Imperial Guard, as well as my personal physician and alchemist to be at your disposal."

"Excellent." Culain bowed and added, "My people will work tirelessly with them to find out more information about the changeling. In the meantime, one thing to consider is a blood test."

Aristide's brow creased and he looked confused. "I don't understand?"

Culain explained it "As you know, Your Majesty, Rose managed to stab the creature. The blood is a thick gray fluid, not red like ours. Though it may have the skill to shapeshift to look like us, can it change its blood too? I would suggest a tiny prick on the finger should prove if a person is human or changeling."

"Then see to it, if you think it warranted."

They were leaving when the Emperor asked, "Bardess Greenleaf, why do you keep a dagger under your pillow?"

"My best friend is a Ranger named Meg Sparrow. She says a woman alone is never safe and should carry protection, even in a palace."

"Your friend is very wise," Aristide confirmed with a dark grin.

"If it pleases Your Majesty, Commander Sparrow would make an excellent candidate for my team," Culain interjected. "She has a sterling reputation as an investigator and is ideal to protect Rose from further harm. Rose injured the changeling and it will retaliate. They are spiteful creatures. I would personally feel better if my bardess had a warrior woman who could protect her at all times."

She could have hugged Culain right there.

"I will agree to this," Aristide nodded. "Commander Sparrow is well known to me. She's a fine warrior. She's also coming from outside the palace, so Sparrow is a safe addition to palace security, since we have no idea how deep this goes. I will accept her inclusion in this private matter."

Rose was overjoyed. She curtsied deeply. "Thank you, Your Majesty."

After they left the Emperor's chamber, fatigue and excitement bubbling inside her simultaneously. Robert followed behind, huffing and puffing to keep up with Culain and Rose.

"You should both get some rest," Culain advised. "It's only a few hours until dawn. First thing in the morning, we are going to comb the library for anything about changelings."

"The Imperial library?" Rose asked, feeling bright with anticipation.

"That too, but White Thorn's public library is one of the largest in the world. We'll check there first. Royal libraries are more often about private editions in fine gold leaf and engraved leather bindings."

"I haven't had time to explore the White Thorn library," Rose replied. "I'm happy to help, though I wish it were a fun outing instead of demon hunting. I love libraries."

"Slaying evil is always a satisfactory pastime," Culain replied lightly.

They reached her room and Culain opened her door. "Until that monster is caught, you will never be alone, Rose."

Inside her room, Sally was there waiting, along with another maid. A wave of relief calmed her nerves. She recognized Sally, and was comfortable with her.

"Culain charged us to stay in your room tonight for protection," Sally curtsied. "This is Agnes. She'll also be staying with us tonight."

"Please to help Miss Rose," Agnes nodded.

Agnes was an older woman with a florid complexion and a no nonsense demeanor. Rose liked her immediately.

Culain bowed with a great flourish, the courtly fop again. "Until your friend Meg arrives, they will sleep in your room for protection tonight, plus four guards will be posted outside your room."

"Thank you," she whispered.

He sauntered away, waving to her as he went to his chambers, Robert wheezing along at his heels.

The events had left Rose spent, though she might be too stressed to sleep. She scratched her hand again. *I must be allergic to demon blood,* she thought grimly. Culain said it could cause a rash. She just wished it would stop itching!

# # #

Nashim Tully was in a foul mood when he returned to the inn. He went to his room and removed his cloak. Mathias was there, morose as ever, looking over some papers.

Mathias looked up from his reading. "You're back early. Did you see him?"

"Meeting has been delayed. They would not say why. There were a lot of guards patrolling—more than usual. I use to be a palace guard and have an eye for these things. Something bad must have happened."

"What makes you say that?'

Nashim held up his pinky finger. "They insisted they prick me before I left."

"What? Why?"

"Who knows? But I smell demon trouble when things like that happen. In the east I've heard about a changeling causing mayhem and death. Killed some general and tried to take his place. They executed the creature, but never found the body of the general. The bloody things are like cockroaches lately. Damn. All this way to White Thorn for an audience to meet with the Emperor. I even wore my best shirt. You know—the one without the patches? It burns me that the meeting was cancelled."

"So that's it? He will not see us now?"

"I'm supposed to return this afternoon." Nashim shrugged. "But that does not guarantee I will be heard. You should come with me. A solemn vicar in his black hat will help our petition."

"I will go. There's still a chance. Royalty is often distracted. As long as we get the money we need. I arranged meetings with two other nobles as well. Something will bear fruit."

"It's tricky, Mathias. Aristide may not want to get involved in our troubles. Juraca is a bad subject for folks. No one likes what goes on there, yet few want to help. Civil war is also a very touchy subject for kings."

"Juraca is ruled by two madmen. A king and a cleric who thinks he is a prophet. None of the other countries support Josiah or the faith that ruined our country. We will get aid. It doesn't matter if it is money, grain, or weapons, as long as we can use it for the cause."

Nashim dropped in a chair and pulled off his boots. He grabbed the wine bottle, yanked the cork out and took a long drink. "Your jaw looks badly bruised. I take it your former wife was not happy to be reunited."

"It was my own fault. Perhaps I should have written first when I learned where she was."

"She would have burned your letters in irony."

"I know you think I am a fool."

"Have you considered that you might be doing more harm than good? You cannot change the past. Let it go. She started a new life in a new country. Good for her. You need to do the same. If you're expecting forgiveness, you need to give that up. Some mistakes stay with us forever.

Accept that cruel fact and move on."

"I have a life. It is devoted to overthrowing Josiah and Bel Urgasa."

"Well, at least that's a start."

"I wanted to ask her to join us."

"Well, that's just stupid."

"Why?"

"After what she went through, she will never go back. They tried to immolate her, boy! You should be ecstatic and thank the gods daily that she escaped. Many did not."

"Juraca was her home. We had a life there once."

"Not anymore. Why would she want to go back to you or Juraca? If she had any feelings about revenge or freeing Juraca, she would have returned long ago. She suffered too much. I do not blame her. Many folk resettled in other lands after the Brethren of Ursas took over." Nashim spit and grimaced. "I despise that the stinking brethren use the name of a good god like Ursas for their obscene religion. Does Meg even know Levina and her father threatened your parents with a heresy charge if you even spoke to Meg after she was arrested?"

"No. It doesn't matter anyway. Even if Meg doesn't want to fight with us, I understand. I still want to ask her for forgiveness."

"You're a fool, Mathias. And you know nothing of women."

"And you do?"

"More than you do, boy. I have a wife who adores me and five beautiful daughters who miss their papa. A lot of people have suffered these past ten years. Me included, though I was luckier than most. I got my family out of Juraca. I hate these damn secretive trips, begging for money and arms like a beggar to depose a pair of crazed fanatics. Living in these rat holes and acting like paupers. Well, that last part is true. We are paupers."

"We must try, Nashim. Those fanatics are planning to invade other kingdoms to spread their poisonous creed. If that happens, the pockets of powerful people will empty for us. Right now, we need to convince other kingdoms to help us before that happens. "

"Then focus on that, Mathias. You say you became a vicar to help people. In truth, you joined the clergy because you're filled with remorse about your ex-wife. Forgive yourself. And leave Meg Sparrow alone. She does not deserve fresh pain. Let it go."

Mathias did not answer, but fingered the charred silver wedding ring he wore around his neck.

Chapter Sixteen

The majestic size of the White Thorn library astonished Rose. Even the exterior was an impressive feat of architecture by itself. Built in the center of the city, elevated above the din of human traffic with a few dozen steps leading up to the six massive pillars and the two stone griffins that guarded the entrance. The library in Stone Haven was a modest white-washed building with a few paltry shelves of books. It was a hovel compared to this book palace! Still, Rose loved that place growing up. It was a refuge where she often enjoyed tranquil hours wrapped in book bliss away from her nagging home life.

Rose stepped inside this great building as though entering a church. There were four whole floors of books to joyously wander in! Gazing up at the painted domed ceiling with awe, she felt like a little girl. She examined the exquisite artwork of gods and heroes rendered in vibrant artistry.

"Catch up, Rose," Culain muttered, quickly pulling her along to match his brisk pace, "and be careful or your poor neck will lock like that."

She followed Culain, giddy in her chosen temple—the worship of books. She noticed the librarians wore matching robes of deep gray with badges of different colors with symbols stitched in on the front of their robes, which must indicate some kind of rank. These *book keepers,* as they were called, busily worked in silence within a broad circular table that was the heart of the main floor that serviced the public.

"There must be thousands of books and scrolls here," Rose whispered.

A hooded man in a shabby cloak walked up beside her, his face hidden in a dark green. "Hello, Rose," a familiar voice whispered.

Craning her neck upward as she needed to do among the tall folk. Rose recognized him and relaxed. "Prince Darius? Is that you hiding in that old cloak?"

"Yes he is," Culain confirmed. "I included him in our secret mission."

Darius shrugged and tugged at his hood with a mischievous smile. "Father was not very receptive to my offer to work with him, as you know.

So here I am. I didn't want to attract attention, so I wore a disguise. Do you like it?"

"Very common man, Darius. You blend in quite well. Speaking of disguises though, let's examine if there are any other disguises."

Darius pricked his own finger with his dagger. He exposed his finger to show his blood was red. He wrapped it in a kerchief. "We better find the creature soon. If this keeps up, we will all be drained of blood and too weak to fight."

"What about your good mother, the Empress?" Culain inquired.

"I made all the arrangements my father demanded. My mother is the safest woman in the kingdom. I tripled the Imperial Guards. I commanded that no one, not even Father, should be alone with her at any time until further notice. I did the same thing for him as well, and I am sure he will be vexed, but he assigned me to ensure protection at the palace. So, I am free to help with the research." Darius looked around and asked, "Where's poor old Robert?"

"Robert is negotiating with the Master Librarian," Culain chuckled as he flipped through a book catalog. "He's sequestered in the private office to secure special permission to take any book off the library premises, even those of historical import that could be useful in our investigation. I'm quite sure Robert is pontificating and waiving the royal seal with great solemnity."

"How are you feeling, Rose?" Darius asked. "You went through a devastating experience."

"Fine. Just a little flustered. Culain assured me the rash should wear off soon. I may also need to sleep with a lit candle by my bed for the rest of my life."

"Changelings can have that effect," Darius agreed in a low voice. "In truth, I'd only ever read about them in legends or fairy tales. I never saw one before. What did it look like?"

Rose casually looked down, though inwardly she shivered. "Hideous. Like a nightmare made flesh." Rose tried to focus on the fact a handsome prince was being attentive, but she was miserable as the ointment no longer calmed her irritated skin.

Culain flipped through small cards and scribbled on his notepad. "Ah, my list is complete! Now, let's requisition one of those book trolleys," Culain announced and marched off to his book hunt.

Darius claimed an empty trolley. They followed Culain deep into the stacks, away from the prying eyes of those sitting about with their books at the long reading tables to prevent them from being too curious or annoyed with them. They ended up in a bleak, abandoned corner of the library, and many of the items looked ancient, decaying and crumbling on the lonely shelves.

Walking with purpose toward a one of several tall wooden scroll cases packed with special tubular shelves that rose almost to the ceiling, Culain thumbed through his list of catalog numbers until he found the right row. Each section was equipped with foot stools and wheeled ladders to reach the higher shelves. Culain deftly rolled a ladder over and climbed up to the top.

"I saw Belenus Aylecross perform when I was a boy," Darius said. "The old Bard was very impressive and intimidating. His voice could boom across a room like rolling thunder. Culain knew him quite well because he lived at his court. We had wonderful bards here of course, but Belenus was one of my favorites."

"He's larger than life at times," Rose agreed. "Folks in Stone Haven hardly ever talk to him, mostly because I think they are a little afraid of him. My village is quite tiny, so when Belenus moved there it caused much excitement. People whispered rumors for weeks about him and wondered a thousand things. Was he married? Did the King banish him for loving a forbidden princess or was he was a spy for the realm? Despite their questions about Belenus, which he never answered, they still lined up their sons at his door for tutoring in bardic studies. He turned them all away."

"But he chose you?" Darius said, grinning.

"Yes, he did." Rose tried to hold back her pride at Belenus picking her over everyone else. "I was very lucky to have him as my Bard Master." Rose lightened her grip and the ladder wobbled.

Culain glowered down on them. "Hold the ladder steady, please. I don't want my epitaph to be 'Prince Culain Ironheart perished in a library.'"

"Sorry!" Rose shouted.

An elderly female Keeper, iron-gray hair neatly pinned in a bun and walking with petal soft steps in flowing robes paused before them. She scowled and loudly shushed them before walking away on soundless feet.

Rose pursed her lips and secured the ladder with Darius' help as Culain climbed up to a higher shelf populated with scrolls wrapped in faded blue paper and tied with paper tags with information written on them.

"I'm sorry you had to see that last night," Darius whispered, not looking at her.

Rose sensed it was about the argument Darius and the Emperor had. She carefully put her hand on his arm. "It's all right, Darius. Believe me! I understand the difficulties of a parent you can never please. On that topic, my mother was the *queen*. What you're going through is rougher. You've been away from home for so long. Three years away, even from a parent, can make you strangers. Perhaps you and your father just need to get to know each other. As you are the Prince, I'll humbly relinquish being top champion of parental disappointment to you, though I reserve second place."

Darius laughed. He leaned in and whispered, "It's true. My father and I cannot seem to find common ground. Justin was his favorite and I accepted that. I was relieved even. Now my poor brother is dead and I must step up and be the Crown Prince. I just wish he would let me try."

"He will, Darius. Be patient." Another book keeper walked by, pushing a cart of books for shelving. "What do the different color badges mean on the book keepers?" Rose whispered.

"Ah, most of the librarians are attached to White Thorn's University," Darius replied softly. "All teachers, students, and even the Master Scholars are required to spend some time in the library as part of their duties, and the students are assigned the more menial jobs. The badge colors and the symbols indicate their discipline-blue for literature, green for history, purple for art, red for medicine, gold for mathematics, silver for science, and so on."

Culain shuffled through the stacks, reading labels and sliding out choice scrolls from the tubes. He finally descended with a hefty armload of scrolls balanced in one arm.

"These are some of the oldest scrolls on ancient species of monster or demon designation," Culain whispered. He passed bundles to Darius who arranged them in the trolley.

Rose sniffed and wrinkled her nose. "They smell like old socks."

"Thankfully, wisdom has no odor prejudice," Culain replied.

Rose fought the urge to scratch her hands. Instead, she chewed her lips as Culain led them on to more discoveries within the library. She finally relented and scratched quickly, which was made it worse. She lathered her hands with the cream the court physician prescribed this morning, but the rash is still a torment.

"I loved this place as a boy," Darius said softly when Culain paused to check his notes. "I spent many happy days here, with royal bodyguards of course, reading about all kinds of things."

"You enjoy study?" Rose smiled.

"Yes. I was good at it too. I'm not very athletic nor did I enjoy hunting or sports. My brother Justin was grand at those things. He was dashing, brave, and tall. I was small and scholarly."

Rose glanced up and whispered, "From my angle, you're a giant."

Darius beamed a smile at her and she knew she blushed. She looked down at the trolley again, suddenly tongue-tied.

Culain sent a selection of research down with an assistant keeper to Robert Silverberry and walked up to the fourth floor and acquired a fresh trolley. This floor housed the biology, science and natural history section. Darius was sent to the natural history section with a list of books to acquire and Culain searched through the biology section with the determination of a stubborn bloodhound.

"This next text should be in the general biology section for monsters and creatures," Culain said briskly, taking down a voluminous book from a shelf. He blew on it, creating a cloud of dust. "Ah, here it is."

"What is it?" Rose asked, a little hesitant.

"I've located an old but decrepit copy of *Encyclopedia of Mythical Beasts* by Marcus Sage. I will check the Imperial Library for a better one later, but we will take this one now. But, ah yes! They have *The Biology and Anatomy of Monsters and Demons* by Professor Willem Krancid. It's a ponderous but very detailed tome. Darius mentioned it when we talked this morning. It was penned over two centuries ago by a tall folk physician who actually performed necropsies on various demons and monsters. The sketches alone are quite disturbing but teeming with numerous facts and particulars, so it should be quite useful."

Culain handed her the massive text. It was quite weighty and even smelled timeworn and moldy. "That sounds both disgusting and fascinating." She opened it and glanced through a few pages and grimaced at the gruesome drawings, "Let's just make sure I haven't eaten before studying it." She closed it and dropped it in the book trolley as though it were contaminated by plague.

"Is there a time when you're not hungry?" Culain teased.

"Now you sound like my mother?" Then she frowned and fell silent.

"What's wrong?" Culain asked. "I was only joking."

"Oh, I know that. It's nothing. I was just wondering about my parents. I wrote to them, but I haven't any word from them yet."

"I'm sure everything is fine," Culain assured her. "Give it time. The mail going north from here always goes by ship first. It's faster and cheaper that way."

"I hope so," Rose said softly. "I didn't leave on the happiest of terms."

"Now what?" he asked.

"Now I'm afraid of what my parents might write back—especially my mother. I've always been trouble in her eyes."

"That's because trouble always finds you," Meg commented, walking toward them. "Can't I leave you alone for five minutes without being attacked or abducted?"

"Meg!" Rose gushed in a whisper. Hoping not to anger the various patrons sitting at the reading tables or the prune-faced book keeper. "I'm so glad you're here."

"That's quite a nasty bruise," Meg frowned, examining Rose's cheek. "Did that damn changeling do this to you?"

"Yes, but I got a few licks in. Thanks for the dagger, by the way. It saved me from the changeling."

"Good," Meg grinned and hugged her. "Still be careful with those fingers. I'll teach you some techniques." She looked at Rose's hands. "What happened? Did it bleed on you?" Meg demanded, bending down and carefully taking them into her gloved ones. "That is a nasty rash."

"The cost of combating demons," Rose grumbled. "They gave me some ointment, but it still itches. I should have brought the jar with me!"

"Commander Sparrow is here? Excellent," Culain observed with an arched brow. "I can use another pair of hands. Being a statuesque woman in this case is beneficial to the cause. I hereby assign you the high shelves. I think I'm developing a case of vertigo on those spindly ladders." Culain, ever the courtly gentleman, bowed deeply. "Welcome, Commander Sparrow."

"Thank you, Ambassador Ironheart. Or should I address you as Prince?"

"I will answer to anything as long as it's not insulting, good lady. I pray our summons to this secret but worthy endeavor has not caused you trouble with your superiors?"

Meg shook her head, "The summons came directly from the Emperor, so it actually impressed Captain Nerlis. Not an easy task. Do you want to check my blood?"

"Meg, you don't have to. I know it's you." She also wanted to spare Meg from removing her gloves in public.

"How?" Culain asked.

"Her breath doesn't smell like rotten oranges. I remember that very clearly from last night. It was faint, but very distinct."

"That is a fact I did not know," Culain said.

"It's one fact I wish I never learned," Rose replied.

Darius returned with a few books. "Our party is growing."

"Prince Darius," Meg acknowledged with a graceful bow.

Rose scratched her hand again and then deliberately stuck them in her pockets. "Darius, this is my good friend, Commander Meg Sparrow. She saved me from slavers when I came here. She's ever so brave." The agony flared and she went back to rubbing at her skin. She moaned, "Sorry. I know it's rude, but this itching just keeps getting worse!"

Culain looked concerned. "Rose, we better have the physician look at that again. It's worse than last night. I think it's gotten worse."

Robert, wheezing from climbing up the stairs, shuffled toward them. "We have permission," he whispered triumphantly, waving the document he received from the Master Librarian. He paused and looked at everyone. "What's wrong?"

Meg looked worried as she examined her hands. "The message I received said you were attacked by a changeling, but you were unharmed. This is definite harm. It's not just red. You're developing black spots. This is troubling."

"Imagine my feelings?" Rose retorted, feeling uncomfortable with the attention.

"No, I mean there is something about those spots that mean something, I just don't remember what. I know who can tell us though."

"I think we should take Rose to see the physician now," Culain lamented. He looked genuinely troubled. "I've seen it cause a little rash, but nothing like that. I'm so sorry, Rose. Forgive me."

Robert interjected quietly, "Your Highness, we're attracting attention and should leave. We should get Miss Rose to a doctor."

Indeed, both patrons and keepers were looking at them.

"Yes, let's get out of here now," Culain agreed.

"How much of that creature's blood did she get on her?" Meg asked as they quickly walked together.

"Quite a bit," Culain answered grimly, shaking his head. "Her hands were covered with its blood. It took a bit of effort to wash it off. Rose stabbed it several times in her efforts to escape. She's a very brave girl."

Rose did not feel brave, and had become winded trying to keep up with the fast pace as they ran down the stairs, except for poor old Robert who stiffly took each step slowly.

"Prolonged or heavy exposure to changeling blood can be dangerous," Meg said. "And I don't mean a rash." She grabbed Rose's hands. "Stop scratching or I will tie your hands."

The faint little pink patches flamed red with little flecks of black. It was actually much worse since she woke up. Rose winced with that memory of the monster glaring down at her as it held her prisoner down. "Ghastly creature. I hope it's rotting somewhere. I thought a rash was normal for exposure to demon blood?"

"Demons are not normal," Meg emphasized. "Neither is your rash."

"I requested the court apothecary examine the creature's blood," Culain said. "I will ask if he knows what we should do for Rose."

"Is the court physician trained in treating demonic injuries?" Meg asked, frowning as she examined the rash again.

"Most are of course, but changeling attacks aren't common and neither is their blood," Darius replied. "That is why we are here gathering our research."

"I have a friend I trust. She's a witch named Zula Rutu. She lives in the old part of town, but she has great knowledge. I trust her. I ask that you trust me, Prince Culain. Let me take her to Zula. I will take care of Rose," Meg promised.

"Of course," Culain agreed quickly. "Take my carriage."

"How will we transport the books?" Robert asked.

"Take mine," Darius offered. "I arrived in a carriage also. The books can be delivered to your chambers, Culain," "I think we should get Rose medical attention right away."

As they bantered, dizziness overwhelmed Rose and her eyes blurred. A disturbing image bloomed in her mind, of crawling through dark tunnels, the smell rank and putrid. She actually felt herself creeping through the filthy passageways as though she were there!

"Rose what is it?" Darius asked, concerned, bending down to take her arm. "You look so pale. ROSE!"

Culain caught her as she collapsed. Rose squeezed her eyes shut, trying to will the images out of her mind. The panicked voices of Meg, Darius, Culain, were so far away now. She was linked to the thoughts of the changeling now.

Blood—so much blood that the changeling lost. A sickly chill spread throughout Rose's body and she began shivering as the library fell away from her reality and was replaced by the dark underground with damp walls. The changeling crawled in the shadows. Bleeding from daggered wounds and cursing the stupid dwarf girl! The hatred was so intense Rose flinched. She was suddenly aware of wholesome sunlight and green grass replacing the dim tunnels, but the changeling did not like the golden sunlight. It hungered and must risk exposure or perish. The changeling cowered in a bush by the stables, whimpering, until a lone stable boy walked near, carrying a bucket of oats. The changeling's wounds required blood and flesh to heal. Must heal! The changeling swiftly scuttled from the shadows and pounced! Rose cried out as the creature attacked the stable boy, tearing at his flesh and feeding. It did not just eat the poor boy, to Rose's horror. Its foul deviltry sucked the life out of him, leaving a ravaged husk. Shivering with revulsion, Rose screamed, shattering the connection.

"Damn it!" Rose cried, shaking off the vision. "I just saw the changeling! I don't know how I know, but it just killed someone."

"What?" Meg cried.

"I saw it in my mind," Rose cried. "It had just crawled out of some tunnel where it was dark. Then it was in the sun. It hates the sun. There were stables and horses. I could even smell the hay. A stable boy walked by and it pounced on him. It killed him! It needed to heal so it murdered that poor boy to do it."

"If it has not fled the palace grounds, that would be the royal stables," Darius whispered. "I will alert my guards to investigate right away. They're waiting for me outside."

There was a commotion in the library now with people beginning to gather around them and a sour-faced keeper was briskly walking toward them.

"I'll take care of this crowd," Robert Silverberry whispered quickly. "Just take Miss Rose and go. Now!"

Culain's expression was grim. "Agreed. Go now. Hurry!"

Darius lifted her easily in his arms and hurried down the stairs, Meg keeping equal stride.

"Am I possessed?" Rose cried, terrified. "What is happening to me?"

Meg Sparrow's steely green eyes brooked no resistance. Her bold pace forced the curious gawkers to silently clear a path as she marched toward the great doors. She shook her head grimly. "Not possessed, but I think you're linked to the changeling's mind."

Chapter Seventeen

They arrived in a rundown section of the city; crowded with timeworn wooden structures with slanted roofs, two or three stories high, along narrow dirt streets that teemed with activity. Some were dwellings, based upon the rows of laundry hanging on rickety balconies. Ramshackle shops and people crammed together doing the daily business of living.

"What do they call this part of the city?" Rose asked weakly, as Darius helped her down from the carriage.

"We call it old town," Meg replied, "though richer folk refer to it as poor town."

Despite her discomfort, Rose's curiosity about new places never waned. This older quarter of the city was dirty and smelly, but full of vitality. Vendors hawked trinkets and goods; a fruit merchant was peddling melons and oranges; women carried woven laundry baskets or burlap sacks of groceries.

A reedy boy with shaggy brown hair came running up to Meg. She tossed him a coin and he took Fayre's reigns protectively, stroking her forehead, which delighted the horse.

"They seem to know you around here," Rose commented.

Meg dismounted Fayre. "I've spent a lot of time here."

Another bout of furious scratching shadowed any further curious questions.

"Stop that!" Meg chastised. "Do I need to put you in iron cuffs?"

"That may be inevitable," Rose groaned forlornly.

Darius looked around like a dazed child who heard a fairy tale with an unhappy ending. "I know the poor exist, but I never knew they lived in such poverty in our city. Not even the docks are this squalid."

"First time in poor town?" Meg inquired. "The people here do all right. So don't fret too much over it, Prince. They're just working folk, well most are anyway. They care more about a loaf of bread than a coat of paint or fancy cobblestoned streets."

Darius gently picked Rose up and carried her, careful not to touch her enflamed hands. They followed Meg up a narrow flight of stairs to the second floor with a long narrow porch. A weather bruised sign of a golden crescent moon hung over a narrow door painted in bright blue and red swirls.

Meg opened the door and a little bell chimed when she crossed the threshold. Inside the shop was shadowy with mystery and chockfull of earthy aromas. Candles and crystals of many colors were strewn about on a display table, with assortments of beaded jewelry and charms. The back wall was lined with several unpainted wooden shelves packed with dozens of mysterious clay pots, glass jars, and wooden boxes etched with runes. Darius set her down gently, but remained close.

"Is anyone even here?" Rose whispered.

A beautiful woman pushed back a red curtain at the far end of the room. She sized up her visitors with a casual glance. Her smooth complexion was dark as onyx, framed by a halo of black curls. She beckoned them with a smile that both mocked and welcomed them. Her flame-orange woven skirt was girdled with broad striped sash that showed off her slim waist and the ruffled white blouse was garnished with colorful beads. Her face was strong, with high cheekbones and a strong jaw that gently tapered into a delicate chin.

"Good afternoon, Meg," she smiled broadly. "I haven't seen you in weeks. Have you finally decided to go into business with me and make proper use of your magic?"

"Sorry. I've been busy. Zula Rutu, these are my friends, Rose and Darius."

"Welcome to my humble shop," Zula replied, her almond shaped eyes bright as she examined them.

"Did you teach Meg about magic?" Rose asked.

"Yes I did, little one, at least when she had time for me," Zula answered. "Meg, who is your rich friend? Have you finally brought me a wealthy patron to soften my path in this cruel world?"

"Oh, I'm not rich," Rose protested. "Even my clothes belonged to another."

Zula shook her head, triggering her silver hoop earrings to jiggle. "Ah, little one, you may not be blessed by gold, but he is," Zula purred, circling Darius like a falcon hunting its prey. "Your plain clothes do not fool me, Prince. The Rhulonese girl wears fine velvet, but her origins are humble. Your clothes are simple, but they do not disguise your true self. Do not try to fool, Zula."

"No one is trying to fool you. We just need your help," Meg insisted.

Zula shrugged, "If you say so, Meg. It's not like I am greedy. We've been friends for over ten years. I never even charged you for magic lessons. I was just hoping for a handsome benefactor to support my mystical endeavors."

Exasperated, Meg's temper flared, "This is serious! Stop playing with the prince and listen. Rose was attacked by a changeling. She's suffering. I don't know what to do."

The mocking ceased and Zula's brown eyes became serious. "Are you sure it was a changeling?"

"Yes," Rose replied. She exposed her hands, inflamed with black blotches. "Its blood stained my skin. And along with this hideous rash, I think our minds have become linked together. I've had ghastly visions."

Zula's nonchalant attitude shifted immediately. "Follow me," Zula ordered. "Tell me everything."

They followed Zula to the back room; crammed with stacks of wicker baskets and old wooden chests stuffed with the various sundries of her magic shop. Tapestries of wild designs hung along faded, chipped walls like beautiful masks, and others were images of exotic animals that Rose had only seen in book drawings.

Zula guided Rose to a stool. "Sit. You must not leave out a single detail. Talk while I look for my ingredients."

Rose babbled the details of her raven dream, the dreadful attack, what the creature looked like, stabbing the monster, and the episode at the library. The whole bloody incident of horror.

"Poor child, that is a terrifying tale," Zula remarked sincerely as she lit a lamp and rummaged through a teak chest until she found a yellowed scroll tied with green ribbons.

"I'm a bard, so tales are my livelihood. This is one I don't want to relive in any song."

"Are you sure the beast didn't bite you, Rose?" Zula asked pointedly.

"I'm positive." Another frantic bout of itching forced both Darius and Meg to grab her hands.

"Can you help her?" Meg interjected, patience running thin. "She's suffering!"

Zula's serious expression unsettled Rose. The witch leaned in close and examined her poor hands. "Of course I can help her. Was it a male or female changeling?"

"I have no idea," Rose replied, confused.

"I'm thinking it was female," Zula decided. "Changelings are nasty thieves, but the marks on your hands indicate that it may be so. Their breath smells like bad fruit."

Rose nodded, wiggling with agony. "I thought it was like rotten oranges."

"Definitely a female changeling," Zula confirmed.

"Charming," Rose remarked dryly, gritting her teeth.

"I'm amazed that you woke up when it was there! How could you wake?" Zula muttered, inspecting her ravaged hands. "Changelings use their breath of sleep to keep victims unconscious, especially if they are going to take you."

"Take me!" Rose cried. "What do you mean *take me?*"

"You're lucky to fight off a demon so strong. You're so tiny," Zula commended her.

"I may be diminutive in size among tall folk, but among my people I will have you know I am unfashionably tall for a girl. And I stabbed it too. I stabbed it many times. I made it run," Rose boasted. "Please explain the 'take me' part. It makes me nervous."

Zula let go of her hands and went to work. She untied the scroll and spread it on the table, securing the ends with unlit candles and stray crystals. It looked brittle with age and written in a language that Rose did not recognize.

Darius put his arm protectively around Rose. "If you care about gold, I can pay handsomely for your information."

"Your Prince is so protective, Rose," Zula remarked coolly as she scrutinized the scroll, "I always heal, even if you are poor. Why do you think I live in this hovel? I will tell you what you need to know, but this is precise work. My father was a demon slayer in the old country. My knowledge comes from his teaching. And I know that changelings are filthy creatures."

"What can you tell us?" Darius asked.

"Changelings can masquerade as humans in two ways. For a short time they can pretend to be someone. For that, all they need is to steal the essence of your body, which can be a drop of blood, a strand of hair, or a fingernail; they can wear the image of another for a few hours or perhaps a day or two. If they plan to impersonate the victim for long time, that is more complicated and deadly. It's a terrible fate for its victim.

They use their breath put you into a deathlike sleep." Zula rolled up the scroll and quickly gathered potion bottles, clay pots, and packets of powder and arranged them on the table as she continued to talk. "They cocoon the person in a web and use divinations and charmed gems to keep them bound in mystical slumber, dreamless and dark. This impious creature forges a bond that enables it be anyone for days, weeks even, as long as they have that poor soul hexed and trapped in the magical stasis. That malignant enchantment forms a connection between their minds," Zula answered. "The creature can draw on memories, language, and personality, so it can fool anyone."

"But why?" Darius asked. "That sounds like a lot of work for such a vile stupid creature."

"They are often the underlings for more powerful forces. Usually they are thieves who use their magic to steal food or trinkets." Zula fetched a large green wooden bowl from a shelf and began to sprinkle in bits of powder, aromatic herbs, and drops of fluid from colorful vials that glowed. "Even demons have rules to their bleak craft—the changeling uses an amulet to sustain the image and connection with the victim's mind." Zula grinned and asked, "Did Meg gift you with the dagger of your salvation? She loves her shiny weapons. If Meg loved magic as much as fighting, she would be the witch teacher instead of me."

"But why is this happening?" Rose begged, looking at her ruined hands.

"Changeling blood is deadly to humans," Zula replied. "That is the reason for the black spots. Did a physician look at her?"

"Yes," Darius replied. "My father sent his personal physician."

Rose gasped and bent over. "I'd chop off my damn hands right now if I didn't need them for the lute."

"She needs that remedy now," Meg demanded.

"I know, I know. I'm working fast but need to take care. Don't be afraid, Rose; I will not let you suffer. Almost ready!" The ingredients in the bowl bubbled into a misty airy cloud and Zula mixed in a chalky indigo powder that transformed the concoction into a frothy pale blue cream. Zula scooped a generous portion and rubbed it on Rose's hands. The pain and itch vanished at once, the scarlet skin softened to pale pink and even the black marks started to fade.

"Thank the gods," Rose sighed with relief.

"Thank Zula first," Zula grinned.

"Thank you," Meg said genuinely. "You're a good friend."

Zula wiped her hands with a towel and curiously looked at Rose. "We are not finished. I'm still bewildered on how you broke free from the changeling's sleep hex. You tell me that you had a raven dream courtesy of the Fate Goddess, Karta, and woke up to face this changeling? Then you had a vision of the beast attacking someone. Are you magical, Rose?"

"No," Rose shook her head stubbornly. "Why?"

"You must have magic," Zula insisted.

"Could that be why the creature chose Rose?" Darius asked.

"Who knows? Changelings are not that smart, but they do not act alone in such an elaborate ruse. There are others involved in this nefarious scheme, I'm sure. If it happened in the palace, you have big troubles, Prince. The changeling demons are scavengers and parasites, with ambition only for feeding and trickery. But something more powerful is using them."

"Is that all?" Meg gasped.

"No," Zula replied. "The creature's blood seeped into her skin. Those black blotches are a symptom of that. The effect can be fatal if not treated correctly. My balm will heal her skin but I must make a potion to flush out any remaining toxins from her body. Good that you brought her to me when you did. It could have spread throughout her whole body and even into her organs. Then not even my fine witchcraft could help the poor girl."

Rose shuddered at those words, but the comforting hands of Meg on her shoulders calmed her. "Tell me, in its false human form, whether the changeling bleeds red blood or its foul gray blood? We are wondering if that is a good way to test people."

"Their blood is gray," Zula confirmed. "That is one thing they cannot change, whether they take animal or human form."

"Culain will be glad to know our theory was correct," Rose remarked.

Darius thought for a moment. "We fear it may already have victims hidden away."

"It's possible," Zula confirmed, "a changeling could have some poor soul, even more than one, secreted in some gloomy grave as long as they have enough amulets and a safe hiding place, but not too many. Maybe two or three at most. They must also return to their prisoner to renew the bond with the amulet or its power could fade, so they need a safe place to hide their captives away from prying eyes."

"I guess I'm lucky to have escaped that," Rose murmured.

"You stabbed the demon. It will be vindictive," Zula warned. "You should hide until it is safe for you."

"An excellent plan," Meg agreed.

"Will this link between the changeling and me fade soon?" Rose asked, frightened.

Zula looked into Rose's eyes and then gently grasped her head with her hands. She smelled of cinnamon and sandalwood. "Poor Rose, you have magic inside you. The link between your mind and the changeling is not a side effect. Does anyone of your line have mystical blood?"

"No, no one. I'm just a bard," Rose replied. "I'm not magical at all."

"Your voice is magical," Darius said softly.

Zula shook her head stubbornly. "You have a spark. When I touched your hands, I could sense it, faint and deep inside. But it is not witchcraft or sorcery. The rash is expected. The vision you experienced, is not. Are you having headaches?"

"Yes, a few, but I thought they were due to exhaustion."

"Your magical ability may be breaking open, like an impatient flower. The headaches could be a warning. Certain mage castes, like those touched by the rhapsodé, can detect demons when they are close by. Mage castes with specific magics, like the rhapsodé or seers and even necromancers, have unique magics that do not evolve the same way as it does for witches or sorcerers. You are a good bard. True?"

"She's magnificent," Darius exclaimed proudly. "Belenus Aylecross himself tutored her."

"Bard's have a special quality. All the great ones do," Zula insisted. "But a very rare talent may have the gift of the glamor."

Rose recalled the last conversation she had with Belenus. He had asked her what she would do if she were touched by the glam rhapsodé. Did he suspect? "I've read about the legends. Their music can summon great magic. It has empowered armies, raised ocean waves, summoned animals. Those with the glam rhapsodé can truly enthrall. It can summon powerful magic through song and poetry, but is also dangerous. Some bards have suffered greatly because of the gift. There hasn't been a bard gifted with this unique magic for well over a hundred years."

"True. You are special, Rose, else you would just sit on a corner and beg a coin for a song," Zula said softly. "You have more talent than you know. I sense magic within you and it is strong. Take care."

Rose looked away feeling a little afraid. The tales of those touched by the glam rhapsodé was legendary—and a little frightening. The power of words that can slay or charm with their magic was the stuff of legends. "But some weeks ago something happened that was unusual. When I was kidnapped by two slavers, Albin and Fendrel, and I tried singing to them to prove I was a poor bard, thinking they might have mercy. They did not have mercy, but when I was singing to them, suddenly I felt my body go hot and for a moment they fell into a trancelike state. Then they snapped out of it and took me away."

"You never told me about that?" Meg said, concerned.

Rose hung her head. "I was so scared at the time and tried to chalk it up to my fear and imagination. There are amazing tales about the bards with this gift, but many of them suffered bad fates. I haven't even written Belenus about it."

Zula spooned a large batch of the blessed ointment into a dark amber jar and sealed it with a cork. "You may have been blessed, but do not run from it, Rose. The fates of those you speak of may not have been good folk. Magic is tricky with those it blesses. It will be a curse only if you let it. Your bard master may or may not have detected it when training you. It is a rare mage skill and you're so young. We must examine this later, when you're fully healed. Do not discount it. Do not reject it. For now, keep this balm away from sunlight. The ingredients are fragile." She handed the jar to Rose and then washed her hands in a copper bowl. "Keep my mixture in a cool dark place. Apply three times a day for three days. I will brew the potion for you, but that will take me several hours."

"Thank you," Rose sighed, clutching the jar of her salvation.

"Be careful. All of you! Take her somewhere safe and watch over her, Meg."

"I will, Zula," Meg said with relief. "Thank you."

"All witches are sisters, Meg. Remember that and visit me more often."

"I promise," Meg replied and the two women embraced briefly.

"I don't think we should risk taking Rose back to the palace," Darius suggested. "As long as that changeling is on the loose, it's too dangerous."

"I agree. Becky and Digby will put Rose up for a few days until this is over," Meg suggested.

"I will escort you there myself," Darius said. "Then I'll go back to the palace and inform Culain of our findings, and that Rose is better now, but staying elsewhere." He turned to Zula. "I will send a carriage to escort you to the Digby's at the Red Boar when the potion is done. I would also feel better knowing Rose had both magic and sword protecting her."

"Thank you, Prince," Zula nodded, and glanced at Meg. "Is Digby still cheap?"

Meg and Rose nodded simultaneously.

"He never changes," Zula sighed. "Still, tell him my fee to deliver my potion to your doorstep is supper and a flagon of his best ale."

"Really?" Meg challenged.

Zula shrugged. "What? I don't feel like cooking."

"Thank you, Zula," Rose gushed with genuine gratitude, happy that her hands were at least looking and feeling whole again. "I would love to hear the stories of your father one day."

"Of course I would love to regal you with the adventures my demon hunter papa. You are very welcome, little Rose. Now, I need practical compensation for my mystical healing." Zula glanced expectantly at Darius.

"Of course," Darius exclaimed and fumbled in his vest for his purse. "Forgive me." He scooped out several gold lions and poured them into Zula's open palm.

"Most generous, Prince Darius," Zula smiled broadly, caressing the coins like a lover. "You are an honorable boy, even for an imperial."

"The generosity is for helping Rose and further aid should we require it. May we call on you again for your wisdom?" Darius asked.

She dropped her coins into a ceramic jar. "I'm at your service, Your Highness." She turned to Rose. "If you have the rhapsodé, you will have greater power than the demon who hurt you. Use it. Do not fear the magic. You can charm too, using song and focus. Remember that. If another vision comes, do not fight it. Try to remember what you see."

"Why?" Rose asked, knowing she would hate the answer.

"Because a changeling keeps its captives cocooned; your visions may be the only way to save them," Zula warned. "Once a changeling is done with its mask, it destroys the mold it came from. They always feed on their victims when they are done using them. You may be their only salvation."

Chapter Eighteen

Thera Sule forced herself out of bed, despite her aching head and queasy stomach. She stumbled to the window, rubbing her eyes. Pushing aside the heavy drapes, she squinted against the stark glare of daylight. The sun's high position in the sky indicated it was at least noon! How could she have slept this late? For days her sleep habits had become more and more erratic; that disturbed her. It could not be indulgence, since she only sipped one glass of wine last night. Even from earliest childhood when she was an acolyte at Temple, it was always her habit to rise at dawn for meditation.

She slipped out of her silk nightgown and walked naked to the vanity. She pushed back her mass of black hair, twisted it into a bun and pinned it up without the aid of a mirror. She splashed her face and neck several times with cold water from the porcelain bowl, fragrant with rose petals.

Temple life instructed Thera about the necessity of discipline, focus, balance, and calm. Her duty was to serve; every day must be served with purpose else it was a waste of life. For days her control was slipping away. Her sleep was becoming more and more erratic. She often woke up with a headache, and she had never suffered headaches before. She pushed aside the breakfast tray of tea and fruit on the dining table, her appetite contaminated by confusion. Her thoughts focused first on her prime duty–the Princess! It was afternoon. Where was Lilias?

Thera rushed to the door that adjoined their chambers and flung it open. To her relief, Lilias was still curled up in the enormous feather bed beneath pink satin quilts. Her blonde hair masked her petite features as Her Highness snored. Her annoyance with Lilias' lazy habits was mollified by the fact she was not out wandering like a fool. Thera's tense muscles relaxed and she closed the door. Her pounding headache continued to sour her mood. She wrapped herself in a velvet robe, so as not to shock the servants with her nakedness, and rang the servant's bell.

Two maids promptly entered the chamber and curtsied. "Yes, Lady Sule," they both said.

"Prepare a hot bath and lay out my lavender gown, please. I have things I must attend to." She looked at the two chamber maids quizzically. "Why did two of you come?"

"There is a great commotion in the palace, Lady Sule," one of them answered excitedly. "No one is permitted to be alone right now. They will not tell us why."

"Who commanded this?"

"Emperor Aristide did," the other maid replied, wide-eyed. "Something happened in the palace last night, but no one is talking about it. I was only to deliver this message to you and the Princess this morning when you woke."

"Very well. Thank you. We will of course obey the Emperor's commands without question. Send for two escorts then, if being alone is an issue. I require their presence within the hour. While I am out, I want both of you to stay with the Princess. Do not let her out of your sight, no matter how much she whines and pouts."

They both curtsied and departed.

Thera returned to Lilias' chamber and ruthlessly shook her, "Wake up, lazy Princess. It's past noontime."

Lilias stubbornly rolled over and pulled the covers over her head. "Go away," she moaned. "Can't you see that I'm sleeping?"

"You have been abed too long. Get up! Now!"

"Leave me alone, Thera! I had too much wine at dinner last night," she whined, kicking her little feet beneath the covers. "I feel sick to my stomach."

"Good," Thera replied coolly. "You drank too much last night, despite my warning. Consider it the price of your poor choice. A princess does not swill wine like a whore or act so foolish without consequences. The Prince was being attentive and you ignored him."

"Prince Darius is so dull. At least the Empress approved of moving the wedding date closer. That should please my uncle."

Thera nodded, relieved for the moment that her duty as virgin guardian was nearly over.

Lilias stretched out in her bed, slowing kicking off the covers. "Fortunately, I already have a wedding gown. When Prince Justin died, I never thought I would never get to wear it! Now I can. Isn't that wonderful?"

"If you say so," Thera answered carefully. "Though the Empress was receptive to your plea to wed sooner, it was still a graceless request given that your first betrothed died just a short time ago. To force the issue over tea and cakes was crude. Royal matches require specific etiquette and planning. You are fortunate Empress Isabeau is gracious. You put on a great show of devotion to Darius and then later at dinner you ignored him like a spurned suitor."

"A princess can be changeable, you know. Are you saying I'm too bold?"

"I'm saying you should have conferred with me first." Thera rubbed her temples again. Marriage was the foundation to achieve the alliance her king desired. Thera's own fate was wrapped up in the success of this venture. Being a king's mistress never guarantees safety. "The sooner you are wed, the better, but keep your remarks about the bridal gown to yourself."

"Was it insensitive?" she asked.

Thera glanced at Lilias, frowning. *Was she really that stupid?* She wished Lilias was indeed married and someone else's bane.

Lilias pouted, "Oh, don't worry so, Thera. Darius didn't see me drunk and I'm not sure he likes me that much anyway."

"Then make him love you. A true noblewoman can achieve anything."

"But I'm a princess! He should love me without question!"

Thera's temper finally snapped. "Foolish girl! You're spoiled and thoughtless. If you behaved according to your caste, perhaps Darius would love you."

"How dare you, Thera! I am a royal! You are my servant! You're just my uncle's official whore-"

Thera's icy stare silenced Lilias. "No petulant girl-I am High Priestess of the Elementals and First Mistress of King Krell of Uragon. No other woman in the kingdom is above me in rank. Not even you! Krell personally charged me to look after you and ensure your proper behavior. Instead of behaving like a princess, you shame your royal caste and guzzle wine like a trollop! You must change, Lilias. Others must work to rise above the station of their birth. Look at Rose Greenleaf! Rose wanted more from life and took it. Rose is beautiful, educated, and brave enough to venture far from the security of her home to pursue her dreams. She has made great strides in rising above her caste. Now she is the official Bardess to Prince Culain Ironheart! She has more of a regal bearing than you and yet Rose is born of a simple blacksmith."

"Stupid ugly dwarf girl," Lilias spat under her breath.

Thera's glance could have melted iron. "Do not speak like a guttersnipe."

"Sorry, Thera," Lilias replied, all gentle and dainty again. "Forgive me. You are my only friend in this strange land. The wine has affected me more than I imagined. I will do better. I'm sorry. Please don't be angry."

Thera's ardent and inscrutable gaze forced Lilias to look away. "In the meantime, the Emperor has ordered that no one must be alone. Something strange happened here last night, but we are not privy to what."

"Goodness! That sounds frightening."

"I have errands I must attend to and have summoned escorts. Stay in your room until I return. I've instructed the maids to keep you company."

"Can't I come with you? Please!"

"No," Thera replied firmly.

# # #

Culain instructed the servants to leave the library books on the dining table in his private chambers. They had gathered a vital collection of references on demons and monsters, but he could not focus on his successful acquirement of rare research. He was agitated and concerned about Rose. He prayed she was all right. Don't let it harm Rose. *Not her.*

Robert's graveled, cranky voice rescued him from his revolving prison of guilt. Robert shuffled through the front door, grumpy and stubborn as ever, elbowing the poor guard who tried to help him. The old valet shooed him away like a fly.

"Do you think I should have let Commander Sparrow take Rose?" Culain asked. "Rose's vision was disturbing. Why did that happen to her? It's nothing I've come across in my research."

"Sir, you have not stopped talking about Miss Rose since Meg and Darius carried her away. They will take care of her."

Culain impatiently shrugged off his coat and dismissed all but one of his personal Rhulonese guards. "Rose is my responsibility. I promised Belenus I would look after her. Maybe I should have followed my initial instincts and sent her home when I found her."

The young sentry stationed himself at the door. He almost blended into the wallpaper he was so silent. Culain wished the soldier would make a noise, anything to divert him from agonizing about Rose. Instead, he settled for a glass of wine and methodically began arranging the books, to keep his thoughts distracted. "When the tragedy happened in Rhulon, we were left with only a dead changeling, its slaughtered victims, but no answers. This time, I'm going to get those answers no matter what. Did you send the coded dispatch to the Raven about the current events?"

"Yes, Culain," Robert replied. "These events will not please the Raven, but it's better to know the truth of the situation." The old man shuddered. "Changelings! Repulsive creatures, but unlike other monsters or demons like goblins, trolls and ogres, they possess the ability to infiltrate human populations through shapeshifting."

"I'm sure there's a powerful force behind the shapeshifters' actions and I'm determined to find it. I only had time to briefly research demons before I left Rhungar. I despise the fact a demon infested my home. By the time we killed the changeling at the royal court, we saved my father's life. The deaths of the four brave men who saved him gnaw at me. A hero's funeral and pension for their families can never make up for their sacrifice. Then, I arrive in White Thorn the day after Prince Justin died. My timing is cursed."

Robert settled slowly into a chair. "Demon and monster lore and fact have always been ambiguous. There were volumes about goblins and ogres— because we've had to fight them in the past. Changelings are more elusive. Still, we cannot keep this up for long," Robert complained. "Especially at court. It will break down into chaos. The rumor mill is already churning."

"I know. Keeping people in pairs or groups by imperial command is going to get tedious and arouse suspicion. We need to catch the damn thing and put it out of our misery. What did the physician say when you told him about Rose's symptoms?"

"At first he was not certain, but after looking into some of his older medical reference books, the creature's blood can have poisonous effects on a human, even if the victim was not bitten. The blood is toxic and can penetrate into the body through the skin with venomous effects. He is compiling possible remedies and doing more research, however, there is no reference on visions."

"Possible remedies? Research? He doesn't even know?"

"Sadly, he knows as much as we do. Most of the antidotes he looked up have a magical base and require a witch or wizard."

"I suppose that is reasonable. They are demons after all. Or monsters?"

"Is there a difference?" Robert asked wearily.

"Sadly there is. Demons have origins to the mystical dark underworlds, but exist in this mortal one. A monster is just a strange aberration of nature or even a creature of fey origin. A goblin of any species is a demon whereas a troll is a big ugly monster that mopes under bridges."

"Mysticism and otherworldly studies always give me a headache," Robert replied.

Culain's expression tensed and he hesitated before speaking. "What about the stable boy Rose saw in her vision?"

"They found the body of a stable boy, or rather what was left of him. It was unnatural. The poor boy was a dried up husk."

"Damn," Culain blurted out and banged his fist on the table. "I had hoped it was a fevered whimsy."

"We all did, sir. The Emperor is keeping it quiet for now until we make headway, but he is angry. He is relying on you to put this fiend down."

Culain poured a glass of wine and handed it to Robert. "I will do that, with the utmost pleasure. I just hope that Rose recovers."

Robert sipped gratefully. "The royal physician is looking into any possible remedies ready should Rose need them. Be assured sir. We're doing everything possible."

"Thank you Robert. I don't know what I'd do without you." Culain's facial muscles softened a bit, but he was still concerned for Rose. "I hope that Meg Sparrow knows what she's doing. Maybe we should find Rose and bring her back here," Culain wondered, pacing up and down the plush carpet.

"We have no idea where Darius and Meg Sparrow took Miss Rose, but I think she will be safe in their care. Plus, it's too dangerous here as long as that changeling is free. You took the proper course of action. That redheaded ranger is a formidable woman from what I have gleaned. Her honor is above reproach and she has received many honors for her bravery."

"What of Meg's past? If we are going to recruit Meg Sparrow as well, I need to know everything about her."

"Her past is murky, but there are whispers she is from Juraca."

"Juraca? That is a grim place," Culain shuddered. "No wonder she moved out west. Anything else?"

"She has served with the rangers for ten years, rising swiftly in the ranks on her own merits. The other rangers respect her. She has a temper and enjoys rum and dice. I also learned that when she applied to serve with the Imperial Rangers, she had a letter of introduction from Emperor Aristide himself."

"That is impressive. Do we know why?"

"I couldn't find out why Emperor Aristide intervened for her, but she must have impressed him somehow. He does not grant favors easily, especially to commoners. Meg Sparrow is an expert fighter and a master of several weapons—and she's reputed to be a witch, though she does not practice."

"That is useful to know. Meg Sparrow retains excellent skills that can serve our cause." Culain loosened his collar and sat down across from Robert, "Rose and Meg are such good friends, though they have not known each other long. It is funny how women bond, isn't it? I've never really bonded with anyone, not even my brothers and sisters."

"The price of protecting the crown requires sacrifice," Robert told him. "Few know about what you have done to protect the Ironheart legacy, but I know, Culain, even if your numerous brothers and sisters are oblivious to your true calling."

Culain drained his wine glass, tempted to pour another, but refrained. He needed his faculties to be sharp with danger and demons lurking. "I just hope Meg can help Rose."

"Sir, you must not despair, and in the interim we have work to do."

"You're right of course," Culain agreed.

They cleared the dining table and divided the books and scrolls for study. They had just sat down when a knock on the door interrupted them. The amazingly silent sentinel answered it.

A cloaked woman stood in the doorway, her face concealed by a deep hood, flanked by two Imperial officers.

"I must speak with the Ambassador." The voice was quite familiar—deep and soft as velvet, with a unique accent.

"Lady Thera, this is a surprise," Culain said, rising from his chair.

What could she possibly want? Culain thought suspiciously. He put his hands behind his back and bowed genteelly, his grip on the dagger he kept in a special sheath in his belt.

"I must speak with you now," Thera demanded, boldly gliding into the room, pulling back her hood. She turned and glared at her escort, "You may wait outside." She then turned to Culain's guard, "Close the door," she commanded.

The stunned sentinel had his hand on the door knob but stopped himself, glancing helplessly at Culain.

Culain nodded and said, "It's all right. Go ahead and close the door, but stay at your post." He looked at Thera curiously. "I know you must be aware of the current rule about anyone being alone in the palace right now, Lady Thera, so my valet and bodyguard will remain present."

Thera eyed the room curiously. "It is wise, Ambassador. Your chambers are exquisite, and they have scaled the furnishings to your needs. It's quite charming."

"We find it so, but let's get to the point. I assure you that whatever secret you reveal to me will be bound by silence. Now—what do you want?"

"Is all this because of a changeling?" she asked directly. "And of something that happened here last night?"

"Yes, my lady, it is," Culain replied darkly, his expression somber. "Why come to me? Why not the Emperor or even Uragon's Ambassador?"

"If I am wrong, I would bring shame to my caste and King Krell. I also know that you're the one who, in Aristide's name, declared the edict that no one be alone."

"Lady, you impress me with your inspective skills, but if you possess some knowledge about changelings, I suggest you tell me what you know now."

Culain released the dagger, pulled out a chair and indicated for her to sit down. Thera dropped her dark purple cloak to the floor, revealing a snug lavender gown with tight sleeves in the Uragon fashion that complimented every curve of her body. She gracefully sat down in the small chair.

"What's happened?" Culain demanded, impatience biting his tone.

Thera looked at Culain without artifice. "I fear a changeling has stolen Princess Lilias."

Chapter Nineteen

The strain of keeping her shapeshift weakened Crimson. She crawled back into bed after Thera left. She told the silly maids she had a headache, so they left her alone. Crimson needed to think. That cursed Thera was a problem. The woman watched her like a hawk. She suspected something. Crimson was sure of it. The breath of sleep was losing its power over her. It was ill luck an elemental priestess was the princess's guardian. Those women felt the mystical more than others.

Crimson touched the amulet she wore around her neck. Keeping the guise of the princess was so difficult now. It had to end soon. Lilias was boring anyway. All she did was needlepoint. Her dark enchantment was fading fast. Crimson must find a way to escape. Princess Lillias was dying. But added to this strain was the danger that was everywhere. She had exposed herself. Thanks to that stubborn dwarf Rose they would hunt Crimson. They would cage her. Torture her. Kill her. Saddened by her bleak fate, Crimson whimpered. The wounds the homely dwarf girl inflicted left her feeble. Feeding on the stable boy healed most of her injuries, but she required more sustenance.

Crimson blamed Rose Greenleaf for her misery! The squatty bardess will die for causing her such agony. She licked her lips hungrily. Rose would be fine treat indeed, but her master wanted her alive. Why did her master desire this pathetic human? An insignificant dwarf who sings? She never expected Rose to fight back when Crimson came to her that night. Rose was unaffected by Crimson's breath of sleep and remained awake no matter what Crimson did to her. She had to hold her down and beat her. And still the dwarf fought! And what meek dwarf girl keeps a dagger hidden under her pillow?

Trapped by her human mask, Crimson could not escape to rekindle the bond with Lilias. Her master demanded she bring the dwarf girl—but how? Imperial command was firm. No one was permitted to be alone now in this vast palace. Armed guards roamed the corridors. Despite her despair, Crimson stifled a giggle because she was the origin of this panic.

Servants entered her bedchamber carrying buckets of hot water.

They filled the copper bathtub in the corner with steaming hot water and added oils and powders.

Listless, changeling Lilias sat up, frowning at them. "Why are you doing this now?"

"You ordered this bath, Princess," one of the maids replied gaily. "You requested it yesterday."

"Very well, but after my bath, I plan to nap until dinner. I have the most dreadful headache. And I want to be alone when I bathe."

Changeling Lilias got out of bed and permitted them to disrobe her, but kept the amulet around her neck. "Now go away," she imperiously commanded.

Alone in the bedchamber, changeling Lilias sank into the steaming bubbles, enjoying the caress of hot water on her beaten body. It was the one aspect of humanity she enjoyed. After soaking for a time, she stepped from the tub, naked and dripping on the plush carpets. Crimson shed the restricting human facade of blonde hair, blue eyes, and insipid human features. She walked to the mirror and gazed hungrily at her true image, reveling in her natural shape of changeling perfection—mottled gray skin, long fingers with retractable curved talons, black eyes that enabled her to see at night, tufts of glossy sable hair that sprouted from her head all the way down her spiny back, the lean body, and long muscular legs. Crimson frowned when she touched the blackened scars on her body, the brands of Rose's cruel dagger. Frail and broken, Crimson bowed her head and wept.

The mirror whirled with shadows and the glass flared with incandescent dark fire. The reek of familiar unhallowed sorcery filled her nostrils; she tasted its smoky tang on her tongue, swooning with the effect. Crimson collapsed to her knees, grasping the mirror's gold frame. The image of her hobgoblin king Morziel bloomed at the mirror's heart. He had not abandoned his poor Crimson! He had come, knowing his handmaiden languished in distress. When he spoke, the words formed were inside her head, so snooping humans would not hear. He knew Crimson was surrounded by enemies.

"Crimson, you have suffered much and proven your loyalty. I will reward you for your sacrifice. I know you crave vengeance on Rose Greenleaf. One day it will be yours. That is my promise to you."

"Yes, yes! I will eat dwarf girl's bones."

"Not now—that is my command. Rose Greenleaf is not to be harmed. I

have plans for her. Promise me you will not harm her."

Crimson hunched over, shaking with frustration.

"Promise me, slave!"

"Yes, dread lord. I promise."

"Good. Your time in White Thorn is at an end. You have inflicted chaos and death on my enemies. Leave the princess to die. Leave the mask of Lilias behind. Go forth and kill one more for me as a final test. Then you may return to me."

"Who do you want in the grave, Master"?

"Culain Ironheart."

Crimson grinned, rocking back and forth. "He will die tonight."

"Good. After you kill Ironheart, find Rose and bring her to my altar at the cemetery."

"My Lord, my magic does not work on her. What should I do?"

"That is your burden, Changeling."

Morziel vanished from the mirror, leaving her bereft. Crimson stroked the glass lovingly, absorbing the smoky traces left by the stygian magic, savoring its heat before it vanished.

Crimson shapeshifted back into Lilias, draining the amulet dry. The princess was good as dead anyway. The glow in the stone dimmed. Getting away from her watchers required all of her demon powers at full strength. When her duty was done, she could at last feast on Lilias. She went to the vanity and took the folded handkerchief with the prized strands of Rose Greenleaf's hair. Yes, with these she could kill Culain Ironheart. She was glad to kill an Ironheart, archenemy of the Hobgoblin King. Besides, Crimson hated dwarves.

Crimson was still weak. She needed to feed and regain her powers. Fortunately, she did not have to skulk around to find revitalizing human flesh. They waited patiently in the next room. She smiled at her pasty human reflection, gratified it was the last time she would wear it.

She rang the bell for the maids. She glanced at her reflection in the mirror. Her blue eyes shifted to hungry black. Yes, the maids would do quite nicely.

# # #

Becky fussed over Rose and even Digby cracked a big greasy smile when she showed up at the Red Boar. Rose and Meg took refuge in her old room upstairs. Her head ached, so Becky brought her some willow bark tablets and some water. A fresh application of Zula's ointment almost made Rose feel normal again. It was so stuffy she asked Meg to open to window for some air. Why was it so hot!

Becky brought them a tray of hearty roast beef sandwiches and her favorite hazelnut pudding to 'restore her strength.' Rose and Meg dined together, sitting cross-legged on the bed like schoolgirls. Rose was so hungry. She gobbled huge bites, devouring her first sandwich and moving on to her second before Meg was halfway through her first.

"Slow down, Rose! I think Becky will make more."

"Sorry," Rose apologized between mouthfuls, "but being poisoned by a nasty changeling really ignited by appetite. I'm starved! Since last night, even the thought of food made me ill. I thought it was the rum, but it wasn't, though I've learned that rum and cake do not mix well."

"They never do," Meg agreed, enjoying her sandwich.

"I'm so grateful to Zula. She is a miracle worker. After Zula's marvelous cream, I feel so much better. My hands are almost normal. She's so amazing and mysterious. How did you two meet?"

Meg frowned and felt her forehead. "You're talking awfully fast. You're burning up too. Zula said you might develop a fever. You should rest."

"I'm fine. Really. Once I have the potion, I'll be cured of this changeling poison. Then I want to hear about you and Zula. That must be quite a tale. I'm writing a story about the rangers too. You're the hero."

"Rose, you're flushed and your eyes are dilated."

Strange. She felt so energetic. And ravenous! "I'm fine. Zula said I might develop some symptoms."

"Dangerous symptoms," Meg countered. She took the tray and put it in the dresser. "I suggest you rest until she arrives."

"Can I at least have my pudding?" Rose asked meekly.

Meg handed her the bowl and a spoon.

Suddenly, someone banged on the door so heavily that it vibrated. Rose panicked until she heard it was Skullcap's voice on the other side, bellowing like a cranky dragon.

"Hey, you in there Meg? What's all the mystery about?"

Rose shouted back, "Come on in!"

Skullcap entered cautiously, his bulky frame taking up a good portion of the room, hand resting on his sword hilt. His crow, Owena, was perched on his broad shoulder. "Captain Nerlis said an urgent message from Prince Darius ordered that I meet you here. What the hell is going on, Meg?"

"A lot of hell, actually," Meg replied. "Thanks for coming so fast."

"Old Nerlis didn't even blink or ply me any questions. You know how he needles on about every detail, but he just sent me on my merry way here with no explanation."

"Imperial intervention carries a lot of weight," Meg explained. "Close the door and I'll tell you what's happened since this morning."

"Is that roast beef?" he sniffed, eyeing the platter of food eagerly.

"Yes, and it's delicious," Meg answered. She unsheathed her dagger and demanded, "First, hold out your hand. Then we'll share."

"What? You gonna cut me? Are you crazy wench?"

"Stop being a baby. If you're Skullcap, then there's no worry. A changeling is on the loose."

"What? A changeling? In these parts?"

"Yes, and it attacked Rose last night at the palace."

"What?" Skullcap roared, and looked over Meg's shoulder at Rose. "You hurt sweetheart?" he asked, concern furrowing his brow. "I'll rip that bloody thing to shreds-"

Rose waved her hands, "I'm fine. I was hurt, but I'm better now. We have to be careful because it escaped. That's why we're hiding out at the Red Boar." She started to shiver now. She wrapped the blanket around her shoulders.

Meg rolled her eyes. "Don't fuss. I just need to prick your finger." She removed one of her gloves and pricked her own thumb. A drop of red bubbled on the tip. "See? My blood is red and I'm not whining."

"What other color would it be?" Skullcap asked.

"Gray. When a changeling is in disguise that's the one thing they cannot change," Meg explained. "Just hold still so I don't accidently open a vein."

Rose was rapidly spooning pudding into her mouth when a strange image popped into her head. *Princess Lilias, blonde snooty Lilias, stalking her. When it cornered Rose, Lilias' blue eyes darkened to black. All humanity melted away as she opened her maw, exposing sharp teeth.* Rose shook her head until the hallucination dissipated. Her energy drained, she put her bowl on the table and she lay back against the pillows.

"You stabbed a changeling?" Skullcap remarked, impressed. Then he scowled and finally held up his little pinky finger. Meg pricked it.

Owena cawed loudly, angry that Meg stabbed her human. "It's all right girl," Skullcap cooed, stroking her beak. "Just a simple test, that's all."

"Thank you," Meg replied smoothly. "That wasn't so bad—was it?"

"Speak for yourself, woman," Skullcap grumbled. "A damn steep price for a sandwich. Tell me more about this changeling running about?" He sucked his finger to stop the bleeding.

Meg wiped the blade on her trousers and handed him a sandwich. "See, I told you we'd share."

"That does look good," Skullcap grinned, taking one and breaking off a piece for Owena.

"Stop salivating and just listen," Meg sighed.

A gentler knock on the door alerted them. "It's me, Meg," Zula called. "I have the potion."

"Thank the gods," Rose moaned.

Another flash of Lilias haunted her, but this time it was a different Lilias, entombed in a snowy cocoon, like a dying butterfly.

Zula sauntered in and smiled Skullcap's way when she glimpsed him from the corner of her eye. "How are you these days?"

Skullcap patted his hairless, tattooed head and answered, "Still bald, Zula."

"Such a pity," Zula sighed forlornly. She tickled Owena beneath the break. "I see you're faithful at least to one female."

Rose blanched and gasped, "You're the witch that turned Skullcap bald?"

Zula shook her head, smiling sweetly. "Not intentionally, child. Anyway, it was near twenty years ago. We had a nasty lover's quarrel because he slept with a slutty wench who couldn't keep her skirts down."

"I did not cheat on you. I was very drunk," Skullcap added. "I was barely conscious when the wench crawled on top of me. Plus she stole my money."

"I was heartbroken. I drank too much wine and got carried away with a few mild incantations."

"A few mild incantations? Woman, I use to have to have a thick head of black hair!"

"You turned him bald forever?" Rose asked.

"I honestly do not remember why I did that or if it was even my intention," Zula confessed. "If could remember my little hex I would reverse it. Sadly, he went to a penny a spell wizard for those funny little blue tattoos. I was so young then and easily prone to passion and fury. Now I am much more temperate."

"Good to know," Rose replied. Angering a witch is obviously very risky. "But then, if you were the one that cursed Skullcap, how does Meg-"

"Oh, Skullcap introduced us," Zula explained. "And it wasn't really a curse, more of a spell gone wild. Magic and wine do not mix."

"Neither does rum and cake," Rose interjected.

"Such wisdom often comes too late to be useful in life. But that is the past and I'm a good witch. Meg needed guidance to control her magic and he asked me to teach her. I felt I needed to make amends to Robert, for my accidental hex."

"You will have made amends when I need a comb again, woman."

Rose recalled that Skullcap's birth name was Robert. It was so strange whenever she heard it because the Skullcap suits him so much better.

Zula turned to Meg and held up a finger. "Now, be gentle. I don't want scars marring my perfect skin."

Despite the squabbling, Rose sensed Zula and Skullcap were not angry with each other. There was more love than hatred in their voices. The human voice holds so much, but people are unaware. Their love was not completely broken, but it was damaged. That was sad. Shaky, Rose poured a glass of water.

After a brief nick on the finger to determine Zula was human, she removed her cloak and removed a red potion bottle from her drawstring purse. She held up the bottle triumphantly. "Fresh from my cauldron!"

Relieved to be fully healed, Rose accepted the offered potion. "Thank you, Zula!"

"Now, the potion will make you a little drowsy," Zula warned. "But it will flush the demon toxins from your body." She touched Rose's cheek. "Goodness! You're fevered. Drink it now."

Rose plucked the stopper and held the bottle to her lips. She paused and squinted, "How does it taste?"

"Just like honey, my dear. I never give my patients unpleasant potions to drink."

Rose drank the potion in one swallow. Zula was right. It tasted like honey. But she did not feel better. Then everything went black.

Rose was in a dark room, staring into a mirror. But she was not Rose. She was the changeling, but she wore Rose's face now. She sensed its sinister thoughts. Crimson, the changeling was called Crimson. It laughed at its reflection before it turned away from the mirror. On the floor at Crimson's feet were two dead maids, their pristine white blouses stained with their own blood, their bodies shrunken and desiccated. Repelled by the changeling, Rose struggled to free herself. In the process, Rose realized Crimson did not know they were connected. Rose fought to flee from the demon's tangled mind. She was so bombarded with bizarre memory fragments she thought she would go mad. She saw the changeling as many people, including Princess Lilias! The real Lilias was still alive, but hidden away somewhere. Lilias was dying, soon to be a meal for the vicious changeling. The amulet, with the small red stone that glimmered with enchantment bound Lilias and the changeling. It was fading now. Death would take Lilias if left unattended too long. The amulet the changeling wore was a part of it. Rose could not bear anymore and toiled to break the bond, horrified by what she saw in its mind. Death. So much death. Another unwelcome thought invaded Rose's consciousness that she seized upon. The changeling planned to murder Culain tonight, posing as Rose. Then it was coming after her for her master, the goblin king, Morziel.

The link finally snapped. Rose found herself sprawled on the floor, surrounded by her friends, who looked as terrified as she felt.

"Rose, you're back. Thank the gods. What happened? Where did the demon take you?" Zula asked softly, lifting her head as she held a glass of water to her lips.

Rose sipped and propped herself on her elbows, gasping. "The changeling is still at the palace, but now she looks just like me! I saw many fragments of her memory. It was awful."

"She?" Meg asked. "What are you talking about?"

"The changeling that attacked me! It's a female named Crimson." Rose tried to steady herself as Meg helped her to her feet. "The changeling was pretending to be Princess Lilias. I knew there was a reason why I didn't like her. She works for her master, the goblin king. Now that damn changeling looks like me and she just killed two poor maids! Oh gods! She fed on them!"

Zula's expression became troubled and she helped steady Rose. "This is not an effect of the blood girl, but I think you have magic that has awakened."

"A magic I do not know what to do with. I spent my life reading about the glam rhapsodé and its power. It's also a curse. I'm scared. I wish Belenus were here. He could help me with this."

"Zula, take Rose back to your shop," Meg ordered. "Skullcap and I will go to the palace."

"No," Rose refused. "I'm coming with you."

"Changelings are nothing to play with," Zula warned. "You're still fevered and should rest! Let the warriors hunt the changelings."

"Listen to her. You're delirious and not thinking clearly. That potion will take time," Meg insisted.

"No," Rose cried. "There isn't time. I must go back to the palace now! Culain's life is in danger! The changeling is going to kill Culain and use my face to do it."

Chapter Twenty

Crimson did not grasp a very important fact when she eagerly transformed into Rose Greenleaf–the Princess's clothes no longer fit. Crimson whined and pulled at the now baggy dresses that hung like voluminous tents. Why didn't she think! The dwarf was only four feet tall. She must get to Rose's wardrobe; but she could not walk out of the chamber alone. There were not just guards posted at her door, but patrolling the halls. Crimson restrained a giggle, enjoying the notion that her evil infected the whole palace with fear.

Crimson stripped and shifted into her natural changeling shape. She stepped over the dead bodies of the servants and retrieved the precious stands of Rose's hair wrapped in a lacy handkerchief and tied it to her wrist. She opened the window and looked down. Guards patrolled the grounds, but the fading sunlight and the ability to shroud her presence might keep her safe from detection. She crawled out of the window and climbed up to the roof. She scuttled briskly, her clawed finger pads glands secreted a sticky fluid that allowed her to cling effortlessly.

Crimson was above Rose Greenleaf's window. She hoped Rose was there now. Then she could restrain the dwarf and bind her up for her master. Changeling magic may not work on her, but a hard blow to the head would knock out any human. She would relish that. Killing her would be better, but she must obey her master. She crawled down the sides of the building and glared inside. No one was there. Where was the dwarf girl? Rose should be sick in bed; she had been stained by her changeling blood, which made humans deathly ill. She kicked the window open and slid inside.

The changeling heard voices approach and saw the door open. Crimson panicked. She quickly jumped into the bed and pulled the quilt over her head.

"Miss Rose, is that you?" a young woman asked.

Crimson plucked the slender strands of chestnut hair from the handkerchief and focused on the dwarf girl. She would not have the dwarf's memories, but these were only servants. Rushed to attain Rose's shape, Crimson's body contracted and painfully shifted. It felt so squat and strange. She had marginal information for a perfect shapeshift except for the shallowest exterior. It would have to do.

Changeling Rose threw back the covers, naked but fully shifted into Rose Greenleaf. It startled the two maids, carrying towels and standing at the foot of the bed.

One of the maids gasped. "Miss Rose, I didn't know you were abed? And you're naked!"

"I was so fevered and weak. I just needed to rest." Crimson Rose grabbed a robe on the edge of the bed and wrapped herself in it. She went to the enormous wardrobe and rummaged through the rich clothes. "I think I feel better now. I didn't mean to fall asleep."

"Well, of course dear, after last night's horror, I don't blame you," the older maid exclaimed. "You're just seemed so modest before, it stunned me that's all. Of course, Prince Culain told us not to speak of last night to anyone, but we know what you suffered. Let old Agatha help you get dressed."

"Thank you," Changeling Rose agreed. Agatha handed her silk underwear and a lacy petticoat. Changeling Rose picked a green muslin gown with sheer white puffed sleeves. It was revolting. They dressed her quickly.

Changeling Rose turned to the younger girl with bouncy ringlets peeking from her lace cap. "I'm sorry, but I'm afraid I forgot your name. I just feel so unwell today and I'm still so new here. I tend to forget things."

"I'm Sally."

"Of course! It's Sally! How mindless of me," Changeling Rose giggled. "Forgive me, Sally."

"Let me fetch you a cold pitcher of water," Sally offered.

The maids departed, giving Crimson time to adjust to her new surroundings. She contrived many interesting forms of torture for Rose as she waited. Master may want her alive, but Crimson wanted to inflict pain on Rose. She looked through the lavish wardrobe. The dwarf must be wealthy indeed to have so many fine things! Even Lilias did not possess such an elaborate wardrobe. Silk, velvets, satin! Even the shoes were finely crafted of velvet or satin, with shiny buckles or ribbons. Human fondness for clothing was something Crimson could never fathom. It was so itchy. Perhaps Rose was concubine to the Ironheart? So the ugly dwarf was a whore! That would make it easy for Crimson to get close enough to kill an Ironheart.

Sally returned with a fresh pitcher of water. Her eyes were so kind. Crimson wanted to eat them. Changeling Rose leaned against the wardrobe, genuinely weak. She splashed her face and accepted the hand towel from Sally.

"Why is the door kept open?" Changeling Rose asked.

"It's one of the orders Prince Culain gave this morning," Agatha replied.

"I must see Prince Culain. I need my lute with me," she fumbled, searching the room for it. Bards use instruments, so she must take it. Sadly, she had no knowledge of how to play it. But she should keep it at hand. She could also use it as a weapon.

Anger at her failings simmered in Crimson's mind. If she had been able to cocoon Rose as she planned, she would have had all of her knowledge and memories. She would not be here dealing with nosy servants. She finally spied the lute in the corner and grabbed it. "A bard cannot be without their lute. It's such a comfort to me. I'm so silly, but I need an escort to Culain's room now that I am rested. Do you mind taking me back to his room? I don't want to get into trouble? I know we are under orders."

"Of course we'll go with you, my dear," Sally answered brightly. "Prince Culain will be happy to see you."

Changeling Rose was ecstatic. As Bardess to Culain's household, she would not need to figure out a crafty way to get close to him so she could kill him. Rose Greenleaf may even be his lover! If only she had her memories! Then it would be easy, so easy to snuff out his life. She almost laughed as she walked down the hall with her escorts, but refrained, fearing it would be inappropriate considering the atmosphere of anxiety.

So much spying and death was demanded these past months, but the Dark Lord honored the changeling clan with these commands and they had to obey. No, not only obey but succeed! The Dark Lord will inflict great punishment should she fail.

They moved through the palace corridors at a quick pace. Crimson sensed the unspoken dread of those they passed. It smelled sweet, like nectar. When they reached Lilias' suite, many Imperial guards were gathered there. Changeling Rose's gut knotted in fear and that was not so sweet. They must have found the bodies. Soon she would be gone from this palace–after she assassinated Culain Ironheart.

"What is happening over there," Changeling Rose stammered.

"I don't know, Miss Rose. Best we do not interfere. Poor thing, you were so brave the way you fought it off." Agatha leaned in and whispered, "And you stabbed it, clever girl."

Changeling Rose grimaced and touched her side. "Yes–clever."

They reached Culain's rooms, but the Rhulonese guards forbade her to enter.

"The Ambassador has been summoned away," one of the guards informed her. "It's best to return to your chamber."

"But where has he gone?" Changeling Rose asked innocently. "I was summoned to play for him."

The guard shook his head, but remained stoic. "He did not say, Miss Rose."

"Of course," Rose replied, eyes downcast but bitter with disappointment.

As she walked back to Rose's room, she knew she had to get rid of these annoying women so she could move freely. Of course, she could just kill them now and flee this place. Be done with this spying. She could finally feed on the real Lilias, captive in her webbed cocoon. It made her salivate just to think about it. Maybe she could restore herself if she feasted on these maids?

"Are you all right?" Sally asked.

"I'm just so hungry," Changeling Rose replied, just to explain away her agitation.

"Of course we will," Agatha said sweetly. "You're such a brave girl. You need not fret. We will not leave you. We'll send for a grand meal."

"I'm so grateful to you both," Changeling Rose grinned.

They entered Rose's room. Changeling Rose glanced in the wall mirror and her eyes shifted from blue to black.

# # #

Fallon watched Crimson from his hollow of mirrors, frowning. She was becoming too erratic. He thought if he gave her an objective like killing Culain, it would deflect her vengeful eye from Rose Greenleaf.

He turned to another mirror, where he watched Rose since he suspected her magic. Now he was sure. Rose was just becoming aware of her terrible gift. The witch helped make her aware. She was sick from the changeling blood, but that would soon pass. The gift of the rhapsodé would be more difficult. So many bards who carried this magic were cursed. Would Rose fall to the victim of enchantment or rise above it?

#

"I'll be fine. Please don't fight me on this, Meg. I'm going and that's final," Rose argued.

"You really vex me at times," Meg snapped.

"Then you and my mother will have a lot to talk about if you ever meet."

"Let's hope it's not at your funeral," Meg shot back and then relented out of frustration. "You can come with us, but if you die on me, I'll never forgive you."

"Let me come too," Zula asked. "I know about these demons. I can help keep an eye on Rose. I can help her with the magic too. It could be the reason her body is not responding to the potion the way it should."

"I'm coming too," Skullcap chimed in.

Meg strapped on her sword. "Good. Skullcap, you take Zula to the palace. Ride fast. I'll meet you there. Rose, you ride with me."

Meg threw on her green cloak, imparting a sharp look at Skullcap and Zula. "Can you two work together without resorting to violence or curses?"

"I can stand the witch's company if she keeps her jinxes in line," Skullcap replied, grinning.

Zula took his arm, rolling her eyes. "Ah, you suffer so much. "Let's go, Robert."

They rushed down the stairs. Becky and Digby were stunned they were leaving already.

"But you're still sick, dear," Becky protested. "You can't go out like this. Meg, talk to her."

"I can't stay Becky, but we'll be careful," Rose promised. She hoped the potion would take effect. Still fevered and weak, even walking was a struggle.

Digby jerked his head toward the back of the room. "Hey Meg, before you go, that fool has come back for another beating."

Meg cursed so vehemently a sailor would have blushed. Mathias stoically sat at a table, his wide brimmed hat at his side, jaw visibly bruised and swollen from the last time Meg punched him. When he heard Meg swear, he stood up. Though he looked unhappy, Rose resisted any sympathy for him, knowing what he did to Meg.

"Tell him that having a stuffy vicar hanging around is bad for business," Digby frowned, wiping his hands on his apron. "And if he's going to take up drinking space, he needs to order ale or leave."

Meg marched over to the table. "Do you enjoy being beaten up?"

"Not really," he replied calmly. "But I still must speak with you."

"Damn it Mathias, I don't have time for this. I don't want to see you. I thought I made that clear."

Digby fetched the big wooden club he kept stowed under the bar for the more *unruly* customers. He casually held it in his hands, polishing it with a cloth. "Want me to take care of him, Meg? I'm happy to do oblige."

"No Digby. I'll take care of this," Meg replied evenly. She walked toward the door, casting a harsh glance at Mathias. "Outside," she ordered.

Rose was unsure what would happen, but Mathias obeyed and followed her out the front door. Rose, however, was not prepared for him to fall to his knees before Meg and bow his head when they reached the road. Skullcap and Zula watched from a distance, so silent Rose wondered if Zula had cast a spell.

"We are passed words or gestures, Mathias," Meg warned him, taking Fayre's reins. "My fist should have resolved any questions you had for me the last time."

"I know you're angry, Meghan."

"Don't call me that."

"I'm sorry," Mathias apologized quickly. "I went to the Ranger Station, but was told you weren't there, but they refused to tell me anything else. I only know that this is a place you visit often, so I decided to wait here."

"Just leave it alone. Leave me alone. I'm on an assignment."

"I know words mean nothing. I know I'm a wretch. For years I searched for you. I only recently learned you resided here in White Thorn and had become a ranger. I just came to say how sorry I am. I failed you. I will not ask for your forgiveness, because I don't deserve it. Know only, that since that day I have lived to save others living under the same persecution as you. I took the vows of a cleric. I'm a Vicar now, though it has made me an outlaw too in my own country. Our land is controlled by brutal religious insanity, but many people now have banded together to restore freedom and make things right again. That's why I'm here. We are gathering support and arms for the cause. I did not fight for you. I regret that. But I am fighting now."

"It can never be right again. Our country is dead. A mad king killed it."

"And it destroyed us," Mathias replied. "But there's a rebellion now-"

"That's not my problem. I serve this country now. I serve its Emperor. I have a new life now and I'm happy here. You need to do the same, Mathias. Fight to free Juraca. You want forgiveness? Very well then-I forgive you. But you cannot change the past. Make a better future for what we once hoped to be. My life is here now. If you mean to save Juraca, then go with my blessing. Fight. Save the innocents. Do the right thing. The past cannot change. Let it go," Meg shouted, lifting Rose up onto the saddle.

He nodded mutely, face a mask of regret.

Skullcap marched past Mathias and deliberately spit on the ground where he kneeled. Skullcap mounted his horse and pulled up Zula behind him. She wrapped her arms around Skullcap. "I would curse him, knowing what he did to our Meg, but I think he lives in his own hell." Skullcap spurred his horse, Zula clinging to him. Owena took to the air, following the pair down the road, cawing loudly.

Meg rode away without another word or looking back at the man she once loved. Rose gripped the pommel, fearing she would be thrown. She glanced back to see Mathias kneeling in the dirt, watching Meg ride away. Fayre's hooves beat the earth hard and fast for the palace. Despite the wild race, Rose could hear Meg crying.

Chapter Twenty-One

Crimson's shapeshift was dissolving. She dreaded this in a crowded room. She shut her eyes, desperately fingering Rose's hair tucked in her bodice. It was fading too soon. Not now! Too many people watched her. Guards were everywhere with sharp swords. Crimson forced herself to calm down and opened her eyes. They were blue again. She sighed with relief.

She must finish her killing for her master so she could leave before they found her out. Her head ached when she thought about taking Rose for her master. Her magic did not work on the dwarf. At least she could feast on Lilias before she left this terrible place. She licked her lips, hungry. Lilias was in a crypt, safe and sound. Well, safe and sound for Crimson. Death was Lilias' companion now in that old cemetery. The dying amulet that bound them was just a pretty trinket now. No matter. She had other pressing issues for her master—kill Culain. Crimson's ability to remain Rose would not last. A few strands of her hair were not enough to maintain her image for long, so she must get to Culain soon.

They brought a platter of food and laid it before her. Not what she hungered for. Typical human fair she had tolerated these past weeks— roasted fowl, bread, cheese, fruit, and little iced cakes. It was revolting. Cooked flesh was so unnatural. She had endured eating during her interlude as Princess Lilias, but it had become a struggle. At least Lilias had delicate eating habits. Lilias would never need to worry about her slim figure again. Crimson Rose snickered, feeling clever. She feigned an appetite for her captors, because the dwarf was reputed to enjoy eating. How the dwarf could eat so much and not get fat amazed her. Changeling Rose chewed and forced herself to swallow as they heaped more on her plate. This was torture!

All these soldiers were making her jumpy. She forced herself to remain calm and asked for more water with the extravagance of ice, which was easily granted. She finished eating and excused herself from the table. She must find a way to shake the guards. She wandered over to the far side of the room when the maids began clearing away the dishes.

Crimson glanced in the mirror again on the wall and her eyes shifted to black again. No! That was always the first thing she lost when the shapeshift lost power—the eyes. She must get away before Rose's image diminished. She closed her eyes and focused on the image of the homely short dwarf. Just a little longer. Thankfully, the maids were occupied with cleaning up and the guards at the door were not watching her. She concentrated, touching the strand of hairs; when she opened them her eyes were blue again. Crimson was resolved. She must act now or leave.

Changeling Rose moved to the opposite end of the chamber. Desperate, she picked up a marble paper weight and hurled it through the window and screamed!

"Help! Help me! The changeling! Guards!"

They swarmed around her instantly. She dropped to her knees and hunched over, sobbing.

"What happened?" Sally cried, rushing to her side.

"The changeling was at the window!"

She lifted her head and pointed to the broken window. "It was staring at me through the window. It was the changeling! It was horrible. I threw the nearest thing at hand. Oh, it was hideous!" Changeling Rose crumbled into a ball and wept. There was chaos. Crimson loved chaos, as long as she wielded it. More soldiers were summoned for the protection of the helpless bard.

When they sent word to Culain, she was finally gratified. She quivered with tears and allowed them to help her to the bed. Her hands may have covered her face as she sobbed, but Crimson grinned behind them. Agnes and Sally comforted her as she wept.

Crimson looked up at the guard with teary eyes. "Oh, please, when will Culain be here? He vowed to protect me. I think I have important information about the creature."

"Ambassador Culain sent word that we are to escort you to him, Miss Rose."

"Are you truly taking me to my master, Prince Ironheart?" she asked hopefully.

"Yes Miss, he's there waiting for you now," Sally replied. "Fear not, we will catch that depraved thing. We won't let it hurt you, Rose."

"Thank you!" Crimson Rose cried, wiping away false tears.

Several guards escorted her through the halls. Changeling Rose plotted to kill Ironheart as she walked. It must be quick. Then she would run. She was glad she did not have to cry anymore. Blubbering was so tiring. She wiped her face and blew her nose. Why did humans cry? It's so silly. Plus, she did not know if Rose was a crier and she was afraid they would note a discrepancy in her character. But human females were so weak and emotional.

They finally approached a set of double doors protected by Imperial soldiers.

Changeling Rose would soon be rewarded with a prize kill. Then she would flee; flee for Mordok and the glorious thanks of her lord and king! Morziel, the Goblin King of all Mordok, would welcome her with open arms. Praise would cover Crimson at last. She would glory in it and sit at the feet of her beloved king in the throne room, his favorite pet.

"Prince Culain awaits you within," the guard promised her.

Two Rhulonese attendants opened the doors and stepped inside the very large room, elegantly furnished.

Culain briskly strode toward her. He was happy to see her, judging by his broad smile. Maybe Culain and Rose were lovers?

"Rose, thank heavens you are all right," Culain exclaimed.

She summoned a fresh batch of tears as she relayed her joy. "Oh, Your Highness, I'm so relieved to see you at last! I was so frightened."

Too many guards remained in the room to act hastily, both imperials and Culain's personal Rhulonese attendants. They suspected a demon in their midst, but like frightened children, they did not know what waited for them in the dark. If only they knew!

Culain was so full of trust. He would be so easy to butcher, but for the force of men around them! Patient! Be patient! She swayed, dizzy with bloodlust. She centered herself. Soon, soon she would slay him.

"Oh, Prince Culain, I've been so afraid of this evil around us," Changeling Rose whispered, so close now, almost close enough to bite. Her bite had a strong chance of being fatal. If she did it quickly, maybe he would die?

"There's no need to fear anymore," Culain replied solemnly, stopping a few feet from her. "I will defeat the evil—and you."

Changeling Rose was too stunned to react when a barbed net dropped over her from above. Panic slowed her response. She tried to throw it off the heavy net, but an angry, tall redheaded woman struck her in the face with the flat side of a sword. Changeling Rose wailed in pain, crashing to the floor. Several guards surrounded her and brutally beat her down with the butt of their spears. Crimson coiled into a ball and shrieked with agony. "NO! Stop! This is a mistake. I am the true Rose Greenleaf. Please don't hurt me!"

"Hold it down," Darius ordered, removing his helmet.

Panting and shaking, she glared at the young prince. What was Darius doing here? She snapped her head around. It was a nasty trap. All planned to torment Crimson. Foolish Crimson. Stupid Crimson. Guards with sharp spears encircled her. Crimson thrashed in its bitter grasp, howling.

Shifting her focus from attack to survival, her frantic mind scanned the room searching for an escape that did not exist.

The redhead grinned and stepped back. "I thoroughly enjoyed that."

"I found it inspiring, Commander Sparrow," Culain complimented her.

Prince Darius observed Crimson coldly. "It's safe now, Father. We captured the changeling."

Aristide entered the chamber and joined the gathering, his stony expression edged with cruel intent.

Panic gnawed the changeling. "You tricked me!" Crimson screeched.

"You tricked yourself, changeling," Culain declared. "I will not be on your death list today." He turned to the maids and bowed, "Thank you ladies for being so brave."

She bitterly squinted at the servants, Agnes and Sally. They actually smirked at her! Then they were led away from the room.

"They knew you weren't Rose, by the way." Culain bluntly told Crimson. "There are many reasons for this. You were clumsy. Greedy. Injudicious. A changeling usually takes better care to know their enemy, but you were quite reckless. The servants knew Rose was sent elsewhere for her safety out of the palace. They alerted me of your presence when they discovered you in Rose's room. Rose is also modest, does not whine or cry, and she never forgets anything. She has flawless memory recall. This is a necessary talent for any bard as they must memorize ridiculously long poems and even whole books. It's a talent one is born with, I believe. You couldn't even remember the names of two chambermaids who knew her, Changeling."

The strain of the dark magic cloaking her true shape was a hindrance now. Crimson sighed, shedding the human image and resumed her natural form. The tiny dress she wore as Rose now ripped and ruined.

She noted the shocked expressions on their faces. It was gratifying in her moment of despair that she frightened them. "Never seen a changeling before? Well, feast your eyes on me. Few see us and survive."

Culain's flinty stare was unmoved. "You're hideous, but hardly frightening."

"Heartless humans," she whimpered, "you struck without thought or positive proof. What if I had been your treasured Rose Greenleaf?"

One of the Rhulonese guards removed their helmet and stepped forward. It was Rose Greenleaf! Deceitful bitch! The dwarf Rose had been among her escort the whole time! She did not even notice the sly bitch! Crimson realized how careless she was. Now she would perish. She should have run when she had the chance! Foolish and shamed, she would die a failure.

Rose stared down at Crimson. "That would be impossible, since I'm the only true Rose Greenleaf. And my blood is red—not demon gray. Since I stabbed you that night and your grotesque blood soiled on my hands, I not only developed a terrible rash, but somehow the infection of your blood bound me to your thoughts. It awoke something within me too. I am aware of your violent sins. You are evil."

"Thank you, Dwarf," Crimson grinned.

"It wasn't a compliment,' Rose remarked sharply. "I was forced to watch you murder that poor stable boy when you tore him apart and sucked the life out of him! Those poor maids died at your hands too. You will never kill again."

Thera pushed her way between the Emperor and Culain until she stood over Crimson, a dagger in her hands, green eyes venomous. "Good. You trapped the foul changeling."

Crimson cowered, for she knew Thera's temper. "Wait. Don't hurt. Please. I'm so weak," the changeling whimpered. It was a struggle to even move now. "Fiendish Dwarf! Poison! You poisoned the food and wine!"

"Not poisoned," Culain confirmed. "We drugged your food and water, just to be certain. We wanted to make sure you were pliable and harmless; as such a demon could be so we could trap you and interrogate you. Now, where are you keeping Princess Lilias Rhodan?"

A dozen soldiers pressed their spears so deep into her body Crimson feared they would slice her open like a melon.

"How do you know about that?" Crimson gasped.

Rose looked down on Crimson. "Through you, Changeling. I saw a great deal when I was inside your mind. You've done horrible things. I know you were posing as Princess Lilias for a long time. I know she's dying in a dark place somewhere. I saw it in my vision."

Crimson recoiled from Rose. "How could you see? My blood does not do that to people. It infects and even kills."

"None of your business," Culain replied. "Tell us where she is."

Crimson lay back, no longer struggling. "No point. Death is my fate. Lilias can die in the hole."

Thera's temper fumed as stood over the changeling. She edged her way between the guards and slashed Crimson's cheek with her sharp blade. Crimson screamed, blood pouring gray down her pallid cheek.

"Tell us or I will flay you in ribbons," Thera threatened. "I can make you howl for a death that will never come."

"Don't let its blood touch you. It's poisonous," Darius warned, drawing the determined Thera back with some force. "Please, I promise we will get Lilias back!"

"Very well," Thera agreed. "But if it does not talk, let me question the thing. I know things that can inflict much agony on such a demon." She turned to Rose and her voice softened. "Rose, you are the bravest of maidens and an honor to your caste," Thera commended her. She turned her wrath back to the changeling. "But this wretched fiend still has Lilias. We must find her. Where is she?" Thera demanded.

Crimson stopped struggling in her net. "Buried. Safe as bones in the grave where you'll never find her alive! And White Thorn is so big. There are so many places to hide away the bodies. It's a haven for my kind. Without me she will wither away and die. The amulet's dead now. She will be dead by sunrise!"

"Then how do we save her?" Thera asked coldly.

"No one survives the changeling cocoon," Crimson laughed.

"Demon spawn!" Thera spat. When you called Rose Greenleaf a 'stupid, ugly, dwarf girl,' I knew you were not my Princess. You manner grew more common each day. My sleep became erratic. I sensed dark magic too late. You used your foul breath to keep me asleep when you escaped the palace at night didn't you?"

"Be glad I did not kill you, Priestess."

"You cannot blame yourself, Thera," Culain consoled her. "They're devious creatures. I know the tragedy they bring."

"Are you sure Lilias still lives?" Aristide asked.

"Yes, Father," Darius replied. "The witch Zula knows a great deal about these demons. She is working on a truth potion to force the changeling to speak. Zula assures us the victim must be kept alive for this long period of shapeshifting to work at all. We still have a chance if we can reach her in time."

"That thing is wearing an amulet that connects them and somehow maintains her human form for long blocks of time," Rose said. "It's important."

"We could not have this beast without Darius' assistance," Culain proclaimed to the Emperor. "Darius planned this charade to trap the changeling. Lady Thera came to us with her suspicions, certain Lilias had been taken by a changeling. When we discovered Lilias missing and two dead maids her room, we knew the appalling truth. When Commander Sparrow and Rose rushed to the palace and warned us it has taken on Rose's form, we quickly made a plan. We knew the changeling was pretending to be Rose to assassinate me. Darius arranged everything. The trap and drugging were all his idea."

"Changelings are quite strong and we needed to weaken it to ensure its capture," Darius added. "I grieve that this monster killed that poor boy and the two women before we could act. But Father, I swear to you, I'll rescue Lilias," Darius declared.

"You've done well, Darius," Aristide commended him. "I had no idea you could be so strong."

"Thank you, Father."

"Torture will never make me talk. Death will only silence my tongue," Crimson taunted. "Fools! You will never find your precious Princess. She will die with me."

"When it's bound in chains and securely caged, send for me," Darius ordered. "Zula can tell us how to extract information from it."

"Rose, you said you saw the amulet in your vision?" Culain asked.

"Yes. It's wearing it now," Rose confirmed. "It has dark magic, but I don't know how it works. I know it is part of the connection the changeling used to pretend it was the Princess."

"Then I suggest the changeling hand it over," Culain said.

"Mine!" Crimson hissed out of spite.

Culain gestured to the guards and they pushed their spears in deeper until Crimson shrieked with agony.

"Stop, stop!" Crimson wailed. "Take it! Take it. Useless now anyway."

They men stepped back, a few spears stained with gray blood. With quivering hands, Crimson ripped the amulet from its neck. It was so small, she could push it through the metal netting.

One of the guards extended his spear to catch it by the chain and passed it to Culain, who collected it in a piece of cloth.

"Now, take that monster to out of here," Aristide commanded. "Use the witch, Zula. And if her craft does not work, torture it until it confesses. I want to know who it works for and if that demon killed my son."

Crimson cackled with glee. "I will tell you that for free, Emperor. I killed your prince. I, Crimson of Mordok, sabotaged his saddle so cleverly that when Prince Justin was riding hard, his saddle snapped—along with his royal neck."

Aristide's fury burst. He snatched a spear from a guard and raised his hand to spear Crimson. Darius and Thera forced him back.

"It killed my son!" Aristide thundered. "It must die."

"It will die! We'll punish it for its crimes, Father," Darius shouted. "The beast will be executed. I swear to you, in my brother's memory, I swear it. But we need it alive to find Lilias."

"Please, Your Majesty," Thera pleaded. "This dirty changeling stole Princess Lilias. Do not let her perish. She is also a victim of this devil. I know what these demons can do. She needed Lilias alive to maintain her fake image for so long. Please! She is innocent, as your noble son was innocent."

Aristide's face was a mask of conflict. Anger and pain intermingled, battling reason and the satisfaction of vengeance. He finally stepped back, lowered the spear and relented. "Very well, but I want it out of the palace. It's too dangerous to keep it here. Lock it up in a dark cell under heavy guard. Put it in the deepest hole in the prison. No one should directly touch it until we know how it shapeshifts. Have the witch Zula cast any magic needed to prevent its escape and find Lilias. When this is over, I will be its executioner."

"Get the cage we prepared and take that thing away," Darius commanded. "My father will deal with this demon later. Be careful of the blood and wash your spears when you have finished."

Trussed in the heavy tangle of metal netting, soldiers lifted the captive changeling and shoved her into a small metal cage. They carried Crimson away, her shrill curses poisoning the air in demon tongue.

Chapter Twenty-Two

Rose winced at the changeling's curses. It added fresh agony to her already aching head. Why wasn't Zula's potion working? She still felt fevered and dizzy.

Meg put her hand on Rose's shoulder. "You better sit. Now that the changeling is captured, you can get some rest. You look terrible."

"Just what a girl needs to hear," Rose quipped weakly.

Despite her condition, Rose still wanted to help. "Prince Darius, one thing is certain, the changeling needed access to the Princess to renew the magic tether to maintain its deceptive shape. She can't be far away. Maybe I can help find out where."

"Don't worry, Rose," Darius assured her. "You've risked enough. We will interrogate the changeling. You still look so ill."

"People keep telling me that."

"That's because she is ill," Culain added. "Commander Sparrow, escort Rose to her bedchamber."

"Don't worry, Rose," Darius added. "We'll get it to confess where she is hiding the real Lilias with Zula's help. You just rest."

"He's right," Meg said. "You're still suffering from effects of the changeling's blood."

"Why hasn't Zula's potion worked yet?" Rose asked.

Meg looked uncertain and shook her head. "I don't know. Zula knows her craft so well, but I'm beginning to wonder if she's lost her touch with potions."

"No, I have not!" Zula interjected, strolling into the room.

Rose was relieved to see Zula. "What's wrong with me? I'm still so sick."

"Your magic is the problem," Zula replied simply, taking her by the hand and leading her to a couch to sit her down.

Rose rubbed her temples, feeling like her head was going to explode. "I don't understand. How is that possible?"

"I think I know," Zula answered gently. "Your magical ability was latent when the changeling attacked you. There is dark magic in changeling blood that, to put it in simple terms, basically activated your magic with full force, like a defense. Your light magic, which has just come to life, is fighting its dark magic. An awakening magic like yours can cause discomfort at first. But the combined stress of the changeling attack and its toxic blood has caused the trouble. I believe your magic is fighting both the demon's poison and my potion, like a confused child. Your fever is out of control because of it. It has been forced to assert itself in defense against the dark. That's what's making you sick."

"So, because I have this magic your potions won't work for me?"

Zula smiled patiently. "They will work, but I must make you a new potion to counteract the effects of what is happening to you. I know what to do now, but we need to do it fast, or your fever will continue to spiral and even kill you."

"I never knew magic and potions could be so tricky," Rose replied.

"It's vexatious, I know. You have the glam rhapsodé and you must accept that, Rose," Zula said. "There is no other explanation. I do not sense that you're a witch, like me. I heard that creature howling curses when they were taking it away. What was it saying?"

Rose shivered. "Most of it was filth. There was a curse on Culain's loins I will never repeat and how the demons are going to eat our flesh when Morziel rises. She also called me a hideous pudgy dwarf. "

Zula leaned in and whispered. "There, you see?"

"I'm not pudgy," Rose insisted.

"Not that," Zula laughed, "you have the rhapsodé, because that creature was spewing out its curses in demon tongue and you understood its language. That is one of the elements of your ability."

"To speak demon? Not very appealing."

"To understand languages, once you have read them or heard the words, or in this changeling's case, been infected by their blood. I can make a potion to compensate for your body's reaction now that we know what we are dealing with. I must return to my shop and brew it for you. Then I will come back. But you must rest and keep your fever down. Your life may depend on it."

"Zula can make the potion here," Darius offered. "Our alchemist and doctors should have all the ingredients you need."

"I agree,' Culain added, "Rose needs to be healed fast."

"Thank you," Zula smiled. "It is rare that two such handsome princes are so generous."

"Stop flirting, Zula," Meg chastised.

"I can help too," Thera offered, joining their circle. "I will help care for Rose."

"Now, take my bardess to her bed and tuck her in," Culain ordered with a smile. "That is my command."

Rose nodded in agreement and allowed Meg to lead her away. When she saw the small red amulet Culain held in his hand, she sensed its dying glimmer pull at her. "That amulet can still be useful. Maybe Zula can use it for a scrying spell." She touched the stone at its center. A flare of dark light burst and Crimson's chaotic thoughts pierced Rose's fevered mind again. Rose's knees buckled.

"Oh no, the changeling is in my head again!" Rose shouted.

Meg shouted. "Resist it. Just snap out of it." Meg was shaking her by the shoulders. "Can you keep it out? ROSE!"

"Not so simple," Rose gasped.

Meg's shouts faded into the distant murmurs and then into oblivion. Reality shifted. Rose was drawn into a chasm where reality and dreams merged. Everyone around her vanished from sight. The last image she gleaned from this mortal realm was Culain's strong hands cradling her head when she collapsed to the floor.

Weird pictures from the changeling's mind merged with her consciousness as Rose was conveyed to a strange limbo. There, in an ethereal plane of light and shadows, she floated among the changeling's memories. Rose became an intruding ghost in the sinister realm of Crimson's mind. Rose was rattled by the chaos. The changeling's thoughts were in its native demon tongue, bizarre sounds punctuated with spattered, harsh consonants and guttural vowels interspersed with hisses, grunts, and clicks. Yet, as Zula told her, she understood its callous language. She remembered Zula advice that she could save the changeling's victim, so she allowed the mystery to take her.

"Go deeper," Rose whispered to herself and the strange ether carried her down. She did not resist as she tumbled deeper through the demon's mind, searching for a sign to lead her to Crimson's trapped victim.

The changeling's incensed brain sent phantasmagorias into Rose's consciousness. Crimson wrapped herself in a ball of hatred and regret. It spat and growled, berating itself for failure, crippled by fear. Crimson's anarchic nature was frightening. The changeling retreated into its past and Rose found herself an invisible spirit among hundreds of demons in a great cavern. A giant scarlet Kobalos goblin in flowing black robes stormed like an angry god about the coming war. Demon clans knelt at his feet. Wiry common goblins with gray or green skin, squat hobgoblins, ugly changelings, rock goblins with stony pale features, and so many more breeds of demons gathered to worship this new goblin king. Crimson worshipped this goblin king. This was Mordok, where the goblins dwelled beneath the earth.

At first, Rose shrank from the hideous visions. The roar of demons thundered and she covered her ears, squeezing her eyes shut to be away from this hell. How could Rose garner information to help if she could not find a cohesive thought?

Her body ravaged by a rising temperature and infection, Rose feared she would perish in this ravaged dream. What if she were trapped here forever? She imagined being dead and buried, but her poor soul cursed to wander in this devil's netherworld.

Her deliria expanded to her mother's spotless, sunny kitchen. Her mother frowned, crimping a pie and reprimanding her. "Foolish Rose! I told you so. Mother is always right. Girls should stay home and bake pies. Adventure leads to demons and death, but you never did listen to your poor suffering mother, you changeling child!"

"Don't call me that!' Rose shouted at her phantom mother. Since she was a little girl, her mother had used that spiteful epithet when she was a naughty girl. It always vexed Rose.

Then her mother suddenly transformed into Crimson, and the chortling, the grotesque gray-skinned demon looked ridiculous in a ruffled pink apron. "I much prefer yummy princess pie," the changeling tittered, shoving the pastry into the fiery oven. "Soon I'll dine on Rose Greenleaf pie! That's a plump morsel to saver. A bit fatty though." The changeling ironed out dough with a rolling pin that began to bleed red.

Rose recoiled from the wild monstrous hallucinations. "Stop it! Stop it! Stop it!"

Now was not to time to obsess about her mother or stray from the path. She began to hum a tune to calm her anxiety, an old habit she engaged in whenever she was distressed after a fight with her mother. Her anxiety softened and her concentration revived. She started to sing the *Raven Song*, a traditional folk ballad she learned as a child.

An idea evolved as she warbled, that the vanity of the creature might be charmed. She had the glam rhapsodé. But how could she use it? Zula had urged her to try. The legends always referred to summoning the magic through music. Rose only knew it involved more than singing, but how can she summon it? Rose recalled that brief moment when she charmed Albin and Fendrel in the woods, but she was scared and it was a defensive reaction to the trauma.

Rose delved into the ethers of demonic consciousness to connect to Crimson directly. She had no time to think of clever rhymes, but she could sing her words to the changeling.

"How clever you are Crimson," Rose sang. Nothing. She paused and focused, feeling the music and when she sang, something else happened. A warm tingle, rising from her core with airy grace, enchanted her music. Was this it? Was this the power? She continued, using her song to ask the questions. "So sly the way you stole the princess! You fooled us all. How did you do it? We are all so envious. You must tell us how you did it." She felt stronger now, able to stand the terror that walled her in this strange medium. She sensed Crimson's pride bloom with Rose's musical praise.

Images of Crimson's past fluttered into Rose's mind now as she hummed and its ego gloated over its many victories. Rose guided her to the more recent victory of Lilias. Infiltrating the kingdom was easy for the changeling. Crimson thieved the Princess from her own bed and bound her by sinister magic into a dreamless waking sleep first. Then Crimson lead an enthralled Lilias to a forsaken crypt where she was cocooned by the demon's own excretion of webs, spinning the silken, sticky material from its own finger pads until the Princess was mummified. Crimson clutched two amulets of small dark jewels on a chain. One she placed on the entombed Princess and the other it placed around its neck.

It was a cemetery, but which one? Rose directed her thoughts to Crimson directly, singing her questions.

Where is Princess Lilias?

Rose stumbled and suddenly found herself in the royal courtyard beneath the night sky. Crimson fled the palace in the darkness, hidden beneath the voluminous purple cloak. Rose recalled that damn purple cloak when she saw a woman running across the courtyard, when she was feeding the raven on her windowsill at the palace.

If only I had known what you were then!

Rose's chased the changeling's memory. It was oddly freeing for her consciousness to run alongside the swift demon on its night journey. The flight ended in a stark wilderness, choked with weeds and tall yellow grass. The changeling absconded for a gloomy ruined church surrounded by ancient graves overlooking White Thorn. Crimson sprinted up the steep peak to a ruined church, shrieking with joy, driving the small nocturnal animals to flee from its violent wail.

Rose dashed through the forgotten graveyard like a stubborn ghost, pursuing the changeling. Tombstones covered a weedy hillside, the timeworn stones etched with the names of the dead, so ancient now that some of the gravestones had crumbled into chalky memory of the dead they once marked. Rose watched Crimson beneath the moonlit sky, creeping behind the demon until it entered the crumbling chapel. The rickety place lost its sanctity long ago. Crimson rushed to a broken door in the floor that led to an underground crypt.

Her thoughts bound to the demon, Rose followed Crimson into the underground of rot and death to a forlorn crypt bed where a pale cocooned figure lay in blackness. The Princess was bound in a white death shroud and the red amulet a glowing grave marker set in dark gold. Crimson needed to return often to renew the link; else the spell would have been broken. The mystical bond was nearly severed because Crimson had kept the shrouded Princess enchanted for too long. Rose sensed the waning spell, like a dying song. She knew they had to act fast or the victim would die without mystical help. Crimson did not care if Lilias died. The demon only regretted it would not get to feast on her now. Rose shuddered, wishing she had not heard that. The changeling fled, and Rose was in pursuit. An ancient iron fence, bowed with time and weather, circled the ancient graveyard. She could not make out words in the darkness, but the moonlight shown on the image of a crow or raven wrought from the iron on the main gate.

The changeling's memory was shifting, shaking off the memories that Rose had woke. There was a terrifying shift that gave Rose pause. She was so focused on watching and directly connecting with Crimson, that she did not know that Crimson had finally become aware of her intrusion. Fury replaced memories and her gruesome face loomed; the eyes glinted, like black flames of hate. The images fractured into chaos again when Rose faltered. Rose was trapped and unable to free herself. She was weakening which each heartbeat as fever burned her body.

I'm dying.

Rose desperately fought to free her mind, but she remained trapped in its consciousness as its demonic visage snarled down.

A giant raven burst between them, bringing a rush of wind that hurled Rose across the abyss. Black sweeping wings and sharp talons forced Crimson back into the dark void. Rose was falling now, but the raven's swift wings caught her. Feathers soft and warm embraced her as the raven carried her away.

"Karta!" Rose gasped and opened her eyes.

Culain and Meg hovered over her, looking down at her as though she were past hope.

Rose sat up, head throbbing with fever, but coherent. "I'm not dead yet, so please shake off that mournful look."

Culain's strong hand was on her shoulder. "Lay back and rest. Your friends should be here very soon with the antidote."

Robert brought her an icy cloth to soothe her fever. Culain laid it on her forehead. For a brief second its coolness soothed her heated brow.

"Go to the graveyard," Rose insisted, trying to make them understand. "I think I know where she hid the Princess."

"How? What graveyard?" Aristide started. "There are many in White Thorn. How can that be possible you saw where?"

"I saw where Lilias is hidden. If I describe the place, perhaps you would know where to search. Find some city maps. I know it must be nearby if Crimson had to visit her often."

"Rose, calm down," Culain told her gently. "It was a just a bad dream."

"No! I can't be calm. The light of the amulet on Lilias has faded," Rose choked. "Lilias is dying. She will be lost unless you act soon. The amulet's link is symbiotic in some way. I don't know about dark magic. But I saw her—truly I did."

"Rose, can you describe what you saw?" Darius asked gently.

Rose struggled to get out of bed. "It was very old. Abandoned. Desolate. An old graveyard with an abandoned church."

Thera knelt by her side and pleaded. "I know Karta is watching over you. She guided you to this knowledge. Tell us how to save Lilias. But if you harm yourself, you will both be lost forever. Rest little one. Trust us to listen."

"Bring another cold cloth," Culain whispered. "She's burning up."

Robert Silverberry added ice to a bowl of water. "Coming sir," he answered.

Rose closed her eyes and told them the detail of the gravestones, the years that were still etched on the gravestones, and the ruined church. The underground crypt. Her detail was vibrant and precise, for her recall was always perfect. She described the crow's sculpture on the cemetery's broken gate.

"I think I know this place," Aristide exclaimed with surprise. "That's Crow Hill. The decrepit old church on top is the old Holy Spear of Ursas chapel, located on the east edge of the city. It was abandoned over three hundred years ago. As the empire grew and expanded, it became largely forgotten as the city grew and took different directions. It's the oldest cemetery in White Thorn. We told ghost stories about it even when I was a boy."

"A lot of local folk believe it's haunted. We should go now, Your Majesty," Meg said, "with your permission of course."

"I'll ride with you," Darius said.

Culain glanced at Darius at nodded, "Go be a hero and save the captive Princess. I'll take care of Rose."

"Your Bardess possesses great bravery and is a credit to your house." The Emperor looked down at Rose. "I will pray for your recovery." He turned to Meg. "Commander Sparrow, you may stay here with your friend of you wish."

"No, Meg should go," Rose insisted. "She's so good at rescue. She rescued me from slavers my first day here, you know."

The Emperor marched away with an escort of guards, with his son at his side.

Meg squeezed her hand before she left. "Don't you dare, die," she threatened.

Rose noted Culain appeared to be heartened as Aristide and Darius left side by side. Thera, ever vigilant for rescue of her royal charge, followed them. Rose wanted to go with them, but she collapsed back on the pillow, fever consuming her.

Rose turned to Culain. "You were the one who planned the trap for the changeling, yet you gave Darius all the credit."

"It helped Aristide to see his son in a different light. As an Ambassador, that is what we call establishing good diplomatic relations."

Incessant taps on the window glass from outside alerted Rose.

"Damned birds!" Robert complained.

"What is it?" Culain asked.

Robert grumbled, "I'll shoo it away."

"No, let it in," Rose gasped. "I think it's Owena. Skullcap must have sent her."

Robert opened the casement window and an irate crow flew inside and landed at the foot of her bed.

"Owena," Rose laughed. "Did Zula send you?"

Culain carefully approached and the crow patiently waited as he untied a small vial the crow had carried. "It's a potion bottle."

"Owena is such a good crow," Rose whispered. "Skullcap's crow for the crown."

Culain uncorked the blue bottle and gently lifted her head. Rose swallowed the potion and then laid her head back on the pillow.

"See," Rose said. "Magic will make it all better soon. Tasted just like honey too. I'll be better after a nap. Then I'll have quite a heroic poem to compose. Do you think Belenus will be proud of me?"

"Of course he will," Culain assured her.

In about a quarter hour, Zula and Skullcap ran into the room. Owena flew over to her ranger and perched on his arm.

"Did she get the potion?" Zula asked. "This palace is like a city. So huge. We knew it would take too much time to walk from the Emperor's apothecary, so we sent Owena on ahead with the potion just in case."

"Yes, we received it," Culain answered. "Now what happens?"

Zula went to Rose. "Rose will sleep. We will wait and pray. We should know before morning."

"I wonder if my parents have my letter yet," Rose said. "I didn't tell them about being kidnapped of course. It was such a long journey here from Stone Haven," she murmured in her delirium. "I walked you know," Rose whispered, fever consuming her. "I walked here all the way from Rhulon."

"That's quite a journey," Culain said. "I would love to hear the tale."

"I have so many new tales to tell, songs to write," Rose murmured. "My mother won't be proud though," Rose uttered bitterly as she drifted, a tear welling in her eye. "I always burned the pies."

"Hush child," Zula whispered. "Sleep."

Rose dreamed of ravens watching over her.

Chapter Twenty-Three

Nashim sat at the rickety table with a metal bowl, mixing soap and water into a foamy mound. "I was worried you would come back with a black eye this time," Nashim laughed. "Your former wife has such a volatile temper." Nashim stirred the frothy soap in the wooden mug and creamed his black scalp with it. Then he took his dagger and carefully and quickly shaved his head.

Mathias watched him shave with careful and swift precision. "I don't know how you do that without a mirror or without cutting yourself to ribbons."

"Practice. A lifetime of soldiering in the field, boy. You do or you perish. I do, however, miss the luxury of my wife doing this is for me, but she is beyond my reach right now. I miss my wife. I miss my daughters. I console myself that they are safe in another land. Tell me, Mathias, is your conscience appeased now?"

"Yes," Mathias nodded, sitting on the narrow bed. "We can go back to Shadulai now."

Nashim carefully scraped his left scalp and wiped the blade. His ebony skin glistened. His large dark eyes glinted at him as he shaved. "We did not get weapons, but the king's agents agreed to cash, with the condition there is no mention of them helping us. That will buy us weapons. The King was preoccupied today. Apparently there is some changeling running amok. They tried to keep it quiet, but I heard some servants whispering in terror."

"Well, at least we will leave with something. Maybe we can build that army and regain our homeland. We can finally bring down the king."

"Remember, I served that crazy man until he started to think of people as kindling. He was once a good king, but bad religion and curses twisted his mind. But I agree, now is the time to rid ourselves of King Josiah. To remove a bad king you need a lot of swords. You need support of other realms, money, and men to fight it. Are you done in White Thorn now?"

"Yes."

"Your martyr obsession was becoming dangerous, you know."

"I just needed to see her."

"She obviously did not feel the same way."

"That's my burden."

"There is a great deal of burden now. None of it is going to get better until we remove that madman from the throne. You coming here was a mistake. A time waster, Mathias. We need to get back." He rinsed the dagger and smoothly shaved the right side of his head. "I have men to recruit and train. Bargains to strike for food and weapons. Rebellion is demanding work, Vicar. Did you at least book us passage on the ship?"

"Yes, of course. I took care of everything."

"Good." Nashim wiped his freshly shaven head with a damp towel and stood up. "Let's find somewhere else to eat. I need some good ale and a hearty dish of beef. The food here isn't fit to be pig swill."

"I'm not hungry," Mathias replied. He fingered the burnt silver wedding ring on the chain around his neck like a talisman.

# # #

Meg maneuvered Fayre through the broken headstones on Crow's Hill. She galloped up steep rocky ground toward the ancient derelict chapel on top of the mound that shone like a lonely ghost beneath the full moon. "Best to stop here, girl," she whispered to Fayre and the horse stopped, bobbing her head up and down, anxious. Meg tried to calm her down, stroking her mane. "It's a bad place. I don't like it here either, but we won't be long."

Prince Darius reigned in his horse at her side, "This place does look haunted."

Meg jerked back her hood and dismounted Fayre. "It's a cemetery. It's supposed to look haunted." Fayre was still agitated and Meg stroked her head soothingly to calm her.

"The horses are nervous here," Thera commented, alighting from her horse with smooth grace. "Even I sense the aura of wickedness here."

"Blame the changeling for that." Meg approached the open entrance, a black hole with broken doors, with care, noting the rotted beams and the collapsed roof. The other riders, a handpicked team of warriors, including a wagon to carry the Princess, dead or alive, arrived. Meg immediately began handing out orders. "Set up a circle of defense around the chapel. I want four men to accompany me inside to look for the Princess. I want the Emperor and the Prince guarded at all times. We have no idea if the changeling has friends lurking inside."

"I'll come with you," Darius volunteered.

"I'm coming too," Thera added. "You can't stop me, so just accept it." Her defiance brooked no refusal.

Meg's temper splintered with their bravado. As warriors, they were both mere amateurs and it pricked her temper that Darius or Thera thought they could cope with any unforeseen trouble. Her distress about Rose rattled her mood too, but she kept her tone tethered. "No, Your Highness, it's not fitting to risk your royal person in such a reckless manner. If the Princess is within, I will bring her out to you. Trust that. We have no idea who else is inside either. And Lady Thera, the danger from a building in shambles is hazardous even without demonic influence. Plus you are wearing silk slippers."

"I am High Priestess of the Elemental Temple. Demons and ruins don't scare me, Commander."

"As your Prince, I must overrule your orders," Darius told her. "So I'm going with you. It is only right that I be part of this. Lilias is now my betrothed and I owe her my protection."

Aristide, calming his own agitated horse, walked toward them, scowling. "What is delaying us?"

Meg turned to him and bowed. "Your son is determined on endangering himself. He is being stubborn, Your Majesty."

"I must do this, Father," Darius insisted. "It is only honorable that I save her."

Aristide's face was inscrutable, but Meg detected a trace of humor in his tone. "Commander Sparrow is correct, but I will permit this, Darius, but if you get hurt or eaten by a demon it's on your head. However, I do sanction Commander Sparrow with full power to decide on how you will proceed once you walk into that church. Understood?"

"Yes, Father."

Meg bowed to Aristide's decision. He had always been a fair and admirable man, and she owed her career to him. She turned to Darius with a severe look. "Your Highness, when we enter, you do this my way. I will precede you for your own protection, and your rear will be covered by two guards. Also, I charge you to protect Lady Thera, though I doubt she really needs it. Now follow me."

They lit lamps, knowing it would be too dangerous to take torches into the decrepit building. Meg ventured inside the chapel first, followed by the others. Cobwebs covered everything, and the old religious house was a jumbled pile of broken timber inside. Thin beams of moonlight lit fragments of stained glass scattered on the ground.

"It smells revolting, but I don't see any evidence of animals or birds nesting here," Darius commented, holding up his lamp. "Not even bats."

Meg lowered her lamp on the altar and looked around. "Not for a while. When the changeling used this old shrine as its lair, they must have fled. Animals don't like demons and any living here cleared out when Crimson came to roost."

The entrance to the underground necropolis was found easily enough, just as Rose described, but Meg paused.

Darius crouched next to her. "What's wrong?"

"Demons are tricky. I was just wondering what traps that thing might have left for any intruders. If you have a valuable hostage, you want to keep it protected from outside forces."

"In this desolate place it may have felt secure," Thera suggested. "But then changelings are also stupid."

Meg pulled up the creaky door in the floor that led to the underground crypt and pushed it back. "All right, let's rescue a princess." She handed Darius her lamp. "Hold it over the entrance so I can see my way down better. Don't drop it on my head."

The stone stairs were crumbly but silent as they descended. The stench of dark magic escalated as they descended into the catacombs

"Even with the lamps, it's too dark to see anything," Thera commented.

"I can fix that," Meg sighed. She conjured three shimmering ball of lights, casting a soft blue-white glow as they hovered in the air. The brightness did not make the tomb less grim, but they could move through the rank crypt without tripping on something.

"Nice trick," Darius complimented her.

Thera's green eyes scrutinized Meg with fresh curiosity. "You're a witch?"

"Yes," Meg replied simply.

Thera shook her head in wonder, deftly stepping over a fallen skull. "A warrior witch is a potent combination, yet you do not vaunt your talents. In my kingdom, your caste would be ranked high and you would be greatly valued."

Meg shrugged as she treaded carefully through rows of bone beds. "I am valued, but I prefer my sword to speak for me. But I thank you for the compliment."

They walked through the ossuary, stacked with finely carved stone crypt beds that lined the walls. Not even a rat was heard scuttling. The lights reflected on the tombs that cradled the rich patrons or noble families of the past, but their funeral finery was lost to time ages ago and now only remnants decayed fragments of moldy cloth clinging to skeletons, remained.

The changeling's profane incantations contaminated a sacred keep. Meg sensed the magic in the room, but more than changeling dark lingered here.

A pale shadow shimmered ahead, human-sized and it matched the cocoon Rose described from her vision. Meg paused and raised her hand for them to halt. "Wait. I found her."

Thera rushed to the white shrouded shape laid on a stone crypt, garnished with only a small red amulet that had ceased glowing. "My poor Lilias," she cried.

"I said WAIT!" Meg grumbled.

"Now what do we do?" Darius asked. "The amulet isn't glowing. Do we tear it open?" He leaned in and whispered so Thera would not hear. "Is she dead?"

"We don't know that," Meg replied quickly. "First, we get the princess out of this hell pit. We'll take her to Zula at the palace. She will know what to do."

"Can you do anything, Meg? You have magic and-"

"This is magic far beyond my skill, Prince. Be quick and take her outside."

The warriors jumped to her orders. She knew they were uneasy touching the changeling's cocoon, but they lifted captive Princess with care. Thera followed them out.

Deeper into the shadows, a shimmer caught the corner of Meg's eye. "Stay here," she commanded Darius and approached with care, hand on her sword.

Darius followed her.

She stopped her tracks. "What did I say, Your Highness?"

"I'm sorry, but it looks dangerous. You need someone to watch your back." Darius did not retreat but stayed at her side. "Curiosity has been a lifelong fault."

Beyond the crypt beds, a corner of the filthy tomb was swept clean of refuse and bones. Meg cautiously approached, her spheres of light following her. On the floor lay a broad circle of obsidian glass framed with red ochre that faintly shimmered in the shadows.

"What the name of Ursas is that?" Darius asked.

"I'm not sure. Maybe an altar," Meg whispered. Kneeling down, careful not to touch the red ring around the mirror, she gazed into its stygian ripples that shifted to liquid shadow.

She backed away and unsheathed her sword. "More than changeling dark lingered here. Get behind me."

"You do love to give orders," Darius complained.

"Call it my contribution to the Crown's succession. I'm keeping you alive." Meg picked up a stray bone and tossed it on the altar. The circle whirled and the red pool flared with sorcerous light. Her balls of light burst and disappeared. "We're leaving. Now!" Meg backed away and headed back to the stairs.

"What was that?"

"Trouble," she said sharply, pushing him toward the murky exit. "I'll post guards here to make certain no one touches that thing until Zula can examine it."

Outside, they were carrying the cocoon to a wagon. She heard Skullcap shouting from a distance. Distracted by the unknown sorcery in the tomb, she shook it off and turned to see him riding up the hill.

"Meg!" Skullcap shouted again, waving to her. Zula was with him to, clinging for dear life. They quickly reached the chapel and dismounted.

Meg's fists clenched and she ran over to them. "Is it Rose? She's not dead?"

"Rose still lives," Zula wheezed, trying to get her bearings. "Such fast riding made me breathless! She is alive. Culain and Robert are watching over her."

"Of course," Meg said, relieved. "She can't die. She knows I'd never forgive her."

"Rose is sleeping. She drank my potion, but we will not know anything until morning if I was in time. That's all we can do now. She's a very special girl."

"That's why she gets into trouble so much," Meg said dryly.

"Zula, why are you here?" Darius asked.

"I'm here to help, Your Highness. Take me to the victim," Zula demanded. "If she still lives, we need to get her out of that thing now, but we cannot just rip her out of it."

"The amulet's glow has vanished," Meg warned in a whisper.

"We need to hurry then," Zula replied.

Meg unsheathed her dagger, but Zula shook her head and stayed her hand. "No. This must be done the witch way, Meg. Watch and learn."

They led Zula to the wagon where they had laid Lilias' entombed shape. The bizarre image of a giant cocoon was unnerving, as though a monstrous moth would emerge. Zula climbed into the wagon with Skullcap's help. Thera and Darius stepped away, mere bystanders now as the mage invoked her witchcraft.

"Releasing a victim from the changeling web must be handled with great care," Zula said, examining the husk with nimble fingers. "It could kill her otherwise. I pray she still lives." Zula whispered words, which Meg recognized a little from her mystic tutelage, which had gone quite rusty. It was the old magic tongue from her people's country. Meg's body tingled with the familiar essence of Zula's witchery.

"Now give me a knife," Zula commanded, holding out her hand.

Meg passed her the dagger and Zula made blessing signs over blade and the silvery cocoon. She removed the amulet and then she carved the shell carefully with the shape of a heptagram, a seven pointed star.

"What's she doing?" Darius asked.

Thera shushed him with an unforgiving glance.

"Without the magic ritual, we risk killing the prisoner." Zula chanted a few mystical words and then she cracked the cocoon like a watermelon with her fists and swiftly peeled off webby sections of it, revealing the human captive within.

"Does she live?" Thera cried.

The young flaxen-haired girl in the broken shell lay still as death. Pallid and frozen, she was unresponsive. Zula listened to her heart. "She is near death, still bound by dark enchantment."

"Can you help her, witch?" Aristide asked.

"I'm trying!" Zula closed her eyes and mumbled rapid words. A bright blue nimbus covered her hands, then she touched Lilias' chest and mouth. Lilias briefly glowed with blue light then shuddered, followed by a deep intake of breath.

"She lives!" Zula exclaimed and sat back, relieved.

Darius and Thera joined Zula in the wagon. Zula shucked more of the broken cocoon off the wagon. "Filthy changeling web! Bad magic. Very bad. I want that vile shell burned until nothing is left but ashes."

Lilias gasped and opened her eyes. Terrified, she gazed at them, but was too weak to move. Tears flowed down her cheeks.

"It's all right, Princess," Thera cried, soothing her. "You're safe now."

A faint voice emerged with great effort. "Where am I? Where is Prince Justin? What's happened to me?" She turned her face away and wept harshly. She was not a princess now, but a frightened girl.

Thera and Darius exchanged knowing glances.

"Tell her nothing yet," Thera cautioned. "I will take care of it. She is my responsibility."

"The Princess is truly restored to us?" Aristide asked.

"Yes, Your Majesty," Meg answered, jumping down from the wagon. "Thanks to Zula and Rose, we have Lilias back.

"Thank you Meg," Aristide whispered. "I knew I could rely on you. And Zula, you shall be richly rewarded."

Zula bowed her head, a smile curling her lips. "Your Majesty is generous."

"Walk with me, Commander," Aristide ordered in a low voice.

"Of course, Your Majesty," Meg replied.

They only hiked a short distance from the others. Aristide spoke in soft tones so they could not hear. "This could have gone badly. I feared explaining a dead princess to King Krell of Uragon. Without you, and your friends, we would be planning a war, not a wedding."

"Conflict seemed to have been the changeling's plan. It is odd though. Invoking political strife and war is not the normal pastime of these creatures," Meg replied. "Why? They are just pathetic parasites. There must be other forces involved."

"A friend of mine was recently telling me the same thing," Aristide commented. "I believe him now. Looking into secret conspiracies can be dangerous. You saved my life once, Meg, and I do not relish risking yours. But I trust you. I may be sending you on a journey for a new assignment, Commander."

"I will be ready," Meg bowed.

He walked back to the others. "Transport Princess Lilias back to the palace and see to her care," Aristide commanded. He mounted his steed and raced away.

Darius ran down the hill and shouted after him. "Father, where are you going?"

"To execute a changeling!" Aristide shouted.

Chapter Twenty-Four

Weary of screaming and weakened by drugs, Crimson could only moan her misery when they thrust her into a cage and loaded her into a wagon. She was so cramped she could barely move; not that she could, since they kept her in the weighty barbed netting. She was wound into it like a spiny cocoon. Guards surrounded her in the back of the wagon. They drove fast to the edge of the city where the prison loomed. It was an archaic building constructed during one of the earlier imperial regimes, constructed of black stone to instill despair and warning. She glimpsed the barren prison yard, void of grass or trees, as they carried her inside. She liked its grimness, but not the fate that awaited her within.

Within the bleak penitentiary, the guards of this human jail did not wear polished armor or fine crafted leathers like the palace imperials. These men were hardened wardens in stark black uniforms who carried whips and swords to maintain order. Men even rougher and harder, criminals of all ranks from thieves to murderers were stabled in his keep behind iron bars. Crimson could smell their violence.

They did not lock Crimson in one of these ordinary cells, but conveyed her cage down many winding steps to the prison's old dungeon. They dumped her in the center of a cavernous room. Imprisoned with no chance of freedom, she now waited for death as a dozen stony-faced guards mutely stood watch over her.

Crimson studied the dismal chamber. It was surprisingly large and barren of any furniture or torture implements. No other jail cells were this deep underground. This room was different. Only barren brick walls with a few torches on brackets burned here. It would be her death place. It would become her unmarked grave. She sniffed traces of blood that lingered from the past.

Heavily armed guards lined this pit watching her, but none dared touch her. Crimson shivered in the cold cell. Pain pulsated throughout her body. Gashes from spears left her weak and shaky. The drugs made her sleepy. Her wounds still seeped, but no one offered to bind her wounds or help her, even if they wanted to. Changeling was the enemy they despised; well, she despised them even more. She weakly cursed in her demon tongue until even that became a strain. She sank into wretched self-pity and embarrassment. Not only was Crimson a doomed prisoner fated for a gruesome death, but she still wore fragments of the ridiculous puffy sleeved gown she took from Rose's wardrobe. Crimson would die dressed like the village idiot. She sighed, better to die here than at the punishing hands of her master, Morziel the Hobgoblin King. He would not only slaughter her, but he would roast and eat her.

Exhausted, Crimson fell into an uneasy sleep marked by strangely vivid dreams. Images of her past danced in her slumber. Her nightly escapes to the old cemetery to renew the bond with Lilias and the secret lair in the underground tomb, peppered with long forgotten bony tenants. The memory of her master, Morziel, spoke to her through the enchanted black pool. The trickery she had played on the humans, the murders she committed, invoked joy. All these happy memories bubbled to the surface in the freedom of her dreams.

Then Crimson sensed something nasty in her dream- a ray of wretched light staining her dark comfort. Rose Greenleaf was with her in her dreams! She was singing! Ugh! The effect of the voice was so strange. Everything became hazy until Crimson reasserted herself. How could this be! She refused to have dwarf girl contaminating her dreams. The intrusion angered Crimson. She raged at Rose, pushing her back into an abyss. A monstrous raven appeared, majestic and powerful, spreading her black wings wide in anger, shielding Rose. The raven barred Crimson from touching Rose Greenleaf. Infuriated, Crimson fought back, but the raven swiftly attacked without mercy, hurting her with nasty, sharp talons.

Voices stirred her to wake, and most of the dream's imagery fractured when she opened her eyes. Fragments floated in her brain of ghostly haunts, Rose Greenleaf, her nemesis, and an angry raven. Why did she dream of Rose? She hated her. In her declining will, she lay there for what seemed hours, fearful to sleep lest the raven come back to kill her. She knew they would kill her soon. At least Lilias would die. She at least had that satisfaction over her enemies.

Crimson was so involved in mourning her future demise and gloating over Lilias, that she vaguely noticed when the men began to whisper and scurry like rats. Someone was coming. Her executioner perhaps? Maybe it would be a swift end.

Emperor Aristide strode into the chamber. The men bowed their head in obeisance, but did not take their attention off of her. Crimson hissed at his arrival.

Aristide smiled callously at Crimson, but kept his distance as he circled her cage. "You failed, Changeling. Princess Lilias is alive, thanks to some very brave people and good magic, despite your efforts."

Crimson twitched with disappointment. "How could my prisoner Lilias live? How? Her hiding place was so secure. The amulet's enchantment was dying!"

"Her secret crypt was found. She has been saved by light magic."

Then Crimson recalled her dream and how the stupid dwarf girl was there. Maybe it was not a dream! "Rose Greenleaf did this to me! Ugly dwarf must be magical in some way. I should have known. She resisted my breath of sleep. Wicked, sneaky dwarf tricked me!"

"That upsets you, Changeling?"

"Princess not matter now," Crimson mumbled, looking away.

"I would interrogate you, but that is too tricky. Your blood has disturbing effects on the human body. Minions never know much anyway."

Crimson's inky eyes flashed at Aristide. "I'm too deadly too touch."

"It does not matter. Your guilt is confirmed. I know you're a murderer, many times over. I'm going to execute you myself. Fortunately, demons are not entitled to trials, only death. You killed innocents, for which you must die. You assassinated my son, Justin. For that there is no reprieve, no mercy."

"Then kill me, human," Crimson spat. "End my misery."

"Gladly," Aristide agreed.

"Fortunately, this ancient lower dungeon is no longer used. My reign as emperor has not made a habit of torturing people, so this torture chamber has fallen into disuse over the years. It's a room no one will miss. Best forgotten, like you. I know better than to touch you or risk letting you out, even to run a sword through your wretched body or to cut off your head. I want to make sure you die. I also want you to suffer before death takes you to Hel."

The Emperor's gesture summoned men who carried jars of oil. They poured it over the cage, the thick fluid dripping through the bars, coating her with the flammable liquid. Crimson wailed, tangled in her barbed net, knowing what end the cruel emperor planned for her.

"You're going to burn me alive!"

"I'm going to incinerate you until not even ashes remain."

The guards put down the jars and departed, fleeing up the stairs.

Crimson panicked and wailed, "Not fire! Please! No fire! Please have mercy!"

"No mercy," Aristide declared, seizing a burning torch from the wall sconce and hurling it at the cage. The flames ignited the fuel soaked floor. Aristide stayed long enough for the fire to engulf the cage before he walked away and slammed the metal door shut. Crimson screeched with agony as flames cloaked her immobile body.

Then the flames vanished. Crimson howled, but the fire was snuffed out in an instant, leaving only smoke and heat. Crimson suffered severe burns, but was not consumed anymore by the raging fire. She huddled in her prison, in pain and confounded. Maybe she was dead? Maybe death took poor Crimson away? This was not Hel? She was still locked up too. Why? Crimson sniffed the air, which burnt with fire and something else more powerful. Magic! A strange, aphotic magic coated the air. A familiar mystical singe lingered in the air that Crimson recognized from her pilgrimages to the old crypt where she contacted her master and held Lilias captive.

A willowy figure appeared, cloaked and hooded in shimmering scarlet. Shaken, Crimson feared this strange apparition and the mystical scent that emanated from it. A slender, fair human extended a hand, and the burdensome net fell away and the cage door opened. Eager to flee, Crimson crawled out of the cell, relishing this malevolent chance at life and revenge. She stared at her mysterious liberator. The red-draped body gracefully approached her.

Crimson salivated, eager to feed. Hungry to heal the burns that wracked her body. This was a foolish human to be so kind to her! Crimson snarled and jerked forward, seizing the hand of her rescuer. *So crazy to help me*, Crimson thought, but her spells were useless on this stranger. Her magic could do nothing! Something frightened her when she gazed up at the stranger. The being before her was so alien. The hand she touched was filled with power and magic so sinister that terror overwhelmed Crimson. She withdrew her clawed hand, shivering. Not demon. Not human.

The stranger pulled back the concealing hood, revealing narrow, delicate features, iridescent white skin, long silver hair, and black eyes that glittered like diamonds.

"You cannot exist," Crimson cried, shrinking back from her savior.

"You know what I am, don't you?" the stranger asked, his voice honey smooth. "You cannot copy me nor harm me in any way. You will never spell me into sleep. You cannot touch me. I am immune to your petty powers."

Crimson cowered in her burnt rags, rocking her head back and forth. "No! No! You cannot live in this world. You were banished in the forgotten times."

"Name me, Changeling!"

"You are *Siabur*," Crimson sputtered, head bowed in fear. "*Shadow Fey.*"

"Yes. Very good. You do know what I am, don't you, Changeling? I am Siabur, among my many names and titles. It is nice to be remembered, even by a parasite like you."

Crimson nodded violently. "How can you be here in this world? Siabur died in ancient war."

"That is not your concern. We once ruled this world, eons ago. Humans and demons have called us so many names throughout time, all to describe what you cannot possibly understand. But the names fey, sprite, and elf are not of my kind. We are antagonistic cousins to them. We were stronger. We were the first mage race. Older than the fairy races people still sing about. Siabur no longer reside in this realm, though it was the place of our origin. Nor did we all die."

"How are you in this world?"

"That is a long story that you will not hear." The Siabur touched Crimson's head, as though giving a benediction. "I saved you from death, Changeling. You belong to me now. You will obey me from this breath, forever."

Crimson nodded quickly, afraid to look at him.

"Good. You know you must, for none of your kind would be in this world if it were not for my ancient race. Now you must look at me, slave."

Crimson reluctantly gazed up into his black eyes.

"I need a pet to spy for me," he responded softly.

His words were so strong. Compelling. Enthralled by his magnetic presence, Crimson was now unable to look away from his austere beauty. A frightening thought interrupted Crimson's veneration. "But my master, the goblin king Morziel, gave me commands."

"I am your *master* now," the Siabur avowed. "I have always been your master. I sent you to White Thorn. I am the dark lord in the mirror who has guided you, tested you for the honor of serving me. I am your God. It was destined. Accept it."

"Yes," Crimson surrendered, bowing in supplication.

He stroked Crimson's head gently and the changeling clung to its new savior, weeping.

"What do I call my god?" Crimson whimpered.

"You may call me Lord Fallon, pet," he offered.

"Yes, Lord Fallon."

"Now go, seek out a victim from the criminals above and prove your worth. Feed on them with abandon. Be furtive and slip from this prison. Do not return to Mordok."

Crimson hung her head. "But I failed to bring you Rose Greenleaf."

"I will forgive that. It is best she learn more about her rhapsodé. It is so frail and unpredictable, a magic driven by emotions. When she is ready, I will take her myself."

"Where do you command I go, Lord Fallon?"

"Travel southeast to the desert kingdom of Hazda."

"But there are so many guards here. How will I escape the prison?"

"They are all returning to their standard routine. The Emperor is riding back to his palace. They will not expect you. Go. Prove you are worthy to serve me. I have enemies, as do you. Cling to that as you strive to live."

Crimson's face twisted with hatred. Yes, she had many enemies to slay, especially the Emperor, Culain Ironheart, and that damned Rose.

"I forbid you to seek out your personal enemies now." It was as though he could read her mind, but then, Fallon was a god. "Many kingdoms will fall when shadows return to this world. Rose Greenleaf, however, is special. I may need her in the future. She must not be harmed, for now. Revenge must wait, my pathetic pet. Go to your freedom and be grateful your god watches over you."

Fallon knew her secret thoughts. Gods know all things. Then Lord Fallon vanished and Crimson was alone.

The heavy iron door was open. Her god saw to that. She crawled up the stairs, her scorched flesh an agony. So many flights until she smelled the prisoners, licking her lips. She kept to the walls, using her changeling magic to meld into the background and scuttle past guards.

It was late and most of the prisoners slept fitfully. She passed an isolated cell where a smelly human was sprawled on a dirty cot, snoring loudly. No guard patrolled this corridor right now and the cell opposite was empty. She tapped the bars eagerly to wake her victim. Touching the only remnant she still had to shapeshift, a strand of Rose Greenleaf's hair, she transformed, but was a sad image in her scorched and torn gown.

The man started and jumped up when he saw her. "Tiny woman!" he croaked. "Why are you here?"

"You know me?" Crimson asked.

"Albin knows tiny woman!" he barked, anger propelling him from his bed to the thick bars and thrusting his hands through, choking her. "They're sending me to the mines. For life! They gave me a life sentence because of you!"

"Then I will take that life," Crimson laughed, welcoming his hands around her throat. She grasped his neck and licked her lips with human craving as her eyes shifted to black fathoms.

Albin screamed.

Chapter Twenty-Five

Impatient, Beleth of Mordok watched for moonrise, cursing time and its crawl. She loathed the light as any goblin would. Cursing it with vehemence; wishing for the blackness of night to banish the sun. Swallow it with a brutal hunger. Beneath her sandaled feet was the deep underground cavern of her home, a magnificent fortress hidden from the upper world of sky and sun, a dominion of darkness; safe from human eyes. She loved Mordok's harsh landscape; delighted in the flames and gases that spewed from cracks in the earth. It was demon country. A land of fire and blood made for all the demon clans, led by the goblins.

The long days of spring hindered her pleasure for going outside. Goblins of most castes could endure the sun—but abhorred its light. Beleth longed for the bleak winter days of hunting. Not that she needed to hunt for herself, for she was hatched with the markings of a queen, chosen to be the mate of the goblin king. Others waited upon her, but she often hunted for pleasure.

The day gradually faded, deepening the blue sky. The chill of coming night prickled her skin and she pulled her fur cloak tighter around her shoulders. The tunnels were always warm, thanks to rivers of magma running deep beneath the mountains of her home.

But in truth, her impatience was for an important event. *Her wedding.*

At last the sky darkened to black and the moon rose in the night sky. She retreated back into her haven of tunnels and walked to her private chambers. Her old slave, Crone, awaited her. Crone was a pale, twisted creature of rock goblin caste with coarse gray skin, cold to the touch, and a withered face and beady black eyes. In contrast, Beleth's skin was red as blood and hot as flame.

Beleth dropped her cloak on the stone floor. "It is moonrise, Crone, time to prepare me for the ceremony. Do not dawdle."

Crone disrobed Beleth and anointed her crimson flesh with sacred oils while Beleth stared at her reflection in a polished copper mirror. Her handmaiden laid out the sheer black spider silk dress, embellished with flecks of garnet stones and a long train woven like a spider web. Slaves had spent weeks weaving her wedding garment. It was magnificent. The dress required no jewelry to enhance its perfection—only Beleth.

"This is an important night, Crone. I was hatched into a world of foul humans who fear us, force us to live hidden away. Dwarfs, Tall Folk, and Giants waged war upon us, all but annihilating our demon clans centuries ago. Since then we have secreted ourselves away in the earth, scavenging like vermin in the pits. Now is the time to rejoice, for the goblin kingdom grows strong and proud again. The new goblin king, Morziel, is fierce and shall lead us all to greatness."

"We bless this dark day," Crone chittered, stroking the pretty material of the dress. "You will be the most haunting of brides."

Tuffs of whitish hair bordered the slave's wizened face, causing Beleth to wonder if Crone had ever been young. Her curiosity about the old slave vanished as quickly as it came, and she returned to her chief concern. Herself.

"Morziel's coming was foretold long ago by our seers. Now that he is chosen as King, I can truly fulfill my destiny as queen. His mother will pass the crown to him at our mating ceremony. Then a new and wicked age; an age of misery and terror shall arise, and I will bear witness as Morziel's wife and queen. It will be the humans' turn to suffer. The old gods, the Grim Gods, trapped beneath the ocean of chaos shall be released and this world will be reborn; anointed in fire and blood."

"Yes, My Lady," Crone kept her head bowed, gnarled fingers struggling to fasten the delicate fabric laces. "How does King Morziel plan to set the Grim Gods free?"

"That is no concern of yours, slave. It is enough to know he shall do so and I will be at his side. When the dark primordial gods are released, we shall become gods ourselves."

"Thou art already a goddess in mine eyes," Crone whispered lovingly.

Beleth grinned, revealing sharp fangs. She permitted herself a moment of pity for her servant and stroked her head. Common rock goblins were lowly creatures, suited only for slavery or fodder on the battlefield. The impish Crone was annoying, but had been her personal slave since the day she hatched.

Beleth returned to her mirror and admired her reflection. Heavy forehead ridges, accentuated by the thick black brows that swept upward like raven wings above ebony eyes. Her nose and jawline were strong and proud, and her cheekbones prominent. Mottled red skin, burnished like night fire, was truly enhanced by the black gown. Her dark eyes glittered and hair writhed with tiny living serpents sprouting through the black and thickly twined arrangement. Only the most superior female Goblins of the Kobalos breed had this highborn trait; true nobility.

Beleth smiled, satisfied she looked flawless.

The goblin clans all considered her demon beauty a perfection of the race and an honor to her clan. Many of the noble bloodlines were exterminated by humans during the last war, so when Beleth hatched from one of the great dark clans, she was treasured above all others.

The old queen had hatched many goblins in her lifetime, but only Morziel bore the mark of kingship. How the clans cheered that day! Beleth hatched shortly afterward and the seers proclaimed her to be the proper mate for Morziel. From that moment to this, she was kept pure for him alone. She was made for a king and none dare touch her but *him*.

Crone gently tugged at her hem and with head bowed, waited for permission to speak.

"What is it?" Beleth demanded, annoyed at the interruption to studying her reflection in the polished copper mirror.

"It is near time for the ceremony, blessed Beleth," Crone whispered.

Without reply, Beleth swept from the stony chamber and walked the long winding corridors of the rocky tunnel to her destiny. Crone straggled after, stooped and head still bowed, scuffing across the stony floor as best she could keep up.

Beleth cared nothing for any ill-treatment she might inflict upon her handmaid. The worship and loyalty of all underlings was her birthright, as chosen of the shadow priests, and the hardship of servants was a privilege due her. Now, it was time to fulfill the most important part of her birthright, to become Queen of all the goblin clans!

The entrance to the underground temple was guarded by two giant scorpions, rare, large as horses and savage, their foot long stingers certain death to any who dared trespass.

Beleth strolled past the two scorpions without the slightest hint of fear. Crone scuttled behind, whimpering as she held aloft the train of Beleth's fragile gown. It seemed to the old goblin servant the horrible creatures actually bowed at Beleth's passing.

Sconces made of bone were set at regular intervals along the corridor walls. The torch wood had been dipped in sacred fire salts before being lit it so each crackled with a deep red flame.

The pungent odor of incense grew stronger as they neared the sacred temple. Coming to a giant archway, with carved images of demons and terrible goblin gods set deep into the stone, the flickering torchlight seem to cause the effigies to move.

She entered the vast temple and welcomed the attention of all eyes fixed upon her glory. At the black stone altar, goblin demon priests prayed. Tall and menacing in their frayed black robes, festooned with chains, bones, and amulets as they swung iron globes smoking with incense in rhythmic arcs. Beleth strode regally toward the altar, and her chosen husband, certain every goblin here envied Morziel.

The hundreds of goblin clans gathered here to witness this ceremony were really here to partake of the coming celebration feast of moss wine and real meat instead of gruel and bugs. They were savages, born of the dark caves and hell pits of Mordok, hiding from light and the world. That would change when they rose to war. Besides the gathered goblins, there were the ogres, changelings, and trolls; lowly castes compared to goblins, yet permitted to witness this most sacred and important rite.

Crone left Beleth before she reached the altar, taking her place with the slave caste of huddled rock goblins. In the center of the raised altar, two royal figures waited. The ancient Queen Mother, Gurza, direct descendent of Raziel the Fallen. Though her back was crooked with age and her face a death mask of age and infirmity, Gurza's eyes still glittered with the fury and bloodlust of a true queen.

Beleth imagined her in the glory of youth and felt a flicker of envy, which was mollified by her aged face and broken body. Gurza had ruled for many long years until a new leader at last hatched. Now, at this appointed time, she could finally rest.

At Gurza's side was her son, the chosen one and Beleth's husband, Morziel, the Goblin King. Towering over his mother like a god, he stood more than seven feet tall; molded of fire and night. Beleth worshipped him. Her heart raced, longing to be his forever. Keen to savage and kill side by side with Morziel and bring rightful darkness to the world.

Morziel was garbed in black robes, inscribed with sacred runes and wore bracers strapped to his massive wrists; stitched of human flesh, dyed black with pitch and adorned with bloodstones. How else should such a king stand before his subjects?

None but Morziel could ever humble her to such obeisance, falling at once to her knees and prostrating upon the altar steps in rare humility.

She remained for countless breaths until his booming voice at last broke her genuflection.

"Rise, my bride in blood," he commanded, "Take my hand and be bound to me forever."

She obeyed, standing proudly as she grasped his hand, his claws piercing her skin. She faced him on the altar as the priest offered a cup of blood for them both to drink from. After the dark priest consecrated their union, they faced the old queen and bowed as one.

"Morziel, you are now King of all the goblin castes," Gurza proclaimed. "And you, Beleth, are his Queen. I have ruled and kept the clans secreted for too long. Hidden away from humans, suffering in the darkness. My time is done. My blood has thinned with age and grief, yours is young and burns as fire. Go forth and set ablaze the world above. Reclaim the world."

Gurza removed her bronzed crown and offered it to Morziel, who placed it on his head without hesitation. The throng bellowed their approval, the beating of sword and thundering drums swelled. Morziel raised his mighty hand and all fell silent.

"Beleth is now my queen," Morziel decreed, and the dark priest handed him a smaller, delicate circlet of bronze. "I bestow upon you this crown. From this day, you are mine. Our blood and hearts will blaze as one before the Grim Gods."

Her snakes danced like joyous handmaidens as he set the circlet upon her head. She smiled broadly for her new husband, her fangs sharp and enticing his lust.

The newly crowned king took the ancient sword of his Goblin ancestor, Raziel, from the priest and raised it high in triumph. He declared to all the goblins and creatures in this sanctorum of shadow, "My rule will mark a rebirth of blood and fire for all the clans. We will rise. We will kill. We will conquer. This time we will destroy all the humans of this world."

Shrieks of bloodlust shook the massive temple.

Filled with the same savagery, Beleth wallowed in the moment of rapture, but deep within her mind, a vision flashed with a dark revelation, shattering her joyous mood. Beleth foresaw a black seed swirling in an ocean of chaos and fire, imprisoned by the Kraken and rings of blinding light. Could this be the Grim Gods? Did her vision bear fruit of their salvation form the Light? The Kraken, fearsome warrior angels of her enemy gods, Ursas and Ishar, guarded this celestial prison alerted to the threat. She despised these servants of the Light. Beleth winced, the bright glare unbearable as she stood within it and she was terrified of the blackness within, though she worshipped it since birth.

Something in that darkness had awakened, stirred by an ancient power she had yet to name. In the distance, another figure in scarlet robes with white hair and black eyes, observed the Kraken and their prisoners, as though patiently waiting. She sensed his primordial power. He frightened her as much as the Grim Gods that swam in the vapors. Beleth barely grasped what she was seeing as the Kraken raised their fiery blades in response to the unseen shadows stirring in the forbidden vortex.

It should have made her happy, this dark and ancient power rising against the light, but instead it filled the new goblin queen with foreboding.

Hours later that night, she suffered nebulous dreams of that strange man in the red robes. A snowy mane of hair framed sharp, pale features and his black eyes full of ancient power. He was standing before the goblin armies and they bowed to him, even her husband! She jerked awake. Beleth knew who was in her dreams and felt doom fill her very soul. They were legend among her race, for they once served them! He was a Siabur. Shadow Fey. They were banished from the world millennia ago after a mystical battle with the Light Fey. Death always followed the Siabur. Death would take them all.

Chapter Twenty-Six

"Gerta, come quickly!" Jack Greenleaf shouted, walking into the kitchen. "Come see this!"

The kitchen was a hard place to be these days. Every shelf and counter seemed always jammed with breads, pies, and cakes from Gerta's daily baking. Peony helped deliver these goods to the needy and the church.

"Who was it at the door" Gerta mumbled, without pausing from her bread kneading board. "Is it Peony? She knows I don't want to see anyone right now. Tell her she can pick up the pies later for the church social. I just want to be left alone. I have so many things to do."

"Gerta, it's a letter. It's important. Stop and listen!"

Gerta beat at the dough with her fists. "Is it from Rose again? Her last letter was lacking."

"No, but I think we should stop this silence nonsense and write to her."

"Never," Gerta swore. She attacked the bread dough with the rolling pin, crushing it across the board. "All that dreadful wait and worry; not knowing if she was dead, or worse. And what does she write to us? Hardly anything! One meager letter! That's all. And me being worried sick for weeks."

Jack braced himself. His wife's turn of phrase often bothered him. What could be worse than *dead*? For weeks now, ever since their daughter ran away, he could not get Gerta to make sense. She rarely slept, and neither did he. The constant worry over Rose made him feel his years and he left the smithy, more often than not, in Simon's hands.

To Simon's credit, he had not let what happened damage their partnership. He was not a bad boy; he just was not right for Rose. He should have realized that. Everyone should have realized that, including Gerta.

Now Jack had just received a letter by special post. The letter received carried the Ironheart royal seal. He did not know whether to be glad or afraid. Jack glanced up from the mysterious dispatch, to see his wife continuing her tirade.

"One would think a so-called bard could write a better letter to her suffering parents," Gerta complained. "Rose flees a perfectly good marriage to do what? Work in a tavern like a common servant! She could have been married good and proper to Simon—but that was not good enough for Rose! She runs away like a criminal and abandons her family and tradition for a selfish whim. That girl will worry me to death! Ungrateful child! Changeling child!"

"GERTA!" Jack shouted, startling his wife into silence. With Gerta's mouth momentarily closed, Jack took a deep breath, and held up the letter. "This was just delivered by a *royal messenger*. It has the royal seal, Wife! And look at the special water stamp. That means it came by ship first. A private, not a regular postal, messenger delivered it to our door. This is important."

Gerta paused from her ferocious bread kneading to look at the golden letter with the red wax seal. "Why would we receive a royal letter?" she whispered, putting floury covered fingers to her quivering lips. "What could this possibly be about?"

"I suggest we read it and find out," Jack offered dryly.

Jack considered it to be a near miracle that his wife chose to forego an immediate opinion on this unusual occurrence. For weeks, since Rose ran away from home, her mood had been fragile and he tolerated the erratic behavior, hoping Gerta would work through her anger and disappointment.

The amount of baking and cleaning she had done these last weeks was gargantuan. Never stopping from dawn to dusk. Giving away pies and cakes she baked to anyone close at hand, because the kitchen was too crowded to contain them. The house sparkled like some enchanted fey cottage; smelling of roses or lemon oil, depending on which room you dared to wander into. Of course, upon Gerta's standing orders, he had to take his shoes off on the porch so as not to dirty the floors she scrubbed daily.

Jack seized a butter knife from the counter, wiped it on his trousers and carefully broke the seal, as though marring it too badly might be treason. He deftly unfolded the letter. Not even he was prepared for its contents.

"Well, what is it!" Gerta cried. "What does it say?"

Jack's eyes skimmed over the letter, and gasped. "It's from the Prince!"

"What prince? A real prince? You're not serious, Jack."

"An Ironheart prince!" Jack added gruffly.

Gerta's brow creased with wonder and at last pressed, "Well, which one? The King does have fifteen children! Or is it fourteen?"

"It's from Prince Culain Ironheart. I believe he is the youngest prince. You know that Queen Fiona has blessed this land with so many heirs the bishops actually want to make her a saint."

"That is true," Gerta piously agreed.

"Prince Culain says that upon receipt of a letter from an old family friend, and former Royal Bard to the house of Ironheart, *Belenus Aylecross*, he discovered the location of Rose Greenleaf in White Thorn. He has her safely in his employ as a bard in his household. Prince Culain! He is the new Rhulonese Ambassador to Tirangel, but he says he is returning to Rhulon for official business for his father, King Grimkel."

"Rose is working for the Prince?" Gerta gasped. "One of the Ironhearts! Are you sure?"

"I can read woman!" Jack protested, clutching the letter to his chest. "And he also says Belenus actually knew the king! You never believed that!" Jack sniffed and resumed his reading, squinting to read the elaborate script in the fading afternoon light. "Not only knew him, but Belenus is apparently a close family friend and was confidant to King Grimkel for years."

Jack refrained from reminding Gerta how gravely she insulted a friend of the king, deciding to save it for an opportune time when it might carry some weight. This was too good. He loved his wife, but her opinions and forceful demands had all but ruined the Greenleaf family. He wanted Rose settled, but by pushing the marriage, and turning his back on her, he had lost his daughter. What Rose did was wrong, yes, but he was partly responsible for this wretched mess.

"Well, go on," Gerta insisted.

Jacked cleared his throat, allowing time to find his place again before continuing.

"The Prince says Rose was previously in the excellent care of a kindly tall folk family and has friends of good and noble rank. Members of the Imperial Rangers, who protected her and saw to her safety in this large city. She had managed to incorporate her bardic talent with the humble job of waiting on tables at the 'Red Boar' Inn."

"Waiting tables," Gerta harrumphed. "A common serving girl!"

Jack deliberately paused until Gerta quieted again before reading further.

"Rose was found unharmed and healthy, her honor and good name intact. Her work for the tall folk family was 'wholesome and respectable,' the Prince assures. He adds that Rose is now safely at the palace in White Thorn under his care, as his official Bardess."

"Is that a real title?"

"Would an Ironheart lie? Prince Culain goes on to say Belenus had praised her talent, but when he saw her perform and learned how truly gifted Rose was, he thought it best to bring her into the care of the Ironheart family. Such a talent should not be claimed only by the tall folk, but by her own people."

"He praised our Rose?"

"Again, let me finish! The Prince ends the letter with, 'So fear not, dear Greenleaf family, I shall watch over her as Belenus requested and keep her safe from harm.'"

When he finished the letter, Gerta seemed, for what seemed to Jack the first time since knowing her, speechless. He neatly folded the letter, put in his pocket and went to the foyer for his overcoat. He took one of the freshly baked apple pies.

"Jack, where are you going? It's almost dinner time."

"I am going to see Belenus, Wife, and I am going to apologize for any insult we have given him."

"Jack you wouldn't!" Gerta begged.

"And I am going to thank him for interceding with the King to help our daughter. After I make peace with the old bard, I am going to invite him to dinner tomorrow night."

"That old man caused us nothing but grief since he moved here last year. Filling my Rose's head with all that barding and adventure nonsense. That's why this all happened! It was all him! How could you even talk to that man?"

Jack lifted his hand and gently put them to his wife's lips to silence her.

"'That man' likely saved our daughter's life. She is now protected and in safe hands. We *will* thank Belenus for that; you will thank him tomorrow night, should he choose to accept my apology and our invitation.

"Rose is not like other girls, Gerta. She has always been different. Trying to force her into someone she wasn't would have broken her. I only agreed to that damned wedding because you insisted. Simon is a good boy, but he and Rose were poorly matched. I think she would have left us one day, no matter what, to pursue those foolish dreams; but it would not have been in the middle of the night, and not in secret, if we had just let her be!"

Jack opened the door, balancing the pie with one hand. "Rose is alive, thank Ursas and Ishar. You should also offer a prayer of thanks. And then think about dinner, wife, but please, stop the damn baking."

# # #

Belenus crammed his leather satchel with clothes, boots, journal and his writing utensils. He belted the straps closed and prayed the bulging bag would not explode. He chose his second favorite lute to take along. He carefully slid the lute into the soft leather case, patting it affectionately and calling it my name. "Fear not, Mathilda, you're my new favorite." He always appointed his lutes with feminine names, for they were much like women, mysterious and demanding.

He gave Rose his favorite lute when she ran away. What a crazy night that was! He still didn't know what possessed him to this day to leave her the instrument that night.

Gerta was a storm determined to have her daughter wed, even to a big oaf, to breed grandbabies and to avoid the brand of spinster. Frankly, he never understood the appeal of babies. They were undeveloped and messy tiny creatures who smelled. Children were not interesting until they began to read and think for themselves.

Most girls would have surrendered to their parent's stern decree of matrimony, but he knew his Rose was made of stronger metal. She fought to the bitter end. Belenus wavered when he heard she had agreed to the marriage and hoped it was a ruse to give her time. The night before the wedding, he crept around like a thief in the night. He left his lute for Rose leaning against the house gate. If she was going to run away, this would be her last chance to do so. He prayed Rose would not submit to her mother's will and marry the big onion boy, Simon. He waited in the dark for hours, his butt sore from sitting on the damp chilly earth, hidden behind a yew tree on the hill. He still had the grass stains on his trousers. He was not sure if she would truly leave her home, but she did. Rose needed that instrument if she were going to make her way in the world. He also suspected her parents might probably hide Rose's lute away as punishment, especially her mother, Gerta. So he wanted Rose to have his lute, if she were brave enough to take it.

He almost burst with pride when he watched Rose quietly leave the house dressed as boy and carrying her satchel. She found the lute and his letter, and she accepted the gift without a glance backward as she walked away. He should have tried to warn her about his suspicions. That she had the gift. He was not sure. Now he was, thanks to both Rose and Culain's most recent letter. He would be able to help Rose soon enough with the glam rhapsodé.

Of course, after she left home, Belenus worried like an old hen about Rose. That's why he wrote to King Grimkel. When he received Rose's letter from White Thorn, it made things easier. He was still relieved when Prince Culain found her. She was in White Thorn and apparently scrappier than he ever imagined. The reports of the changeling attack disturbed him. He would learn more later when he was back at Rhundoran Keep. Despite his latent feelings of guilt over sending her alone into the world, he was proud of her. It was mad of Rose to run away of course, but youth was the time to be mad.

Belenus was years past his own mad juvenescence and considered a man of *venerable years* now. Belenus detested that term. It brought to mind creaky bones and wrinkles deep as the sea. Even the word venerable sounded dull, like he was already decrepit and gumming his porridge.

He searched his cramped home one last time, fretful he had forgotten something. He cleaned out the cupboards so mice would not completely infest his cottage while he was gone. He swept the floor. He had his bag of gold tucked in a special belt he wore under his robes. What had he missed?

He cursed and dropped into his musty velvet chair, exhausted. Age assaulted his body and mood. He loathed feeling so *venerable*. Maybe he would be gumming his food soon? Travel was simpler and easier when he was a young man living on the road, before he became a housebound antique. As an unencumbered boy, he possessed only a knapsack and his prized lute, without so much as a copper penny in his pocket. Too many sentimental artifacts of life wrapped in memories weighed heavy now in his gray years. It was damned indulgent of him to become so complacent and lazy.

Someone knocked on the door, infringing on his sulking.

Now what?

Irritated, he shouted, "It's unlocked," and stuffed his pipe and tobacco into his pockets. "And if you're Mrs. Butternip, go away! I'm not accepting any students, including your tone-deaf son."

Jack Greenleaf cautiously walked in, carrying a pie. "Good thing I'm not Mrs. Butternip."

"Ah, Mr. Greenleaf."

"Call me Jack." He handed him the pie. "I brought a peace offering."

Belenus graciously accepted the edible gift, and realized he had forgotten something today. He forgot to eat! The pie tin was still warm to the touch. He sniffed the rich pastry and the intoxicating aroma of baked apples bathed in sugar and cinnamon filled his nostrils. "Thanks, Jack. Ah, apple pie! My favorite sin." He squinted at Jack and whispered, "Gerta didn't poison it, did she?"

Jack laughed, "Only with her thoughts."

"Well then, Jack, come on in and sit. How's the smithy doing?"

"Simon is running things pretty well. I have more time for fishing. I wish I could say I missed the work more."

"I heard that boy has a new sweetheart. How's your wife taking it?"

"She's coping. Gerta is still baking too much. Frankly, I'm surprised there's even a bag of flour or sugar left in the village. But thank you, for looking after my Rose. I'm glad she is safe."

"I worried too. I'm sorry you had to be concerned for her. But it turns out she is tougher than either of us imagined."

"I heard in town that you're leaving us for a while."

"For such a small village, folks here can spread news faster than a hummingbird. It's true, Jack. I'm going to visit Rhungar for a spell. I'm going to see your daughter there. The Prince is returning on royal business and bringing Rose with him. Coach should be here in a couple days. Reminds me how much I hate to pack. Sit yourself down and share a drop of whiskey and a piece of pie. Don't worry. I won't tell the wife."

"Don't mind if I do."

Belenus poured two whiskeys into ceramic mugs that were almost clean. He cut two large slabs of pie and grabbed a pair of forks. They sat sipping spirits and blissfully eating pie for a few moments in silence.

"Is Rose going to Rhungar too?" Jack finally asked.

"Yes," Belenus confirmed. "She is accompanying Prince Culain as his official Bardess. You know Jack, if you want me to take anything to her, I'm happy to do it."

"Thank you," Jack replied, drinking down the whiskey and putting the mug down on the wobbly table. "Rose is special, isn't she?"

Belenus looked at Jack evenly. "That she is."

"It's not just because she can sing, is it?"

"No, Jack, it's not. Don't fear for our Rose. I will watch over her, but don't ask me any questions, at least not yet."

His inner thoughts still tormented him. Should he tell Jack his daughter had the ancient bard magic? That she had the glam rhapsodé. Only a handful of bards in history possessed it. Poor Rose did not even know she had this gift when she ran away. Neither did he, not for certain. Now he did and he had to help her through it.

"Keep her safe then. I will ask that of you."

"Done."

"And since you're not hiking to Rhungar, would you mind taking her lute as well? I just want Rose to know that we love her."

"I will," Belenus agreed quickly, fearing an outpour of parental recrimination. He chuckled, pouring more whiskey for them. "Me? Hike to Rhungar? Those fine days and strong limbs are long gone. My poor old hips would never carry me there now. My days of wandering are restricted now to coaches with padded seats." He ate another forkful of pie and shook his head appreciably. "Do compliment your wife for me. This is scrumptious pie. I'd compose a song praising her baking, but she might get the wrong idea."

"I will. I must compliment you on this whiskey too," Jack said.

Belenus chuckled and poured more of a potent brew, which had been a birthday gift from Grimkel a few years ago. "Then have a drop more, Jack, and thank the Gods for wonderful whiskey that eases painful joints and lifts life's sorrows."

Chapter Twenty-Seven

Rose's bright blue gown was the essence of spring, though the low cut bodice was a bit daring. A personal gift from Empress Isabeau, she insisted it was modest enough. Rose even put up her hair with Sally's help and tucked in a few white flowers, but she was sure it would fall no matter how many hairpins she used.

"You look lovely, my dear," Empress Isabeau smiled, tying blue satin ribbons to her wrists. "And this is the latest court fashion, or so my young ladies tell me."

"Really? The ribbons as bracelets are quite pretty and so simple."

Isabeau laughed as she made a small bow. She still dressed in mourning for her lost son, but she smiled more easily now. She inspected her charge with a careful eye. "Perfect. Ah, you are so young and pretty, Rose. Enjoy it a little. When you arrive in Rhungar, please send Queen Fiona my best. I have a letter for her, if you would be so kind as to carry it. I assume it will be safe in your hands?"

"Of course, Your Majesty," Rose replied earnestly. "I will deliver it her myself."

"Wonderful. As queens, we have always kept an eye out for each other and our families. It appears that times have become even more dangerous. Aristide tries to protect me, but I see what is happening not only here, but in the world. Be careful, Rose."

"Your Majesty has been so kind to me these last two weeks," Rose said. "I'm going to miss you very much."

"And I'll miss you dearly, along with your lovely songs. You must promise to return to us soon. Know you will always have shelter with us, should you ever need it."

Rose was moved by her genuine affection and bowed her head. "Thank you, Your Majesty."

The Empress had been the soul of motherly concern (minus the nagging) when she was convalescing. She visited Rose each day, oversaw her treatments with Zula and the court physician, and made sure she had every comfort. Isabeau also devoted herself to helping Thera nurse the frail Lilias back to health. Her recovery was much slower.

Isabeau opened the curtains and sunlight streamed into the room. "The weather's perfect today for an outdoor reception too. The palace gardens are blooming with flowers and there's just enough breeze to offer a gentle balm. Now, let's go welcome our guests. Remember to mingle and smile."

Rose resisted the urge to check her hair before following Empress Isabeau to the gardens.

The party was an official farewell banquet for Culain, who was returning to Rhulon on urgent family business; that urgent family business of course was about the rising goblin army. There were rampant rumors about changelings and Princess Lilias, but no one openly spoke of the incident.

Outside in the lush palace gardens, it was indeed a paradise. Tables covered with snowy linen brimmed with fine wines and a buffet of delicacies. Rose was anxious to sample the goodies too, even if her dress was a bit tight. She wished she could kick off her shoes and run barefoot on the green grass.

"You look quite frilly and feminine," Meg whispered from behind.

"I'm so glad you could make it," Rose cried happily, hugging her. She surveyed Meg's elegant dress uniform, which looked much more comfortable than her fine dress and the corset Isabeau insist she wear beneath her new gown. No one ever expected you to wear a corset if you wore trousers. It was a good thing Rose did not have to sing today.

"I've never been in the middle of so much pomp and nobility," Meg laughed. "Will you miss the court and its luxuries?"

Rose shook her head. "I will miss some of the people, of course. And the food! But pomp is not really for me. Prince Culain didn't want an elaborate show for his departure back to Rhungar. Empress Isabeau wanted to give us a party to reward us for rescuing Lilias and capturing the changeling."

Meg nodded in agreement. "It's probably better that way. Aristide doesn't want to announce to the world a princess under his care was kidnapped by a changeling. But how are you? I haven't seen you in a few days. Any recent visions or glam episodes?"

Rose laughed and shook her head. "No, thank Karta. I can still speak changeling and apparently my glam magic is raw and needs training, according to Zula. It will take a long time to learn to deal with it."

"That frightens you."

"Yes. My magic is weird, to say the least. It's one thing to read about such things, but to actually have the magic, is different altogether. With the glam rhapsodé, you do not weave the usual spells or sorcerous implements of magic. It's more complicated."

"You've been studying, I see."

"I had little else to do when I was confined to my bed. Legends are full of tragic tales of bards with this ability. Talasyn was one of our great bards who wielded this cursed gift with great power, but even if he did not suffer, he had a bizarre end. No one knows how he died or when. They say the Fey carried him through the veil that separates our worlds, but how much of legend is fact and how much is pure myth? At least I will see Belenus when I return home." Rose paused mid-step. "That feels so odd to say. Rhulon does not feel like home now. Neither does White Thorn."

"You think too much," Meg laughed, fetching two little stuffed pastries filled with meat and spices from the table and handing her one.

Rose bit into the pastry, careful not to spill on her new gown. "At least my headaches are gone. It's strange to learn that I am basically a demon detector now because of my ability."

They walked pass Lilias, who sat between Empress Isabeau and Lady Thera, eating chilled fruit. Pallid and weak, Lilias leaned against her pillows as a servant waved an enormous feather fan over her. Though occupied with her royal charge, Thera flashed a warm smile in her direction and Rose returned the greeting. She studied the differences between the soft blonde and the steely dark woman, finding it strange to imagine Lilias and Thera were even from the same kingdom.

"How is Princess Lilias doing?" Meg whispered when they were out of earshot.

"She's still recovering, but at least she's out of bed. Zula said it was a miracle she survived at all. She may not be as frail as we suspect. I feel sorry for her. Zula thinks she was trapped in that cocoon for weeks. Darius sees her every day, but it's hard for them both. He thinks she's still mourning the loss of Justin, his brother. Darius is so shy."

Emperor Aristide and Captain Nerlis were talking beneath a shady an oak tree. When Aristide summoned Meg over, she excused herself for a moment and joined them.

Rose wandered the garden among the other guests, though she did not feel like mingling. She greeted Robert Silverberry in passing, who sat beneath a shady tree, sipping a cordial, ignoring the court as he relaxed. He had been so caring during her recovery. He was not cranky with her even once.

The sundrenched gardens beckoned Rose. She retreated from the elegant reception to enjoy a moment of solitude in golden sunlight, just far enough away from the others to be secluded among a grove of flowers. She welcomed the soothing embrace of quiet nature away from the gathering. She closed her eyes and imagined her favorite stream and woodlands back home, banishing the darkness of the past days to the far corner of her mind. Rose remembered hot summer days of hiking and fishing with her father, whom she missed so very much.

Time softened the sting of her father's betrayal. Rose received a letter from her father yesterday. He wrote of familiar little things and wished her well. He referenced her mother's love in the letter, but Rose knew too well the bitterness of her mother's feelings from years of recriminations and endless battle. There was no forgiveness from her mother yet. It was a fate she must accept, at least for now. Her father's letter was warm, tenuous, and full of unspoken feeling and regret. She cried when she read it.

Rose sensed someone near and turned around, shading her eyes against the noonday brightness. Prince Darius was standing there.

"Your Highness," she curtsied.

"Please, you never have to curtsy to me, Rose," Darius insisted genuinely. "I didn't mean to disturb your privacy. I just wanted to say goodbye and wish you a good journey."

"Thank you, Darius. I never liked goodbyes. Too final and sad."

"Then I will just wish you a good journey."

"How is Princess Lilias faring? I am glad to see she is at least out of bed."

"The doctors say it will be some time before her strength is fully restored. The witch Zula has brewed some droughts to increase her vitality, which seem to help her. She does not remember anything though."

"Perhaps that is for the best."

"Father agreed that we will postpone the wedding until her health is fully restored."

"That will at least give you time to get to know each other."

"I agree. Frankly, I'm also a little relieved. I haven't prepared myself to be married just yet. Not that I find her repellent, it was just so unexpected to be engaged. How does one fall in love?"

"I can empathize with that," Rose laughed. She blushed when she recalled the crush she had on Darius when they met, but decided to keep that her secret. "The sudden prospect of arranged matrimony surprised me too when I was in Stone Haven. My mother decided on a husband named Simon for me. He smelled like onions and hated music."

"A grim fate indeed. What did you do?"

"I ran away. It has been hard for my parents, I know. I should have just kept refusing to marry Simon. I was impatient. In truth, they could have dragged me down the aisle, but they'd never make me say 'I do.' I don't regret coming here, even though I was kidnapped by slavers and attacked by a demon. I've made great friends and achieved more than I ever imagined."

"I wish I could run away," Darius whispered.

"Running causes it owns troubles."

"Perhaps. I sometimes wonder if Lilias ever wanted to run away from all of this."

"Maybe, but you'll never know unless you ask her. That's the trouble with political marriages. The heart is never involved. I have happily noted that she's less shrill than the changeling version of her. Thera told me Lilias was a little frivolous, but was never cruel or selfish. I think Crimson's personality seeped through the mask after so long pretending."

"Come to think of it," Darius laughed, "the changeling was strangely pushy as Lilias. The real princess is so different. I know she's sad, but I cannot find a remedy to make it better."

"Lilias suffered a terrible shock. She must be very lonely, even with the formidable Thera at her side."

"I wish I could help her. Thera Sule does not make it easy either. She oversees our visits like a mother hawk ready to pounce, talons first."

"She's an unusual woman," Rose laughed. "But if you get on her good side, I think you'll find that you have a strong ally."

"I will consider that a personal quest."

Rose knew she was fortunate. Escaping wedlock caused her trouble but in the long run it was worth it. She regretted the pain she caused, but not the freedom. A prince would have a far more difficult time escaping an arranged marriage than a commoner.

"You're a courageous woman, Rose. The bravest person I have ever known. Lilias would have perished in that forgotten tomb with no one to know, if it hadn't been for your sacrifice. You saved her life. You risked so much to recover a stranger without reward. That's what makes you brave."

Rose shook her head, flushed and a bit embarrassed. "No, I'm not so brave, truly. I was terrified the whole time. Whenever I think about it my hands itch."

"You are fully recovered now, I hope?"

"Oh yes. I'm guess I'm too tough to defeat, even by a changeling."

"Still, your life was imperiled. That upset me, Rose."

"So was being in the changeling's mind."

"What was that like?"

"Bizarre and terrifying. I know Crimson is dead, but I feel like she is still out there. I saw such wicked creatures in her memories that would frighten hardened warriors. The goblins are raising an army. That much is true. Culain did not seem surprised by this. But there is something more that haunts me. I cannot name it and that troubles me."

"What is it?"

"It's just a shadow in my mind. Something dark watching me, but then, my imagination was always too ripe, according to my mother. Never mind all that. I hope you will write to me."

"Of course I will," Darius promised.

Rose brightened. "I would like that. A lonely bard always has need of a friend."

He kissed her hand, and answered earnestly, "I would never turn from you, Rose. You will always have my friendship and devotion."

"Now go sit with Lilias and bring her some cake. Cake always makes me smile."

After Darius departed, Rose could not bring herself to return to the festivities. Instead, she walked away from the gaiety.

Culain met her on the path and greeted her with an exquisite white rose, grinning ear to ear. "A rose for a Rose."

"How long have you been waiting to say that?" she replied dryly, plucking it from his hand and breathing in its fragrance.

"Since I met you that night at the Red Boar, so I think I deserve an enormous amount of credit for my restraint."

"If I do, will you answer one question for me," Rose bargained, looking him in the eye.

"If I can answer it, I will."

"You did not discover me at the Red Boar by chance, did you?"

He sighed and shook his head, resigned. "Alas, in life there is no such thing as coincidence and I never believed in chance. Belenus wrote to my father when you ran away. Since I was coming to White Thorn anyway, he asked me to find you. Believe me, it wasn't that hard. A young Rhulonese girl coming to White Thorn alone, and then becomes a key witness in an imperial criminal case against slavers was not exactly secretive. You also worked in a local tavern I often frequented during my visits here. It was not a grand quest, even in a city as large as this one. Belenus is an old family friend who wanted you safe. He was just concerned, knowing how cruel this world can be. But when I heard you sing that first night, your talent was far grander than I imagined. But then, crusty old Belenus would not tutor just anyone. I offered you a position in my household because of your talent. You have other qualities too."

"As a potential spy to train? A bard with the rhapsodé magic?"

Culain guided her gently away from any eager ears that might lurk nearby until they were safely alone. They walked a narrow path between immense oaks. "You're still free to refuse my proposal about the secret matter. Being my bardess will keep you busy enough, but what I do for my family is risky. If you don't want to remain in my household, I understand."

"I will admit that I'm a little frightened by it all," Rose conceded. "That you're a spy, that I have a strange new magic that I can't control, and this darkness that seems to be looming. What I saw in Crimson's mind left me shaken, I will not hide that."

"If you weren't apprehensive, you would be a danger to yourself and to the Crown."

"That's the thing, isn't it? The danger already exists. You told me Rhulon may be threatened by it. Not just by an invading army, but something more sinister. There is a new goblin king and they are preparing for war. There is something else too, a shadow I cannot name, but it has haunted me since I was in Crimson's mind." Rose was torn by duty and fear, but also attracted to the thrill. Perhaps something was wrong with her? "When I was still recovering, you admitted you were a spy for the Crown. Why tell me that?"

"Because I trust you, Rose. If you serve my house, you would be at risk too. I don't declare this to just anyone. To many, I'm Culain, the roguish prince who dresses in bright silk suits. The indolent royal awarded aristocratic posts by his disappointed father to keep him out of trouble. Not even my brothers and sisters know what I do for Rhulon. I feel I can tell you the truth, and it will be safe."

"You live in two worlds. That must be hard for you."

"I'm good at it. I've convinced Aristide to join Rhulon in a private alliance. I call it the Cabal of Light. It's not about conquest, but a genuine experiment to keep kingdoms at peace. I know there is trouble looming. What you saw confirms my suspicions. That's why I am good at my job. As my bardess, there will be times when you will be entrusted with vital information. Some things are too risky to put to pen and paper. Plus, the glam powers you have will be of great value to Rhulon. Your gift is rare. I just hope it doesn't hurt you."

"The rhapsodé frightens me more than espionage."

"There is a genuine danger in my profession, Rose. Because of that, think hard before accepting my offer. There is no going back once you start down that path. It's a nebulous existence to be trained as one of the Raven's Eyes."

"Things change. When I left home, I wanted to be a bard and free to see the world."

"Then be that and stay safe," Culain encouraged. He handed her an envelope with a blue seal.

Rose opened the enveloped and nearly cried when she saw what Culain offered. "It's from the White Thorn Bard Academy. They are offering me a place with them beginning this summer with full tuition paid and lodgings at the academy, with you as my official benefactor. You would do this for me?"

"You deserve a chance for happiness and freedom."

She looked into his eyes, usually so candid and gay, now tinged with sadness and longing. She could not leave him now. From the moment they met, he vexed and challenged her. She could not imagine being away from him now. She only knew she must stay with Culain, no matter what. But what did he feel? Dare she ask?

Rose was haunted by the memory of Thera's views on castes. Caste was important to her culture, and was it so different for her? What was her place in the world? She still did not want to marry. Yet, she felt bonded to Culain, but was hesitant to use the word *love*. She could not express her feelings in words and she was a wordsmith! Rose was not born of royal blood and Culain was a prince from an ancient line. She was a common girl who broke from tradition to pursue freedom as a bard. Culain was a prince who lived a life outside of his caste as a spy. They were both outcastes in a way. No matter what their beginnings, Karta has put them both on the same path together. She would follow it.

Culain took her hands into his own. "My life is dangerous. I could not bear it if you were hurt again. The academy was your dream. Stay here and be free, Rose. "

"It was my dream, but I had the best bard master in the world-Belenus Aylecross. I realize now he gave me more than any academy could offer. I have been gifted with something more important that I can offer my people. You know it's true, even if I try to run from it, the magic will follow me along with its danger. I freely want to stay and offer you my talents, if you still want them."

"When people learn of your ability, it will make you a target for unscrupulous people. I swear by Ursas and Ishar that I will protect you."

"I know you will. I trust you too. I just hope Belenus can help me with this magic that I do not understand."

"There are too may mysteries of late," Culain said grimly. "What Zula found in that crypt was dark magic more powerful than any changeling could conjure."

"We're all in jeopardy. I would rather fight evil than be oblivious to it."

"Gods, you're so young and so terribly stubborn. Also, your hair is tumbling down."

Rose's hands flew up to her head. A few long locks had escaped the pins. "These are all faults I can't change. I would rather help the side of right than turn away. Just promise you won't tell my mother. I don't think she could adjust to me being both a spy and a bard."

Culain grinned, a rogue again. "Then welcome, Rose Greenleaf, to the Cabal of Light."

Chapter Twenty-Eight

The cold sea wind nipped at Rose as she waited on the deck, bouncing up and down to keep warm, despite wearing her woolen cloak and scarf. Digby and Becky Crofton hugged her goodbye before turning to Meg with fresh tears.

"Now Becky, please don't cry," admonished Meg.

"I can't help it," Becky wailed. "I feel like I'm losing two more daughters."

"You're not losing us," Rose assured her. "I'll write so often, you won't know I'm gone."

Digby put his arm around Becky to comfort her. She blubbered uncontrollably against her stout husband, wiping her eyes with a damp hanky. Even dour old Digby flushed with sentiment, his lower lip quivering.

"Well, I'll be praying for you both. Be good girls now," Becky sniffled, handing her and Meg large baskets overflowing with foodstuffs for the voyage.

She looked through the basket, filled to the brim with cheese, apples, bread, oatmeal cookies, and a small bundle of oranges and limes. "By goodness, these are amazing. I could live on this for days!"

"Not the way you eat," Meg teased. "You know they will feed us on the ship, but these are wonderful."

"The oranges and limes will prevent the scurvy," Digby informed her.

"Thank you so much, but I don't think we'll be on the ship that long," Meg said, smiling.

"They're still good for you," Becky told her. "I've also included a packet of special tea from the apothecary. He swears it prevents sea sickness."

"He charged you a high enough price for that packet of weed too," Digby complained.

"Oh, stop being such a skinflint, Digby. The man swears it will ease even the most severe seasickness," Becky protested.

"Good to know,' Rose grinned. "Thank you. I've never sailed before, so being prepared is a good thing. I'll miss you both so much. Thanks for giving me a home. I will always be grateful for that." Rose felt her eyes welling and blinked back her tears, knowing it would unleash a fresh flood from poor Becky.

Skullcap and Zula arrived just in time to say goodbye. Owena was perched on Skullcap's shoulder, cawing loudly. Rose secretly hoped Skullcap and Zula could find love again. She also prayed Zula had truly tamed her tempestuous temper.

Zula rushed over and hugged her tightly. "Goodbye, little Rose." Rose was comforted by her scent of cinnamon and sandalwood. "I just know the Rhulonese court will be at your feet! Just be safe and stay away from those nasty changelings!"

"I shall definitely do that," Rose laughed.

Zula wildly threw her arms around Meg, embracing her with gusto. "My life is so tragic. How can I lose my dear friend, Meg? It's so cruel. Despite my deep sorrow, I wish you bright luck. May the light spirits watch over both of you! But I still hope you return home soon."

Zula turned back to Rose and whispered in her ear, "I know you're healed, but please send me a letter now and then so I don't get lonely."

"Of course I will. We are both magical, so in a way we are truly sisters. I wish you were coming with us too."

"Yes, so do I," Zula laughed. "And we are the best kind of sister. Ah, banish that frown, little one. It makes wrinkles, though I make a cream for that too."

"That's enough! It's my turn, Woman!" Skullcap grumbled and edged between them. Owena hopped to Zula's waiting arm. Skullcap swept Rose off the ground with a boisterous hug and spun her around. "Goodbye Rose! If you ladies ever need me, just send word. Promise?"

"I promise," Rose cried. "Take care Skullcap, and Owena too. Give her some treats for me."

Skullcap gently put her on her feet and turned to his fellow Ranger. He crumbled a bit when he embraced Meg. "Farewell, Commander Sparrow. Don't go looking for another drinking chum either. I won't stand for it."

"I wouldn't dream of it," Meg replied.

Zula linked her arm with Skullcap's and gently drew him away. "Come away now Robert, they will be taking off soon. We can drown our sorrows together with wine."

"Ale," Skullcap sniffed, wiping his face with the back of his hand. "Wine is for fancy folk."

After more tears and hugs, their friends departed.

Rose felt a pang of loneliness when she saw them on the docks waving.

She asked Meg, "Have you ever traveled by ship before?"

"A few times," Meg replied. "But never to Rhulon. I hear Rhungar the capitol is magnificent. I just hope they took my height into account when they assigned my berth below as well as my chambers at court."

Rose laughed, but she did relish being on a vessel which was Rhulonese. The Dwarven sailors were stout, rugged men, though clean and uniformed in dark blue and white since this was a royal vessel. She had almost forgotten she was actually a statuesque girl among her own people.

"I just pray I don't get seasick," Rose said. "That would be too embarrassing."

"Hopefully the tea Becky gave us would cure that, just in case," Meg answered. "Something tells me you are too sturdy to be swayed by the sea."

"I'm glad the Emperor chose you to come with us," Rose said in a low voice.

"I've done my fair share of spying before as a Ranger, but this is different. Now I'm an agent of the Tirangel Empire working with other countries under a shared goal. Rhulon is the heart of this alliance, so that's where Aristide is sending me."

Rose studied her friend and asked, "I suspect you and the Emperor have an interesting history. Is it something you can tell me?"

"You are always the bard looking for a story, aren't you?"

"It's a curse," Rose quipped.

"Another time perhaps," Meg suggested. "But rest assured there is no impropriety involved. I saved his life once, that's all. He remembers. Not all kings remember, but he does. Perhaps over a glass of rum I will share my story, as long as you promise not to put it in a poem or song."

"Very well, but keep my rum well diluted with tea. Hangovers are wicked. My curiosity is even more piqued. It's so strange. I was just getting used to White Thorn and the tall folk. Now I'm leaving. It's not just a diplomatic exchange, but an alliance of crowns for a single purpose." She looked at Meg, wearing black leather trousers and boots, a blue and black brocade vest, white shirt, and of course, gloved as always. "It's also odd to see you out of your Ranger green. The only other time I ever saw you out of your uniform was when we met in that awful cave when I was kidnapped."

"I do feel peculiar," Meg admitted, looking down at her elegant clothes. "My role now is not as a ranger, but as the special agent for Emperor Aristide."

"Do you know why he picked you? Did Culain ask the Emperor to choose you?" Rose asked. "I'd feel guilty if you were pushed to accept and had to give up your ranger status."

Meg laughed and shook her head. "No worry. My status as a ranger is not endangered. I'm on special leave, sanctified by Aristide and only Captain Nerlis and Skullcap know why. I think the Emperor just wanted someone he could trust. He also chose me because I'm not officially attached to the court. Though your influence with Culain is considerable, I doubt it extends to confidential imperial appointments."

"I doubt I influence Prince Culain that much."

"If you say so," Meg noted dryly.

Meg looked at her so strangely Rose finally asked, "Why are you looking at me like that?"

"No reason. I'm going below deck to check on Fayre. Poor girl has never sailed before. I'm going to give her some of these apples. I'll be back in a bit."

After Meg left, Lady Thera Sule boarded the ship and strode toward Rose like a goddess embodied in mortal form. The sailors parted swiftly for her as she walked past, gazing on her regal beauty. They also kept a respectful distance.

"Lady Thera!" Rose exclaimed. "I'm surprised to see you here."

"Before you left us, I wanted to say farewell and to give you a gift, little Rose." She removed a parcel from her drawstring bag and placed it in her hand.

Rose unfolded the yellow silk. Within was a delicate, small gold pendant on chain. It was gorgeous, with a brilliant blue stone at its center and marvelous intricate engravings on the round disc. "It's breathtaking. It's too extravagant, Thera."

Thera closed her hand over Rose's and smiled, brooking no refusal. "It's for you, Bardess. This is not just jewelry. I know such trinkets would matter little to you. This is a sacred temple seal. It will bestow certain rights to the bearer, like a token but more powerful. The symbols engraved on the gold are runes of our ancient language. They represent the ancient Elementals of my faith. If you're ever in my kingdom and require shelter, food, sanctuary, or even protection, go to any Elemental Temple and show them this emblem. They will help you freely. They will even fight to the death for you. They must do this, for only a High Priest or Priestess can bestow this holy gift and it must be honored."

"Thank you, Thera," Rose gasped, genuinely moved.

"Walk in the Light," Thera replied, bestowing the ancient Uragon blessing. "May your enemies be as dust beneath your feet, little Rose. We will meet again one day, of that I am sure. We share the same patron goddess, Karta, so that makes us sisters."

"I hope we meet again," Rose replied earnestly. "Walk in the Light, Thera."

Thera inclined her head and walked away without another word.

"What did Lady Thera want?" Culain asked, joining her.

"To give me a parting gift," Rose answered, wrapping the exquisite piece in the silk and putting it in her pocket.

"Thera is an unusual woman," Culain commented. "She is usually aloof as an owl, but for some reason she likes you."

"I cannot explain it," Rose shrugged, equally pensive. "But then I have come across a few mysteries since running away from Stone Haven. She is just one."

The ship pulled anchor and headed out to sea. Even in the brisk morning air, buffeted by gusts of cold sea air, Rose was warmed by the affection of friends as she waved a final farewell to them. Among them in the background, she glimpsed Darius standing on the pier, apart from the others, wearing a wide-brimmed feathered hat and a gray cloak. He was foolishly alone, without guards. He bowed to her and tipped his hat when she looked his way. A twinge of sorrow threatened to shadow her mood. She watched her friends vanish as she sensed the speed increase beneath her feet. Soon there was only ocean. The kingdom of Tirangel faded to a bittersweet memory with the distance.

Rose refused to endure sadness today. The threat of evil may still lurk in the world, but she decided it must be cast off for this moment. She clutched her lute like a talisman as she looked across the water.

The ocean was so amazing. She felt transported and free. Her life had changed so much and it was still changing with every breath. So far her stomach remained calm, even if the wind was not, the gales lashing her. She welcomed the brisk cold. Despite the mercurial events since she left Stone Haven, Rose remained her own woman and free to become the person she imagined.

Rose whispered a quiet prayer to Karta, thanking the goddess for her good fortune and blessings. She took Thera's gift from her pocket and put it around her neck.

Meg joined her on deck and together they watched the ocean in comfortable silence. She was grateful for Meg Sparrow's companionship and knew she had found the truest of friends.

Culain joined them and leaned against the side of the ship next to her. "The sea is magnificent, isn't it?"

Rose nodded and smiled, studying her royal companion, the man of so many secrets and contradictions. Culain was enigmatic and a constant challenge. He intrigued her and infuriated her. She trusted him with her life and knew Culain would never abandon her. It was more than friendship and certainly more than benefactor and bard. She had no name for it. But they were together. She was free to choose her life. She accepted that as enough for now.

"You are unusually quiet, Rose."

"I'm just enjoying the moment. My life has been so tumultuous of late, I had forgotten to stop and breathe."

"Are you excited about going home to Rhulon?" Culain asked.

She smiled and looked directly at Culain, her answer honest. "I'm a Bard. My home is the road."